PLAY DEAD

Also by Angela Marsons

Detective Kim Stone series

Other books

Angela MARSONS
PLAY DEAD

D.I. KIM STONE
BOOK FOUR

Bookouture

Published by Bookouture

An imprint of StoryFire Ltd.
23 Sussex Road, Ickenham, UB10 8PN
United Kingdom

www.bookouture.com

ISBN: 978-1-78681-008-3
eBook ISBN: 978-1-78681-007-6

This book is a work of fiction. Names, characters, businesses,
organizations, places and events other than those clearly in the
public domain, are either the product of the author's imagination
or are used fictitiously. Any resemblance to actual persons, living or
dead, events or locales is entirely coincidental.

This book is dedicated to my mum and dad – Gill and Frank Marsons – whose pride and encouragement continues to inspire me.

Thank you for sharing this journey and for helping to make it fun.

I love you both.

PROLOGUE

Old Hill – 1996

I knew before I touched her she was dead. And yet I touched her anyway.

The skin was cool to my touch as my finger trailed along her forearm. It paused at the mole beneath her elbow. Never again would it enlarge with her movement. Never again would I see it as her arms came towards me, encasing me in her warmth.

I caressed the side of her face gently. There was no response so I stroked the skin more forcefully, but her eyes remained fixed on the ceiling.

'Don't leave me,' I said, shaking my head as though my denial would make it untrue.

I couldn't imagine my life without her. It had been only us for such a long time.

To be sure I held my breath and watched her chest to see if it would rise. I counted to twenty-three before the breath burst out of me. Her chest hadn't moved – not once.

'How about if I put the kettle on, Mummy? We could go and play our favourite game. I'll get everything ready,' I said as the tears began to fall. 'Mummy, wake up,' I cried, shaking her arm hard. 'Please, Mummy, I don't want you to go. I thought I did but I don't.'

Her whole body rocked with the force of my pushing. Her head thrashed about on the pillow, and for a moment I thought she was saying no. But as soon as I stopped so did she. Her bobbing head was the last thing to fall still.

I dropped to my knees sobbing into her hand, hoping my tears were made of magic. I willed the muscles to flex, ached for the palm to engage. To feel those fingers combing through my hair.

I grabbed her lifeless hand and placed it on top of my head. 'Go on, Mummy, say it,' I said, rolling my head beneath her still fingers. 'Tell me… tell me that I'm your best little girl in the world.'

CHAPTER ONE

Black Country – Present Day

Kim crouched behind the wheelie bin. After fifteen minutes in the same position the feeling was leaving her thighs.

She spoke down into her jacket. 'Stace, anything on the warrant?'

'Not yet, boss,' she heard in her earpiece.

Kim growled. 'I'm not gonna wait for ever, folks.'

From the corner of her eye she saw Bryant shake his head.

His body was hunched over an open bonnet, positioned directly opposite the target property.

Trust Bryant to be the voice of reason. His cautious nature dictated they do everything by the book and she agreed. To a point. But they all knew what was going on in that house. And it had to end today.

'Want me to come closer, boss?' Dawson asked eagerly into her ear.

She was poised to respond in the negative when his voice sounded in her ear again.

'Boss, IC2 male approaching from the other end of the street.' A brief pause. 'Five foot seven, black trousers and grey T-shirt.'

Kim edged back even further. She was two properties away from the target house, wedged between a wheelie bin and a hydrangea bush, but she couldn't risk being seen. Presently they held the element of surprise and she didn't want that to change.

'Any ID, Kev?' she asked into her jacket. Was it someone they knew?

'Negative.'

She closed her eyes and wished for the figure to pass. They didn't need a third male in the property. Currently the numbers were on their side.

'He's entered, guv,' Bryant said from across the road.

Damn it – that could mean only one thing. He was a customer.

She hit the microphone button. Where was that damn warrant? 'Stace?'

'Nothing yet, boss.'

She heard the greetings between the two men as the door of the target property opened.

Kim felt the blood surging around her body. Every muscle she could name ached to sprint for the front door, barge in, cuff the occupants, caution them and worry about the paperwork later.

'Guv, just give it a minute,' Bryant said from beneath the bonnet.

Only he would know exactly what she was thinking.

She keyed the radio without speaking to acknowledge his words.

If she entered the premises without a warrant, the case would probably never get to court.

'Stace?' she asked again.

'Nothing, boss.'

Kim heard the desperation in her ear and knew Stacey was as eager to offer the right answer as she was to hear it.

'Okay, guys, I'm going to plan B,' she said into the microphone.

'What's plan B?' Dawson asked in her ear.

She really had no idea.

'Just play along,' she said, straightening.

She escaped the clutches of the hydrangea bush and stamped life back into her lower limbs. She smoothed her hands over her black canvas jeans in case any flower sap had attached itself to her clothes.

She strode purposefully to the front of the house and along the pavement, as though she hadn't just crept out from a neighbouring garden. As she walked she pushed the wire from her earpiece into her hair.

Yes, the warrant was imminent but that man was most likely a customer and that was a thought she couldn't stomach.

She positioned herself slightly turned so that her earpiece faced the road.

She knocked on the door and pasted a smile on her lips. Bryant hissed into the earpiece, which was still audible in her hair.

'Guv, what the hell…?'

She raised her finger to her lips to signal silence as she heard steps from inside heading down the hall.

The door was opened by Ashraf Nadir.

Kim kept her face neutral as though they had not been watching his every move for the last six weeks.

His face instantly creased into a frown.

'Hello there, I wonder if you could help me? We've broken down over there,' she said, nodding towards Bryant. 'My husband thinks it's really complicated, but I think it might just be the battery.'

He glanced over her shoulder and Kim glanced over his. The other two occupants were talking in the kitchen. A wad of notes was passed between them.

Ashraf began to shake his head.

'No… I'm sorry…' The voice was thick with accent. Ashraf Nadir had arrived from Iraq only six months earlier.

'Do you have any jump leads we could try?'

Again he shook his head. He stepped back, and Kim saw the front door moving towards her.

'Sir, are you sure…?'

The door continued to close.

'Got it, boss,' Stacey screamed into her ear.

Kim thrust her right foot into the opening and launched her weight against the door. She felt a rush of air as Bryant materialised.

'Ashraf Nadir, this is the police, and we have a warrant to search…'

The front door slackened to her touch. She pushed it open and saw Ashraf charging through the house, knocking over the other two occupants like bowling pins.

She tore after him, following out the back door.

The rear garden was dense with overgrown shrubs. An old sofa protruded from the vegetation against a broken-down fence to her right. Ashraf tore forwards, heading through the garden. Kim hurtled after him pushing aside the tall grass trying to entangle her ankles.

Ashraf paused for a split second and frantically looked around.

His eyes rested on a garden shed partly obscured by a wild ivy plant.

He leapt onto a bucket and scrabbled with his feet for traction against the brick. Kim lunged forwards from the ground and missed his foot by a couple of inches.

'Damn it,' she growled, tracing his route, step for step.

As she hauled herself onto the top of the shed Ashraf was easing himself down the other side.

Kim sensed she had lost ground and he sensed it too. A smile began to form on his thin lips as his face disappeared from view.

His look of triumph lit a fuse that led all the way to her determination.

She took a second to assess the garden into which he'd jumped and saw what he had not.

The property was open and tidy with a manicured lawn and a paved patio area. The right-hand side was adjoined to the next property.

The left was secured with a fence that rose seven feet high topped off by cat spikes. But in front of the fence stood two things that were far more interesting.

Kim sat on the shed and dangled her feet over the edge. And waited.

Two German shepherds rounded the building and Ashraf stopped dead.

Kim heard Bryant's voice in her earpiece.

'Guv… where are you?'

'Take a look out back,' she responded into the microphone.

'Umm… guv, you're sitting on the shed.'

Bryant's powers of observation never ceased to amaze her.

Knowing that her number-one suspect was not going anywhere, her thoughts turned immediately to the reason for the Sunday-morning raid.

'Have you got him?' she asked.

'Affirmative,' he answered.

Kim rested her hands either side of her thighs and watched as the tan and black dogs advanced towards Ashraf, reclaiming their territory.

He began to back away from the animals, his body desperate to flee, his mind searching for other possible escape routes.

'Need any help there, guv?' Bryant crackled in her ear.

'Nah, I'll be back in a minute.'

Ashraf took another two steps backwards and turned her way.

She gave him a little wave.

The German shepherds matched his two strides.

Although moving slowly their intention showed in the focus of their eyes and the tension in their necks.

Ashraf took one more look at the dogs and decided he'd be better taking his chances with Kim.

He turned and bolted towards her. His sudden movement unleashed the pent-up aggression in the dogs, who charged after him, barking. Kim lowered her right hand and pulled him to safety.

The dogs leapt and barked, missing his heels by an inch.

The man she had grabbed bore no resemblance to the man who had opened the front door.

She could feel the trembling of his whole body through the conduit of his thin wrist.

His forehead was mottled with beads of sweat. His breathing was hard and laboured.

Kim reached into her back pocket with her left hand, securing his right wrist before he had the opportunity to gather his nerve. She wasn't chasing him again.

'Ashraf Nadir, I am arresting you on suspicion of the kidnap and false imprisonment of Negib Hussain. You do not have to say anything. But it may harm your defence if you do not mention when questioned something which you later rely on in court. Anything you do say may be given in evidence.'

She turned him around on top of the shed so he was facing the target property.

The whole six-foot height of Bryant stood with his arms folded and his head tipped.

'Any time you're finished, guv?'

She moved Ashraf closer towards the edge. She would happily have pushed him forwards, head first, but the code of conduct frowned upon gratuitous violence towards apprehended suspects.

She leaned on his shoulder and forced him to a sitting position.

'Cautioned?' Bryant asked, easing the male down to the ground.

She nodded. On top of a garden shed was not the strangest place she'd made an arrest but it was probably top five.

Bryant took hold of Ashraf's cuffs and pushed him ahead.

'What stopped him running?'

'Two German shepherds.'

Bryant looked at her sideways. 'Yeah, I'd probably have taken my chances with the dogs.'

Kim ignored him and entered the back door first.

The second target and the customer were cuffed and under the guard of Dawson and two uniforms.

She looked at Dawson, the question in her eyes.

'Living room, boss.'

Kim nodded and took the next door off the hallway.

Stacey sat on the sofa a good foot and a half away from the thirteen-year-old boy clad only in underpants and a T-shirt beneath Bryant's suit jacket, which dwarfed him and made him look like a toddler playing dress up.

His head was bowed, legs together, and he was sobbing quietly.

Kim glanced down at the hands that were strangling each other.

She covered the hands with her own.

'Negib, you're safe now. Do you understand?'

His flesh was cold and clammy.

Kim took one hand in each of her own to stop the trembling.

'Negib, I need you to go to the hospital and then we'll get your father…'

The head shot up and began to shake. The shame shone from his eyes and Kim thought her heart would break.

'Negib, your father loves you very much. If he hadn't been so insistent we wouldn't be here now.' She took a deep breath and forced him to look into her eyes. 'It is not your fault. None of this is your fault and your father knows that.'

She could see the brave effort it took for the boy to hold back his tears. Despite the pain, the humiliation, the fear this child was feeling, he did not want to break down and cry.

Kim remembered another thirteen-year-old who had felt exactly the same way.

She reached across and touched his cheek gently. She uttered the words she had longed to hear back then.

'Sweetie, it's going to be okay, I promise.'

The words unleashed a torrent of tears accompanied by loud, heaving sobs. Kim leaned in and pulled him close.

She stared over the top of his head thinking, *Go on, sweetheart, just let it out.*

CHAPTER TWO

Jemima Lowe felt the palms close around her ankles.

With one sudden movement she was yanked from the tinny van. Her back landed on the floor followed by her head. The pain shot around her skull like a star bursting through the darkness. For a few seconds the shards of pain were all she could see.

Please, just let me go, she offered silently as her mouth was unable to move.

The muscles in her body had been severed from her brain. Her limbs no longer obeyed her. Her mind screamed messages but the rest of her body wasn't listening. She could run a half marathon with ease. She could swim the Channel and back. She could ride a bike a triathlon distance, but right now she couldn't even make a fist. She cursed her own body for letting her down and succumbing to the drug ravaging her system.

She felt herself being turned on the ground. The gravel bit into the small of her back where her top had hiked up.

Her body was being dragged along by the ankles. She had the sudden image of a caveman dragging a freshly killed carcass home for the family.

The texture beneath her changed. It was grass. Her head bounced up and down as her body was pulled along by invisible hands. The angle changed. She was being pulled up hill. Her head was thrown to the side. Her cheek hit against a small rock.

She sent an instruction to her hands to grab on to the ground. She knew her only chance was to slow this down. It was her only way to live.

Her thumb and forefinger almost grabbed at a small clutch of grass but then slid away as the digits refused to hang on. She knew the drugs were deep in her system. The tears of frustration stung at her eyes. She knew she was about to die – but also knew she couldn't stop it.

A laboured sigh from her captor punctured the silence as the incline grew steep and the angle of her body changed.

Please, just let me go, she prayed again. Her thoughts had sharpened, but her muscles refused to catch up.

Her body came to a halt. It was level, her legs in line with her back.

'You want me to stop, don't you, Jemima?'

There was the voice. The only voice she'd heard for twenty-four hours.

It chilled her to the bone.

'I wanted you to stop, Jemima. But you wouldn't.'

Jemima had already tried to explain, and yet she had been unable to find the right words. How could she ever explain what had happened that day? In her mind the truth had sounded so inadequate and once out of her mouth it had sounded much worse.

'One of you put a sock in my mouth so I couldn't scream for help.'

She wanted to apologise. Say sorry for what she had done. She had spent most of her adult life running away from the memory of that day. But it had never worked. The shame of it had always been with her.

Please, just let me explain, her mind screamed through the numbness. If she could just have a minute to think she was sure she could say the right thing.

She managed to open her mouth. But before she could summon the strength to speak something was forced in through her lips. Her tongue recoiled from the thick dry substance.

'All I hear when I go to sleep is the sound of your laughter.'

Another handful of dirt entered her mouth. She could feel it travelling down and clogging her airway. A scream was building in her throat, but it couldn't find a way out.

'I will never hear your laughter again.'

Another handful was forced in and then a palm clamped over her face. Her cheeks bulged as the dirt tried to rearrange itself to make room. The only exit it had was to try to escape down her throat.

She could feel the breath leaving her body.

She tried to writhe away from the hand covering her mouth. In her mind the movement was strong and forceful. It emerged as a pathetic wriggle.

'And then you held me down, didn't you, Jemima?'

Is this what it had felt like? she wondered, as her body fought for breath.

She could feel the life draining out of her and into the ground. Her mind screamed the protest that her body could not.

For a second the hand moved and Jemima had a fleeting hope that it was over.

Something hit her in the middle of her face. She heard the sound of cracking bone a second before the pain exploded around her head. Blood spurted from her nose and cascaded over her lips.

The agony travelled to her mouth, causing her to cry out even though she could make no sound. The action sent more dirt travelling down her throat.

Her gag reflex tried to eject it, and she began to choke. She tried to swallow the arid ground, but it was sticking to the sides of her throat like freshly poured tar.

Tears forced themselves from her eyes as she tried to find a breath somewhere in her body.

A second blow landed on her cheek.

Her mind screamed out with the agony.

She writhed against the ground. Her cries of terror were held in the dirt.

A third blow landed on her mouth. Teeth burst away from her gums.

Every inch of her had succumbed to the pain as the calm voice reached her once more.

'I will no longer see your face in my dreams.'

She had one last thought before the darkness claimed her.

Please, just let me die.

CHAPTER THREE

Kim knocked once before entering the domain of her boss, Detective Chief Inspector Woodward, who resided in a corner office on the third floor of Halesowen Police Station.

The landline was at his ear. Mild annoyance shaped his features before he ended the call abruptly.

'Didn't feel like waiting for the word "enter"?' he growled.

'Er… you asked to see me, sir,' she said. It's not like he didn't know she was coming.

He checked his watch. 'Almost an hour ago.'

'Really, that long?'

She stood behind the chair that faced him.

He sat back and offered her an expression that her best guess said was a smile. But she wouldn't bet her house on it.

'Congratulations on a positive result yesterday with the Ashraf Nadir case. Had you not been so insistent that there were more people involved in that prostitution ring we would never have found the second property.'

Kim accepted the compliment. Woody had managed to condense her dogged effort into one single sentence. If she recalled correctly it had taken four separate requests to investigate Ashraf Nadir after she'd spotted him talking with a male suspected of involvement in the publicised Birmingham case. She hadn't exactly camped outside his office but she'd been close to buying a tent.

She took a step back to leave.

'Not quite yet, Stone. I have a couple of questions.'

Oh, if only she'd been called to his office just for a pat on the back. Too late she realised the completed statements from her team on the Nadir raid were neatly piled on his desk.

He popped the reading glasses onto his nose and lifted the first page of the top statement, which he really did not need to do. Kim knew that any questions he wanted to ask her were already in his head.

'I'd like you to clarify the time difference between receipt of the warrant and entry to the Nadir property.'

'Marginal, sir,' she answered honestly.

'Minutes or seconds?' he asked.

'Seconds.'

'Double figures or single?' he asked, removing his glasses and staring at her, hard.

'Single.'

He placed the glasses on the desk. 'Stone, was the warrant in place before you entered the property?'

She didn't hesitate. 'Yes, it was.' She didn't add the word 'just'. She also decided it was best not to add that she'd been about to go in anyway. She tended to get in enough trouble for her impetuous acts of judgement. Adding in near misses was a whole new story.

He eyed her suspiciously for a few seconds before tapping the statements with his fingers.

'Other than that, watertight,' he said.

She nodded her understanding and again took a step backwards towards the door.

'So much so, I think you and your team have earned yourselves a little treat.'

She narrowed her gaze and opened her ears. Now she was suspicious.

'Do you remember being briefed about that facility in Wall Heath?' he asked.

She nodded. 'The one carrying out forensic research? Of course.'

Everyone down as far as detective-inspector level had been briefed when the place had originally started work. It was called Westerley and focussed on studying the human body after death.

Kim wondered if the mid-July heat was getting to her boss. Outwardly the twenty-three-degree heat had only prompted him to loosen his shirt cuffs but maybe he was melting on the inside.

Completing cases was not like bowling. Solving one didn't knock the other ones down. There were many more cases spread across the desks of her team, and Woody knew it.

'Sir, any chance of a rain check?' she asked. 'My team has six new cases that have landed over the weekend.'

Again, that almost-smile appeared on his face.

'No, Stone. I've been waiting for an opportunity for the last few weeks but delayed it while the Nadir case was live. But you will take the trip today.'

She had learned to accept when her boss would not be moved, and she now chose her battles more wisely. Still she had to give it one last try.

'Is there any particular reason why now is…?'

'West Mercia have solved two cold cases in the last month based on the research being carried out at Westerley,' he said, with a look that left her in no doubt that the discussion was over.

They were going.

CHAPTER FOUR

Her team piled into her ten-year-old Golf, which was only with her today after dropping Barney at the groomers. Normally her Kawasaki Ninja provided all the space she needed.

Bryant folded his six-foot height into the front while Stacey and Dawson shuffled in the back.

'Buckle up, kiddies,' Bryant said over his shoulder.

'Bloody hell, Kev. Move over a bit, will yer?'

'Christ, Stace, you've got loads of room.'

Kim drove the car out of the car park as Dawson and Stacey continued to bicker in the back.

'Hey, you two…' Bryant said. Thankfully he was going to restore some order before she had to. 'Hope you both went to the toilet before you got in the car.'

Dawson groaned and Stacey stifled a chuckle.

'Hey, Bryant,' Dawson said, leaning forwards. 'Did you bring us all a packed—'

'One more bloody word,' Kim snapped, 'and you'll all be walking. This isn't a school trip to the zoo.'

At least in the office she could retreat to The Bowl, a term used for her tiny office in the corner of the CID squad room. In her small car there was really nowhere to go.

Silence descended like a curtain.

Eventually Bryant broke the peace.

'Guv?'

'What?'

'Are we there yet?'

'Bryant, I swear—'

'Sorry, what I meant to ask is where exactly are we going?'

'Just on the outskirts of Wall Heath.'

The facility was right on the border where the West Midlands met the Staffordshire police force.

Wall Heath was primarily a residential area located on the edge of the West Midlands conurbation bordering Staffordshire to the west. It was at the very edge of Kim's safety zone before the roads narrowed, traffic lights disappeared and roadkill was waiting around every corner.

'That's Holbeche House,' Bryant said as she passed what looked like a stately home. 'It's famous for being where the flight of the Gunpowder Plotters ended. The mansion was originally built around 1600 but is now a private nursing home.'

'Splendid,' Kim offered. 'Apparently we're looking for a place called Westerley Farm,' she said, glancing to her left.

'Not signposted as a site of rotting corpses then, boss?' Stacey asked.

'Funded research?' Dawson asked.

Kim was relieved that they had returned to grown-up questions.

'Yes but not exclusively,' she answered. 'The programme is funded by a mixture of universities and police forces.'

'Unlikely to be featured on the annual "look how we spent your money" leaflets,' Stacey acknowledged.

Kim suspected not. It was definitely on the 'not for public consumption' list.

'And you just passed it on the right,' Bryant said, looking behind.

The lane was a one-track road. She drove along for almost a quarter mile before reaching a driveway she could use to reverse.

She drove back down the lane and slowed as she saw the break in the seven-foot-high hedgerow. A simple wooden sign with the name burned into it hung from a gate that offered a one-foot gap either side of the car width.

Bryant jumped out and unlatched the gate, waving her through. He closed the gate behind.

'No lock?' Kim asked, frowning.

The road narrowed further and became two strips of dirt with a central line of grass and weeds. The hedgerow grew higher and began to impose itself around them. Kim was reminded of taking the car through the car wash.

The track ended at a second wooden gate but, unlike the first, this one rose to a height of eight feet and was made of solid wood. The gate wore a hat of black, wrought-iron spikes. This gate was locked. She was guessing they'd reached the business end of the property.

Kim lowered the window and spoke into the speakerphone on her right.

'DI Stone, West Midlands Police.'

There was no reply but the solid gate began to move along a single runner. Halfway across it juddered and then continued. Kim drove the Golf through as soon as the gap was wide enough. Although the thought of viewing the facility held some interest for her, real police work was stacking up on her desk. Her mind was already apportioning the one armed robbery, two sexual assaults and a vicious ABH to her team.

Kim brought the car to a halt beside a light grey prefabricated structure that was probably the length of two eight-berth caravans. Two red doors punctuated the row of perfectly square windows.

A collection of cars and pickup trucks were parked beside a double Portaloo.

The vehicles were all squeezed into a small gravel patch. Kim could see that some effort had been made to provide a line of gravel from the makeshift car park to the Portakabin, but the majority of the stones appeared to have been trodden into the ground.

Kim was forced to park the car on the dirt behind a red pickup truck. Bryant looked at the vehicle before a slight frown shaped his face.

'Glamorous, eh?' Stacey noted, opening the rear door.

'Shit, these shoes were expensive,' Dawson said, trying to find a place to put his feet where they wouldn't get swallowed by the mud.

A figure walked towards them with a smile and an outstretched hand.

Kim guessed him to be mid-fifties with a well-stocked girth giving him an ambling gait as he approached. Black wellington boots rose over green corduroy trousers to the knee. A patterned jumper completed the look of a farmer who still lived with his mother.

'Detective Inspector Stone, so pleased to meet you. Chris Wright, Professor of Human Biology and person in charge of Westerley.'

His palm was warm, fleshy and pumped her hand enthusiastically.

Kim took a moment to introduce the rest of her team and the professor ensured that he shook the hand of everyone.

She followed as he led them to the red door on the left that had two wooden steps denoting it as the main entrance.

She was immediately struck by the TARDIS element of the space as her team filed in behind her.

The door had opened into the mid-section of the Portakabin, which was clearly the office. Fixed to the walls on either side were light beech-effect counters. The front edge was fluid with indents for the ergonomically positioned chairs pushed snugly underneath.

There were three clearly defined working spaces. The first, directly opposite the door, held three flat-screen monitors, the largest keyboard Kim had ever seen and a mouse lying idle next to a wrist support. The screens on either side of the workspace had been turned to form a wall of privacy from the next workspace.

'Jameel is running late,' Professor Wright said, nodding towards the screens. 'I'm hoping he'll be here before you leave to demonstrate the analytical software systems we use.'

Kim would swear she could see the envy dripping from Stacey's eyes.

He pointed to sliding doors that took up the final third of the Portakabin. 'That's our preparation area. The second door leads directly into there to avoid us having to bring corpses through the office.' He smiled widely. 'But I'd imagine it's our residents you really want to see.'

What she really wanted to see was that heavy wooden gate closing behind her, but she did not wish to offend the professor. She understood that the work carried out here was valuable, but the vision of important witnesses forgetting vital information related to the cases on her desk was ever present in her mind.

She stepped to the side as the professor turned away from the sliding doors and moved back towards the centre of the space. The rest of them filed around and followed like some kind of disjointed snake.

The professor moved through the office section to the far end of the space. The left-hand side held a kitchen area with all the normal appliances. Kim wasn't so sure she wanted to take a look in the fridge or the freezer. The rest of the space was taken up by a three-seater leather sofa and a round meeting table made of the same light beech as the desks.

A woman stood before a boiling kettle, spooning instant coffee into an array of mugs. Her legs were encased in dark jeans and what appeared to be compulsory-issue wellington boots. Her tawny hair was pulled back in a functional ponytail that rested on the back of a college emblazoned sweatshirt.

'This is Catherine Evans, entomologist. She's our resident maggot lady.'

The woman turned her head, smiled and nodded. The smile was neither warm nor welcoming. It was functional and reminded Kim of a toddler being told to smile for a tolerated aunt.

She couldn't help but feel that Catherine Evans had heard that introduction a hundred times already and briefly wondered how the woman felt about her extensive journey of education and study being reduced to a description of 'maggot lady'.

Professor Wright stopped and turned, clasping his hands before him. 'We have a couple of consultants roaming the site at the moment but they are currently observing Ant and Dec so will not interfere…'

'Excuse me?' Kim said, perplexed.

He smiled. 'I will explain,' he said, leading them outside. He closed the door behind him and began walking slowly, heading east.

'Officially we are categorised as a research facility specialising in forensic anthropology and related disciplines,' said the professor. 'More commonly known as a body farm.'

'Isn't there one in America?' Dawson asked.

'There are actually six in America. The largest belongs to Texas State University and covers an area of seven acres.'

Dawson frowned and shook his head. 'No, that's not the…'

'You'll be thinking of the original body farm in Knoxville, Tennessee, founded by Doctor William Bass in eighty-one and made famous by the author Patricia Cornwell. Westerley is much smaller than the two and a half acres of the Texas facility but is used in the training of law enforcement in scene-of-crime skills and techniques. I visited the place some years ago and modelled Westerley on many of their ideas and theories.'

'So how much land do you have?' Dawson asked.

Professor Wright nodded forwards. 'As far as the eye can see and a little bit beyond the south border.'

Kim followed his gaze. The area he'd indicated totalled seven or eight football pitches and although the ground undulated in places it was a downhill slope from the Portakabin.

He pointed to the west. 'Those trees mark the barrier to Staffordshire. The entire south is blocked by hedgerow beyond the oak trees and to the east is a brook that separates us from our closest neighbours.'

'And how do they feel?' Dawson asked.

He smiled. 'We don't place a weekly advertisement but our closest neighbour is a food-packaging factory. It's a half mile in any direction to the nearest resident.'

Dawson seemed satisfied.

'How many bodies do you have?' Bryant asked.

'Currently seven.'

'Where do you get 'em from?' Stacey asked.

'Donations from family members, a person's own wishes as stated in a will—'

'Hang on, Professor,' Bryant interrupted. 'You're telling me that family members actually donate their loved ones to this research?'

Professor Wright hesitated. 'Donations to medical research rarely state the nature of the research. Few family members would wish to know the details, but they are content to know that the death of a loved one may be of scientific benefit, and of course it is.'

Kim stepped in. 'And some people will themselves here?'

'Not necessarily to this exact location but to the benefit of research. Texas State has some one hundred bodies donated each year and over 1300 people have registered to be donated there specifically upon their demise.'

'It has a waiting list?' Kim asked incredulously.

Professor Wright smiled and nodded.

'Are the bodies in varying states of decay?' Stacey asked.

'Yes, my dear, I think you'll get a good idea of what we do from the two residents I'm heading towards.'

Kim caught Stacey's slight stiffening at the endearment, but she smiled through her irritation.

They all followed as the morning sun finally broke through the white cloud and changed the face of the day completely.

Kim matched the professor's stride. 'It must be quite a unique funding system you have here?'

He nodded. 'We are fortunate indeed that the majority of institutions we approached had an interest in our research and yet no one wants it on their doorstep. So we share our findings with all parties and offer assistance where we can.'

'To current investigations?'

He nodded as he walked. 'Of course. We intend to replicate as many scenarios as we can that will not only aid our research aims but assist the police with both current and historic investigations.'

And had already helped West Mercia solve two cold cases. Damn, Woody. Now she was bloody interested. Kim would not scoff at any additional police resource. Cold cases were frustrating to any officer on the force. They stayed in the back of your mind like a conversation that had ended before you'd had your say. They embedded themselves into your subconscious until you could put it to bed. And that was if you were lucky.

Sometimes they didn't even make it to the back of your mind to be machinated over while you continued with the current workload. Now and again they remained at the forefront of your thoughts, doubts constantly gnawing and shredding your brain. *Did I interview the correct witnesses? Did I miss a vital clue? Could I have done more?* It was Kim's opinion that it was cold cases that were responsible for much of the alcohol abuse within the police force.

'So here we are,' Professor Wright said, regaining her attention.

Kim noted two perfectly cut rectangles in the grass. As she got closer, she saw that they were makeshift graves.

'Please meet Jack and Vera,' Professor Wright said, pointing like a proud father.

'Their real names?' Stacey asked while Dawson rolled his eyes.

The professor shook his head. 'No, they come to us with unique reference numbers, which remain their official identification, but we prefer a more personal approach out here in the field.'

Kim glanced to the foot of a nearby tree. Two bouquets were in their last throes of life. Roses and lilies.

'Flowers?' she asked.

His eyes followed her gaze. 'Yes, just a mark of respect from us.'

Kim liked the small touch.

He stood at the head of the graves and peered down. They all followed suit.

The grave to the right held Vera, whose body displayed the incision of a post-mortem. The flesh was immersed in water and Kim noticed the grave was angled towards them.

She looked towards Jack who was also immersed in water but there was no post-mortem incision and no angle to the grave.

'We have much to learn about insect activity in the water,' Professor Wright explained. 'Vera is immersed in water being fed from the brook. We've cut a channel and angled her grave away from the stream.'

Kim swatted a fly away from her ear and looked to the small slip of moving water five feet away from the tip of the graves. Now she understood the angle. It was so the stream water would drain away from the water source, ensuring that no contaminants from the body re-entered the slow-moving brook.

'We take any opportunity to use the elements around us,' he stated and then raised an eyebrow. 'The decision to site the Texas facility at Freeman Ranch was questioned due to the presence of vultures but this now provides a new area of study focussing on the effect of scavenging on human decomposition.'

Kim nodded her understanding. She was all for using the resources available but vultures?

'Jack is immersed in rainwater so his liquid contains no insects, unlike the water in with Vera.'

'Bugger off,' Dawson said, swatting the air around his head.

Professor Wright smiled at Kim's colleague. 'Never complain at seeing a blowfly, young man. They don't fly below fifty-two degrees Fahrenheit so it's a good indication the weather is warming up.'

'Well, this one's a bit keen,' Dawson moaned.

It wasn't the only one Kim realised as another one tried to land on Bryant's shoulder.

She looked down at the bodies in the water. The flies were paying no attention to them.

'Occupational hazard of what we do, I'm afraid,' the professor said. 'Okay, on to the next.'

They stepped away from Jack and Vera and began heading across the site to the western edge of the property. Kim looked back to see if the flies were following. They were not. They had retreated to an area just beyond the brook. Kim could see they were not alone. Multiple flies hovered and then dived with the excitement of a new discovery.

Kim saw the professor was guiding them towards two males in the distance surveying a lifeless form positioned above ground encased by a chicken-wire guard.

She hesitated. 'Professor, could we just go back…'

'Aww… guv, let's just keep going towards those two guys over there,' Bryant said, with a glint of amusement in his eyes.

She had no idea what the source of his amusement was, and she didn't much care. If there was a fresher body for her team to view, where they could observe the beginning of insect activity, then she was ready to hop off the official tour and learn something useful.

She turned and started walking back towards Jack and Vera.

'Inspector, there's nothing else over there,' Professor Wright called.

She covered the ground quickly and was back at the two graves by the time he caught up with her.

'I'm not sure what you want—'

'Don't worry, I'm sure it won't be too much for my team to handle,' she said, wading through the slow-moving stream. The water reached above her ankles. No threat to the leather biker boots but the bottoms of her black canvas jeans were sodden. She didn't mind. Water dried.

'It's not that, Inspector. I'm just not sure what you're hoping to…'

His words trailed away as they rose out of the brook on the other side and discovered the source of the insect activity.

A fully clothed woman with a smashed-in face stared, unseeing, up to the blue sky.

A hundred flies hovered above the blood-covered face.

'Can you tell us what you hope to learn from this one, Professor?' Kim asked as her team finally caught up with them.

The professor's face had drained of all colour while his eyes remained fixed on the body.

There was a long pause before he finally answered. 'I'm sorry, Inspector, but I can't tell you a thing because this body is not one of ours.'

CHAPTER FIVE

'Kev, go find me anything to help us cordon off this area. Stace, go back to the Portakabin and look at the footage to see if there's anything at all that helps us.'

The professor shook his head, slowly, his eyes still fixed on the body. 'The CCTV doesn't cover…'

'We'll see,' she said, nodding towards her team. They turned and headed up the hill. For her, the shock of the discovery had worn off and now it was time to get busy. The professor still appeared to be reeling.

Thoughts of the cases on her desk faded from her mind. The victims in every one of them were still alive, injured but still breathing.

From the corner of her eye she could see that the two figures in the distance were moving towards them.

'Bryant, keep them away. I don't care what they're consulting on. This one's not for public view.'

'On it, guv.'

Her phone was still in her hand. Her first call had been to Keats, who was despatching a forensic team immediately. She had moved everyone to the other side of the brook where they would remain until that team arrived.

'Detective Inspector, is there anything I can do?' Professor Wright finally asked from the other side of the water. As he wasn't forensically trained any observations would need to be made from outside the immediate area.

Kim shook her head although she noted that the colour was slowly returning to his washed-out complexion.

She scrolled through her list of contacts and pressed to call. Woody answered on the second ring.

'Sir, we have a body,' she stated without preamble. Greetings and salutations were not normally high on her priority list, but in a case like this they were non-existent.

She heard the smile in his voice as he responded, 'Oh, Stone, your humour…'

'No, it's a live one.'

Kim heard the paradox of her statement but he'd know what she meant.

She continued. 'Female, difficult to age as her face has been badly beaten. Fully clothed and she hasn't been here long.'

'Okay, stay with it. I'll draft a holding statement for the press. Have you called Keats?'

She kept her irritation in check. Of course Keats had been her first call. The pathologist was bringing a forensic team to analyse the scene and offer her clues to help find the person responsible. Woody was drafting a press release. Priorities.

'Yes, sir,' she responded. 'First call.'

Maybe she hadn't been able to tame every bit of irritation.

His voice was curt. 'Full briefing later.'

He ended the call, and Kim shrugged and put the phone in her back pocket.

She turned to the professor, whose complexion was now approaching a normal hue.

'Any idea how long she's been here?'

He coughed and met Kim's gaze. 'We know that warm-weather bodies attract blowflies by the hundreds in a matter of minutes. On a day like today it would only take a few hours for the nose, mouth and eyes to be filled with fly eggs.'

The previous day had been warm but she couldn't see any evidence of the grainy yellowish eggs as yet, indicating the body had been left sometime during the night.

The professor continued. 'We've had thousands of pregnant females swarming around a body shortly after its arrival and, as you know, one female can lay hundreds of eggs at a time.' He paused. 'It's interesting that the flies are targeting only her face.'

'How so?' she asked, glancing across to Bryant in the distance talking animatedly with the other visitors. He was taking his time, no doubt advising them to keep away.

Kim's attention returned to the professor, who was still talking.

'… indicate there's no other wound. If they smell blood that would be their target location.'

Give the man a prize, Kim thought. Already she could estimate that the body had been dumped during the night and there was unlikely to be any other wound on it. At this rate she could give Keats the day off.

'Oh, thanks for joining us, Bryant,' Kim said as her colleague returned. 'I told you to warn them off, not take them for a meal.'

He stopped short of the stream and spoke to the professor. 'Lack of coffee makes her snarky.'

Kim shot him a look.

'Cavalry's here,' Bryant said, glancing up the hill.

Keats, the diminutive pathologist, charged towards them. He paused at the stream before wading through. A group of forensic scene investigators flanked him. West Midlands Police had a team of more than a hundred civilian technicians who would photograph, sketch and collect all evidence before the pathologist was able to remove the body.

Suddenly Keats stopped dead, raising his hand above his eyes before waving at someone in the distance.

The pause was brief and he landed beside her within seconds.

A smile lifted his pointy beard. 'Oh, Inspector, only you could find a body here.'

'Keats, how about you just—'

'Does she know?' Keats asked Bryant.

She caught her colleague's quick shake of the head.

'Know what?' she asked.

'Oh, excellent,' he said, smiling. 'Now, let me see our victim.'

Kim looked to her colleague for clarification.

'Bryant…?'

He held up his hands. 'I'm gonna go find coffee. You're going to need it.'

She had the sudden feeling that everyone had been told a joke and she was the only one not to get it. She couldn't help thinking it had something to do with the two consultants now standing in the middle of the field.

She shrugged and then turned to the professor. 'I need to ask you to leave the area.'

'I understand. It's a crime scene. I'll go and check on my other visitors.'

Kim took the protective footwear being offered to her.

'So, Detective Inspector—'

'Keats, don't even start with me today. This was supposed to be a reward,' she said, snapping on blue gloves.

They often bickered at a crime scene. He called it banter. She called it a pain in the arse. Last year, Keats had lost his wife suddenly after thirty-five years of marriage. The loss had hit him harder than he'd allowed anyone to see. But she had known. And so she let him have his fun. Now and again.

The technicians worked around her and she blocked out the surrounding chatter. For a moment Kim was as still as the body. Everything faded away as she focussed her senses on the woman before her. The only thing that mattered was the clues she still held. Anything other than the victim disappeared from her mind as she allowed her gaze to start at the partly exposed feet.

The woman's toes peeked from gladiator sandals with two strap fastenings above each ankle. Only one of the straps of each sandal was tied.

The skirt was long and flowing, a gypsy skirt formed of vertical patterns up to the elasticated waistband. Kim took a closer look. The skirt rested just above the sandals all the way around, as though placed with care. A lilac vest top with thin straps showed the absence of a bra. The slight frame didn't require one. A simple chain with a gold cross hung below the neck, falling on the breastbone.

Her arms were placed a couple of inches away from her torso. The wrists were barely discernible from the rest of her arms. A thin strap of white showed where her watch should have been on the left wrist, but it was the right wrist that caused Kim to pause.

A perfect line encircled the wrist and a graze had removed some of the skin from the top of the hand. Kim needed no more information to deduce the mark and the graze were from the presence of handcuffs.

Her heart beat faster for just a few seconds as her eyes lingered on the injury. She remembered how that same red ring had looked on her own six-year-old hand. The memory of soreness from the scraped skin passed fleetingly through her, causing her to rub the top of her own hand. Sometimes she needed to remind herself that it was long gone; although new flesh had grown and healed it away she would still be able to draw its shape back onto her skin twenty-eight years later.

She shook her head to release her mind from the past.

Her gaze travelled up to what used to be a head. The skull was distorted as though someone had taken a bite out of it like an apple. Dried blood covered every inch of the skin and had formed rivulets over the woman's jaw and down her neck. The right-hand side of her hair was coloured red from blood and the left was blonde. Kim guessed it was where she had turned her head slightly into the ground to try to avoid the blows.

The nose appeared to be pointing to the left. The flesh would have swollen immediately upon impact. Injuries inflicted after death didn't swell, indicating the victim had been alive during the beating.

'What the…?' Kim said, leaning down. Her attention was drawn to the line between the upper and lower lip. A brown substance had rested there.

'Easy, Inspector,' Keats warned, watching her every move.

'What's that?' she asked, tipping her head to get a better look.

Keats leaned down from the other side of the body and took a deep breath before placing his face next to to the victim to get a closer look. He didn't want to exhale and blow away valuable evidence.

'Looks like dirt,' he said, meeting her gaze.

'In her mouth?' Kim asked.

Keats pressed a single finger to a couple of areas of the woman's swollen face. How he knew what he was touching was a mystery to Kim.

'Don't quote me until I get her back but I think her mouth is full of it.'

Kim stood and looked around. 'Here,' she called, spotting an area that had clearly been disturbed. A tech marked where she pointed as she moved out of the way. If the killer had scraped at the ground to loosen the dirt he could have left something behind.

Bryant appeared beside her and held out a cardboard cup. She took it and sipped as she turned her attention to Keats. 'I already know she's been here less than twelve hours and there's no other wound, so…'

'Hear that, guys? The detective inspector knows it all so let's just pack up now and bury her tomorrow.'

For a split second Kim wondered if he was referring to the victim or her.

Both she and the technicians ignored him.

'The professor was very informative while we were waiting for you.'

'So you won't be grilling me for an early post-mortem then?' he retorted.

'You wish. Speaking of which…'

'Tomorrow at nine and I'm not budging.'

'Fine.'

'Bryant, feel her forehead. No fight. She's sickening for something.'

She offered him a brief smile.

The timing of the post-mortem suited her perfectly. There was no handbag close by or pockets in the victim's clothing so identification would be the priority of the day.

Kim took one last walk around the body, committing every detail to memory. She paused. There was something she hadn't noted before. She reached towards the left hand, but Keats swatted her away.

'Don't even think about it. They need to be bagged.'

Kim raised an eyebrow. This was not her first dead body.

The hands were one of the most important elements of a body at a crime scene. There could be anything under the fingernails: skin, a fibre, a clue.

She moved along the body to the feet and found the same clue there.

She touched the nail of the big toe gently, rubbing the tip of her finger back and forth.

She felt footsteps approach behind her as she knelt down and brought her face closer to the toes.

'Well… Detective Inspector, it appears we meet again.'

Kim's eyelids snapped open at the voice she recognised all too well.

CHAPTER SIX

'Doctor Bate,' she said, raising herself to a standing position.

'Surely it's Daniel by now,' he said, offering his hand.

Kim touched his hand briefly.

Now she understood Keats's amusement and Bryant's collusion at her anticipated discomfort.

She and Daniel had met the previous year during the Crestwood investigation. He had been the forensic osteoarchaeologist despatched from Dundee. They had not hit it off initially. They had shared three shallow graves and a stirring of fascination. But the case had ended. He had left. End of story.

His hair was slightly lighter than she remembered it. Possibly bleached by the sun. His eyes were the same green that seemed to brighten at times with mischief and yet darken behind the thin-rimmed glasses he normally wore while at work.

He wore light jeans and a khaki T-shirt. The muscles in his arms from his love of outdoor activities remained the same, although there was a fresh scar just below his left elbow.

Suddenly she felt like the main event of a boxing fixture. The first punch had been thrown and now three interested people awaited her reaction.

She smiled brightly. 'How lovely to see you again, Doctor Bate. I hope you're well.'

Keats stroked his beard and Bryant coughed into his fist.

She looked at the pathologist. 'Are you ready to move her yet?'

In terms of importance, nothing trumped her victim. Amongst the other bodies placed at Westerley, this one didn't fit. The woman was no experiment, either gifted or donated.

Despite his faults, Kim always felt relieved when the victims were back with Keats. He treated all of his charges with respect.

'As soon as I can, Inspector.'

She returned her gaze to Daniel. The amusement lit up his eyes. If he wanted to come here and play games he'd be playing this one on his own.

She turned and waded through the water before turning back.

'Keats, I'll see you tomorrow at nine.' She glanced to his right. 'And it was nice to see you again… Doctor Bate.'

She stormed up the hill and didn't slow as Bryant appeared beside her.

'Judas,' she spat.

It all made sense now. His gaze lingering on the pickup truck. His smug smile, his lengthy chat with the visiting consultants. If she remembered correctly, Bryant and Daniel had got along very well.

'You knew he was here and didn't bother to tell me?'

He shrugged without apology. 'I like my knackers where they are, thanks. And anyway, why is it a big deal? It's not like anything happened when—'

'It isn't a big deal,' she snapped. Yes, there had been a brief attraction between them but they had both been too busy to acknowledge it.

'Yeah, clearly. But, er… guv, more importantly, why were you peering at the dead girl's feet?'

Kim lifted her hand and rubbed her forefinger over the nail of her thumb.

'The nails on both hands and feet were dull and rough. They felt like matte paint.'

He shook his head. 'No, still not getting it.'

'Nail-polish remover. It takes the shine from your nails. Recently done.'

'And you think that means something?' he asked doubtfully.

'Bryant, I would have thought you'd have learned by now that everything means something.'

CHAPTER SEVEN

Kim replaced the receiver and stepped out of The Bowl into the main office.

'Okay, Stace, get the board. Kev, get the coffee poured and Bryant, get the window open.'

The squad room had filled with the stench of death and whether it was imagined or had been brought back on their clothes and shoes it was definitely attached to them now.

Stacey stood on tiptoe to label the top of the whiteboard. The words 'UNKNOWN FEMALE' were written with a perfect underline.

Kim hated that phrase. She detested anonymity in her victims. In life they'd had a name, a personality, a past, facial expressions, loves, hates, fears and dreams. They had weaved through the world interacting, imprinting on others. A smile at the lady on the checkout. A brief exchange with the barista in the coffee shop. A donation to charity. Every victim had left a footprint somewhere.

Finding her name was the top priority.

'Okay, facts first. Height approximately five foot four. Weight no more than eight stone. Natural blonde. Age: late twenties, early thirties based only on clothing. Time and cause of death we'll have first thing in the morning. Stace, put a line down the middle of the board.'

Dawson handed her a mug of coffee. It was hot. She placed it beside her on the spare desk.

'Just notes now. Identification, location, suspects, motive.'

She paused and sipped while Stacey caught up.

'Fully clothed, nail polish removed,' Kim stated.

'She could have done it herself,' Bryant offered. 'We don't know exactly when she was taken. Could have been last night after she'd been for a meal or something.'

Kim nodded. 'Those were day clothes she was wearing.' She shrugged. 'Might mean nothing but I want it noted anyway.'

Stacey stood poised.

'Handcuff marks to the wrist,' she said, staring at the board. She moved on quickly. 'Face beaten beyond recognition.' She paused. 'Is this to hamper identification, slow us down – or is there another reason? The dirt in the mouth, accidental or meaningful? Where are her belongings? Most folks have at least a phone and a small amount of cash.'

Stacey was summarising Kim's sentences to two or three words and noting them.

Kim cast her eyes over the board, satisfied that the main aspects had been covered, and waited for the detective constable to resume her seat.

'Okay, Stace, I want you to start by seeing what you can dig up on the staff at Westerley. Without an identification we'll work our way out. The land on the other side of the stream is not officially their property and the facility is secret so what's the significance of the dump site? Also, I want you to look at the access point. How did he get there and how did he know about it?'

'Got it, boss.'

'Kev, get on to missing persons to see if we can get a match.'

He nodded and reached for the phone.

She took a sip of her coffee. 'And I'm off to brief the boss.'

Bryant smirked. 'Have fun.'

'And apparently you're coming with me.'

His face dropped as Dawson offered a snigger.

'So, Bryant, what you done wrong now?' Kim asked as they headed up the stairs.

'I was just gonna ask you the same question.'

Woody's instruction had been specific. Bring Bryant. As his superior she would be present for any bollocking for him, but Bryant had never been present for any of hers.

'Ready?' she asked, as they arrived at the door bearing the brass nameplate of the detective chief inspector.

She tapped and entered.

'Sit, both of you.'

They did so.

'Update, Stone,' Woody said, glancing her way.

She reiterated everything they had just noted on the board downstairs.

He nodded and then looked from her to Bryant. 'I wanted to speak to you both. This case has the potential to get complicated if it becomes known where the body was found. The facility is still a closely guarded secret, and I don't want it to be us who lets it out.'

Was that it? Kim wondered. She had worked that much out for herself.

'And another thing…'

Of course there was.

'I want to make sure you haven't forgotten about the weekend.'

'Er… the weekend?' she asked, casting a glance at Bryant. He offered no clue.

'The award ceremony, Stone.'

'Oh, that. Yes, sir.'

Jesus, was that here already? She had forgotten. She was being honoured for her work on a recent kidnapping case.

Kim hated to be ungrateful, but awards were not something she craved. As ever it had been a team effort and glory hunting was not in her make-up.

If she could cut up the commendation into pieces she would offer it to her team who had worked the same hours she had without complaint. They had put their entire lives on hold for the sake of that case and had been happy to do so.

Next she would offer some to the police officers who had guarded the site for days while the forensic technicians secured the evidence once she and her team had left.

After that she would send it to the medical staff who had sewn up the girls and repaired their injuries. And then a portion for the psychologists and counsellors who would help put the kids back together again.

'So I certainly don't want any complaints landing on my desk between now and then.'

'Of course not.'

Honestly, from his tone you'd think it happened all the time, she thought.

'Forgive me for not taking your word for it, Stone. I would recommend you stick closely with Bryant on this one.'

Kim felt her toes curl inside her boots. It seemed to be the natural order of events anyway but she resented the hell out of being directed to do so.

'Sir, if you don't mind…'

'It wasn't a request, Stone.'

She stood abruptly. 'If that's all—'

'Sit back down,' he instructed. 'Don't sulk, Stone, it doesn't suit you. I say this because there are some cases that require a different approach. No one doubts your skills in getting the job done but occasionally a little tact and diplomacy—'

'With all due respect—'

'Stone, get my right fist open,' he said, sighing heavily.

'Sir?' she said, raising an eyebrow at the closed fist he held across the desk.

He looked from her face down at his clenched hand.

'It's a simple instruction. Get my right fist open.'

She leaned forwards and used her left hand to turn the fist upwards. She followed the length of his fingers into his palm and tried to dislodge them. She pulled at the thumb that was helping to hold the fingers in place. It didn't move.

She took her other hand and tried to lift the thumb with her left and prise the fingers away with her right.

Nothing budged.

She let go and sat back in her chair, unsure exactly what her boss was trying to prove.

He moved the closed hand towards her colleague. 'Bryant, get my fist open.'

Kim expected Bryant to reach out, but he stayed exactly where he was.

'Sir, would you mind opening your fist, please?' Bryant asked.

Magically the fingers came away and splayed apart.

Kim groaned.

'Point proven, Stone. Same problem, two different approaches. It never occurred to you to use your mouth.'

Well, it had, Kim reasoned, just not in the way he thought. Biting her boss's fingers would definitely have come up in her performance review.

Kim moved in her seat. 'May we…?'

'Go on, Stone,' he said, waving his hand towards the door.

She could feel Bryant's smirk burning into the back of her head all the way back to the squad room, which was silent when she entered.

Stacey was staring hard at the computer as Dawson glared dolefully at a pile of paper that stood like a tower block in the middle of his desk.

'We need to weed out the youngest and the oldest and—'

'I did. This is what's left.'

The process attached to missing persons was much more involved than people thought and was not as simple as passing on a few facts in a simple report.

Missing persons had historically been recorded only on paper but were now logged on a computerised system called 'Compact' and the procedure now split into two parts.

The person taking the initial call was required to ask sixteen very important questions in order to establish whether the person was actually missing from home or was just absent. The details included the usual – full name, date of birth, home address, description of the person, clothing that they were wearing, mental state and physical state – from which they built up a picture.

Once answered, the details were logged on the command and control system called OASIS. At this point a duty inspector was informed and had to make decisions on escalating the misper report or not.

The electronic system was vast and not always speedy so they worked through the paper copies of reports filed at Halesowen and the electronic system for other stations.

'Okay, divide the pile into four and let's get cracking.'

There was no higher priority than giving their victim a name.

Kim sat at the spare desk, and the room fell into silence. Only the sound of pages turning could be heard.

Kim used the process of elimination. The two most common forms of description were hair and eye colour. The eye that had remained visible through the swollen flesh had been blue.

Any report that didn't contain both blonde hair and blue eyes was turned face down onto the desk.

'Bloody depressing,' Bryant said, shaking his head.

She noted the way he gently placed each report that wasn't a match. She got it. The investigator in him wanted to delve deeper into every single one of these missing females. The father in him wanted to bring them home.

'How far back did you go, Kev?' she asked.

'Three months.'

So bloody many in so short a period of time.

'Got her,' Dawson said, holding aloft a piece of paper.

Everyone except Dawson looked at each other doubtfully.

His eyes moved over the details as he nodded. 'Yeah, boss. There's a picture. She's wearing that cross.' He began to read. 'Been missing since Saturday lunchtime. Reported by her parents. Her name is Jemima Lowe.'

Kim felt a bit of peace rest in her mind.

Her victim had a name.

Now Kim just had to find the bastard who'd killed her.

CHAPTER EIGHT

'Go on then. How much?' Bryant said.

She knew what he was asking. They often mused at house values. The property concerned was that of the Lowe family.

Dawson was bringing the family home. Kim hated that they had to see the body of their daughter in such a condition, but it was necessary for them to progress with the case.

She knew that Keats would have done his best to minimise their distress, but he was a pathologist, not a miracle worker. The truth and brutality of Jemima's battered face could not be hidden. There were no kind words that could disguise the pain their daughter had felt immediately prior to death. It was a picture that would never leave them.

It had been a positive identification based on clothing, jewellery, an appendix scar and a poorly formed bone in the little finger of the right hand.

Their victim was definitely thirty-one-year-old Jemima Lowe.

Kim narrowed her eyes and assessed the property. It was double fronted with a door nestled between two leaded bay windows.

The house was detached and the two-car garage ended the row of three similar properties.

'Three ten,' Bryant guessed.

Kim shook her head. No way was it over two hundred and eighty grand.

'Come on. It's gotta be four bedrooms if not five.'

She explained her disagreement. 'On the other side of that treeline is a busy road and the Merry Hill shopping centre. Look at the bigger picture.'

'Yeah but—'

'They're here,' she said as a vehicle rolled slowly towards them.

As the car stopped, Dawson got out of the front passenger seat and opened the rear door.

Mr Lowe stepped out and assisted his wife, who in turn held out her hand for the third occupant. Their other daughter.

Mr Lowe offered a brief nod to Dawson, who offered a respectful nod in return before getting back into the car.

She noted, as the family walked towards her, the absence of direct eye contact with each other. To do so would destroy their defences. To see their own pain reflected in the face of someone else would confirm what their hearts were not ready to accept.

Yet there was a physical connection threading the whole family together. Mr Lowe draped his arm loosely around the shoulders of his wife whose hand clung to that of her daughter. Sara Lowe had the same blonde hair as her older sister but she carried a few more healthy pounds.

'Mr Lowe, Mrs Lowe,' Bryant said, stepping forwards. 'Detective Sergeant Bryant and Detective Inspector Stone. May we come in?'

Mr Lowe hesitated before nodding yes. Every other inch of him begged them to go away. And Kim sincerely wished that they could.

Intruding on the grief of a family was like entering their bedroom in the middle of the night.

They followed the family as they walked slowly across the drive.

Mr Lowe opened the front door and stood aside for his wife and daughter to enter. Once inside, the family paused in the hallway, not knowing what to do. Everything was the same but strange now. Their house looked different because their daughter would never be there again.

No one knew what to do. Normality had been suspended until they found a new one.

'I'll make tea,' Mrs Lowe said to no one in particular.

It was an action, a movement, a minor distraction. The family liaison officer would arrive soon and even that small task would be shared.

A door to the right led to an informal lounge decorated in shades of beige. Kim saw a flat-screen TV in the corner.

Mr Lowe guided them inside. He took an armchair while she and Bryant took the sofa.

'We are sincerely sorry for your loss,' Kim offered.

Good manners prompted a nod as though the platitude meant something. It meant nothing. Anything other than it suddenly all being a mistake was meaningless to the grief-stricken man. And she understood. She had seen what he had just been forced to see. For her it was horrific enough; for him it was a trauma she couldn't measure.

Kim guessed him to be mid-fifties. The white shirt and charcoal trousers showed the body of a man who had stayed fit and trim. His hair was short and unashamedly grey. His face carried an outdoor complexion.

'Can we excuse Sara from this?' he asked, looking from her to Bryant. The sudden concern took its place in his eyes amongst the worry and the grief.

Kim nodded. She would speak to Jemima's sister only if absolutely necessary.

Mrs Lowe entered the room and placed a tray onto the glass coffee table. The tray contained a teapot, sugar bowl, milk jug but no teacups. No one commented as Mr Lowe stood for his wife to take the chair.

She was a woman who matched her husband's height inch for inch with the assistance of high heels. Her hair was a mass of unruly red curls being held in check by clips and a rubber band. As Mr Lowe stepped behind the chair and placed a hand on his wife's shoulder Kim couldn't help but notice what an attractive couple they made.

'Can you tell us when Jemima went missing?' Kim asked.

'Saturday afternoon,' Mrs Lowe offered. 'She was late from work. She's never late from work.'

Kim wondered if it was something the thirty-one-year-old did every Saturday. Come home for tea with the parents.

'Was Jemima married? Children?'

Mrs Lowe shook her head. 'I got the feeling it was something she was beginning to think about, but her career has taken precedence since she left university. She's an equine specialist but she's been working locally and living here until she could get everything sorted.'

'Sorted?' Kim asked.

'Oh, I'm sorry she's… she's…'

Mr Lowe took over from his wife, whose thoughts had been diverted by her own use of the present tense.

'Jemima suddenly made the decision to move to Dubai about five years ago. She went to work for a family of horse breeders. She's been back less than a month.'

Kim nodded her understanding.

'Did Jemima have a boyfriend?' she asked.

'She'd been seeing someone. Just a couple of dates, I think.'

Bryant's pen was poised above the notepad.

'His name is Simon Roach, someone she met while shopping over the road. Deputy manager, I think.'

'Did you meet him?'

'Once,' Mr Lowe confirmed. 'One night she brought him round for a meal.'

'And?' Bryant asked.

'I don't like to judge on first impressions.'

The message was loud and clear.

'Had Jemima had any problems with anyone that you know of?'

Mr Lowe frowned. 'Not at all. Jemima is… was a gentle soul.'

Mrs Lowe stifled a sob on the past tense. Mr Lowe squeezed her shoulder again.

'Jemima was not confrontational. She detested arguments and would always walk away.'

Kim stood. She had asked enough questions for now. They had intruded on the grief of this family long enough for one day.

Bryant followed suit and spoke before she had a chance. 'Thank you for your time and, again, we are sorry for your loss.'

Kim headed through the hallway.

A shadow moved at the top of the stairs followed by the gentle closing of a door.

Kim hesitated for just a second before leaving the house.

CHAPTER NINE

Kim switched on the iPod. Bach was a composer she hadn't listened to extensively before, but the string work in the Brandenburg Concertos complemented her work on the bike.

He had scored the concertos for several instruments: two natural horns, three oboes, a bassoon, two violins, a viola and a cello. The artistry required to bring all of those components together to produce a piece of music was not unlike the task of forming the parts strewn over her garage floor. One day it would grow up into a 1954 BSA Goldstar.

She had called time on the working day following the meeting with Jemima's parents. Dawson was getting paper cuts from the missing-persons reports. Stacey was going cross-eyed staring at the screen, and Bryant had been stuck with her since first thing. They all deserved the opportunity to get home before seven p.m.

She hated this part of a case: the beginning, when the letters on the whiteboard in the office had room to breathe. To her it always felt like trying to stack pebbles. Without some kind of mortar it was going nowhere.

She had taken the time to clean all her windows and take Barney for his night-time walk. He now lay straddling the threshold of the doorway to the kitchen. At the tip of his front paws lay a portion of antler bone. The treat was supposed to last a long time and give the dog something to work at. In Barney's case, he tried every now and again and then just left it. At this rate he could pass it on to his children, Kim mused.

Her dog was all about instant gratification.

Barney had come to her from one of her earlier cases. He had been the faithful pet of a convicted rapist who had been murdered on the Thorns Road. Following the attack the dog had not run away to freedom but had chosen to sit beside his master with his blood-spattered fur. And although the marks were now gone Kim still pictured him sitting there.

Clearer still was the image of him being led away from an old lady unable to take care of him and placed in the 'no-go' area of the dog's home. His kennel had lacked even a nameplate. So sure was the facility that he would not be re-homed again.

Unfortunately, for whatever reason, the dog didn't play well with others and had seen more homes than a Barratt's digger.

Kim gave him one last rub and stood, fully aware that she had more in common with a dog than anyone else in her life.

She tipped her head at him. Much the same way he did at her. 'Want a carrot?'

His ears pricked and his tail whooshed the floor.

'Yeah, I thought—'

Her words ended as the mobile phone next to the iPod began to ring. Good news didn't usually come after midnight.

She checked the display. It was a number she didn't recognise. 'Stone,' she answered.

'Ah, Inspector, I thought you'd be up.'

At first the lazy, baiting voice didn't register, but when it did she groaned into the mouthpiece.

Tracy Frost, local reporter, national pain in the arse and someone who should not have had her number.

'Is it not midnight under your rock, Frost?' she asked.

'Oh, you know us reporters. We never sleep.'

Kim thought the term 'reporter' held a little too much dignity and professionalism to apply to Tracy, but she let it pass. The woman had been the pea beneath her mattress during her last major investigation, threatening to expose a kidnapping story despite a media blackout. The timeliness of the search had been imperative to the well-being of the girls, but Tracy Frost had added just that bit of extra pressure.

'A bit like you police officers, eh? We are so much alike.'

Kim held the phone away from her ear and looked at it as though it had just licked her lobe. Was this woman on medication?

'I'm hanging up now so…'

'I wouldn't if I were you. You're going to want to hear—'

'Tracy, you do know that we're not friends, don't you?' Kim clarified.

'Of course,' she said, chuckling.

'And you know that I can't stand the sight of you and will never give you the heads-up on any case I'm working?'

'Absolutely,' Tracy answered.

'Then why the hell are you on the other end of my phone?'

Kim held her breath, praying that the news of Westerley had not yet broken. She didn't want to have to get Woody out of bed to fight fires at this time of night.

'Well, I'm writing a feature about West Mercia having recently solved a few cold cases. To be honest the article focusses more on the fact that West Midlands Police have not, and your name does come up a bit so I thought I'd give you the chance to comment.'

Kim sighed with both relief and disgust at the same time. Trust Tracy Frost to concentrate on the negative. She also knew that the chance to comment realistically meant opportunity to defend herself.

'Frost, I'm going to hang up now,' Kim said, moving the phone away from her ear.

'Keep your knickers on, Stone. I already asked your boss for a quote and he refused, so I thought I'd come to you, seeing as your name will be all over it.'

Of course it would. Kim's refusal to play nice with the woman often meant she was front and centre when Tracy mentioned anything to do with West Midlands Police. Frost's call to Woody further explained the timeliness of the visit to Westerley.

'One of the cold cases I'm going to mention is that guy named Bob…'

'Who the hell is…?'

'Unidentified male found in Fens Pools reservoir two years ago with his fingers chopped off. I refer to him as Bob—'

Kim wrinkled her nose in distaste. 'You called him Bob because he was found in the water?'

'I called him Bob because he reminded me of my uncle Robert. Fuck me, Stone. I'm not that cold.'

Kim's inner jury was out on that one.

Kim placed the phone on loudspeaker and put it on the worktop. She moved back to the pile of parts in the middle of the garage and knelt. She was far more interested in fitting the connecting rod to the piston assembly than anything this low life had to say.

Kim said nothing to encourage her to continue but Tracy chose to anyway.

'You remember it, surely?'

'I remember it, but it wasn't my case,' Kim answered, reaching for the blowtorch.

It had been handled by Brierley Hill, which was a stone's throw from the location the body was found. She'd had no involvement.

'His killer was never found.'

'And?' Kim asked. That's what happened sometimes. No police officer liked it but never forgot an unsolved case. It prodded at you periodically like an unscratched itch.

'Come on, Stone. Surely you're intrigued by a guy with no fingers. Doesn't that pique your interest? A killer does something to make sure you can't identify the victim and gets away with it. Is that not offensive to you?'

Yes it was and this infuriating woman bloody well knew it.

Kim noted with a smile that Barney had turned around and now lay with his behind facing the phone. He really was a clever dog.

Kim put down the blowtorch and began moving things around on the workbench.

'Bloody hell, Stone, what are you doing?' Tracy shouted.

'Looking for a tool, so if you're done with our late night—'

'Come on, Inspector. If this had been one of yours there's no way it would—'

'Aaaah, spanner,' Kim said.

'Excuse me,' Tracy said.

'Found it,' she said, reaching for the tool.

'This poor guy has no identity, no name. I mean, imagine if that was one of your family members, eh? He wouldn't have been dismissed quite so—'

'No victim is dismissed,' Kim snapped and realised too late that she had given this woman exactly what she'd been seeking. A reaction. 'I'm hanging up now, Frost,' she said, reaching for the phone.

'And just to let you know I've bought new shoes for your commendation cere—'

Kim switched off the phone and enjoyed the sudden peace that entered the room. It had been no less invaded than if the woman had marched right in and sat down.

She reached over and brought Bach once more into her special place.

What had Tracy Frost been thinking? Like Kim really needed to take on cases unsolved by other teams in the borough. Her own local policing unit kept her busy enough.

And yet, as she tried to fit the connecting rod to the piston, Kim found herself thinking about a man named Bob.

CHAPTER TEN

Tracy Frost let herself into the small rented house at the bottom of Quarry Bank high street. Although it didn't fall under the postcode for the more affluent area of Amblecote she used it in her postal address anyway.

Before doing anything else she stepped over to the laptop on the dining table and hit the space bar. The computer hummed to life and revealed that the white Audi TT, her most prized possession, filled the centre screen.

In Quarry Bank high street a car like hers could attract negative attention. Groups heading to one of the chip shops further up the hill sometimes stopped and admired it. Kids looking in the window of the motorcycle shop opposite might pop across the road to take a peek. Jealous neighbours might flatten a tyre or two. A regular occurrence before she'd had the camera installed.

It was almost one in the morning, and there'd be very few people passing her car tonight.

She left the screen open as she removed her five-inch heels. She hated the damn things, but she wouldn't be without them for anything. She loved her car more than anything, but, given a choice, she would keep her heels. Her sanity depended on it.

All day she'd been plagued by a feeling of unease. She'd done all the things that normally quieted any anxiety within her. She had checked her online bills and found nothing outstanding.

Her bank balance was hovering exactly where it always did, just below her overdraft limit.

She had gone backwards and forwards in her diary to make sure there were no birthdays or anniversaries forgotten or imminent.

She had phoned her mother and listened to the minor details on just about everything since her last phone call. As usual she had pretended that everything was fine and that she really would try to go round to see them both sometime in the coming week. She hated that both statements were lies and hated even more that her mother knew it.

She'd hoped that a bit of goading of her least favourite police officer would help lift her mood, but it hadn't.

What she hadn't admitted to Kim Stone was an element of guilt that accompanied any thought of Bob. Two years ago, when she'd watched his body being loaded into the ambulance, Tracy had vowed to expose whoever had done this to him. She had fully intended to speak to her editor about a human-interest piece focussed on finding out who he was.

Two days later she'd been covering the story of a local footballer whose cocaine addiction had been leaked by one of his mistresses. She had been unable to resist a sex and drugs piece, and her story had amassed the second highest circulation of the *Dudley Star*, beaten only by a commemoration edition for Princess Diana.

When she'd spoken to her editor the following week about Bob he'd had trouble recalling the man pulled from the lake and had denied her request. She wasn't part of the police force tasked with investigating his murder, but she felt some kind of responsibility that his murderer still walked free. It was one of the things that periodically jumped into her consciousness and slapped her around a little. The news that West Mercia had been successful in clearing a few old cases had brought Bob back to the forefront of her mind.

During the course of the day she had tried everything she could think of, yet the feeling had not cleared.

Maybe she just needed some sleep. These feelings rarely accompanied her into the next day.

She carried the pair of Jimmy Choos up to the bedroom and opened the door. She placed them behind the other pointy-toed stilettos in the Anouk range. So far she had six pairs. And every one of them had a support in the left shoe.

She knew people laughed behind her back as she tottered around on them, and that was fine because what they didn't know was that the shoes helped her hide the real problem.

The one that had plagued her for most of her life.

CHAPTER ELEVEN

Oh, Mummy, I miss you every single day.

I have trudged through the sludge of years since you left me.

How strange that I always phrase it that way in my mind. You left me. You didn't leave me. You fucking died.

Sorry, Mummy, you don't like swearing and neither do I. It is a sign of a limited vocabulary, you said.

I always agree with you, Mummy. Eventually.

I remember one time when I didn't. I woke up and my clothes were laid out at the bottom of the bed.

It was a brown pinafore dress that buttoned up the front. It was dark brown. The colour of mud. It was a rectangle that fell at a no man's land between my knees and my ankles. A long, shapeless block of dirt with two flaps as mock pockets on the front. Not even real pockets.

I liked pockets.

I hated it. I didn't want to wear it, and I told you I wouldn't.

You asked me if I would reconsider.

I said no.

You gave me that sad smile, and I knew I'd made a mistake. But I couldn't go back.

And neither would you.

Without speaking you marched to my room. You brought down all my favourite clothes. You took the scissors, the sharp ones you used to cut my hair. I knew they were sharp because one time you nicked my neck while giving me a trim.

You sat at the kitchen table, a smile playing across your mouth, and I was happy to see any expression at all.

Cut. Cut. Cut.

I watched as you began to snip them to smithereens – like streamers, slivers of material fell to the ground, intertwining with each other like a pit of snakes.

The pinafore lay folded on the table between us.

You didn't cut along seams. You cut so they could never be repaired. The damage was done.

A lesson to be learned.

I started to undress and the scissors slowed but they didn't stop. I looked at you, but you didn't look at me because you knew.

You had won.

I slipped on the yellow T-shirt and then the slab of brown. It hung like a block of unyielding chocolate.

You placed the scissors on the kitchen table, gently and without speaking, and stood at the sink.

I stood in the middle of the kitchen, staring at your back. The only sound was your hand swishing the warm water as you turned the washing-up liquid into bubbles.

But still you didn't speak. What else had I done wrong? I had done what you asked but still that wall of silence and a spine bent with displeasure.

'Mummy…'

You turned. Your face was impenetrable, but somewhere beneath was the promise of a smile.

This was my moment, my opportunity to make our world right again.

If only I said the right thing.

'Mummy, play with me.'

And, finally, you smiled.

But you're not here to play with me any more, are you, Mummy?
But my other friends are.

I must go now.
My next best friend is waiting.

CHAPTER TWELVE

'Okay, folks, let's get to it. Stace, what do we know about the team at Westerley?' Kim asked, eager to get moving on the first full day of investigation.

'Professor Christopher Wright was born in 1959. His father died when he was two years old and his mother never remarried. He's a confirmed bachelor and has worked in various medical fields before settling on human biology. He has written countless papers and is listed as a consultant to seven universities that I've found so far.'

'Clever chappie,' Bryant observed.

'Oh, there's more,' Stacey said, continuing. 'He is a qualified expert and has testified in at least three murder investigations and two appeals. He's got a reputation for remaining calm even under robust cross-examination. Also, in addition to his full-time job at Westerley he's still pretty active on the lecturing circuit.

'There was a complaint lodged against him in his early teaching days by one of his students, but it was unfounded and later retracted. Oh, and he has a cat named Brian.'

'Bloody hell, Stace,' Kev said snidely. 'What did you do, take him out?'

'To be honest he's plastered all over the internet. He wasn't hard to find,' Stacey admitted.

Kim opened her mouth to ask a question, but the detective constable beat her to it with the answer.

'No criminal record, boss. Three parking tickets all paid on time.'

'Bit of an open book,' Bryant said. There was nothing there that warranted any kind of note-taking.

'Catherine Evans, on the other hand, is a completely different story,' Stacey said, raising her eyebrows. 'No articles and no published papers. Found her on LinkedIn but no Facebook or Twitter. Really weird.'

Not that strange, Kim thought. LinkedIn, she knew, was a type of Facebook for professionals. She wasn't on it. Neither was she on Facebook or Twitter. Some people just chose to live their lives away from social media.

'Next.'

'Jameel Mohammed is twenty-two, was top of his class for statistical analysis at Loughborough University. You can find him on Facebook, Twitter, Snapchat and Pinterest. There are six video clips of him on YouTube, playing the guitar... badly. Lives at home in Netherton with his mum and dad and two older sisters.'

Okay, Kim mused. Nothing there was screaming 'I'm a murderer'.

'Keep digging on Catherine and I think we need to cast the net a bit wider. Get on to Professor Wright and get a list of people involved with setting up Westerley.'

'Will do, boss.'

Kim rubbed at her chin. 'Stace, before you start that, can you get me the aerial view of the site?'

Stacey tapped a few keys and Kim moved to stand behind her.

As the camera zoomed in Kim waited until she could make out the whole area. 'I want a better idea of how he got her in there.'

Google continued to rotate the world before her eyes.

'Stop. There's the stream running through which marks the boundary of Westerley land so we know that Jemima wasn't actually dumped on their property.'

Kim couldn't help wondering if that was significant.

'Zoom back out… slowly. Is there anything else in the area?'

Both she and Stacey stared as the camera view backed up.

'Is that a road, Stace?'

Stacey zoomed back in. 'Kind of.'

It was barely a single-track carriageway that on closer inspection was a dirt track. It was little more than a few tyre tracks driven into the grass.

'You really think one man carried her up that grass bank alone, guv?'

'She was delivered somehow, Bryant, and it wasn't by Royal Mail.' She turned back to Stacey. 'Zoom back out. Jesus, there's nothing around there.'

The choice of the location was becoming a real source of intrigue for her. There had to be a significance, and she wanted to know what it was.

'Okay, Stace, you know what you're doing. Kev, I want you focussing on access and CCTV. How the hell did he get her up there?'

Already something here was not making sense.

CHAPTER THIRTEEN

'Guv, can you remind me what I did to deserve the pleasure of coming back here with you?'

'You're just lucky, I suppose,' Kim said as they waited for the gate to open.

'Oh yeah.'

'Bryant, you know I have a very fair way of choosing who gets the shit jobs. Whoever pisses me off the most. Simple.'

'Ah, that explains why it's always me.'

Kim opened her mouth to argue but no, he was right.

And still the gate hadn't opened.

'It wasn't this hard for our bloody murderer to get in,' Kim moaned, giving the button another press.

The gate began to move.

Kim drove through and across the gravel.

She glanced to the line of cars and groaned inwardly when she saw the red pickup truck of Daniel Bate.

'Not one word,' she growled at Bryant.

'Yeah, I appear to be in enough trouble as it is.'

She parked up at the end of the row beside a silver Aston Martin. It was a car she hadn't seen parked there the previous day.

'Okay, I'm gonna get Catherine to take me on a bit of a tour and I want you to chat to the others.'

She got out of the car and turned to lock the door.

'Ah, Kim. I hoped you'd be back,' Daniel Bate said, approaching his vehicle.

'Why are you still here?' she asked.

'Nothing too urgent back in Dundee so I thought I'd hang around. Annoy people for a while.'

'Must be nice to have that level of flexibility,' she observed.

'I've earned it,' he stated simply.

Annoyingly, she knew it to be true. Their time spent on the Crestwood case had shown her Daniel was not afraid of hard work.

'Well, just don't annoy me,' she said to his back.

'Believe it or not, I'm not even trying. Yet.'

He swung open the passenger door. Lola, his one-eyed dog, jumped down to the ground, shook her body then wagged her tail. The dog turned, stared for a second and then bounded towards her at the end of the pickup truck. Kim wasn't sure how the dog's vision was affected but it didn't seem to bother her one bit.

Kim instantly held out her hand for the dog to sniff.

'Pretty pointless doing that,' Daniel said, walking towards her. A lead dangled from his hand. 'Dogs' noses are so powerful she could smell you before you came through the gate.'

Yeah, Kim knew that, but it was still her natural reaction to show the dog she was no threat.

The dog started sniffing madly at her boots and offered a couple of playful barks.

Daniel shook his head, bemused. 'She likes you. God only knows why.'

Bryant chuckled, knowingly. 'She can smell Barney.'

Kim threw him a murderous look.

'Who's Barney?' Daniel asked, looking from her to Bryant.

'My goldfish,' she answered.

Daniel looked down to where Lola's attention was still fixed on her boot.

He raised an eyebrow. 'What did you do, stamp on him?'

'Yeah, because he pissed me off,' she said, walking away.

She heard Daniel laugh somewhere behind her.

She opened the Portakabin door and walked into the chest of a navy blue thick-knit jumper. She looked up but then levelled her gaze as the man stepped down onto the dirt patch.

The first thing she noticed was that the sun had disappeared behind either his wrestler's body or his shaved head.

'And you are?' she asked.

'Darren James, security and going home.'

He plucked at a lanyard around his neck and produced a security licence.

He'd obviously spent the night at the facility guarding the bodies and was under the illusion he could simply finish his shift and leave.

'Well, you got the first two right but not the third,' Kim advised. 'You won't be going anywhere until Bryant here has had a word with you.'

'No way, love. Me bed's calling after a thirteen-hour shift.' He nodded towards the open door. 'Me boss is in there, and you can take it up with him.'

She peered at his badge. 'Instead of "love" try "Detective Inspector" and don't make me cuff you to the door.'

He looked to Bryant.

She rolled her eyes. 'I can't actually do that, Darren, but we do need you to stay.'

He was still looking at her doubtfully. Honestly, could no one take a joke any more?

'Bryant will speak with you first so you can get off, okay?'

He nodded. 'All right if I have a smoke first?'

'Go for it,' she said, walking around him.

She stepped into the Portakabin.

Jameel and his companion turned. Jameel nodded briefly and turned back to the screen. The gaze of the man next to him lingered.

Kim met the look squarely. The expensive grey suit told her she was looking at the owner of the Aston Martin outside. He was a man that wore a pricey suit well. Not too tight and not too loose. His shirt was a crisp white with a burgundy silk tie. His chestnut hair was cut stylishly and professionally short but he had the blackest eyelashes she had ever seen on a man.

He stood and offered his hand. She reached out and shook it.

'Curtis Grant, Managing Director of Elite Systems Security.'

Kim recognised the name. It was embroidered into Darren's jumper.

From the corner of her eye she could see the quad grid on Jameel's screen. 'You set up the CCTV here?' she asked.

He nodded. 'We offer a complete security service to meet all your needs.'

He began to reach into his suit pocket and Kim held up her hand. He may have been in the habit of offering a business card to everyone he met but she wasn't in the market for his services.

He took another step forwards. 'Professor Wright asked me to come in. We're looking at an upgrade.'

The words horse and bolted sprang to mind but this was not her business.

She turned away and took two steps further into the Portakabin.

'Morning, Professor,' she offered. Now that was progress. She had learned to offer a morning greeting. Woody would be so proud.

'Please, Inspector, call me Chris.'

She nodded the acknowledgement. She very rarely allowed people to drop her title. The use of her first name was an intimacy that she did not invite. It was good for people involved in a case to remember they were dealing with police officers and not friends. Although the title dropping could be used to her own advantage sometimes.

His voice dropped to a whisper as he turned his back towards the others. 'Have there been any developments on the case – anything you can share with us?'

Kim could understand why he was asking. He was in charge of the facility and he'd been right there with them when the body had been found. However, he was a civilian and she could no more share details of the case with him than she could with anyone else.

'I'm sorry, Professor, but I can't really discuss our lines of enquiry.'

She had been unable to force his first name out of her mouth.

She ignored the surprise on his face and continued with her reason for being here. 'I'd like to take a walk around with…'

'Catherine is just about to start her morning checks. Perhaps you could tag along.'

Perfect.

She nodded her agreement and headed towards the woman whose concentration was fixed on the clipboard.

'The Professor said I could—'

'I heard, Inspector. I'm not deaf,' Catherine said without raising her head.

Clearly not a morning person, Kim surmised. She didn't hold it against her. She herself had yet to find any time of day that enhanced her mood.

However, she was not a patient person. She offered a small cough.

Catherine finally turned and looked at her. There was neither a smile nor a frown.

'Subtle,' she said, standing and towering over Kim. The loose jeans and plain black vest top enhanced the woman's androgynous shape. 'I am now ready to make a start.'

Kim transferred her mobile to the back pocket of her black canvas jeans and removed her jacket. The temperature was around nineteen and humid.

She followed Catherine out the door and turned left. The discovery of Jemima's body had curtailed their guided tour and Kim could see they were now taking the other route.

'So you're an cntomologist?' Kim asked as they left the gravel and stepped onto grass.

'Yes,' Catherine answered.

'And you've worked here for—'

'I'm thinking, Inspector. I work as I walk.'

So do I, Kim thought. *Or at least I try to.*

Catherine's words were not unpleasant or rude. Merely cool and detached. Not unlike herself, Kim conceded.

'Am I a suspect?' she asked and Kim saw the first evidence of an expression. It was the hint of a smile.

'Everyone is a suspect,' Kim answered honestly. 'So…'

'I have worked at Westerley since it opened, having been asked by Professor Wright to leave my old job.'

'And you two met…?'

'I was a student of his at Aston University.'

'So what appealed to you about… oh my God!' Kim exclaimed.

'I'd like you to meet Elvis,' Catherine said.

A body had been placed half sitting, half lying against the trunk of the tree. Kim was glad Catherine pointed out the name as she honestly could not have fixed a gender.

It wasn't the sight of the body that had startled her. It was the volume of wasps.

One buzzed close to her ear and she instantly swatted it away. Two hovered close to Catherine's right eye, but she made no move to displace them.

Nerves of steel, Kim noted.

'Elvis is helping us learn about wasp activity on the body.'

'How?' Kim asked.

Catherine leaned down closer to the body. Kim did not. She had seen many dead bodies that were combed for clues to help her do her job. Somehow the sight of corpses deliberately abandoned to the insect and wildlife community for feasting and housing was a new experience for her.

'We all know that clumps of fly eggs hatch into thousands of maggots in as little as four to six hours. But yellow jackets and wasps show up within the first few hours too. Some feed on the body itself. Others snag flies in their wing, carry them off and decapitate them with one swift bite of their jaws. Others feast on the masses of fly eggs or the young maggots hatching in the body's openings.'

'So what are you hoping to learn about the wasps?' Kim asked, taking a step back. Catherine's movement around the body had caused a clump of them to emerge from the left eye of the corpse.

Catherine didn't move a muscle.

'I want to analyse the level of wasp activity against the level of decomposition. The fresh stage, the bloated stage, the decay stage and the dry stage.'

Kim could verify from the unique aroma that Elvis had not yet reached the dry stage.

'Is there a reason Elvis is under a tree?'

Catherine nodded as she pushed herself to her feet.

'Bodies left in the sun tend to mummify. The skin becomes tough like leather, impervious to maggots.'

Kim was prevented from asking anything further as Catherine began to write. Kim watched the hand move across the paper but it was the joints that caught her eye. All four knuckles contrasted with the tanned skin. Each one of them was white with scar tissue.

'You can speak,' Catherine said.

The woman tried to write something and then shook the pen up and down.

'You really do like your insects, don't you?'

'I am fascinated by their ability to survive. I only hope they never learn to communicate with each other.'

'Why?' Kim asked, finding the statement a little strange.

'Because there are over a million species of insect and they represent more than half of all known living organisms. So if they ever managed to communicate with each other, we're in big trouble.'

Kim had never thought of that. But perhaps Catherine had thought about it enough for both of them.

Catherine shook the pen again and then looked at Kim.

'Do you…?'

Kim shook her head.

As Catherine spun it between her palms Kim glanced over towards the location she'd stood in just twenty-four hours earlier. There was no activity.

'Have the techs gone?'

Catherine nodded. 'Just before I got in this morning.'

Kim hadn't been informed they'd finished collecting evidence.

She took out her phone and dialled Woody's number.

'Stone,' he greeted.

'The techs have gone, sir. It's a pretty big area. I can't believe they've finished combing it already.'

'I know,' he responded. 'It was my instruction. They were called off first thing this morning.'

'May I ask…?'

'Not that I have to explain my decisions to you but a deserted terror cell was discovered in Digbeth yesterday afternoon.'

Ah, she needed no further explanation. That was a priority job. Every inch of an abandoned cell would be analysed. Over here, Kim was dealing with one person who was already dead. Clues in Digbeth could lead to saving hundreds if not thousands of people.

But just because she understood it didn't mean she had to like it.

'Okay, sir, thank you for letting me know.'

She ended the call before he could respond to her little dig about being kept in the dark.

Catherine glanced back towards the Portakabin that was only three hundred feet away and held up the empty pen.

'I need to get…'

'Can you send Bryant out?' Kim asked. Her mind had already left Catherine and was heading back over to the crime scene.

Catherine nodded and headed back.

Kim took a few steps away from Elvis and his occupants and watched as Catherine strode back towards the office.

It took a very special kind of person to derive so much pleasure from the activity and habits of insects, Kim couldn't help thinking.

CHAPTER FOURTEEN

'You could have removed your jacket, Bryant,' Kim said as he approached.

'Happy the way I am, thanks.'

Kim shook her head. She had rarely seen him without a jacket outside of their squad room.

'Get anything from inside?' she asked, walking across the field.

'In that amount of time?' he retorted.

'Well… something… anything… '

'And you found out what exactly?' he asked.

Kim smiled. 'Well, since you ask, I found out that Catherine appears to like insects more than she likes people. She has very curious scarring to her right hand and is not easily rattled.'

Bryant let out a breath. 'All that without any threat of waterboarding?'

'Yeah. Your turn.'

'I found out the security guy's name.'

She growled.

'Okay, he lives half a mile down the road and although the place gives him the creeps it's convenient. He used to work the doors, but the boss moved him here.'

'Anything else?' she asked.

'Yeah, he's supposed to do a full patrol every two hours but most nights he doesn't bother and just signs the sheet off as checked.'

'Fabulous,' Kim said. 'I suspect he'll be doing his patrols now if he wants to keep his job.'

Bryant nodded towards the location of the crime scene. 'So why the early withdrawal?'

'Abandoned terror cell in Digbeth.'

Bryant sighed his understanding. 'So are we forensics now as well?'

As detectives, he knew they became whatever they needed to be to get the job done.

They'd reached the other side of the field. She stepped across the brook and located the exact spot where Jemima had been dumped. The ankle-high grass had been flattened underfoot like a crop circle. A single trail had been trodden down the hill where the tech van would have been parked while they worked.

Kim stood at the crest of the hill. The land started rising in height about six feet from the path, climbing steadily for about thirty feet, before dropping down towards the entrance gate.

From where she stood, the direct route down to the path was quicker but steep, so the techies had walked along the brow until the incline had lessened, making it far less hazardous.

'Unlikely there's anything left to find, guv,' Bryant said, using a handkerchief to wipe his forehead. Although the techs had left the area, a line of tape stretched the 150-feet gap between two trees.

'But not definite,' she said, walking past him but continuing to look down over the descent. The area behind them was meaningless now it had been examined but worse, trampled. And a line search wasn't going to do any good with just the two of them.

But activity had occurred before her. The killer had parked his vehicle, extracted Jemima, dragged and carried her up the hill and then laid her down and killed her.

She walked another few steps to the east and then turned back.

'Wait here,' she said as she trod the path that the techs had made and arrived at the foot of the hill. She walked along the path until she was level with Bryant's position.

She assessed that she was now at the shortest, most direct but steepest route from the path to the top.

'Bryant, come down,' she called.

By the time he reached her she had already found what she was looking for.

'Look at the grass,' she said, pointing to a flattened area a foot away from the path.

Bryant shrugged. 'What am I looking for exactly?' he said, stepping to the other side of the line.

'This is his trail,' she said, walking up the hill, following the line of flattened grass.

The route was not completely straight and where the route adjusted slightly, a circular indent was faintly noticeable in the grass.

As they continued to follow the line it was clear they were headed for the exact spot Jemima had been found.

'What do you make of those other marks, guv?' Bryant asked as they headed back down the hill.

Kim paused halfway down and lowered herself to the ground. She lay in the grass and adjusted her position until she fitted into the shape that had been made by Jemima's body. Taller grass and nettles rose up either side of her.

'Guv, is there any need…?'

'It's her head,' she said, ignoring him. 'As she's being pulled along her head is bouncing around, freely.'

While she was being dragged in a straight line Jemima's head would have made no impact in the grass already flattened by her body but when her killer changed direction, even slightly, her head would have taken a second to catch up.

She was about to raise herself up when she heard a familiar voice.

Daniel Bate called to her from the bottom of the hill. 'Hey, Inspector, is this a private picnic or can anyone join in?

She sat up. 'Daniel, how many times do I have to tell you to—'

'Piss off?' he asked. 'Not at all, Inspector, as I didn't come looking for you.' He looked up to the hill. 'I think you'll find I actively tried to avoid you.'

Good – they finally understood each other.

He stroked the head of Lola beside him. 'Although it was worth it to hear you use my first name.'

Okay, maybe they didn't. And she hadn't noticed the slip.

'Bryant, take photos,' she instructed.

'Of what?' he asked.

'Just take one of exactly where I am, then the line back up the hill and the top of the hill.'

He took out his phone and took a photo, trying to hide his smirk. Daniel didn't even try.

'Isn't there somewhere you have to be?' she asked him, making a move to stand up.

He chuckled and shook his head. 'Actually, no, I'm quite enjoying myself.'

Kim responded with a sound of disgust as she placed her hands either side of her to push herself up.

'Shit,' she cried as her right hand met with something in the grass. It was the hand she'd cut almost to the bone on her last major investigation and which still gave her a little discomfort now.

'What?' Bryant asked, stepping forwards.

She reached down, gingerly, and retrieved the object.

'What the hell is that?' Bryant asked, as she held out the palm of her hand.

It looked to her like a hairgrip. White plastic covered the wire that shaped it. A brass-coloured motif decorated its centre.

She looked closer. The motif was a heart cut into two with a jagged edge. The section that had dug into her palm. It reminded Kim of a necklace that she'd seen somewhere that came in a pack of two and each person wore one half of the heart.

'My missus uses something like that,' Bryant said. 'Without the heart, obviously, but it's for holding her fringe back when she's straightening her hair.'

Yeah, that was exactly what she'd been thinking.

Bryant took an evidence bag from his jacket pocket. She dropped it in and turned to Daniel.

'Well, it's been lovely to see you again…' she reached down and patted the dog '… Lola.'

She smiled and turned on her heel.

Her mind was already focussed on the hairgrip. And getting it over to Keats.

But she'd learned much more than she'd mentioned.

She no longer needed to wait for the toxicology report to know that Jemima had been drugged. The only question remaining was with what.

Additionally, the knowledge that she had been dragged, probably by her ankles to the top of the hill, instead of carried, indicated to Kim that their killer was working alone.

CHAPTER FIFTEEN

Kim found the cold sterility of the morgue refreshing. The heat outside was already early twenties on what promised to be another heavy, humid day.

The hairgrip in Bryant's pocket was still on her mind. At this point she had no idea if the object was even connected. It could have been lost by anyone.

A quick phone call to Jemima's mother had ruled out their victim using any type of grip at all. She preferred her hair loose and her mother had said she wasn't a heart embellishment type of girl. Only a simple elastic band, she had said, with a catch in her voice.

Keats turned as they entered.

'Oh, Inspector, I am gladdened we meet again. Yesterday, our parting was—'

'Not soon enough,' she retorted. 'Now must we really do this every time?'

He considered for a second. 'Yes, I feel we must or people would get the idea we liked and respected each other.'

'Not from me,' she said, moving towards their victim.

Jemima's body was covered by a simple white sheet that was just slightly tucked around her shoulders.

And that was one of the reasons Keats was allowed a little fun. It was the small things.

'Shall we begin,' Kim asked.

'Already done. I made an early start. I have two new customers from a motorway accident on the way.'

He reached for the clipboard from the metal counter.

'Okay, first thing to note. Her panties were on backwards. Not sure if that means something.'

Kim looked at Bryant who took out his pocket notebook.

'Any sign of sexual assault?' Kim asked.

Keats shook his head. 'Unlikely. No bruising, no redness and no trace of semen.'

She nodded and he continued. 'Cause of death was asphyxiation caused by soil blocking the airway. There was enough dirt to plant a small herb garden.' He pointed to a plastic container the size of a takeaway tub. 'That's what we removed.'

Kim stepped over and held it up. She couldn't imagine that volume of dirt forced into a person's mouth.

'We've sent off samples to see if there's anything in there that can help.'

Kim nodded. 'Anything else?'

Keats frowned. 'Yes. There are no defensive wounds, but there is some bruising to the upper arms and more recently to the ankles.'

Keats pulled up the sheet around Jemima's feet.

Kim immediately pictured her recent experiment at the site. She already knew.

She stepped to the end of the body and looked at her. 'He dragged her up the hill,' Kim said, forming her hands around the ankles. Her fingers matched the bruise marks almost perfectly.

'He, Inspector? You're already assuming it's a male without the presence of sexual assault?'

Kim nodded slowly.

He shrugged. 'Your suspicion may explain the fresh graze mark on the small of her back and the small pieces of gravel embedded in her skin.'

Kim lifted up the sheet and viewed the faint marks on the upper arms. 'I think these are from when she was taken.' She paused for another ten seconds. 'And I'm guessing our guy is about five foot seven or taller.'

Keats sighed. 'Inspector, you cannot possibly...'

His words trailed away as she removed her jacket.

'Oh dear, you're not staying, are you?' he asked.

She stood beside Keats. His five-six stature fell three inches below hers.

'Okay, now move me from here to the door,' she instructed.

'Excuse me.'

'It's simple enough, Keats. Move me from here to the door,' she repeated.

Keats looked at Bryant who shook his head.

'Must I stop this side of the door?'

'Just do it,' she snapped.

He shrugged and stood behind her.

'Are you dead?' he asked.

'You wish, Keats. Not dead but let's just say I'm pliable...'

'Now that would...'

'Don't think about it, just do it.'

'Okay,' he said, placing his hands above her waist but beneath her breasts.

He began to propel her forwards towards the door. Like air from a tyre she let some of the rigidity fall from her legs. She stumbled and weaved. Keats's hands moved all around her back and to her waist to keep her steady and moving.

She put the brakes on her feet just short of the doorway.

'Okay, thanks,' she said, returning to the starting point.

She turned her back on Bryant. 'Now you do it.'

He stood behind her and she knew that the top of her head was level with his nose.

Instinctively he grabbed her upper arms and marched her forwards. She did the same with her gait but still she moved at speed, propelled towards the door.

'And what has that little role play told us?' Keats asked.

'Height,' she said, pointing at the spot on her arms. She looked at Keats. 'You are… umm… shorter than I am so you had to grab me around the middle. Bryant is taller and his natural instinct was to grab my arms and push me forwards.'

Bryant considered. 'Either a male or a very tall woman.'

Kim conceded the point.

'Well, if the floor show has quite finished, the stomach contents have been sent for analysis. Not easy to identify, just mush.'

Kim stood at the top of the metal tray. As she looked down she noticed two kinks in the front of the thin blonde hair.

She held out her hand towards Bryant. Like any assistant surgeon he knew exactly what she wanted.

The evidence bag landed in her palm. She held it forwards, towards Keats.

'Not sure if this is anything…'

'Where the hell did you get that?' Keats asked, staring down at the bag.

He took it from her and turned it over to get a better look.

'Near to where Jemima's body was found,' she explained, surprised by his reaction. 'What's the problem?'

Still carrying the bag, he moved towards the table in the corner. 'I have a matching one here,' he said, holding up an identical bag.

Kim was confused. 'I didn't see that yesterday.'

'You wouldn't have done, Inspector. I had to dig it out of her face.'

Bryant's gasp preceded a veil of silence that fell between them. Kim knew they were all pondering the level of force required behind the blows to bury that object in her skin.

Eventually Keats broke the silence. He coughed before he spoke. 'So time of death – I would say you're looking at between one a.m. and three a.m. yesterday morning.'

'Okay, Keats, is there anything else I should know?'

'How to speak to people would be a start.'

'About our victim,' she growled.

'Actually, there is one curious thing.'

He drew back the sheet gently and Kim's gaze immediately rested on the handcuff ring that circled the thin wrist.

Razor bumps and skin irritation on Jemima's legs were visible beneath the bright white lights of the morgue. Kim got the impression that she had been preparing herself for a good night out.

Keats gently touched the body an inch above the belly button. A faint red line stretched across her waist approximately one inch wide.

Kim briefly considered that she'd been tethered but the mark would have been wider and not as straight.

'On her back?' Kim asked. Perhaps it was something that had been placed around her.

'Not her back but here.'

Keats rolled the body slightly so that she was lying on her side.

The same line stretched perfectly halfway between her buttocks and her calves.

She looked to Keats who shrugged.

No, she'd never seen anything like it either.

CHAPTER SIXTEEN

'Jesus, I'm gonna get car sick in a minute,' Bryant said sarcastically.

The journey from Russell's Hall to Dudley Wood had taken less than ten minutes. The address they sought was directly opposite the old site of the Cradley Heath Speedway track.

The speedway team was formed in 1947 at the Dudley Wood Stadium. The club was one of the most successful in the sport throughout the eighties and nineties, winning seven Speedway World Championships.

In 1995 the team were evicted by their new landlords, who had bought the stadium to redevelop it into housing.

Kim couldn't pass the stadium without a pang. Most of her Saturday nights between the ages of ten and thirteen had been spent standing between Keith and Erica watching the bikes race around the track.

She could easily recall the sound of the tyres on the red gravel track above the Saturday night crowds. A noise that to the locals was unbearable yet was missed once it had gone. The smell of methanol used for bike fuel mixed with cheap hot dogs was a combination she would never forget.

Initially Kim had not understood their fascination for speedway. Round and round the track until one bike won. A bike was a bike was a bike. She had never supported any kind of team in her life.

But their enthusiasm had been contagious, her foster parents fervent in support of their local team. She cheered them on not because she felt any kind of pride in them but because Keith and Erica did. The fish and chip supper on the way home remained the same, win or lose.

But whether she got it or not, those nights had been magical.

Hidden behind the spacious houses that lined Dudley Wood Road was a small development of newbuild properties. The mixture of townhouses and apartments were set around a small paved courtyard.

The property of Simon Roach appeared to be a ground-floor flat with an old BMW-series car on the communal drive.

The paintwork on the door had been patched up with a shade of blue that didn't match.

Bryant pressed the doorbell but there was no connecting sound in the property.

Kim knocked on the door. Three sharp bangs and listened. Nothing.

Bryant tried again. Kim stepped back and surveyed the area. No activity.

She looked at her colleague. This male was not at work. His car was parked outside and his girlfriend had been murdered less than forty-eight hours ago. Bryant got it.

He nodded. 'Yeah, I think this time I'm gonna agree with you.'

Bryant pushed on the door and established the exact location of the lock.

Kim got into position beside him. She would kick beneath the lock at the same time he threw his weight above it. It wasn't pretty and could look like a standing variation on the game Twister. But they'd done it before and it had worked.

'On three,' Bryant said.

She raised her leg, ready.

'One… two… three… '

The force of their joint weight both above and beneath the lock forced the door open.

The momentum bounced it off the inside wall.

'Police,' Kim shouted, entering the small, dark hallway. A number of closed doors cut off any light source to the poky space.

The second door along opened. A beam of light appeared before the shape of a stark-naked male.

'What the fuck…?'

'Simon Roach?' Kim asked.

'Fuck, yeah. Who are you?'

Bryant produced a warrant card and introduced them to the man who was making no effort to cover any part of his anatomy. Kim couldn't help thinking his confidence was misplaced.

'What the hell…?'

'Simon, what's going…?'

'Nothing, Rach,' he called back without turning.

He moved forwards, bringing himself just a little too close to the boundary of Kim's personal space.

She stepped to the side. He closed the bedroom door behind him and opened the door to the next room.

Kim followed him into the lounge, keeping her gaze on the back of his head. Roach's hair was long, dark and tousled.

Two sofas faced each other over a wooden coffee table. He aimed for the furthest seat from the door and sat.

Kim sat opposite.

He raised his left foot onto his right knee.

Kim didn't miss a beat.

'We're here about your dead girlfriend,' she clarified. She knew his failure to cover up demonstrated a lack of respect and was an attempt to unnerve her. It would not.

'Jemima?' he asked, causing Kim to wonder just how many dead girlfriends he had.

Kim nodded.

'Girlfriend is probably a bit formal,' he said as a lazy smile spread across his face.

And that was when she saw it. His blatant and unabashed charisma. Kim's brief time with this man had already prompted the question of what the hell Jemima had seen in him.

The lazy smile had transformed his face. The humour in his mouth travelled up to his eyes and made them sparkle with challenge and danger.

He locked his gaze with hers.

Kim was unimpressed. Men who were truly dangerous did not need to advertise it. But she'd play along.

'What about Rach? Is she your girlfriend?' Kim asked.

He shook his head slowly.

'Ah, friends with benefits,' Bryant said.

'Something like that,' he said, without removing his gaze from hers.

Simon leaned forwards and took a pack of cigarettes from the table. He lit a match and the smell of sulphur filled the air. He continued to hold the match as the flame burned along the shaft, staring right at her as the flame met with his fingertips and died.

Kim struggled not to laugh. Overt sexuality had never been her bag. Now if he'd taken the match and extinguished it in his naked arse that would have been a party trick worth seeing.

He threw the match into the ashtray on the table.

'You do know Jemima was murdered?' Kim clarified. It was kind of hard to tell.

'I'm not stupid, Sergeant,' he drawled as a flash of irritation appeared in a gaze that someone else might have called smoldering.

'I didn't say you were, Mr Roach. And it's Inspector. You just appear to have dealt with your grief very quickly.'

The irritation fell away and the smirk returned.

'Let's not play with each other, Inspector. I'm not exclusive, okay? I'm not your monogamous type. There are far too many beautiful women in the world.'

His gaze fell to her breasts.

'Did Jemima know this?' Kim asked.

He shrugged before flicking his ash. 'Not sure if I remember mentioning it specifically, but if she didn't know, she should have. I mean, look at me,' he said, glancing down to his crotch. Kim didn't follow his gaze. 'It wouldn't be fair to limit all this to one person.'

'So you never actually told her you were sleeping with other women?' Kim asked, eager to see any kind of remorse.

He shook his head. 'Works better as a break-up line and we weren't quite there yet.'

'How about Rach – does she know she's not the only recipient of your charms?'

A soft chuckle escaped from his lips. 'I like that, Inspector. And, no, we haven't had that conversation yet.'

Kim was imagining the tip of her biker boot grinding his testicles like a discarded cigarette end. She couldn't help wondering what a date with this charmer might entail. She would guess it wasn't candles, music and flowers.

'How did you and Jemima meet?' Kim asked.

'Oh, you know. I saw her around.'

'Where?' Kim pushed.

His expression held a distinct lack of interest in trying to remember. 'Honestly couldn't tell you, Inspector.'

Kim realised it wasn't worth pursuing. He wasn't being difficult. He just didn't give a shit.

'When was the last time you saw Jemima?' she asked.

'Friday night. She was getting on my nerves. Quiet and sulky. Said she thought someone was following her. I cut the night short and met my mates for a game of snooker. It was obvious I wasn't gonna get anything from her.'

'You took her home?' Bryant asked.

Kim hadn't needed the answer to that one.

Simon shook his head. 'No, just told her I wasn't feeling so good and was heading home.'

Kim ignored his childish grin and focussed on the only thing he'd said of interest.

'Did she say anything else? Any hint about who might be following her?'

'Sorry, Inspector, but I was already thinking about last orders.'

She could see from his expression that there was nothing else.

'Where were you on Saturday?' she asked.

He tipped his head. 'Oh, Inspector, you can't believe I had anything to do with it. Honestly, I couldn't even be bothered.' He looked down at his crotch proudly. 'I'm just your average kind of guy.'

Kim offered no reaction. 'So you were…?'

'Here, in bed.'

'Can Rach verify that?' she asked.

He smiled. 'No. Unusually I was alone. It was a rare—'

'Thank you, Mr Roach,' she said, standing abruptly. 'If there's anything further we'll be in touch.'

Quite frankly, she couldn't bear another second in his company.

'You'd best get someone back here to fix this door,' he moaned from behind her.

Oh yeah, it would jump right to the top of her priorities list, Kim thought as she stepped outside and almost gulped in the cleansing fresh air.

Bryant stepped past her and headed towards the car. Kim turned to follow him. Simon filled the doorway in all his naked glory.

Kim stepped back towards the repulsive creep. Her skin started to recoil at each inch she closed.

She spoke loudly, confident that her voice would carry. 'By the way, given your sexual activity, I would strenuously recommend you get yourself checked for sexually transmitted diseases. We are awaiting those results from your last partner.'

His shocked silence gave her just long enough to hear the sound of movement from the bedroom behind him.

Result.

Simon Roach opened his mouth to speak but Kim beat him to it.

'And for the record, whoever said you were average…' she cast her gaze downwards '… was just being kind.'

She offered him a sad smile and turned away.

'Honestly his name should be cock for a number of reasons,' Kim said, getting into the car.

Bryant thought for a second. 'Oh I get it. Last name and all that.'

'Jeez, Bryant, I'll wait while you catch up.'

Her gut was taking the fifth on Simon Roach. If she was looking for the cockiest moron this side of the River Severn he'd be cuffed and on his way to the station, but she was looking for a murderer, someone who had actually possessed the passion to beat Jemima's face to a pulp. Was Mr Personality capable of that? She really had no idea.

'Where to, guv?' Bryant asked as her phone began to ring.

'Stace,' Kim answered, checking her watch. It was almost six and she wasn't surprised the detective constable was still at work.

She listened as her colleague revealed the reason for the call. A frown began to form on her face as she ended the call.

'Change of plan, Bryant,' she said, taking a deep breath. 'Head back to the Lowe house. There's something this family hasn't told us.'

CHAPTER SEVENTEEN

The door to the Lowe house opened as Bryant parked the car.

A woman in her early sixties stepped out and turned to hug Mrs Lowe. The absence of a handbag or purse told Kim it was probably a neighbour offering condolences for the family's loss.

Kim noted that Mrs Lowe tapped the woman's back as they hugged.

It was a gesture of reassurance. A physical 'there, there' as though the neighbour had suffered the loss.

She was not surprised as the woman walked across the driveway that separated the Lowe property from the next.

Any irritation she had felt at the family's omission faded away when Mrs Lowe offered a weary wave, the exhaustion and grief shining from her eyes.

'Sorry to bother you again,' Kim said and meant it. 'But there's something we need to clarify.'

'Of course, come in,' she said, stepping aside.

Kim automatically moved towards the lounge they'd occupied the previous day. She caught a movement from the top of the stairs. It was Sara. Her eyes were red and puffy, and she had a tissue clutched in her right hand.

Kim nodded in her direction and Sara nodded back. This time Sara didn't skulk back into the shadows but lowered herself and sat on the top stair.

'How are you doing?' Kim asked once the three of them were seated.

The woman considered for a moment before answering. 'People visit and mean well. They bring me their grief, and I don't need any more. A bit of it stays when they go. Another realisation of what the loss of my daughter means to someone else.'

Kim heard the tinge of bitterness and understood it. Swimming alongside someone in the sea of misery was not helpful to a grieving person. It offered them nothing, no respite from the hollow feelings of loss. Share something funny, an example of their clumsiness, innocence, humour, naiveté. Offer the grief-stricken a memory to add to their own portfolio that would grow no more.

'Mrs Lowe, we need to ask you about something that happened to Jemima before she left for Dubai.'

The confused expression as the woman looked from her to Bryant was genuine. There was no deceit. It had been an honest mistake and obviously something she had forgotten in the intervening years.

'We have an incident report filed by Jemima dated just a few weeks before she left. It details an attempt of forced entry into her flat.'

The woman's hand flew to her mouth. Her eyes had widened in horror. 'Are you serious? Are you telling me that some kind of madman tried to get into her home?'

'She didn't tell you?'

Mrs Lowe shook her head as her hand rubbed furiously at her chin. Her eyebrows raised as a memory seemed to jump to the front of her mind.

'What is it?' Kim asked. She'd take anything.

The woman nodded slowly. 'She came home to stay, before she left for Dubai. She said that her landlord was carrying out emergency repairs to the building.' She paused as the rest of the memory caught up. 'She also took some time off work. Said the job was getting her down, and she needed something new. She heard about the job in Dubai from an old college friend. She spoke to the family for two hours on Skype and she clicked with them straightaway…'

'So she moved back in and then rarely left the house?' Kim clarified.

The woman nodded again. 'Come to think of it, yes. She didn't even accompany us out for a family birthday. I just never thought for a moment that anything like that…'

'Are you saying that she never told you?' Kim asked incredulously. Jemima had felt frightened enough to report the incident to the police. She had moved back into the family home and had pretty much left the country as a result – but she hadn't told her family?

'I swear that she never—'

'It was me she told, Inspector,' Sara said quietly from the doorway.

Mrs Lowe's head whipped around as Sara took two steps into the room.

'What are you… when did she… why…?'

Sara held up her hands in defence. 'I'm sorry, Mum, but she swore me to secrecy. She didn't want you to worry. She called me the night it happened. It was me that advised her to come home.'

Kim could see the hurt that had settled on Mrs Lowe's face. That her daughters had kept such a secret from her seemed just too much to bear under the weight of everything else. Kim couldn't tangle herself up in that right now. Sara had spoken to Jemima on the night of the attempted break-in. She might have said something that hadn't made it to the report.

Kim turned towards the younger sister.

'Sara, did she talk to you about what had happened?'

Sara nodded. 'Only that night on the phone. Once she was back here she swore me to secrecy and then tried to pretend that it had never happened. She never spoke of it again.'

Kim could feel the frustration growing in her stomach, but she had to push the girl.

'Is there anything at all that your sister said that night about the incident that might help us now?'

Very slowly Sara's head began to move in an affirmative direction.

'Go on,' Kim urged.

Sara took a breath. 'She said she thought it was someone that she knew.'

CHAPTER EIGHTEEN

Kim tried to leave the day on the doormat as she turned the key in the lock.

Her detour to the Brierley Hill station on the way home had been brief but fruitful.

A small smile tugged at her lips as she heard the familiar tap, tap, tap on laminate.

She hated bringing negativity home. Her best friend had had enough in his few short years.

'Hey, boy,' she said, leaning down to rub at his head. Barney jumped up, trying to press his head even closer into her hand. She took off her jacket and lowered herself to the ground.

'Come here, you little terror.' She laughed as he jumped all over her legs.

As usual the dog walked behind her. The Border collie was busy rounding her up towards the food cupboard.

He sat and looked up at her expectantly.

As she looked down his full tail swished across the floor. She smiled and reached into the cupboard. She took a teeth-cleaning chew and asked for his paw.

He gave his left then his right then his left again, doing a little dance that never failed to raise a smile from her lips.

He took the chew and trotted proudly to the rug in the lounge, the place he always took his booty.

As she filled the percolator jug, she knew that she would never be without him.

But even his enthusiastic welcome had failed to lift the cloud for more than a few minutes.

She had tried to convince herself that it was her current case.

She hated this stage of a new investigation. It was the most frustrating part, getting to know her victim, trying to get inside the mind of the killer.

Some clues came from the life of the victim and others came from their death. So far, other than a complete dickhead for a boyfriend and a break-in attempt at her home, there was very little of Jemima's life to pick apart. She'd only been back in the country for a short while and it was unlikely she'd made any new enemies in that time. Unlikely but not impossible.

Waiting for the clues of her death was like being stuck in the middle lane of the motorway at rush hour. You look for different ways to go but you're just not moving anywhere.

Kim tried to superimpose the photo she'd seen of Jemima at the Lowes' home on top of the bloody, battered mess that she'd been left with.

There was so much about this murder that was personal. Her instinct was telling her that Jemima had not been some random woman taken with no thought or care. Her killer had wanted her for a reason.

Kim applied her usual logic of deeds done past, present or future. Jemima appeared to be no threat to anyone. She wasn't involved in any project that was going to harm or threaten anyone. Her present was equally vanilla. Although Kim thought that if she'd been able to collar Roach for it and get away with it, she might be tempted. Any loss to the human race, women in particular, he was not. But the more she pictured the viciousness and passion that had gone into the attack, the more certain she became that he was not their man.

Which left only Jemima's past – and that's where they would begin tomorrow.

She knew it wasn't the only thing bothering her.

It was the bloody commendation that was at the core of her misery, for more reasons than one.

Kim disliked public recognition for doing her job. Yes, it had been a hard and trying case, and yes she had eaten, breathed and slept the investigation. But that's what she'd signed up for and receiving a piece of paper in front of a few hundred people was not what had prompted her application to the police force.

The commendation meant little to her but would have meant everything to Keith and Erica. The irony was that the ceremony was to be held on the anniversary of their deaths.

This time of year brought forth many cherished moments of her time in their care, but it also prodded at a day that, when recalled, had the power to bring her to her knees.

Kim did what was second nature when memories from her past threatened to overwhelm her.

She turned to work and opened the file of a man named Bob.

CHAPTER NINETEEN

Oh, Mummy, I remember a little girl named Lindsay. She lived just down the street with her two daddies.

I found it strange that she had two and I had none. Her daddies were named Maxwell and Clint. You showed me my birth certificate when I asked. And my daddy's name was 'unknown'. You convinced me we didn't need one; that families were made of all different types of people and some families didn't have a mummy and some families didn't have a daddy. And like everything else I accepted it.

One of Lindsay's daddies dropped her at our house one day. She was such a pretty little girl. Her hair was blonde and curly, natural curls that constantly invaded her face.

She had an adorable little head shake to dislodge the unruly curls from her eyes. I remember her eyelashes. They were long and black, framing eyes that were as blue as the summer sky. Her cheeks were rosy and round and she had happy lips. That's how I've always remembered them, Mummy, as happy lips because even when she was frowning her lips looked like they were having fun.

I liked her, Mummy, and you liked her too.

I was so excited when she came for tea that night. It was the very first time and I couldn't wait. She was dressed in a bright yellow frock that reflected her golden hair. She wore brilliant white stockings that made her legs look like chubby little tree trunks. Her white buckle shoes were finished off with polka-dot bows that matched the one in her hair.

She was excited and so was I.

We played so nicely at first. A game that you chose. We giggled and chuckled and you smiled at us both. Oh, Mummy, how I loved to see that smile.

You left the room to make our tea. It was going to be sausage, egg and beans – my favourite.

Lindsay nudged me and I fell over. I giggled as I nudged her back. Within minutes we were wrestling all over the floor. We were laughing and playing, our dresses and best clothes were getting creased and ripped, but we didn't care. We were too busy laughing to notice.

You stepped back into the room and the look on your face had changed. I knew I'd done something wrong.

You called Lindsay's father to collect her and she never came back again.

You always made my friends leave, Mummy, and now I must do the same.

CHAPTER TWENTY

Kim had read through the file before she'd taken Barney for his nightly walk.

The humidity of the night had dissuaded her from the drive to the Clent Hills. Even with all the windows down, the small car was like a Dudley furnace working overtime.

She wasn't sure Barney was all that bothered about where they walked. A field was a field and his nose went into overdrive picking up the new scents wherever they went. Owner projection, she considered, made her think Barney preferred a car trip to the local beauty spot.

He plonked himself on the rug in the middle of the room while she returned to the paper explosion at the dining table. Her mind had been busy as they'd walked the park.

Yes, Bob appeared to be a mystery but surely not an unfathomable one. Many questions were rattling around in her head.

Why that particular reservoir – did it hold any significance? Was Bob a fisherman? Had the locals known him? Why had it been so important to hide his identity? Were his stomach contents important? What about the items found in his pocket… what help could they get from some pound coins and a raffle ticket?

There was nothing remarkable about Bob. He was an overweight middle-aged man who had been found on the edge of a reservoir. He was an average guy that no one seemed to have missed, but he was something to someone and that was what bothered her. If nothing else he had been someone's son.

'Damn it, Bob,' she said, picking up the file. She already knew that this man's story had wormed its way under her skin. Tracy Frost may not have known that she was pressing Kim's activate buttons, but they had been pressed all the same.

Her interest wasn't purely due to the mystery of his missing hands; it was because nobody fought for the average guy. Unsolved cases were periodically reassessed, but Bob was unlikely to be the cream that rose to the top. He was low profile and nobody was chasing for a result, so other cases would always take priority. He would remain the property of the coroner with a tag of 'unidentified male'.

Not if I can help it, big guy, Kim thought.

The précis report she'd picked up from Brierley Hill offered her an overview of the basics but no detail of the investigation, posing even more questions in her mind. How much effort had gone into trying to find out who this man had been? Was he a father? A grandfather? Had he known his killer was coming?

Her mind was fragmenting into so many lines of enquiry that the sound of her phone startled her.

Instantly she bristled. If this was Tracy bloody Frost again, she'd arrest her for harassment.

'Stone,' she answered.

'In-Inspector, is that… that you?'

The trembling male voice ruled out Frost.

'It is,' she answered, frowning.

'Professor Wright from W-Westerley.'

She sat forwards, her mind cleared of everything except the voice on the other end of the line.

'Professor…?'

'There's a… another one, Inspector.'

Kim was already on her feet and reaching for her jacket.

'Professor, don't let anyone touch—'

'Please hurry, Detective Inspector. This poor woman is still alive.'

CHAPTER TWENTY-ONE

As Kim waited for the gate to move aside, Bryant's Astra pulled up behind her. The gate began to move, and she drove through once the gap was a foot and a half wide.

She was off the bike and heading into the office as Bryant parked the car.

Darren, the night security guard, sat at the small round table. His hands were trembling around a mug of something.

The colour of his skin had not yet returned to its natural state.

'Did you touch her?' Kim asked urgently.

He shook his head.

'Then how did you know she was still…'

'She moaned,' he said brokenly. 'Oh God, the sound…'

He shook his head and stared back into the mug.

'Is the professor with her now?'

He nodded without looking at her.

Kim looked at Bryant. 'Stay with him and get the gate open for the ambulance,' she instructed.

He nodded.

She headed out of the door and took her torch from her pocket.

The light from the Portakabin aided her only to the end of the car park. The moon offered her the promise of a direction of travel, but she was stepping into a sheet of darkness with only a general idea of where she was going.

Kim walked into the blackness and each stride confused her senses more. She took a few steps and was no longer sure she was moving in the right direction.

Bryant would question Darren, find out about his patrols. Kim guessed they'd be more accurate this time around. He'd almost lost his job. After his recent discovery, Kim suspected he might be wishing he had.

'Professor,' she called into the darkness.

Suddenly a shaft of light lifted from the ground and illuminated the single figure beside the oak tree.

Thank goodness, she'd already been starting to head away.

She sprinted to his location, feeling the long grass whip her ankles as she ran.

She detoured slightly to the left, remembering Jack and Vera in the sunken graves not far away.

As she reached his side the professor shone the torch down but not before she'd seen his ashen face.

Kim dropped to the ground, her knees sinking into the dirt thanks to a brief shower that had occurred around sunset.

A soft moan sounded but Kim could see the colour red seeping along the grass.

Kim knew she needed to assess the scene for evidence, but the priority was the woman who was still alive. She gently touched her bare arm.

'It's okay, we're here with you and the ambulance is coming.'

She had made a second call to Ambo Control to clarify the exact location. It was difficult for them to find a place that was trying to hide.

There was no further moan or acknowledgement that the figure had heard her.

She looked up to the professor. 'Can you get down here and place your hand where mine is so she knows there's someone here?'

He knelt beside her and touched her hand, replacing it.

Torches shone from the Portakabin that was now illuminated by the lights from a squad car and the ambulance but, God help her, she needed to look for clues.

'Shine your torch there,' she said, pointing to the woman's head.

The hair was brown, short and matted with blood and dirt. She couldn't see the face, and she dared not touch it in case she caused further injury. She followed the light beam down the body to the breastbone. Flecks of brown, like freckles, mottled the area below her chin.

Shit, her mouth, Kim realised as she leaned down and inspected the woman's lips. Specks of brown were present. Damn it – her mouth was full of dirt!

Kim realised she had no choice. She took hold of the woman's chin and slowly pulled down her lower jaw. What should have been a gaping hole was packed with dirt. Kim used her index finger to gently prod and then sweep the dirt from her mouth. She knew she had to be careful not to dislodge the packed mass too quickly, for fear of sending the soil down her throat to her airway. After the first sweep Kim leaned down and placed her cheek as close to the woman's mouth as she could without touching.

She could hear the rasp of some air making it in and out. She wanted to just dive in and scrape it all out in one go, but she made another sweep and removed another small portion.

'I'm just trying to make it easier for you to breathe,' Kim said calmly. The woman still had her nose but the effort of using her nostrils only was causing her chest to rise and fall quickly.

Another gentle sweep and Kim had removed as much dirt as she dared.

'Paramedics are here,' the professor said. The relief in his voice was evident.

The irony that she had more freedom with the dead was not lost on Kim. Not nice but true all the same. Although a dead body couldn't offer a description, she reasoned.

From what she could see, Kim was guessing that their killer had begun his ritual of filling the mouth and beating the face to a pulp, but there was a slight difference. The blows to this victim had landed on the side of her head rather than in the middle of her face, indicating this woman had been able to move her head around more to avoid the blows.

The additional body weight of the woman before her could have meant that the same level of drug in her system hadn't had quite such potent or debilitating effects as it would have had on the slight frame of Jemima Lowe.

That there was also less dirt in the mouth told Kim he'd been rushing. It was possible he had seen Darren's torchlight in the distance but had still been compelled to finish the ritual. The specks of soil on the woman's chest confirmed to Kim that he had filled her mouth with the dirt around them. Had he done it earlier they would not still have been present after she'd been dragged up the hill. Even under duress, the ritual was important to him. But he must have given up completely once Darren had come closer.

'It's okay,' Kim soothed the woman as she assessed. 'The medics are here and they're going to take care of you.'

As the torch moved down her body Kim saw she was wearing a floral halter-neck dress made of cotton and the smell of soap drifted up from the bare skin. The dress was not raised above the knee and Kim could see no sign of trauma.

Except for the back of her head being caved in.

The torches and voices were coming closer. The torchlight rested on the woman's bare feet.

'Shine it around,' Kim instructed the professor.

He plunged her body into darkness as he raised the torch to light the area.

There was no evidence of her footwear.

She could hear words now passing between Bryant and the paramedics and the grass being trodden underfoot. She quickly leaned back down to the woman as another soft moan sounded.

Kim gently reached for her hand and rubbed her thumb across the nail. As with Jemima, it was coarse to the touch. Both women had chosen to strip their nails right before going out. It was a coincidence that didn't sit comfortably in her mind.

'Step aside, please,' said the first paramedic as he knelt at the victim's head. 'Name?' he said, looking to her. Kim shook her head. The dress had no pockets and there was no handbag.

'Unknown,' Kim answered. 'There's dirt in the mouth and she's probably been drugged.'

The head injury they could see for themselves.

'All right, love,' he said to the victim as he reached into his bag. The second paramedic took the place of the professor.

Kim took a few steps back and drew level with Bryant.

The work of the paramedics was far more important than hers. For now.

'Darren's in a bit of a state,' Bryant said. 'But his log is in order. He swears on his daughter's life he did a patrol at eleven and the next at twelve. He happened on to the victim at around twelve fifteen.'

Kim nodded and turned her attention back to the medics.

The first medic took a dressing from the bag while the second raised the woman's head slightly.

'Worst of the bleeding is over but we'll dress it anyway, Jeff,' he said.

Another soft moan sounded from the victim.

'It's all right, love, you're okay now,' said Jeff without taking his eyes from the bandage being looped around her head. Once the task was complete, the first medic spoke again.

'Okay, Jeff, place the stretcher.'

Kim took one step forwards. 'How is she?'

Jeff shrugged. 'Need to get her in. She's breathing, so best to get her to hospital quickly for the head injury.'

The two paramedics managed her carefully onto the stretcher and lifted her on three.

The professor offered to carry the rest of the equipment and headed off across the field behind them.

By Bryant's torchlight she could see three crime-scene techs heading in their direction.

'What do you reckon he used?' Bryant asked.

Kim took the torch from him and shone it around the area just away from where the woman had been found. No weapon had been found at the crime scene of Jemima and she suspected this time would be no different.

'Well, Darren might be feeling shitty right now, but he needs to know he saved this woman's life.'

Kim was in no doubt that Darren's torchlight as he had patrolled the grounds had scared the killer off before he'd had a chance to complete the task. Because of Darren, their second victim still had a pulse and still had a face.

'It's not just about the death,' she said. 'It's all about what he's doing with them first.'

'Jemima showed no evidence of sexual assault,' Bryant reminded her.

The techies arrived and took control of the scene.

Kim moved and stood beside her colleague with a slight shake of the head. There was one thing that had been puzzling her since finding Jemima and was even more disturbing to her now.

'Bryant, why the hell is he leaving them here?'

CHAPTER TWENTY-TWO

Kim took a swig of coffee before resting her behind on the edge of the spare desk.

The mug had appeared on her desk on her last birthday, a day she never celebrated.

Originally the caption above the picture had read 'World's Best Driver', but some bright spark had inserted the word 'Slave' into the sentence with permanent ink. And not one of her team was brave enough to own up to it. But she had her suspicions.

'Okay, you all know about our second victim, who remains both unidentified and alive. The priority with victim two right now is keeping her alive and we will speak with her as soon as we can. So right now we continue the focus on Jemima. Bryant, have you got the toxicology report?'

'Circulated, guv.'

Everyone nodded.

'So what do we think?' she asked.

'Obviously drugged,' Dawson offered.

The level of Rohypnol in the bloodstream had been enough to subdue a medium-sized horse. The drug was used as a hypnotic, sedative and skeletal muscle relaxant. It was often referred to as the 'date-rape drug' due to its high potency and ability to cause amnesia.

'Why?' she asked. 'There was no sexual assault.'

'To make her easier to handle?' Dawson asked.

'Oi, Dawson, I had my hand up for that one,' Bryant moaned.

Dawson smirked. 'You snooze you—'

'Both get a kick up the arse if you don't stop it.'

Kim continued speaking, after her look had the desired effect. 'So does the fact he needed her pliant mean anything, Stace?'

'He knew exactly where he was going to dump her?'

'Bingo,' Kim said.

'I had that one too,' Bryant mumbled.

Kim ignored him. 'That's what I think. There are much easier places to dump a body. To get there he had to drive narrow lanes across two fields and then haul her up a hill. Why?'

No one answered. They knew when her questions were rhetorical.

'Stace, I want you to find out everything you can about the land around Westerley. I want to understand the significance of the dump site and I want to know more about Catherine.'

Stacey nodded.

'Also, the last document of Keats's email is a photo of the hairpins. Do some digging and find out just how common those things are.'

'Will do, boss,' she said, making a note.

Kim used her phone to flick along to the second report sent by Keats. 'Next – stomach contents. A mixture of sausage, beans, pastry and custard.'

'Easy to get?' Stacey offered.

'And?' Kim pushed.

'Easy to cook?' Dawson said.

'And?' she said, a little more forcefully.

'He gave her dessert,' Bryant answered.

And there it was. The man who had abducted, beaten and killed Jemima had also given her dessert.

'A little bit weird,' Dawson observed.

Kim reiterated. 'So our kidnapper subdued her, snatched her, kept her, undressed her, fed her and then smashed her face in.'

'Like I said – weirdo,' Dawson said.

'One weirdo or two?' Bryant said, as though asking about sugar lumps.

Kim thought for a moment. 'I still think just one,' she offered. 'Jemima was chosen for a reason. She is not some random victim discovered by chance, which means it has to be someone she's been in contact with at some stage.

'Kev, I want you on that. I want you to go to her old address and see if anyone remembers the incident before she left for Dubai. We don't know if it's linked to her murder as it was so long ago but Sara said that Jemima felt she knew the person concerned. We need to follow it up.'

Her mobile phone rang. She frowned when she saw the name of the pathologist at the top of the screen.

'Keats?' she said. He rarely contacted her by choice.

'Inspector, we've had the results back from the soil that was forced into Jemima Lowe's mouth.'

'Go on.'

'It definitely matches the soil at site,' he said.

She had worked that much out for herself. 'And?'

'There are traces of blood. Well, more than traces to be accurate.'

Kim pictured the killer forcing dirt against the soft gum line. He could easily have caused a small injury. 'The inside of her mouth could have been—'

'Too much blood for that, Inspector,' he said, cutting her off.

Kim stood. 'Are you saying it could be from our killer?'

'Not unless he cut off a digit during the course of the crime…'

Kim stopped listening as her heart began to hammer in her chest. She knew what he was going to say.

The blood in Jemima's mouth was not her own. The blood had not come from the killer – which could only mean one thing.

Someone else had been killed in that spot.

CHAPTER TWENTY-THREE

'Sir, we need to get a team out to Westerley.'

Woody didn't even chide her for her failure to knock.

His eyebrows narrowed. 'What are you talking about? Forensics have just stood down from the site. They've been there all night and found a total of nothing.'

He thought she meant a team of techies. He was going to have to dig deeper into his annual budget for what she was about to request.

She shook her head. 'No, sir, I need detection equipment, probably extraction and I need a full team of forensic—'

'Calm down, Stone. What's the development?' he asked calmly.

Sometimes she wished he would just act before asking her twenty questions. It reminded her of calling an ambulance in an emergency situation. You wanted to shout, *'Just get it on its way – then I'll give you the details.'*

'The sample taken from the soil in Jemima's mouth. It was scraped up from the scene and forced in. The dirt contains traces of blood that do not belong to Jemima.'

'The killer?' he asked.

Kim could swear she'd just had this conversation. 'Unlikely. Too much of it and it's been there a while.'

'You're sure?'

She nodded. 'Keats tested the soil with luminol and, to use his phrase, "it glowed like a beacon", sir.'

'Any indication how old the blood is?'

'No. Keats is doing further tests, but he said it can be detected for years, at least six to eight,' she said, sharing with him something she hadn't known before the phone call.

He sat back in his chair and sighed. Time to sell herself and get what she needed. She had a sudden flash of *Dragons' Den*.

'Sir, I think there's going to be another body buried at the site,' she clarified in case she wasn't making herself clear.

Kim knew he was weighing up the expense of the operation against the likelihood of a find. She was eternally grateful that financial planning fell under his remit and not hers. She was also grateful that he was not guided solely by budgetary constraints. Like her, his priority was always the journey to the truth. Only his job description said he had more questions to answer if it went horribly wrong.

'Any change with the second victim?' he asked.

She understood his logic. If there was a chance they could make an identification in the near future from the second victim, the expense was unlikely to be sanctioned without further justification.

'Called first thing. They're still stabilising her after surgery to the head. They'll let us know if and when we can speak to her.'

He paused and rubbed at his chin thoughtfully. 'I understand that Daniel Bate is on site at Westerley.'

Kim frowned. 'He was, I'm not sure he's still—'

'Probably a good idea to try and keep him there. I'll get it authorised.'

'He's not the only osteoarchaeologist in—'

'He's the only one who is on site now. If you want this to move as quickly as you normally do, I'm surprised you haven't made the call already.'

She stared at him for a moment, unable to find the right words to argue. She had experience of Daniel's expertise in determining sex, age and health of human remains in the past.

He stared right back and then frowned. 'Probably best get moving, Stone. Daniel Bate is an opportunity you don't want to miss.'

'Sir, I…'

'It'll take hours, if not days, to get another scientist of his expertise on site. If I were you I'd hope that he hasn't already left.'

Kim turned and left the office, annoyed that she had to converse with Daniel Bate. Her boss could not have been clearer. *Use the resources available and this will go ahead.*

Okay, Woody had won this one. If Daniel Bate was still at Westerley she would speak to him.

And, if it helped find the killer sooner, she would even ask him to stay.

CHAPTER TWENTY-FOUR

Kim entered the Portakabin and was faced with a wall of despair. She supposed having one dead body and one battered woman turn up in a matter of a few days was enough to crush your workplace morale. That they were all still turning up for work was a testament to their professionalism.

And now they were to be told it was probably going to get worse.

'You're still here?' Kim said to Curtis Grant.

He smiled. 'I have been home. Different suit,' he said, flicking at his jacket.

She acknowledged his response. 'Are you almost finished, Mr Grant?'

He glanced over at Jameel, who nodded.

'I'll be back later in the week to add two new cameras and upgrade the software.'

Kim nodded and headed further into the space as Bryant and Dawson came to a halt behind her.

Catherine sat at the meeting table. A quick glance acknowledged their presence.

Professor Wright and Daniel Bate stood at the furthest point from the door.

'Morning everyone,' Kim said. 'We have some information that we need to share following some test results.'

'And that is my cue to be on my way,' Daniel said, shaking the professor's hand.

He stepped past her on his way out and offered a nod in her direction.

Bryant coughed.

She glared at him before stepping past Dawson to the door.

Kim followed Daniel outside. Two steps away from his pickup truck he turned.

'Excuse me, are you lost?'

She rolled her eyes. 'We need to talk.'

He leaned his arm on the side of the vehicle as his gaze narrowed with interest.

'About?'

'This case,' she clarified.

He stepped away and opened the passenger door. Lola tried to jump down from the passenger seat. He held her back and wound down her window before closing the door again.

Kim could see his overnight bag in the foot well.

'I'm not sure I can offer anything to help,' he said, walking around to the driver's door. The keys jangled in his hand.

'I think there's another in the ground,' she said.

He paused.

'Don't ask me to repeat what I know, and Bryant is explaining it inside right now, but my boss has asked me to ask you to stay and help.'

Daniel paused at the door and turned, leaning against the pickup section of his truck. He put the keys in his pocket and looked up at the sky before turning his head towards her.

'So let me get this straight: your boss, Detective Chief Inspector Woodward, has asked you to ask for my help should you find a body buried underground?'

She nodded.

He smiled widely. 'And you're just hating every single minute of it, aren't you?'

She dug her hands into her pockets and said nothing.

He placed his arms on top of the cab and then rested his chin and stared at her.

'What are you doing?' she asked. His blatant stare was as annoying as his delay in giving her an answer.

'Oh, I'm wringing every second of enjoyment I can from your discomfort.'

'Not childish at all though?' she asked.

'Probably,' he said. 'So if you just ask me nicely, I'll give it some thought.'

She felt the heat burn in her cheeks. 'Daniel, this is no longer funny.'

'I disagree, and hearing my actual name from your lips is almost enough to persuade me to stay.'

'Are you prepared to assist on this case or not? I need to call my—'

'You can't do it, can you? You can't actually ask me to stay,' he said, still amused.

She faced him squarely. 'Daniel, I'm asking for your help but if you'd rather this bastard—'

'One condition,' he interrupted. 'I'll stay if you just do me one small favour.'

Kim frowned. She wasn't agreeing to anything until she knew what it was.

'Drop the Doc and the Doctor Bate and continue to call me Daniel.'

She considered for a moment then nodded. That, at least, she could do.

From behind she heard the truck door open and four paws landed on the gravel.

'Come on, girl. It looks like we're hanging around.'

Kim hid the satisfaction in her smile.

CHAPTER TWENTY-FIVE

'He's like a dog with two dicks,' Bryant said as they headed out of Westerley.

Kim knew her colleague was referring to Dawson, who was happy to remain at Westerley as the first point of contact for both the staff and the tech experts as they began to arrive.

During the Crestwood investigation eighteen months ago, Dawson had been stationed at site and had done an exceptional job. Kim didn't believe in fixing things that were not broken.

Bryant drove and talked. She had already told him where she wanted to go.

'So the doc is staying on then?'

'Bloody hell, nothing gets past you, does it?' she said.

'You mean like the smile that you were trying to hide when you walked back in?' he observed.

'That'll be because I won,' she admitted.

'Won what? I didn't realise there was a prize on offer.'

'Don't worry about it,' she said.

'You do know he likes you,' Bryant stated.

'And you do realise that this is not high school and there'll be no need for you to pass notes between us.'

Bryant glanced her way.

'And I'm sensing you like him just a little bit too.'

Kim ignored him. That wasn't strictly accurate. To state that she liked him was a little exaggerated. She just disliked Daniel less than a lot of other people.

'Bloody hell,' she said as they entered Russell's Hall hospital. The car park already looked fit to burst.

The super hospital was an amalgamation of three local hospitals that had either been closed down completely or their A&E departments removed. Unfortunately the parking had not been increased pro rata with the expansion.

Bryant spotted a space at the furthest point from the hospital and parked quickly.

'Wait here – I won't be long. Just want to see how she is.'

Bryant grumbled.

She ignored him and headed in through the maternity entrance, up the stairs and across to the Surgical High Dependency Unit. This ward, together with ITU, provided the critical-care element of the hospital. High dependency normally took emergency surgical patients and was staffed on a ratio of one staff to two patients. ITU provided care on a one-to-one basis.

She spoke at the intercom to gain entry.

As she pushed the door open she was again struck by the absence of chatter or daily noises. No televisions hummed quietly. There was no clink of the tea trolley doing its rounds. No conversations that travelled from bed to bed to fill the hours before visiting, no occasional moans of discomfort and pain.

None of that was present in this unit. This area was reserved for the sickest people in the building.

Kim held up her badge and smiled at the ward sister named Jo. She was late thirties with blonde hair that fell in a short but shiny bob around a plump face.

Jo took a good look at her identification and nodded.

'A woman was admitted last night.'

'Head injury?' Jo asked, turning to face the whiteboard behind. Kim nodded.

'No identification, so for now she's Jane.'

Many facilities had now adopted the American procedure of labelling unknown victims John or Jane.

'She's in bay two, bed three,' Jo said.

'Is she…?'

'Conscious?' Jo asked and shook her head. 'She's in an induced coma. Her brain has taken a battering.' She leaned over the desk and looked up and down the corridor.

'Doctor Singh is still on his rounds. I'll ask him to come and have a word.'

Kim nodded her thanks and headed around to bay two.

Jane lay in the top-left corner closest to the window.

Kim suspected that the rich chestnut hair that had been matted and tangled with blood and dirt was now gone, leaving a bald, shaved head beneath the bandages.

The index finger on her left hand was being clutched by a white plastic pulse oximeter measuring the oxygen saturation in her bloodstream and her heart rate. The results, along with her blood pressure, were being transmitted on the screen to her left.

Her right hand was covered in white plaster holding down the intravenous cannula. Blood had seeped through the tape, indicting they'd had trouble accessing the vein.

Kim's eyes travelled to the woman's left wrist and the circle mark she knew so well. She wondered if Jane would still rub it for years after the mark had disappeared. Would she now and again just feel, for a split second, like it was still there? The mind could be cruel that way.

Kim's hand fell and touched the red band. This woman had moved her wrist considerably to try to free herself. There were the telltale marks between her wrist and her knuckles where she had tried to force her hand through. Just like Jemima. And Kim herself, many years ago.

The memory of her own six-year-old hand scraped raw by her numerous attempts to free herself was sudden and painful. Kim pushed it away and rubbed gently at the skin of the girl nicknamed Jane as though trying to erase it from her flesh.

Her thumb passed over an area of raised skin. She rubbed her thumb back and forth a couple of times, frowning.

She turned the wrist over gently and saw what she would not have been able to see last night. Four very definite lines of scar tissue ran across the wrist. This girl had attempted suicide, and she hadn't been messing about.

'Officer…?'

Kim turned to an attractive dark-skinned man she presumed to be Doctor Singh. His white coat was unbuttoned and revealed plain black trousers and a white shirt. There was a kindly smile in his eyes.

Kim briefly wondered how long it would take the NHS to knock that out of him.

He stood at the end of the bed and picked up Jane's chart.

'Our patient here suffered a depressed cranial fracture and was in surgery until six this morning.'

Kim heard a slight trace of his Indian accent but only on certain words. His voice was caring and warm, and she liked him instantly.

Kim knew that depressed meant that the injury had caused the skull to indent or extend into the brain cavity.

'There are many types of fracture but only one cause,' he explained.

Kim knew the only cause was a blow to the head strong enough to break the bone.

'The surgeon has released the pressure on the brain, but she has scored six on the Glasgow Coma Scale.'

Kim frowned. It wasn't something she'd heard before.

'It is a scale used to assess head injuries from a score of three to fifteen. A score of three is the most severe, but any score between three and eight reflects that the patient is in a comatose state.'

'What's that?' Kim said, pointing to a wire leading from the back of Jane's head.

'Intracranial pressure monitor. It is monitoring the space between the skull and the brain. It will alert us to any changes in the pressure inside the skull.'

'Will she survive?' Kim asked, adjusting her voice to match the doctor's soft, gentle tone.

He took a few steps away. 'We don't know. Really she should not have survived the injury, but somehow she managed to hold on. We must hope she continues to be strong.'

'Can she hear?' Kim asked, realising he had stepped away to speak.

He shrugged. 'I like to be sure, especially when discussing chances of survival.'

Kim understood. 'Do you have any idea how long…?'

The doctor was already shaking his head. 'I can't answer that. The brain is more complex than any of us can comprehend. People we expect to survive often don't and then others…'

His words trailed away and Kim got his point.

'And if she does wake?'

'Inspector, you are asking me every question that I cannot answer.'

His voice was still kind but with a hint of amusement.

Kim smiled at his easy manner. It was a bit like her conversations with Keats, the pathologist – only this doctor was pleasant.

'Well, thank you for your help… oh, actually there is one more thing,' she said.

'Of course.'

'There is something I need to check on her body but I wouldn't…'

He nodded his understanding. She would never handle Jane's body without seeking permission.

He stepped back towards the bed and drew the curtain around him. 'Where?'

'The back of her legs.'

He lifted the sheet and gently moved the woman slightly onto her side.

'May I?' Kim asked.

He nodded.

Kim gently lifted the bottom of the hospital-issue nightgown.

The marks were there.

Two one-inch red lines stretched across the back of her lower thighs.

Kim took out her phone and clicked a couple of photos.

'I need to check her stomach.'

Doctor Singh placed Jane onto her back and lifted the sheet up to her midriff before raising her nightgown.

The line stretched just above her belly button. Kim snapped a couple more photos.

She reached for the sheet to cover Jane back up and then paused. A tiny red cut to the skin of the lower leg caught her attention. She moved around the bed, taking photos of the woman's legs from the knee down.

'Significant?' Doctor Singh asked.

Kim smiled. 'Now it's my turn to say I don't know.'

He acknowledged her answer. 'Is that all?' he asked.

'May I just have a minute more?'

'Of course,' he answered before turning away.

He drew back the curtain and stepped towards the patient opposite.

Kim put the phone back into her pocket and placed her hand back onto Jane's wrist. 'I'm sorry I had to do that, but I want to catch the person who did this to you.'

Once more Kim felt the scar tissue beneath her touch.

This woman had suffered in the past, and now she was suffering again.

'I promise you will not be a Jane for long.'

CHAPTER TWENTY-SIX

Jane could feel a soft pressure on her hand. She wasn't sure if she was in some kind of dream.

Sometimes there were voices and sometimes not. Sometimes there was a soft bleeping sound that was swallowed only when the darkness came again.

In her stomach there was fear. It began in her belly button and worked its way out.

The blackness around her kept moving, rearranging itself then snatching and stealing her thoughts.

There was pain echoing around her body. She didn't know from where but the blackness took it away. The darkness consumed it along with her and then spat her back out.

At times she was at one with the darkness

She wondered if this was death and if so how she had got here. Was it possible to feel pain in death? And if she was dead was this her eternal state?

Any further thought or realisation was taken away by the dark.

She wanted to open her eyes but the blackness took her before she could.

If she was alive she knew she was in hospital. She knew that someone was holding her hand.

She tried to open her eyes.

She knew she had something to say.

The panic rose up to her throat before the blackness took her again.

CHAPTER TWENTY-SEVEN

Instead of heading back out to Bryant's car, Kim went straight to the morgue.

Keats was sitting at his desk, head bent in studious concentration.

'Ahem…' she said.

'I know you're there, Inspector. It's a stomp I would recognise anywhere, but I'm hoping if I ignore you, you'll go away,' he droned without raising his head.

'Yeah, you and most people I've ever met, but I need your help.'

He looked up and narrowed his eyes suspiciously. 'Are you mauling me, Inspector?'

She stifled the smile that played at her lips. He knew her too well.

Blowing smoke up the behind of the pathologist was not worth her time. She knew from other people's experience that it didn't work. He would either help her or not.

'Three years ago a male was found at Fens Pools,' she said.

'You'll need to be a bit more specific than that.'

'His fingers had been cut off.'

'Aaah, yes, I remember it. I didn't do the post-mortem, but I recall the case. Still unidentified?'

Kim nodded and sat down. 'I have the reports, but I could do with a bit of expert translation.'

He tipped his head. 'Only if you stop being so damned pleasant to me. It's a little bit frightening without Bryant to protect me.'

This time the smile escaped. 'Okay.'

He looked above her head and then began tapping away at his keyboard. 'I have five minutes until my next customer arrives, so make it quick.'

Kim recalled the post-mortem report she had pored over at home and recalled the one thing that had struck her as curious.

'The only wound visible was a knife mark above the left chest, two – maybe two and a half – inches long, possibly a stab wound?'

He glanced back at the screen. 'Well if it was a stab wound, it wasn't deep. The cause of death was definitely drowning.'

'The fingers were removed after death, is that right?' she asked.

Keats nodded and continued to read.

There had been no pain or torture inflicted by the killer to prolong the agony. The removal of the digits had been purely functional.

'What can you tell me about him, Keats?' she asked.

'Shush,' he said and continued to read for a couple of minutes. 'In layman's terms, his age was estimated at mid to late fifties. He wasn't a heavy drinker but was definitely a heavy smoker. He ate too many fatty foods and didn't take enough exercise. No obvious broken bones, tattoos or other distinguishing characteristics.'

Pretty average then, Kim thought. Except that every finger had been severed from his hand. Yeah, there was no escaping that particular fact.

Kim sighed. She had not learned much at all.

She stood. 'Thanks, anyway, Keats. I'll—'

'Not so fast, Inspector. Just take a quick look at this.'

She stepped around to his side of the desk. The image on the screen had been zoomed, and she wasn't sure what it was she was looking at.

She tipped her head sideways. 'Is that the chest wound?'

Keats nodded. 'And there's something there that looks a little odd.'

Her ears pricked up. Odd was good.

As she stared she began to see what he meant. She'd attended enough crime scenes to know how knife wounds normally looked on the skin. Regardless of the type of knife used the cut was consistent and clean. Close up, this one appeared lumpy and uneven, as though the knife had been dragged across the skin.

'It looks more like a cut than a stab,' Kim observed.

Keats nodded. 'And I think I know why.'

He zoomed in one more time. 'I think he was cutting scar tissue.'

'You think he was opening an old wound?' Kim asked, as thoughts began to form in her mind.

'Or taking something out…'

They looked at each other as the realisation hit them both.

'Pacemaker,' they said simultaneously.

CHAPTER TWENTY-EIGHT

'How is she?' Bryant asked as she reached the car.

'Unresponsive right now and the doctors aren't really committing to anything in terms of her recovery.' Kim paused. 'Head towards Brierley Hill,' she said as she processed everything she'd learned in the last hour.

'She has the same marks on her back and thighs as Jemima,' she continued.

Bryant shook his head as he drove. 'Never seen anything like that. It doesn't make sense.'

Kim agreed. They already knew that the restraint was a handcuff to the wrist, so what could those straight lines mean?

'There's something else,' she said as he crossed a set of traffic lights. 'Her legs are covered in little nicks and cuts.'

'Well, that makes sense. She was pulled over a gravel path and up a hill to the dump site.'

'She would have been pulled around on her back, like Jemima. These marks are on the front of her legs, just like Jemima. It's like a shaving rash.'

Bryant rubbed at his chin. 'Yeah, I get it sometimes.'

Kim pondered. 'Why only sometimes?'

'If I want a closer shave I'll go against the grain. Gets a cleaner look but irritates the skin more.'

So now she had both girls scrubbing the polish from their nails and giving their legs a close shave. Who the hell did they think they were meeting?

'Hang on, turn right here,' Kim instructed as they passed through Brierley Hill.

She continued to direct him until they arrived at a warden's office at the junction of Pensnett Road and Bryce Road.

'Ummm... guv...' Bryant said.

'Are you coming?'

He followed her past the warden's office to Fens Pools.

The area was a nature reserve that had once been part of Pensnett Chase, a medieval hunting ground of the barons of Dudley. Like most of the rest of the Chase, it had been gradually turned to industrial use, including coal mining, clay extraction and a brickworks.

Part of the Earl of Dudley's private railways ran across the area. The collieries and clay pits closed in the early twentieth century but the brickworks and railway only closed in the 1960s.

Some of the ponds had been formed from old clay pits but the three largest reservoirs, Grove Pool, Middle Pool and Fens Pool in the north-eastern part of the reserve, had been constructed by the Stourbridge Canal Company in 1776 and were the largest areas of open water in Dudley. A fourth pool called Foot's Hole lay to the south-west and was separated from the others by the Dell Sports Stadium.

Kim knew it was a popular spot for fishing and the ninety-two-acre site had been designated an area of special scientific interest.

She looked beyond the first pool to the grass bank that ran between the water and the canal.

'That's where he was found,' she said, pointing.

There were areas one could sit and feel miles away from the built-up industrial area close by and other places where the sprawling housing estate and trade units were clearly within view.

'Who?' Bryant asked.

'Unidentified male with his fingers cut off, a few years ago.'

'Didn't Brierley Hill solve that one?'

Kim shook her head. 'No, Bob is still a guest of the coroner in a cold, dark drawer.'

'Bob?' he asked, narrowing his eyes.

'Not my term, but it'll do until we find his real name.'

And Kim wasn't exactly sure how she was going to do that. Her only potential clues had been removed. All that was left was his clothing, the change in his pockets and an old raffle ticket. Dental records were a good form of identification, but you had to know where to start.

There were no family members harassing the police force for progress reports on the murder of their father, brother, uncle. The missing-persons reports would have been searched when the body was first found so no one cared enough about Bob even to file a report.

He appeared to have been missed by no one – and that in itself was enough to burrow under her skin.

'Ah, bittern,' Bryant said.

'By what?' she asked.

He shook his head. 'Bittern the bird. Over there by the tall grass.'

'Didn't have you down as a twitcher,' she said, turning away.

He sighed heavily. 'Ummm… remind me again why we're looking at this?'

Kim was about to say, 'Because no one else was,' but the thought was cut off by the ringing of her mobile phone.

The number was withheld.

'Stone,' she answered.

'Inspector, it's Jo. You were here just a little—'

'Is Jane okay?' she asked urgently. She had left a card with the ward sister and asked to be informed of any type of development.

'Yes, she's fine. No change. Except her name's not Jane. It's Isobel.'

'How do you know?'

'That's what her boyfriend told us. He called and is on his way here.'

CHAPTER TWENTY-NINE

Stacey stared hard at the computer. Something about the entry of the records for Catherine Evans was not quite adding up.

Her birth certificate was there but new documents out of place always left a trail, no matter how skilfully inserted into the records. And this one was highlighted by a software change.

A different file type had been in use up until the late eighties so if Catherine's birth certificate had been issued back then it would have been the old file type. It was the one that matched the system upgrade in 1999 prior to the widespread panic over the millennium bug. Software companies had injected the fear of God into everyone and especially the government, local councils and health authorities, hinting that older systems would be unable to maintain date and time facilities once the clock tried to click into a new century, never mind a new millennium.

Worldwide, private companies had sought confirmation and guarantees from suppliers that systems would not fail. Contingency arrangements, business continuity plans and disaster-recovery manuals had all been set up to prepare for the second it switched over.

The whole thing had fizzled out like a damp firework as the anticipated chaos failed to materialise.

Catherine's birth certificate stated 15 June 1983 but had not been entered on to the system until 2001, when Catherine was eighteen years old.

Fifteen minutes later, Stacey had tracked the issue of a medical card registered to Catherine Evans. Also registered as June 1983 but entered in the late nineties.

Stacey sat back in her chair. The palm of her hand rested on the mouse but her fingers tapped absently.

Why the eighteen-year delay in registering the details?

The words 'new identity' screamed in her head. Documents being inserted at a later date trying to look like authentic records hinted at an invented identity. This was not a name change by deed poll instigated by the woman herself. This level of expertise pointed only one way. The state.

Why the hell would Catherine Evans have been given a new identity?

Stacey felt the excitement building in her stomach. She was on to something and she knew it.

She went back to the date of insertion and began to work back from that.

Whatever it was, it would have made the news.

CHAPTER THIRTY

Kim stepped into the ward for the second time that day.

Jo smiled as she approached the desk. 'He arrived a few minutes after I got off the phone.'

'May I?' she asked, taking a step away from the desk.

Jo nodded.

A dark-haired male sat beside the bed with his back hunched and his head bowed. He wore a black T-shirt and jeans and was holding tightly on to Isobel's right hand.

'Excuse me…'

His head snapped up and she saw a handsome face ravaged by fear and worry. His skin was pleasantly tanned as though he'd been working outside or just returned from holiday. A quick assessment of his height gave her a guessing measurement of one similar to her own five foot nine. He wore hiking boots, adding to her theory that he worked outside. His arm muscles were not overly developed but were definitely used. Light stubble was peeking through his lower jawline.

'Detective Inspector Stone,' she said. 'And you are?'

He offered her a shy smile. 'Duncan… my name is Duncan Adams and I'm Isobel's boyfriend.'

Kim looked around. 'How did you know she was here?'

He coloured slightly. 'She didn't text me on Monday night. I always sent her a goodnight message and she would send one back if she could. I sent one but got no reply. I didn't think too much of it as we were due to meet on Tuesday anyway. When she didn't turn up I knew something was wrong.'

'Did you try and call?' Kim asked.

He nodded. 'All through the night and when I got no response I rang the police to see if there had been any, umm… incidents. They noted my call and advised me to try the local hospitals. I spoke to admissions who confirmed there was no one under Isobel's name but an unidentified woman had been rushed into the HDU.' He nodded towards the nurses' station. 'I was put through to Jo who asked me some questions and then I got here as fast as I could.'

'How did you confirm the woman was Isobel?' Kim asked.

He pointed to his wrist.

Of course – the scars, Kim realised.

'How long have you been seeing Isobel?' she asked.

'About two months,' he said.

'Do you know Isobel's last name?'

'Jones. Her last name is Jones,' he answered emphatically.

Bloody great, Kim thought.

'How did you meet?' Kim asked, praying they had met at work.

A smile spread across his face, which lit the affection in his eyes. 'Believe it or not, I swept her off her feet – or rather knocked her off them. I was hurtling out of the phone shop and she was coming out of Costa. We collided and I'm sorry to say that she got the worst of it. Her coffee was all over the floor and I insisted on buying her another. It was the least I could do.

'We got talking and something just clicked. It was as though…'

'Do you know where Isobel works?' Kim asked. She hadn't meant to cut him off so sharply, but she'd already established there was nothing in their meeting that would help her at all.

'I picked her up from 157 Plaza in Erdington, but I never went inside.'

Kim made a mental note. It was a starting point at least.

'Her address?'

Duncan coloured further and Kim could see that his inability to help was as troubling to him as it was to her. She noted that he went to bite the inside of his lip and stopped himself.

There was something this man was not telling her. She quickly replayed their conversation so far and remembered something he'd said earlier.

'You said that Isobel replied to your texts when she could. What did you mean?' she asked.

He looked to Isobel regretfully and lowered his voice.

'She's married, Inspector, that's why she insisted on secrecy, and I respected that.' He squeezed Isobel's hand. 'Please don't judge her. She told me straightaway, and I chose to continue seeing her, but she was beginning to talk about leaving her husband. She hadn't been happy for a long time. They separated a week ago, and Isobel was planning on speaking to him about divorce.'

'Was he abusive?' Kim asked, thinking about the scars on her wrists.

Duncan hesitated, as though it pained him to be discussing her most intimate secrets behind her back.

'I think he'd been physical with her, the odd push and shove…'

'That's why you called the police and the hospital?' Kim clarified.

He sighed heavily. 'Yes, I was worried that she'd told him it was over and he'd hurt her.'

Kim had no feelings either way about the secrecy and deceit. People spun their own webs, and she couldn't get caught up in them all.

His eyes travelled up and to the left, recalling something. 'She did say something about shopping in Wolverhampton, so…'

Kim smiled her understanding and made a mental note.

His hand had not left Isobel's. His thumb stroked her skin tenderly.

'Do you know how she got those scars on her wrist?' Kim asked.

He shook his head. 'I first saw them on our second date, but she covered them quickly. Eventually she admitted they were from a long time ago, but I didn't push her. I knew she would tell me when she wanted to.'

He let out a breath. 'Inspector, I am so sorry that I can't be more help.' He looked back to Isobel and his face softened. 'But I will be here if you need to ask me anything else.' He squeezed gently on the hand. 'If she can hear me, I want her to know that I'm here for her and that I'm not going anywhere.'

He turned back to face Kim fully. 'Although it was only a few months I felt like we were getting along very well. I had high hopes for us… still do in fact.'

Kim couldn't help but think about the inconvenient husband that would need to be dealt with first. If Isobel woke up, she would need a lot of help. It would not be a fast recovery.

'Can I take the mobile number you have for her?' Kim asked, taking out her own phone.

He recited it and Kim keyed it into her phone.

'Do you think she'll make it?' he whispered with a tremor in his voice.

'I spoke to the doctor and he…'

'Won't commit to a damn thing,' Duncan said, shaking his head.

Obviously he'd had the same conversation with Doctor Singh as she had.

She passed the man a card from her pocket.

'If you think of anything at all that might help, however irrelevant you might think it is, give me a call.'

Duncan slipped the card into his pocket and she offered him a smile before she turned away.

Kim hoped to God he came up with something – because at the moment she was feeling as though she had no clues at all.

CHAPTER THIRTY-ONE

Kim stepped out of the hospital into a twenty-four-degree wall of heat. The clouds had cleared, and the sun was shining proudly in the sky.

Bryant was parked on the double yellows across the road with a face like thunder. She stood still as he brought the car around to the entrance.

She jumped in as he used a tissue to wipe at his forehead.

'No air conditioning in this thing?' she asked, buckling up.

He wound down the passenger-side window. 'There you go.'

'Who pissed on your chips?' she asked.

'It's this damn heat,' he said, pulling out of the hospital grounds. It wasn't the heat that was bothering him at all. It was a morning of inactivity. He was a police officer with a keen brain and a gift for solving puzzles. Not a chauffeur.

'So our girl's name is Isobel Jones and that's about it.'

He glanced her way as he approached the traffic island for the second time that day.

'Really?'

'Yep, that's it. The guy in there has been seeing her for a few months and got worried when she stood him up.'

'So he knows very little about her?'

'Yeah, but I do have a mobile number.' She swiped her screen as her mobile began to ring. 'Stace, I was just about to call you. Can you write this number down?'

She recited the number she'd keyed in.

'That's the number of our victim two whose name is Isobel Jones. Update the board and start looking at 157 Plaza building in Erdington. She may have worked there. Also check the electoral roll around Wolverhampton – there would be a husband listed too. And check the logs and see if we got a call yesterday morning from a Duncan Adams. I know how that sounds, but it's all we've got.'

'Jeez, boss…'

'I said I know, Stace. You've got a lot on your plate so if you need me to call Dawson back…'

'Boss, I'm perfectly capable of doing my job, but I called you because there's something you need to know.'

A beeping sounded in her ear. She pulled the phone away and checked the screen.

'Hang on a sec, Stace, I've got Kev trying to get me.'

She switched calls to Dawson. Whatever he had to tell her took priority. He was at site.

'What is it, Kev?' Kim said into her phone. 'We're on our way back to West—'

'Yeah, boss. You might want to take a detour,' he said.

'Why?' she asked, putting him on loudspeaker.

'Something a bit strange going on over here. It's a bit chaotic at the minute. Machinery is arriving. Identifications are being checked. Looks like Woody has blown a month's budget on this one…'

'Kev…?'

'Sorry, boss. The phone has been going mental. The press has discovered the facility and the shit is hitting the proverbial fan.'

Kim frowned at Bryant, who had glanced to his left. Unfortunate but not wholly unexpected. Only a fool would have expected it to stay secret for much longer.

'There was so much going on that I didn't even notice at first…'

'Notice what?' Kim asked. Whatever he'd missed sounded important.

'She took a call – I was right beside her. She screamed "No comment" and slammed the phone down. Next time I looked she was no longer here.'

'Kev, you're not making a whole lot of—'

'It's Catherine Evans, boss. She seems to have just disappeared.'

CHAPTER THIRTY-TWO

The uneasy feeling in Kim's stomach did not lessen the closer they got to Catherine's house.

It began as soon as Dawson had told her that Catherine had fled her place of work and continued to swirl when she had returned to her conversation with Stacey.

The fact that Catherine Evans was living under a false identity had scattered Kim's thoughts in a dozen directions. Whatever had happened must have been serious and how the hell was it linked to a call from the press?

All she knew now was that she needed to find Catherine and get answers to some of these questions.

Bryant wound the car through the shiny residential estate that had caused controversy on the edge of the green belt that bordered West Hagley. Affordable housing had been the marketing strategy for the sprawling housing complex that had wiped out three fields and a small wooded area.

So far Bryant had navigated the two of them through the outer circle of detached, spacious homes with double garages and mock pillars. Properties valued in the mid three hundreds eventually gave way to single-garage dwellings with half the drive space, which in turn guided them to the affordable housing buried in the centre of the estate.

These houses made no attempt to stand out from each other. Not one facet identified them from their neighbour or the strip of properties over the road.

The house at which they stopped was a two-storey semi-detached property formed of brick that was an unnatural red.

'Compact and bijou,' Bryant observed as they got out of the car.

The narrow, one-car driveway held the Ford Focus that belonged to Catherine Evans.

Kim skirted around it and stepped onto the border between the two properties.

'Start knocking and I'll take a look around the back,' she said, leaving Bryant at the front door.

The side of the house was not fenced, and she had free access to the rear of the house.

As she turned the corner she saw the reason. A CCTV camera was fixed to the corner of the property, covering the walkway to the side of the house.

Well, Catherine would certainly know they were there.

Another camera was fixed to the rear wall, peering down at the back door. It was a small box-like property but covered by two expensive CCTV cameras. Why?

Kim initially wondered if it was some kind of neighbour dispute, but the placement of the cameras said otherwise. The protection was on the approach and entrances.

Catherine was watching for people coming in.

The small garden was grassed without borders or plants. A five-foot fence separated it from the property next door and the property behind.

Kim's path was unencumbered by garden furniture. At this time of year any garden forays were normally obstructed by barbecues, lawn chairs and parasols. But here there was nothing.

Against the fence was an outside storage box about five feet long by two feet high. Beside it was a Flymo lawnmower.

Kim could see straight into the house through the patio door.

Having learned from Bryant in the past, she fought her natural instinct to find something heavy to smash against the glass.

'No answer yet, guv. But she must be here,' Bryant said, appearing beside her.

'Not necessarily. She could have parked the car and gone out.'

Even as the words left her mouth Kim felt it was unlikely.

She wasn't sure exactly what she was hoping to find, but she had to establish why a call from the press had caused Catherine to run away like a scalded rabbit. Catherine had told no one she was leaving Westerley and was not answering her mobile phone.

What did she know about this case and what had frightened her away?

Kim touched the door handle, and the door slid away from the frame.

She frowned. Why would a woman who had every inch of outside space covered by a camera leave her back door unlocked?

'Shit, guv,' Bryant said, reaching the same conclusion. 'You don't think our guy has...?'

'Dunno, Bryant but we now have a reason to enter,' she said, stepping over the threshold.

The room was small and dark. Kim guessed the kitchen was at the front, basking in the daytime sun.

The mauve furnishings brought some light into the property, but there was a claustrophobic feeling about the space.

She stood still and listened. There was no sound echoing through the house. Only the noise of an occasional car driving past. There was no sound of a TV or radio or anything to cut through the silence. Somehow it made the small space even darker.

Kim headed to the kitchen, a room she always found gave the most accurate snapshot of the activities within the home.

All of the property's light appeared to have been filtered to this one small room. The units and appliances were a shiny white, all reflecting the afternoon sun as it burst in through the window.

The space was neat and tidy. She felt a few crumbs underfoot and saw a single plate and upturned mug on the sink drainer.

Her investigating skills were not being tested in deducing there had been coffee and toast for breakfast before heading off to Westerley this morning.

So Catherine had had no time to make any more mess since she'd come home. Kim reached across and touched the kettle. It was stone cold.

Most people on entering home tended to switch on the kettle for a drink. Even if they then got distracted by unloading shopping or tidying things away, the kettle had normally been activated.

'This is starting to look a bit suspect now,' Kim said, heading out of the kitchen.

Bryant had remained in the lounge, as there was only room for one in the kitchen. He followed her as she took the stairs two at a time.

At the top of the staircase was a stubby hallway with three doors, all pulled shut.

The first left was a small but functional bathroom. The second was the spare room, which held no bed, just a couple of pieces of mismatched furniture, a few boxes and a wardrobe.

So the house had CCTV but Catherine still hadn't properly unpacked.

Kim was getting an uneasy feeling in her stomach, which was not helped when she opened the door to the main bedroom.

An open suitcase lay on the bed. It was empty but the top drawer of a chest was open. Kim glanced inside. Underwear. Normally the first thing when packing in a rush, the mind already attuned to need rather than desire.

Women tended to pack from the inside out, essentials first. Men normally packed the opposite.

The rules differed when packing for a holiday. Then you might take time over the clothing first, but in a rush it was underwear first.

'Where the hell is she, Bryant?' she asked, surveying the room.

It was a small house and they had covered every square inch in a few moments. Catherine wasn't here but she had been.

A woman so focussed on security had left her back door unlocked. For some reason she had bolted from her place of work and come home. She had paused for nothing before starting to pack. Her car was still here, she was not and yet there was no evidence of a struggle.

'I think he's got her,' Bryant said, scratching his head.

No scenario made sense to Kim, but she was on the verge of agreeing when her phone shattered the silence.

'Stace,' she said.

Kim listened to Stacey's excited and turbocharged voice. She didn't interrupt her colleague once.

Because what she had to say changed everything.

CHAPTER THIRTY-THREE

Kim pressed the button that ended the call.

She closed her eyes for a second, absorbing everything she'd heard. The pieces began to fall into place.

She exhaled the breath she'd been holding. 'Oh, Bryant,' was all she could say.

'What's going on?' her colleague asked.

Kim took a moment to retrace everything they'd seen since arriving at Catherine's home. Now she knew where to look.

'Follow me,' Kim said, heading out of the room and down the stairs.

She strode out of the back door and stopped at the only place that made sense.

She lowered herself to the ground and sat cross-legged in front of the garden storage box.

'Catherine, it's Kim Stone, and I know you're in there.'

Because the lawnmower was not.

There was no sound and Kim considered the possibility that she was sitting on the ground speaking to an empty plastic box. But she suspected not.

Kim scooted closer to the box and lowered her voice even further. She placed one hand on top of the lid as though offering the woman some kind of reassurance.

'Catherine, I know who you are, and I know why you're scared.'

There was the faintest of sobs.

Kim heard a sharp intake of breath from Bryant, who was standing behind her. She glanced around to find him shaking his head with bewilderment. She turned back to the container.

'It's okay, Catherine. I know you're the orange-box kid.'

Kim heard another sob and she knew Stacey had got it right.

'I also know your name was Janet Wilson and you were abducted from your front garden in Walsall. You were kept in an orange storage box for seventeen days before you managed to get away.'

Kim now understood the scarring on her hand. It was from trying to escape.

The sobbing became even louder. Bryant stood behind her, not making a sound.

'I know why you're scared, Catherine. Will you please come out and talk to me?'

The sobbing had stopped and Kim knew she could throw open the lid and haul the fully grown Catherine out. Only it was nine-year-old Janet who was hiding in the box.

Stacey had read her everything she'd been able to get her hands on.

'The doctors couldn't understand how you'd managed to stay alive, could they?' Kim asked.

But Kim knew. The nine-year-old had lived on insects and it was why she showed them such great respect now. They had kept her alive.

'Catherine, I promise you can trust me. Please step out of the box.'

The lid began to open and a contorted body began to unfurl.

Kim held the lid open as Catherine resumed her normal shape.

Bryant offered his hand to help her step out of the box.

Her face was pale, tear-stained and looked much younger than her thirty-two years.

'May we go inside?' Kim asked.

Catherine nodded and stepped through the patio door.

Kim followed and Bryant stood in the doorway.

Catherine sat on the sofa and stared at her hands. This was not the self-assured, aloof woman Kim had met at Westerley.

Kim sat beside her. 'Catherine, I know you're still in hiding. The men that took you were never caught, were they?'

It didn't matter how many years passed, the fear that they were coming back for her would always be there.

Kim had experienced dreams for years that her mother had managed to find her and put the handcuffs around her wrist again. Her mother had been locked in Grantley Care psychiatric facility for more than twenty-five years. And yet still the dreams came.

'Trust me, Catherine. I get it,' Kim said, meeting her eye.

Kim was saddened by the fear she saw there.

'I can't go back,' she whispered.

'To Westerley?' Kim clarified.

Catherine nodded and lowered her head. 'I'll have to move again. Once the papers start printing the story my name will appear and someone might make the connection. It didn't take you long. He'll find me. I know he'll find me.'

Kim could see her point, although not everyone had a Stacey up their sleeve.

The fear was not rational anyway. Catherine was now a grown woman with a different name and a different life, but the fear came from the nine-year-old girl who knew her torturers were still out there. She had worked through her education safely, although she'd moved university twice, and she'd found a job doing what she loved in a place where she could never be found. Finally, she had felt safe.

But Catherine was correct. Westerley would be examined in depth, staff members and all.

'I was happy there,' Catherine offered. 'I haven't felt so safe since leaving Bromley…'

The very name sent a frisson of fear through Kim. She knew of Bromley. Every kid in the care system knew of Bromley. Twenty years ago it had been a closed psychiatric unit for youngsters and a place surrounded by mystery and fear. It had been the threat that lived on the lips of every care worker that couldn't handle an unruly or spirited kid.

Catherine caught her expression. 'You know of it?'

Kim nodded. 'I was a care kid, Catherine. It was often used as a threat to keep us in line. We were terrified of the place,' she admitted.

Catherine looked surprised. 'Really? I was happy there. I couldn't cope, you see. Afterwards. I went home to my family, but it wasn't the same. They tried to make me feel safe, the police even arranged for panic alarms to be fitted throughout the house, but my mind found a way around everything.

'They could disable the panic alarms, cut the power, take me again while I was sleeping. It was the fear… it consumed me. I couldn't eat or sleep and nowhere felt safe. I just cried every day. They tried drugs first, but nothing worked until I was sent to Bromley. They took care of me there. They protected me.'

'Did you stay there?' Kim asked gently.

Catherine shook her head. 'My first stay was two weeks. The second I heard those doors close and lock behind me I felt safe. I felt relief. Amongst all that craziness, I finally felt sane.'

Kim understood that she had hated it for the very reasons Catherine had loved it.

'The second I got home the old feelings returned. Two days later I was back at Bromley. The trips home became less frequent, and that was fine by me. My parents visited as often as they could, and my father consulted a solicitor who made a case for a new identity.'

Catherine's expression saddened further at the mention of her father.

'By the time I left Bromley for good I no longer knew my parents. They just reminded me of what happened, and so I stayed away.'

Kim realised from the dates Stacey had given her that Catherine had been at Bromley until she was eighteen years old. No wonder the outside world was difficult for her to navigate.

'At Westerley I thought I was safe,' Catherine continued, looking around the small living room. 'But I have to leave now. I can't possibly go back.'

'Sleep on it, Catherine,' Kim advised. 'Don't do anything rash. It might not be over yet.'

'I don't understand. You know everything, so you have to understand that I can't go back there. If it's about the investigation I'll let you know…'

'It's not about the investigation. I'm just asking you to ease off. At least until tomorrow. Will you do that for me?'

She could feel safe here for the moment. The article wasn't out for the next hour or so and she had CCTV.

Kim handed her a card. 'If you have any trouble, any unwelcome visitors or even noises you can't explain, call me. Got it?'

Catherine nodded eagerly. Kim had given her options. The logical mind of the grown woman knew her captors were not coming back, but the fear of the little girl would never go away.

Catherine used her index finger to trace a line around the edge of the card. A slight tremble was still present and some tension in the jaw.

'What is it?' Kim asked, sensing there was still fear in this woman's mind.

'Do you have to tell them – at Westerley, I mean?' She bit the inside of her lower lip. 'I just don't want to be treated any differently and they'll have questions which will take me back to that time. And I don't think I can bear that.'

Kim understood that better than anyone. She saw no reason to divulge what she'd learned to the woman's work colleagues. She had made her life as Catherine Evans and it was her prerogative to share her past with whomever she chose.

Kim shook her head. 'It won't come from me but you'd better start thinking up an explanation for your sudden departure today.'

Catherine swallowed and tipped her head. Her face had lost some of its ashen colour.

'Inspector, you're not quite the person I thought you were.'

Kim offered a half-smile. 'Neither are you, Catherine Evans.'

Kim stood. 'I'll call you tomorrow, okay?'

'Thank you,' Catherine said.

Bryant followed silently to the car.

'You know, guv, I hate to have to say this but none of what I heard in there completely rules her out.'

Kim knew he was right. But despite her team's suspicions, she still felt they were looking for a man.

She opened the passenger door and tossed Bryant the keys. A clear indication that she needed to think.

'Bryant, drop me home and head back to Westerley. I'll meet you back there later.'

He frowned. 'What the hell are you going to try and do for her?'

Kim said nothing but stared out of the window. She couldn't tell Bryant what she was considering.

Because it meant bedding down with the devil.

CHAPTER THIRTY-FOUR

Isobel crawled along the darkness of her own mind.

There was no light anywhere. The blackness was trying to consume her.

The warm sensation on her hand had disappeared. Had it ever really been there?

She wasn't sure where her body had gone. She had the sensation of being only a head. A picture came into her mind of body parts arranged in place but unconnected.

For a moment the darkness was alight with the vision, only for it to be swallowed again.

And yet it hadn't properly disappeared. The darkness was not as black any more. There was a greyness somewhere in the distance. The vision had left behind a trail of light. A cord for her to reach. A guide out of the dark.

But she didn't know how to reach it. Her heart began to beat loudly in her chest as she pictured the lifeline disappearing completely and returning her to the infinity of the dark.

Please don't go, she cried to the grey speck that both tantalised and taunted her at the same time. *Take me with you. Don't leave me.*

Suddenly the total emptiness of the darkness was terrifying as she began to wonder what it meant.

The beeping increased and hands were touching her. Maybe they were joining her back together again.

Her heart returned to a normal rate and the speck of grey returned.

She didn't feel quite so alone while the speck was still there.

Out of the darkness she heard a voice, words that broke through the haze. But she didn't understand what it meant when it said, 'One for you and one for me...'

CHAPTER THIRTY-FIVE

Kim glanced at her watch. Her companion was already ten minutes late.

She pushed away the weak coffee that had bought her a seat. The culinary offering was not the reason she'd chosen this place. A greasy shed on a Brierley Hill trading estate was not somewhere she would normally have chosen for a meeting. But Joe's Diner was out of the way and they would not be seen.

She itched to walk out but damn it, she wanted this meeting more than the person she'd invited.

She watched as a wasp entered through the open window and landed beside the sugar bowl on the next table. She was instantly reminded of Elvis and, in turn, Catherine, who was her reason for being here.

The bell above the door tinged as the door opened.

Tracy Frost made no effort to hide the disdain as her eyes searched for and then rested on Kim.

Her long blonde hair flowed freely and the five-inch heels tottered over to where Kim sat.

Her legs were clad in black tailored trousers and her upper half in a pastel T-shirt with cuffed shoulders. A burgundy bolero was straddled over a handbag that reeked of expense.

She slid into the chair opposite and placed her handbag on her lap.

Kim didn't blame her. She wouldn't want her personal belongings touching the floor, or the table for that matter. Her own arm had accidentally brushed the top of the table and had almost stuck to the droplets of grease welded there.

Kim glanced at the cup of liquid that was now lukewarm. 'Want one?'

Tracy looked at her as though she'd lost her mind. 'Only if it comes with a tetanus shot.'

The woman at the next table overheard and offered Tracy a filthy look.

And people commented on her lack of social skills. Kim offered the woman an apologetic smile and received an even frostier glare in return.

Tracy didn't even notice, and if she had she wouldn't have cared. The woman's hide was thicker than that of an old aged cow.

'So what the hell is going on, Inspector? You call and request my attendance at a place that's harder to find than a virgin in Dudley. When it's normally all I can get you to do to throw a "Fuck off, Frost" my way.'

The woman at the next table shook her head with disgust. Kim guessed she was from Dudley. If they sat here long enough Kim was sure Tracy could offend everyone in the place.

Kim fought back her smile at Tracy's observation. It was true. She despised the woman and the way she did her job, but right now she could prove useful.

'I want to talk to you about this current case,' Kim said.

'Now I know you've bloody lost it, Stone.'

Kim sat forwards. 'Look, this case is about to get messy. The public will be crying out for answers over the secrecy of the location. The harder I try and keep this to myself the worse it's going to get, and the last thing I need right now is bandana-wearing, placard-carrying protestors causing a major distraction.'

'You want to go on the record?' Tracy asked disbelievingly.

'Unnamed source,' Kim said.

Tracy thought for a second. 'Okay, but I think you're up to something.'

Now for a bit of authenticity. 'Tracy, you know I can't stand the sight of you. I don't really hide that fact, and if there was any other local crime reporter you would not be sitting here right now.'

For once, Tracy's mouth fell open. Yeah, Kim knew this was not the way to get a favour out of someone, but she was dealing with Tracy Frost. Kim enjoyed the bewildered expression for a whole two seconds before continuing.

'I am using you, Tracy. The story needs to come from a local paper and you're the only person there is.'

'Stone, I don't trust you—'

'Forget it,' Kim said, pushing her chair back. 'I'll speak to—'

'No… no… ' Tracy said, grabbing her wrist.

Kim shook it free. 'I don't have time to keep explaining myself to you. Either get your notebook out or I'm off.'

Tracy reached into her bag and took out a shorthand pad with a pen stored in the metal binding.

She used her left hand to wipe at the table before placing her handbag between them.

Kim sat back down.

'Westerley is a research facility for studying the effects of both insect activity and climate conditions on the human body. It is at least a mile and a half from the closest residential property.

'There are a total of seven corpses there spread over a two-acre site. The bodies have all been donated by legitimate means.

'The facility is run by Professor Christopher Wright and he is assisted by Jameel Mohammed. Both have impeccable qualifications and—'

'I spoke to a woman,' Tracy interjected.

'No, you didn't,' Kim said.

'Yes, I did.'

'No, you didn't,' Kim repeated forcefully, wondering when the pantomime horse was going to step out of the wings.

Confusion then understanding registered in Tracy's eyes two seconds before Kim expected it to.

'Bloody hell, Stone, I should have known.'

Yes, she really should have.

'You're getting the heads-up on the understanding that you mention only the staff members that I've named.'

Tracy sat back in her chair, weighing up if it was more beneficial to have the first accurate story or to have every single detail.

'If someone uncovers something juicy then I'm gonna look like a prize dick.'

Kim knew that to be true. 'Yes, you are.'

'I don't know, Stone, I'm not convinced…'

Now for the clincher, Kim thought, offering a wry expression.

'I had a meeting with Keats, the pathologist, earlier today. We discussed Bob, at length.'

Tracy sighed heavily. 'Jesus, that's unfair.'

Kim shrugged.

Their gazes met and held for a long minute.

'Okay, enough foreplay,' Tracy said, turning the page.

Kim was happy to continue.

'One body identified. Second victim not yet named is still alive but in a comatose state.'

'Picture?' Tracy asked.

'In your dreams,' Kim responded.

'Go on,' Tracy urged her to continue.

'We are currently exploring all lines of enquiry. We do not feel that the purpose of the site has any connection to the crimes. All personnel have been ruled out of our investigation.'

Tracy frowned. 'So why's it being used as a dump site?'

Kim had stopped short of just how much she was prepared to reveal. She had to allow Tracy to feel she was earning this somehow.

Kim hesitated. 'The exact location of the body was not actually on Westerley property.' She held up her hands. 'That's all I've—'

'Is there any connection between the victims?' Tracy asked.

She shook her head. 'Not yet established.'

Kim was surprised she had not been asked about the activity at the site. She had hope that this was, as yet, undiscovered. If Tracy knew of it that would definitely have been her first question.

'Is there…?'

'No more, Tracy,' she said, pushing back her chair for the final time. 'I've offered more than I should have already.'

'I know,' Tracy said, raising an eyebrow. 'That's what's worrying me.'

Kim's phone began to vibrate in her pocket. Tracy caught the subtle noise.

'Your phone is ringing,' she said.

'Yeah, I know,' Kim answered.

'Not going to answer it?'

'In front of you? Yeah, right.' Kim placed her hand on her pocket and shrugged. 'Run the story or don't. Your call – but I'm not going to be talking to anyone else.'

Tracy licked her lips. A body-language expert would explain that as a 'tell' that she was excited.

The article would be at least half a page. Tracy would be able to turn what she'd said into some serious column inches.

'I need a name,' Tracy said, as her pen hovered above the pad. 'If the first victim has been identified and next of kin informed, you can give me that.'

Damn this woman. Kim had been hoping to keep Jemima's family out of it for a little while yet, but it would look more suspicious if the identity continued to be hidden.

'Okay, Frost, her name was Jemima. Her full name was Jemima Lowe.'

The pen dropped from Tracy's hand as Kim rose to her feet. She leaned down and picked it up.

Tracy took it without speaking, but Kim noted a slight tremble to Tracy's hand that she hadn't seen before.

She stepped outside as her phone stopped ringing. It started again before she had a chance to remove it from her pocket.

She saw immediately that it was Bryant, who was now back at the site.

He didn't wait for her to speak.

'Guv, we need you back here now. It looks like there's another body.'

CHAPTER THIRTY-SIX

Tracy sat still for a minute and allowed her face to arrange itself into the expression it wanted to form. Confusion.

Damn it – Jemima Lowe was not a name she wanted to hear. Not ever.

She tried to tell herself that the vague trembling in her legs was because of exhaustion. She would take just a few moments to rest her legs. It had been a hard day. She'd been chasing a story around the Black Country all day about a vicious assault on an elderly woman in Bilston.

Right now she wanted to kick off her heels and hurry back to the safety of the car barefoot, but of course she wouldn't. Her feet had been encased in five-inch stilettos since she was old enough to get a Saturday job and buy a cheap pair from the market. But the minute she had, her life had changed.

Yes, people still pointed and laughed, thinking she'd chosen heels way too high to master. And that was fine. Because they were no longer calling her a spastic.

Just the memory of the word brought colour to her cheeks and a rolling anxiety to her stomach.

No matter how you tried to outrun your past there were memories that refused to go away. And with the memories came the rush of emotions, as though it was yesterday.

Suddenly her breath seemed unable to get down her throat. The room before her was beginning to spin. The nausea was rising in her stomach. Not now, she silently begged. Please don't do this to me now.

Tracy tried to stem the panic and get her breath. She tried to remember the coaching. First she must try to get her breathing under control, but the palpitations were vibrating within her chest cavity. She closed her eyes against the onslaught of dizziness.

'Please no, please no,' she whispered through dry lips.

The first episode had happened when she was seven years old. Her mother had thought she was experiencing a heart attack and she'd called for an ambulance. The diagnosis of *panic attack* did not do justice to the severity of the symptoms.

In the years since the first one she'd read that it was her body protecting itself following the shot of adrenaline launched through her system, but it sure as hell didn't feel as though her body was on her side right now.

It will pass, it will pass, she told herself. The symptoms would peak in a few minutes. But as a fresh wave of perspiration broke out on her forehead and the nausea rolled in her stomach, she realised how long those ten minutes could last.

Her hands had wound themselves into the shoulder strap of her handbag. Her fingertips were turning white but she couldn't unclench them.

'Yow all right, love?' asked the woman who had thrown filthy looks her way earlier.

Tracy tried to smile and nod her head, but she could feel that the expression on her face was a lopsided grimace.

Tracy sensed the woman slip into the chair beside her, but the stars in her eyes were threatening to consume her.

'Here yow am, love,' said the woman, unclenching her hands from the strap. 'Hang on to me and squeeze as 'ard as yow con.'

Tracy did as she was told, as she was in no position to argue.

She squeezed her palms around the woman's fingers and told herself over and over that she wasn't going to die. That her breath would continue to come and that her heart would not explode right out of her body.

'Goo on, love,' the woman said. 'I can teck it.'

Another good squeeze and Tracy could feel the tension starting to fall from her fingers. The uncontrollable trembling in her legs was beginning to subside. The stars were receding to the back of her head. Her body felt battered and exhausted.

'All right now, love?' the woman asked.

Tracy nodded gratefully. A few people were looking their way but nothing Tracy couldn't cope with.

'Thank you,' Tracy said, giving her hand one last squeeze.

The woman stood and reached for her shopping bag. 'You're welcome, now teck care, eh?'

Tracy nodded and thanked her again.

Only when she'd gone did Tracy allow the tears to pierce her eyes. An episode was always followed by fatigue and emotion.

She probably had about twenty minutes to get home before the exhaustion claimed her completely.

The shame of her condition was as humiliating today as it had been back then. If she turned she was sure she would see the group of girls and boys who had screamed it as she'd passed.

There had been many other names throughout her school days but spastic had been their favourite.

Unequal leg length was the common term for it these days, or leg-length inequality. All very nice names but not ones you can get kids to shout while they're pointing and laughing.

The discrepancy in her own legs was due to the femur in her left thigh being shorter than the one in the right. The frequent back pain was the result of a now tilted pelvis.

She had tried the heel lifts and the ugly shoes that had been available and none had worked.

They'd just made her feel even more clunky and ugly.

And that was why she wore the shoes.

Tracy took a deep breath and reached for her handbag. Her legs faltered for a moment as she pushed herself to a standing position, but a couple of breaths and she was ready to walk.

The fatigue pulling at her eyelids told her she was already on borrowed time, but she would have to fight it for a little bit longer.

She had to get her jumbled thoughts in order. Her legs were not responsible for the panic attack.

It was due to the mention of Jemima Lowe.

CHAPTER THIRTY-SEVEN

As Kim pulled up at the gate that separated Westerley from civilisation, she wondered how long it would be until this entrance was besieged by reporters and the placard brigade.

The press knew that a body had been found on 'farmland bordering Wall Heath', but as yet the exact details had been hidden. With the arrival of equipment and specialists, they were on borrowed time before the secret was out.

The gate began its slow journey. The CCTV camera had alerted her arrival.

The gravel parking area held three vehicles Kim didn't recognise.

Bryant stood beside the Portakabin as she parked.

Kim felt the full force of the evening sun when she stepped off the bike and switched it off. The passing breeze had kept her cool, but the fact that the temperature had prised the suit jacket from Bryant's back and rolled his sleeves up to the elbow told her they were mid to high twenties.

'They've checked it twice,' he said as she removed her helmet. 'But I'll let the guys explain when you get down there.'

'Where are they?' she asked.

'Furthest point away, opposite side to where Jemima was found,' he said, matching her stride as she headed down the hill.

'Have you called Keats?' she asked.

Bryant nodded.

And she had called Woody, so between the two of them key personnel should already be on their way.

She glanced down in the general direction Bryant had indicated and was dismayed at what she saw.

'Jesus, it's a circus already?'

Although the commotion was in the distance Kim counted at least nine or ten people around the area, including Professor Wright and Daniel Bate.

'Watch out for Cher,' Bryant said, guiding her to the left.

In her haste she had almost missed the cut in the grass and the metal grid that lay across the grave. Kim took a quick glance as she passed. The similarity to the real Cher ended with the long black hair. This version was bloated and waxy and writhing with worms.

'Bloody hell… this place… '

She shook her head and charged straight into the middle of the group.

'Okay, guys, what have we got?' she asked, stepping towards the machine. She sensed Bryant's despair, but there was little point in introductions. Whoever had the information would shout up.

A man dressed in dark blue coveralls stepped forwards, holding out his hand.

'Harry Atkins, I'm the archaeologist from Aston University.'

'Nice to meet you, Harry,' Kim said, offering a quick smile. 'What can you tell me?'

If he was surprised by her brusqueness, he didn't show it.

'If you look here,' he said, moving back to the machine. She'd seen ground-penetrating radar equipment before, but this one looked like a lawnmower.

'What the machine does—'

'Harry, I'm fine with the explanation.'

Realising how churlish that sounded, and with Woody's warning ringing in her ears, she offered a smile. 'But thanks anyway.'

She knew that the machine employed radio waves to emit a pulse to the ground and then recorded echoes.

The picture he wanted to show her was an image built from those echoes.

'The apex of the hyperbolas indicates that there is a mass right there,' he said, pointing at Professor Wright's feet. 'And it's between two to four foot down.'

Kim had the sudden urge to tell the professor to move but stopped herself. If there was anyone down there they wouldn't be hurting now.

She waited for more but Harry shrugged. She'd asked for the condensed version and that's what she'd got.

She took two steps towards the professor. 'Eventually there will be reporters and news crews. Now we will set up a cordon at the end of the lane to keep the vans and vehicles away from the entrance but the quarter-mile walk isn't going to deter them.'

She made a quick appraisal of the people milling around and frowned.

'Security consultant still here?' she asked.

'Needs to update his risk assessment for Darren. A body and an almost-dead body tends to change things for your staff members,' Bryant said.

'Okay, but he doesn't need to be down here. In fact…' She took a couple of steps away. 'Folks, may I have your attention,' she shouted out. 'We need to clear this area and restrict it to necessary personnel only. That means police officers… and Harry. Can you remain with the equipment?'

He nodded.

'Can everyone else please make their way back up to the office…'

'Am I necessary, Inspector?' Daniel Bate asked.

She thought for a moment. 'I'd go as far as potentially useful… Daniel,' she responded. 'Kev, go and find something to place around Cher. I don't want anyone falling in that hole.'

'Got it, boss,' he answered, heading off.

A soft chuckle sounded from Bryant to her left. 'Jesus, guv, it's a good job you sent people away 'cos this field ain't big enough for everyone.'

She turned and followed the direction of his gaze.

Oh yeah, she could certainly see what he meant.

CHAPTER THIRTY-EIGHT

The first group was led by a woman whose five-foot-four height did nothing to diminish her authority. The four taller males behind struggled to keep pace as she barrelled in Kim's direction.

'Oh hell no,' Bryant said from behind her.

'Hell, yes,' Kim said, walking towards the forensic archaeologist.

The woman was clad in grey jeans, plain black T-shirt and Doc Marten boots.

'Doctor A, good to see you,' Kim said. Everyone referred to the woman as Doctor A. Originally from Macedonia, her first name was long and complicated. She had termed the name herself.

'*Dobra vecher*, Inspector.'

The curt nod and brief smile told Kim that was a greeting of some kind.

'What are we having here?' she asked, looking around the group.

Harry stepped forwards to explain his findings as Doctor A took an elastic band from her pocket and tied her ombré hair into a tight ponytail.

'Guv, permission to be moved to another case,' Bryant said from beside her. 'Few of us mortals can deal with both you and her together.'

'Denied,' Kim said in response.

Many people had an issue with the direct approach of the forensic specialist. Kim did not.

She had met Doctor A once outside of a crime scene and had found her to be both charming and effervescent with a wicked sense of humour.

Doctor A nodded knowingly at the screen Harry was showing her.

The second group arrived, headed by Keats. She recognised two of the techies who had been removed from site earlier in the week and transferred to Digbeth. She'd heard that their findings had led to the apprehension of two suspects, and they had gathered intelligence on a third.

Nods and acknowledgements travelled between the two groups and within a few minutes Kim no longer knew who belonged with whom. Her own team she could account for.

Dawson had found some yellow 'wet floor' signs that he was placing around Cher and Bryant was sharing a joke with Daniel Bate.

'No, not like that,' Doctor A cried as one of her team began to spray white paint onto the grass. She stepped towards him. 'I shall show you.'

She spoke to him in hushed tones and began to spray in a gentle motion to and fro, lengthening the line with each stroke. She handed back the can. He followed her example.

'Perfect,' she said, patting him on the back.

The male positively beamed from the compliment.

'Doctor A, good to see you again,' Keats said, offering his hand.

She accepted it and smiled. 'You too, Keatings,' she said, before turning and instructing a second assistant on the equipment she required.

Kim noted the cheek muscle that jumped along the jaw of the pathologist.

Doctor A looked around at her audience as she took possession of a shovel. 'Stepping away from the area please,' she said.

Keats moved forwards. 'Doctor A, it is sunset in two hours' time. You will not have time to recover the—'

'Thank you, Keatings, for the reminder that, surprisingly, it will eventually go dark.'

Keats shook his head and walked away.

Kim leaned in and whispered, 'Doctor A, his name is Keats.'

Doctor A turned to face her. A smile tugged at the woman's lips.

'Yes, of course, I know this.'

Kim coughed and turned away.

'Doctor A,' Keats insisted. 'You will not be able to complete in normal daylight.'

She tipped her head and nodded. 'Then get me the generatings to power the lighting. Chip chip. If there is a lady down here she will be leaving the ground this night.'

And that was why Kim liked her.

CHAPTER THiRTY-NINE

Kim leaned into the back of the car and unclicked Barney from his seatbelt. He remained seated while she attached the lead to his collar. Only when she said 'out' did he bounce past her legs.

He turned, sat and waited for her to close the car door.

Bryant had questioned whether Keats and Doctor A could be left alone. But Kim had every faith in their professionalism. And if that failed, Dawson was there and would soon let her know if anything began to brew.

Right now what she needed was a little space to think, the opportunity to get a little clarity. Very little about the Westerley case was making sense to her. She couldn't help being torn between wishing for the forensic team to uncover something or someone who would help her solve the case and praying that no one else had suffered the same fate as Jemima Lowe. If she received word that there was a body in the ground she would be right back and would not leave until it had been removed.

And then there was Bob. By making a deal with the devil she had removed her own freedom of choice to investigate his murder. Both mysteries were swimming around her head.

The Clent Hills were the perfect place to help her clear her mind. Referred to as Klinter in the Domesday book, the hills rose over a thousand feet and offered 360-degree views.

Their nightly walk was a little earlier than normal. The sun was in the process of setting and they normally walked once it was dark.

Barney wasn't keen on other people and certainly not on other dogs.

Kim often wondered what had happened in his early years to make him such a complex little character. She supposed he wondered the same thing about her.

She'd recently discovered a small wooded area at the southern base of this hill. Most people walking their dogs were heading for the summit to catch a glimpse as the sun set and plunged the Black Country into a hot, sticky night.

She headed towards an overgrown path that had once been a ramblers' route but had been cut off by new fencing to prevent access to a hazardous area. It was perfect for just the two of them.

'Well… fancy seeing you here,' said a deep and slightly amused voice behind her.

Kim groaned inwardly as she turned to see Daniel Bate smiling at her.

'What are you doing here?' she asked.

'Building a sandcastle,' he offered sarcastically as he looked down towards Lola.

Barney had tensed his front shoulders and was staring Lola down. The brief power play ended as Lola looked away.

Instinctively Kim's hand reached out towards the submissive dog. Lola's nose nuzzled into her palm and her tail wagged.

Daniel reached towards Barney.

'Don't,' she advised. 'He doesn't like it.'

Barney hated being approached by strangers and expressed his disgust in a growl. Normally.

Although he didn't nuzzle like Lola, he tolerated the hand on his head and Kim could swear in better light his tail might have moved slightly.

'Hmmm… sounds like a case of owner projection there, Kim.'

She resented that she could not maintain that barrier of 'Detective Inspector' between them, but she had no jurisdiction over him outside of a crime scene. And even then it was tenuous at best.

'So you got yourself a dog since we last met?' he asked.

She should have known the goldfish ruse wouldn't last for ever.

'Yeah, apparently they help you socialise,' she said, raising one eyebrow.

He laughed out loud and his green eyes sparkled. 'I can see that's working out well for you,' he said.

Yeah, she remembered that he was one of the rare people who had actually been able to tell when she was joking.

Silence fell between them. It was charged, and Kim had no choice but to break it.

'What are you doing here, Daniel?' she asked.

'Walking my dog,' he said, meeting her gaze. Unlike his dog, he did not look away.

'Why here?' she asked.

He looked around. 'Local beauty spot. Thought the dog might enjoy it.'

'Owner projection?' she asked.

He shrugged and began to walk. She wasn't prepared to let him off the hook quite so easily.

'In this exact spot, at this time?'

'Just a coincidence,' he said and smirked.

Yeah and its name was Bryant. She had allowed him to tag along on one of her night-time walks but she wouldn't bloody do it again.

'It's a really nice view from the top,' she said, nodding towards a well-trodden path.

He watched as a male with two Dobermans headed in that direction. 'Seems it might be a bit crowded that way. I think I'll head over here.'

So her choice was to bundle Barney back in the car and take him home or to the local park.

Hang on, why the hell was she even considering it? This was her walk, not Daniel's. He lived in Dundee and was no threat to her well-being.

She tugged gently on Barney's lead and strode past the dawdling pair.

'So how's the case going?' he asked, keeping step with her.

'Slowly,' she responded.

'Any suspects?' he asked.

'Perhaps.'

'Oh come on, Kim. I'm sure we can talk about our work without clashing. Ask me something about mine.'

'When do you have to get back to it?' she joked.

He chuckled. 'Predictable, even for you. But to answer you, I'm due back at the weekend. I have two lectures booked for early next week.'

'So what brought you down here?' she asked. It looked like she was stuck with him and talk about work was safe enough.

'The professor wrote to us asking for some advice on the timings of bone decay in sandy soil.'

'And you couldn't have sent an email?'

He shrugged. 'It was worth a visit. I find myself drawn to the Black Country. There's something dark and moody that brings me back.'

'Yeah, it's called smog and grime,' she retorted.

'You do realise just how deeply you're overcompensating, right?' he asked, ducking below a veil of gnats.

'For what?' she asked, tugging Barney away from a stinger.

'For finding me attractive.'

'Ha, you wish,' she said and then offered him a bemused expression. 'Do you think everyone who doesn't like you really wants to sleep with you?'

He lifted one eyebrow.

She continued. 'Because I gotta tell you, Dawson's not that keen on you either.'

He snapped his fingers. 'Damn, and I had high hopes for him as well.'

Kim smiled at the humour that was so much like her own.

'You're like the playground bully,' he said.

'Hey now, just a—'

'Calm down. I'm giving you an example. It's like you go out of your way to show people you despise me but it's really an effort to prove it to yourself.'

'Oh please,' she said, rolling her eyes. 'I'm sorry if you feel I've pulled on your pigtails or stolen your conkers but you couldn't be more wrong.'

'Really?'

'Is it really inconceivable to you that I don't find you attractive? In fact I think you're annoying and aloof.'

Daniel surprised her by throwing back his head and laughing.

'Aloof? You dare to call me aloof?'

Kim stopped walking and he did too. It was time to put him straight once and for all.

'Daniel, I respect you as a colleague. I know that you're dedicated and passionate—'

'Thanks but I already have a CV. What I want is for you to finally take notice and admit there's a spark between us.'

She faced him squarely. 'Not even an ember, Doctor Bate.'

He took a step towards her. His eyes danced with the challenge.

'Want to test the theory and see?'

No, she bloody well did not.

'You take one more step, Daniel—'

Her words were cut off as both their phones began to ring.

CHAPTER FORTY

Kim was back at Westerley within ten minutes of receiving the call.

She parked the Golf at the top of the site and made sure the car was ventilated for the dog.

She'd lost Daniel about three miles behind.

The four floodlights at the bottom of the site guided her way, although Cher still lay somewhere between her and them. The strategically placed wet-floor signs did not glow in the dark.

Dawson met her about halfway. 'They've uncovered flesh now,' he said without any greeting.

His phone call had informed her that less than three feet down they had discovered some remnants of clothing.

'What does Doctor A say?' she asked.

'Dunno, half of what she says is a mystery to me. I think she swears in many languages.'

Kim approached what she now knew to be a grave. The forensic archaeologist was kneeling about two feet down with a soft brush in her hand. One of her assistants was using a small trowel to remove samples of the soil. To the right two others were sifting soil already removed.

Keats was watching intently with two of his aides. Harry appeared to have left the scene for now, but Kim knew he'd be back. The rest of the site would need to be checked.

'Doctor,' Kim said by way of a greeting. 'What do we have?'

'Inspector, you are just in the nook of time,' she said without looking up.

Kim felt the heat of the four floodlights beating down on her.

As she bent forwards she heard the sound of footsteps and the voice of Daniel as he spoke to Dawson.

'Male or female?' he asked.

Dawson tutted. 'Dunno yet, ask Rosetta Stone over there.'

Looking down into the pit Kim could see that a square of sky-blue material had been exposed. She guessed it might be a T-shirt of some kind.

'That is the left leg.' Doctor A pointed with the other end of the brush.

Kim frowned and peered closer. She had thought she was looking only at soil.

'There's still skin?' Kim asked.

Doctor A nodded. 'Peter is working on the head and I am working on exposing the sex,' she said. 'In females the uterus is last to decompose.'

Kim had heard that somewhere before.

She knew that when buried six feet down in ordinary soil an unembalmed body could take eight to twelve years to decompose to a skeleton, whereas an exposed body could be skeletonised within days.

'Any idea how long?' Kim asked.

Doctor A turned to look at her. Kim saw a couple of dirt marks on her face.

'I would guessing at five foot five,' she answered.

Kim realised she would have to be more specific with the doctor.

'I'm sorry, I meant...'

'I know, Inspector,' she said, offering a lopsided smile. Everyone had their own methods of getting through the horrors of a crime scene, whether it be recent or historic.

She continued. 'As you know, many factors slow down decomposition: lower temperature, exclusion of air, absence of animal life, damp, humidity. I could go on.' She turned to face Kim. 'Did you know that in India an uncoffined body is skeletonised within a year?'

Kim shook her head as Doctor A turned back to the body.

Her gaze met that of Keats and she knew they were both thinking the exact same thing. They had been here before during the Crestwood investigation. They had faced each other across too many shallow graves, but it was the career they had chosen. She held his gaze. She got it. He nodded and looked away.

'Aha,' Doctor A and Peter said together, prompting Kim to wonder how long they had worked side by side.

The double exclamation brought all parties to the edge of the pit.

'It is indeed a female,' said Doctor A.

Kim could see that a flowery cotton fabric around the lower half of the body had been exposed but she guessed that wasn't what had prompted the doctor's confirmation.

Kim's gaze travelled up the pit to the highest point where Peter continued to dust.

There was one thing Kim didn't need to wait to be told, because it was already abundantly clear.

The woman's face had been completely smashed in.

CHAPTER FORTY-ONE

Do you remember when I refused my medication, Mummy? I didn't understand why I had to take the pills but you insisted every day. Even though I didn't feel poorly.

I said to you one day that I didn't want to take them any more and that they made me feel strange. I refused to drink the water so you took the water away.

You popped a pill into my dry mouth, but I couldn't swallow it down. You tipped back my head and stroked at my throat until the pill made its slow, arid journey down, like a football passing through a straw.

You dried my tears and wiped my snot and then gave me back the water.

I never complained again.

And I took my tablets every day.

CHAPTER FORTY-TWO

'Okay, I'll go first,' Kim said once everyone was seated. 'As you all know, a second body was found on the Westerley grounds in the early hours. Identified as female and finally removed at two this morning.'

The vision was still with her and would be for a long time to come. She'd sent Bryant and Dawson home around one a.m. and had stood by the grave until their victim had been gently and painstakingly removed. Never before had she seen a body containing so many stages of decomposition. Clean, white bone had protruded in places while others still held a full covering of flesh. It had reminded Kim of an animal carcass part devoured by its predators.

A thick silence had fallen over the area as Doctor A and two of her colleagues had tenderly placed the body onto the waiting body bag.

'*Spij mirno, draga moja*,' Doctor A had whispered before stepping away and nodding to Keats.

Kim wasn't sure what the archaeologist had said, but it had sounded like some kind of endearment or farewell to carry on her way.

'We have her now,' Keats had said, after a couple of deep swallows. And the handover was complete.

Everyone waited until the bag was zipped and on the stretcher before dispersing from the scene. It wasn't a funeral; it wasn't a memorial. But together beneath the floodlights, surrounded by the dense blackness of night, they had offered a moment of respect. It was the least they could do.

Kim took a deep breath and continued. 'We have no further information except that the face of our victim had most definitely been beaten.'

This left no doubt in the minds of anyone that they were looking for the same killer.

'So how does that help our timeline? This lady appears to have been the first...'

'Let's hope so,' Bryant said, and she had to agree.

Harry and his team would be back at Westerley this morning and would sweep the whole area again. Kim prayed there were no more.

'We don't know exactly how long she's been down there but we're clearly talking years. So why has he waited so long to do it again but then speeded up this week?'

Everyone was silent for a minute.

'Come on people, think,' Kim said.

'Something has sparked him off...' Dawson offered.

Kim thought for a minute. 'I don't think so,' she said. 'He's too organised for it to have been some kind of knee-jerk reaction. On both occasions this week he's had the presence of mind to take away whatever it is he's used to beat them, probably a rock,' she said.

'He's been incapacitated somehow,' Bryant said.

Kim considered. 'Possible, but I don't think that's it.'

The room fell silent as three sets of eyes stared at the whiteboard for clues.

'Come on, guys, he's organised, methodical, ritualistic,' Kim prompted. She felt like a parent coaxing a homework answer from a child. 'What must he have?'

'Order,' Stacey said, looking around her own immaculately organised desk.

Kim nodded. 'Go on,' she urged.

'He couldn't get Isobel before Jemima. There's a particular order to the process?' Stacey asked.

'Bingo,' Kim said. 'Stacey gets the prize. Our first victim was murdered years ago but our second victim, Jemima, only returned to the country a few weeks ago. She's been working with horses in Dubai. And then Isobel so soon afterwards. It's as though he was waiting for Jemima to return to carry on.'

She could see she had their full attention. 'So that tells us there is a reason why he's targeting these particular women. There is a link somewhere. It's going to be difficult to tie Isobel to anyone so we need to focus on the other two.'

And using her own logic of past, present or future she knew exactly where they should start.

'We know that Jemima and our latest victim hadn't met recently, so we can rule out present. Jemima was planning nothing untoward that we're aware of, so that leaves only one direction.'

'I'll start digging into Jemima's distant past and work forwards,' Stacey said. 'I've still got nothing on Isobel's place of work or address, but I'll keep at it.'

Kim nodded her agreement. Isobel's husband was certainly someone she wanted to talk to.

Kim turned towards Dawson, who pre-empted her instruction.

'That'll be me on mispers again then?' he said knowingly.

'Yes, but only for an hour or two, and then I want you back on site at Westerley. Forensics will be back by then looking for any clues, and I want you right there if they find anything.' She paused. 'Oh, and Kev, dig away as much as you like. I want to be sure we know everything there is to know about the folks over there.'

'Got it, boss,' he said brightening.

'Bryant and I will be heading over to Keats shortly, so if there's anything likely to help, we'll let you know.'

Dawson nodded and pulled his shirt collar away from his neck.

She had opened the token window at six thirty when she'd arrived, but no breeze had found its way in yet. To make matters worse, the single radiator beneath the window was still kicking out heat. On a day that promised temperatures in the high twenties it was an unwelcome addition. The knob was broken, and the heating did not get turned off globally as the offices on the north side of the building were like the chilled section of the supermarket, whatever the season.

A floor fan stood in the corner, offering nothing more than an occasional lifting of papers from Dawson's desk.

'Stace, anything on Isobel's phone?'

Stacey shook her head. 'It's a pay and go jobby bought from Asda in Brierley Hill. It wasn't registered so the number from her boyfriend wasn't a lot of use to us. It was bought with cash. I've already fired off an email to the networks, but you'll all remember last time.'

Oh yes, Kim remembered it well. Two little girls had been kidnapped and their only lead had been a batch of mobile-phone numbers. The networks had laughed in their faces.

'Are we ruling out female killer, boss?' Dawson asked.

'He's right, guv,' Bryant agreed before she had chance to answer. He continued. 'No sexual assault, drugs used for pliability. It could be a strong woman.'

Kim opened her mouth to argue and decided against it. Her gut didn't think so but on the evidence she couldn't rule it out.

'Okay, guys, there's something else. Another case we're looking at.'

'Because we haven't got enough,' Dawson grumbled.

'Sit it out if you like then, Kev,' she shot back, knowing that nothing would humiliate him more.

'But I like to be kept busy,' he said with an apologetic smile. Kim didn't smile back.

'You all remember the guy found at Fens Pools a few years ago?'

'The Pianist?' Dawson asked.

Kim wondered just how many nicknames the guy had.

'Uggghhhh, Kev,' Stacey admonished as her face scrunched in distaste.

'Yes, him,' Kim confirmed. 'We're looking into it and before you say another word, Kev, yes this was a Brierley Hill case, but it remains unsolved.'

'Wasn't gonna speak, boss,' he said, shaking his head.

'We can all guess that his hands were removed to avoid identification, but I learned yesterday that his pacemaker was cut out also.'

'They have a serial number,' Dawson observed, narrowing his eyes. Now the case had his interest.

'Don't those patients have to take warfarin and get monitored every six months?' Bryant asked.

'And second prize of the day goes to the man on my right,' she said and then looked to Stacey who knew what to do.

'I'll start ringing the clinics and check for anyone that started missing appointments about three years ago.'

'Thanks Stace, and Kev… while you're looking through mispers anyway…'

'Got it, boss. But there's just one more thing.'

'Go,' she said, rising from the desk.

'I appear to be the only person who didn't win a prize.'

She looked at him meaningfully. 'And that, Kev, should tell you something.'

CHAPTER FORTY-THREE

Oh, Mummy, do you remember THAT DAY the same way I do?

You were a year late dropping me off at school. No preschool or nursery for me. No opportunity for a young mind to familiarise itself with other young minds.

A simple lie about my birthday, and I was all yours for another year.

You didn't think I'd find out, did you?

That morning you cried as though your heart was being torn in two. I didn't know what was wrong, but I cried too.

You sobbed as you brushed my hair. Your fingers trembled as you formed two equal pigtails that protruded from the side of my head. You were rough as though it was my fault.

You made me breakfast and gave me my vitamins, but they weren't vitamins at all.

I remember my socks. They were ankle socks with pink butterflies in a line around the top. I didn't like them, but I couldn't say so because I remembered the pinafore dress.

As we walked hand in hand I wondered if I could somehow discard them during the day and then I could blame someone else.

There were tears at the classroom, from us both. I cried because you cried and then you cried some more. I can't remember who stopped first as the teacher pulled us apart.

The other kids looked on, laughing and pointing meanly. I sat in the corner on my own hoping that someone would talk to me and praying that no one would talk to me.

I was sure when I told you how much I hated it you would not make me go again.

Louise was my designated escort. She was so pretty. At break time it was the job of the six-year-old girl to show me around. She took me to the little girls' toilets. I didn't want to go in front of her but the milk from the breakfast cereal weighed heavily on my bladder.

The doors were not full length. If you crouched you could see under, and if you jumped you could see over.

I peed as quickly as I could to the sound of Louise's excited chatter about the lunch choices.

I stood and pulled up my knickers, oblivious to the fact that the chatter had stopped and that Louise was peering over the top of the door.

She was quiet and her eyes were wide. Heat infused my face and I didn't know why.

But I was to find out later that day.

CHAPTER FORTY-FOUR

Isobel held fast to the grey. It was edging along the black like a spreading stain. She knew it was trying to claim her, but she didn't know if it was life or death.

And she no longer cared.

Anything but the unrelenting blackness that suffocated her would be a welcome relief.

The darkness had taken everything away. It had stolen her thoughts. There was nothing upon nothing that lived in the desolate bleakness.

Send her the grey, offer her the white, show her the tunnel that would lead her away.

At times the tide of grey slowed to an agonising crawl, causing her to wonder if she'd imagined its encroaching stealth.

There was also a blurring of the edges as though her consciousness was fraying.

The blackness was not as deep, but the more she reached, the higher the panic rose in the fragmented parts, and so she waited patiently for whatever was about to come.

CHAPTER FORTY-FIVE

'You told him, didn't you?' Kim spat as soon as they were alone in the car. 'You sung like a canary about where I'd be.'

Bryant shrugged. 'I *might* have mentioned that you walk Barney up Clent on a Wednesday night around nine and that you park in the lower car park. Just in passing, you know.'

She swung a hard left and bounced him against the passenger door. 'Bryant, you do realise just how deeply I resent your attempted intrusion into my private life.'

'Ha, is that what you think I did?' he asked, righting himself.

'Isn't it?'

'Nah. Whenever we're working on a big case you get turned all outside in. I know you don't like Daniel Bate, so I thought this was the ideal opportunity for you to blow off a bit of steam. Basically if you're shouting at him you're not shouting at us.'

Kim realised that he'd had far too long to come up with that response.

'And if you insisted on driving just to punish me, it's working and I won't do it again,' he said, grabbing hold of the dashboard.

That hadn't been her intention but she'd bear it in mind for the next time.

'Any change with Isobel?' Bryant asked as she slowed at the Russell's Hall traffic island.

He knew she would already have checked.

'Nothing significant but there is still brain activity.'

'Uggh…'

'What?' she asked.

'Have you ever thought about it?'

Instead of answering she just waited for the inevitable continuation.

'It'd be like being buried alive, wouldn't it? I mean, your brain still working but locked in darkness because your body won't move and your senses are numb. It's like being just a head. Do you know what I mean?'

Unfortunately she did. It was something she had been forced to ponder on one of their earlier cases when she'd met a young girl named Lucy. She had not been in a coma but her body had been destroyed by muscular dystrophy, leaving her only the use of a few fingers. Her brain had worked perfectly.

'It's like your whole existence is being just a head,' he continued then sighed.

'Okay, Bryant,' she said. She'd heard enough. 'If you want something to think about, spend some time working out why Bob had pound coins and a raffle ticket in his pocket 'cos it's got me beat,' she admitted, parking the car.

'Yeah, I'll be sure to give that priority,' he moaned.

She had lost count of the times they had visited the hospital over the last few days but this time they weren't heading to a ward.

'But why eleven pound coins?' she mused out loud, as they headed down the corridor to the morgue.

'Trick question, guv?' Bryant asked.

'Why not a tenner or fivers. Why all coins?'

'I really have no idea,' he replied.

Kim found it strange sometimes how different minds chose different things to dwell on. Bryant had given the detail no thought and yet she'd thought of little else. With so little evidence to dissect, everything had to mean something.

'Hmmm…' she said, pressing the access button into the morgue.

A wall of white coats greeted her.

'Keats… Daniel,' she said. 'What do we have?'

The pathologist shook his head. 'Inspector, if you spent less time on small talk, you'd save yourself… well, no time at all really.'

Kim was grateful that the crisp white sheet covered their victim up to the shoulders.

She knew from the picture that had remained in her head all night that the woman's face was decaying slowly. The injuries she had sustained were still evident.

'How many blows to the face?' she asked and had no preference for whichever one of them decided to answer.

'I've counted seven so far, all to the left side,' Keats stated.

Kim knew he was inferring that the murderer was likely to be right-handed. The blows probably came from above while the killer was astride the victim.

'Mouth?' Kim asked.

Keats nodded. 'Full of dirt. Most likely the cause of death but we haven't finished yet so I'm not prepared to commit, but go take a look on my desk.'

Kim strode to the table in the corner of the room. An evidence bag was positioned in the corner. She picked it up and turned it around.

It was a kirby grip. There was no broken heart, but she could see a gap in the white plastic where something had been broken off.

'Same as Jemima,' she whispered.

'A little bit coincidental, Inspector?' Keats offered.

She nodded her agreement and put the bag back onto the desk. Curious but not much help to her. They were mass-produced and available in two chemist chains and countless supermarkets.

She moved back to the table.

'Any idea how long she's been down there?' Kim pushed.

Regardless of their stage of the process, she needed answers. Anything that would help her identify this woman.

'Given the seasonal and climatic variation, the amount of soil water and acidity, I would estimate four to five years.'

'Seems a bit far gone for such little time,' Bryant observed.

'Bodies decay quicker the higher up they are buried,' Keats replied.

Of course their victim had only been about two and a half feet down.

'Anything that will help me put a name to her?' Kim asked. Her priority on both a professional and personal level.

Daniel stepped forwards. His Clark Kent glasses were like a uniform that converted him to a serious, studious scientist. Gone was the playful, teasing expression she'd seen the day before.

'Over a lifetime the human skeleton undergoes sequential chronological changes normally categorised as foetus, infant, child, adolescent, young adult and so on. Up to the age of twenty-one the teeth are the most accurate indicator of age. From what I can tell so far, our victim falls under young adult, which typically spans from twenty to thirty-five years of age.'

'Can you be any more specific?' she asked. She would have liked to offer Dawson something in his search through missing persons. That was one heck of an age range to cover over the last four to five years. And that was if the woman had been reported missing.

'I would estimate that the female is over twenty-five years of age. The clavicle – collar bone – is the last bone to complete and is fully grown.'

Kim said nothing and waited. She was hoping for a little more than that or she had been seriously short-changed when humiliating herself in asking him to stay.

Daniel continued. 'Throughout a lifetime bone makes new osteons, which are minute tubes containing blood vessels. Younger adults have fewer and larger osteons, but with age they become smaller as new ones form and disrupt the old ones.'

Kim was grateful for the information but wasn't sure she would ever have cause to use it again. If this woman could not be identified by her osteons it wasn't a great deal of help to her.

'And finally the cranium. The bones that enclose the brain grow together during childhood along lines called cranial sutures. During adulthood bone remodelling gradually erases these lines.'

'So age wise are we looking to early thirties like Jemima Lowe?' she asked, determined to force a more accurate answer.

'Except for one key difference,' Daniel said. 'This victim has had a child.'

She exchanged a look with Bryant.

Now the service provided was becoming worth the price she'd paid. But his expression said that he wasn't finished yet.

'Pregnancy doesn't modify a woman's bones, with one exception. During childbirth the pubic bones separate to allow an infant to pass through the birth canal. The ligaments connecting the pubic bones must stretch. They can tear and cause bleeding where they attach to the bone.

'Later bone remodelling at these sites can leave small circular or linear grooves on the inside surface of the pubic bones called parturition pits—'

'Doc… Daniel, what are you trying to tell me?' she asked.

'I suspect she gave birth in her teens.'

And that final statement had sealed the deal.

CHAPTER FORTY-SIX

Isobel looked around the darkness. Her heart beat faster as she realised that it wasn't black any longer but more of a dirty grey.

The black was being bleached out of her mind but not just at the corners any more. And it moved.

There was something beyond the darkness and there was a shadow.

There were voices. She listened carefully to see if they were in her mind. She wasn't sure, but she suspected they were beyond her head and not in it.

The familiarity of the warm feeling on her hand was back. It was reassuring, comforting.

Please, someone, help me, she cried. *I'm in here. Please let me out. I don't know how to leave.*

The effort of trying to communicate with her mind brought about sudden exhaustion. But there were sensations. There was a tickle in her foot. Something cold being placed on her chest. *I'm here*, she wanted to scream but her body wouldn't listen.

For a while she'd wondered if her body parts were scattered around her head but the sensations told her they were connected.

Her body was still whole and she might be alive, not stuck in this silent, eternal hell.

But if she allowed hope then she must also prepare for despair, and she didn't know if she could take the disappointment of being wrong.

Her heart cried with unshed tears as she prayed for the nightmare to end.

Being dead made much more sense and that's why she had so readily accepted it. Being alive was far too complicated, exhausting.

If she was dead, she no longer had questions.

If she was alive, she had too many.

CHAPTER FORTY-SEVEN

'I still don't see why you're quite so, er… animated,' Bryant said, as they exited the hospital.

Kim switched on her phone to see she'd missed a call from Stacey. Just the person she wanted to speak to.

She pressed to return the call and threw the car keys at Bryant. He'd suffered her driving enough.

'What have you got, Stace?' she asked.

'Something I think you're going to like.'

'Go on.'

'I have the address of the old head teacher from Jemima's junior school. I've got a list of staff that were there when she would have been.'

'Good work, Stace. Text the address to Bryant. Now find out from her parents which high school she went to and check to see if you can find anything on a teen pregnancy for any girl around the same time,' she said as they got into the car.

'On it, boss, and one more thing. There are seven warfarin clinics in the area. Spoke to them all and have a list of eleven men who stopped attending around the time Bob was found.'

'Bloody hell, Stace. Are you on fire?' Kim asked. 'Just give me the first names,' she said as Bryant exited the car park.

'Alphabetically, they are Alan, Charlie, Edward, Geoffrey, Ivor, Jack, Lester, Malcolm, Norman, Philip, Walter.'

Kim shouted them out as Stacey said them.

'Guv, you do know I'm driving and I can't write anything down?'

'Use your memory,' she said, moving her mouth away from the phone.

Bryant shook his head and continued driving. He stopped at the Brierley Hill high-street lights.

'Catch up later,' Kim said, ending the call.

She looked to her left as Bryant was forced to brake sharply for a group of teenage boys who stepped into the road six feet shy of a crossing.

'Jesus, sometimes…'

'Pull over, Bryant,' she said, her eyes fixed on one of the shopfronts.

He expertly claimed a space vacated by a white delivery van.

'Guv… what are…?'

His words trailed away as he saw where they'd stopped.

Every high street had one. No matter how deprived the area or the rate of unemployment. There was always the market for an amusement arcade.

'Wait here, Bryant,' Kim said, jumping out of the car.

She pushed open the door and stepped in. Her eyes took a few seconds to adjust from the bright day outside to the false night-time environment of the premises.

Three slot machines along, a man wearing jeans and a white shirt was wiping at the glass display.

'Excuse me,' Kim said, allowing the door to close behind her.

His face was thin and pale but he smiled openly. 'Whassup, love?'

Kim didn't feel like taking the time to explain her position. Her question was a simple one.

'Do you use raffle tickets here?' she asked, looking around. 'For bingo or for…'

She stopped speaking as he was already shaking his head.

Damn it, although it had been a long shot.

'Nah, love…'

'Okay, thanks for…'

'We ain't used 'em for years, five or more,' he said.

Good news and bad news in one short sentence.

'What did you use them for?' Kim asked.

'Prizes. There was a weekly raffle, but we stopped it when business dropped off.'

Kim nodded and began to back out of the claustrophobic space.

'Appreciate your time…'

'You might want to try the one over at Merry Hill. I think they still use 'em today.'

She offered him a warm smile and peered closer at his name badge.

'Melvyn, you've been a great help, thank you,' she said, before heading towards the door.

'You're smiling,' Bryant observed as she got back into the car.

'Down to Merry Hill,' she instructed, securing her seatbelt. It was still a long shot but for the first time she felt like she at least had a field to play on.

It was a short drive from Brierley Hill down Level Street and onto the complex.

Bryant drove into a space that luckily opened up right in front of him. He parked and they cut through the bus station into the amusement arcade.

The dark space was lit by the fast, racing lights of the machines as they tempted with their promises of jackpots and prizes.

Two elderly women looked around sharply as the sound of pound coins falling was heard from the next aisle along. Kim could hear bingo numbers being called towards the back of the property.

'Excuse me,' Kim said, approaching a woman dressed in a light blue overall. A leather bag containing change was strapped around her waist.

Her hands automatically reached towards the bag and Kim couldn't help but think the lady might need a short course in recognising your customer. There was no such thing as a 'typical gambler' look but neither she nor Bryant were dressed for anything of a leisurely nature.

Kim took out her badge. The woman squinted in the light and the wrinkles around her eyes deepened. She accepted the identification and immediately looked concerned.

'How long have you worked here, Jean?' Kim asked, reading the name badge.

'Eight years,' she said, as though she couldn't quite believe it herself. But a job was a job as far as Kim was concerned, and anyone who had the gumption to stick at one instead of looking for easier options had her vote.

'You use raffle tickets?' Kim clarified.

The woman nodded slowly as though she was making some kind of guilty admission.

'May I ask what for?' Kim asked, praying there would be some kind of clue.

She shrugged. 'Many things. Grocery hampers, meat joints, shopping vouchers, free bingo games.'

Each item punched a bit of excitement out of her stomach.

Bryant stepped forwards. 'All these items every week?' he asked.

Jean nodded.

'How do you keep track of which raffle ticket is for which item?'

'The colour,' she said simply.

Kim shot Bryant a grateful look.

'What's blue for?'

Jean smiled. 'Blue is for a bottle of Bell's whisky.'

The hope was being rebuilt in her gut. 'Always?'

'For as long as I can remember,' she said. And Kim already knew that was over eight years. It was a very simple system but one that had worked.

'Do you keep records?' Kim asked hopefully. The normal form of identification for a raffle ticket was an address or phone number. Yes, there'd be one a week for the last three years but that totalled less than two hundred and worth the work to give Bob a name.

Jean shook her head. 'Only for a few months and then we give the unclaimed prizes to Mary Stevens Hospice. We tell people that when they buy the tickets,' she added defensively.

'We want to ask you about a man who may have been a customer here a few years ago. I think he had one of your whisky raffle tickets.'

Just the words leaving her mouth was enough to convince Kim of the futility of this exercise. The woman's expression only confirmed her thoughts. Jean must see hundreds of faces every day. Multiply that by two or three years and Kim was looking for one face out of more than a hundred thousand. But the pound coins had to mean something.

'Love, I'm not being funny but—'

Kim let the endearment pass and continued anyway. 'He would have been in his mid-fifties, dark hair, a bit on the heavy side.'

Jean began to shake her head and handed a clutch of pound coins without speaking to a gangly lad who appeared to her right. She placed the note in a separate zip pocket on her pouch.

Bryant stepped forwards. 'May have been named Alan, Charlie, Edward, Geoffrey, Ivor, Jack, Lester … '

Kim stole a glance at her colleague as Jean frowned. 'Hang on a minute,' she said. 'Did you say Ivor?'

Bryant nodded. It wasn't a common name around these parts.

'We used to have a bloke named Ivor come in here a lot. Used to sit and play the OXO machines for hours. Anything he won he put straight back in.' Her eyes widened in surprise. 'He bought a raffle ticket for whisky every week. Not for the other stuff but always for the bottle of Bell's. Won it a fair few times as well,' she said, nodding. 'He hasn't been in for years though. We assumed he got banged up for something.'

'Why would you think that?' Kim asked, frowning. She wasn't sure that was the immediate conclusion with the loss of every customer.

'Oh, no reason,' she said, colouring, but Kim didn't believe her.

'That's not true,' Kim said. 'Please, Jean, anything you can tell us would be greatly appreciated. We really need to find out more about this man.'

She hesitated and then sighed. 'Hang on, I'll be back in a minute,' she said before walking away.

'Jesus, guv, Woody was right when he said you can make something out of nothing,' Bryant said, once Jean was out of earshot.

'You weren't too bad yourself,' she observed. 'I can't believe you managed to memorise all those names.'

'I assume you don't keep me around for my good looks, although—'

'This is Rita,' Jean said, presenting a woman of similar size to herself but with a shock of deep red hair. She too wore a blue overall and a money belt.

'Do you remember that bloke you had a bit of trouble with, Ivor the whisky bloke?'

Rita nodded and looked suspiciously at her and Bryant.

'It's all right, tell 'em, they're police,' Jean urged.

Rita looked doubtful but Jean nudged her. 'Go on, it might be connected.'

Kim's interest was piqued.

'He was a big guy – overweight I mean. Not tall. A bit creepy, but you just get used to that in here. Don't get me wrong, there's some lovely folks that come in here and—'

'But Ivor…' Kim said, steering her back.

'Well, we get kids in here now and again,' she said, looking at Jean. 'We do everything to stop 'em, but they ignore the signs on the door, and we get 'em out as quick as we see 'em, eh, Jean?'

Kim wasn't interested in a bit of underage gambling on fruit machines.

'I understand, it must be difficult,' Kim said. 'Now about Ivor?'

'A while back, must be a couple of years now, I had a group of girls in and I hadn't spotted 'em until one of 'em came over and said that Ivor had touched her mate.'

'What did you do?'

'Well, I couldn't call the police… she didn't want to make a complaint and, well, she shouldn't have been here in the first place.'

So neither the girl or this woman had wanted to get into any trouble.

'What about Ivor?'

'I told him to get out and not to come back,' she said, nodding, convinced that she'd taken the correct course of action.

'And did he come back?' Kim asked.

She shook her head. 'Nah, and I never saw his mate again either.'

Kim's heartbeat quickened. If Ivor was their man Bob, then his friend could be their first lead.

CHAPTER FORTY-EIGHT

'Okay, Stace, get me everything you can for the guy on the list named Ivor. It's a bit thin, but there's a chance this could be our guy.'

'On it, boss,' Stacey replied.

'And while you're at it, he had a mate named Larry something. Don't know if he might also be listed with any of the clinics. They may have met there, and if we can find him he may be able to help.'

'Got it,' Stacey said before Kim ended the call.

'What do you make of Rita's story?' Bryant asked as he drove towards Stourbridge. On the other side lay Stourton and the home of Jemima Lowe's ex head teacher.

Kim shrugged in response. 'Could have been a harmless misunderstanding and I've got Stacey barking up the completely wrong tree... but right now it's the only tree we've got and for a guy with no form of identity I think every move forwards is going to be a leap of faith.'

'I still don't see why that particular tree has ended up in our forest to be honest,' Bryant said.

Kim was saved from answering by the ringing of her phone. There was no need for him to know it had come from Tracy.

'Stone,' she said.

'Inspector, it's Doctor Singh, from Russell's Hall. We spoke—'

'Of course, Doctor Singh,' she acknowledged.

'I'm calling about Isobel...'

Kim braced herself for the news that she'd been dreading.

'I'm ringing to tell you that Isobel has woken up.'

Kim ended the call and told Bryant to turn the car around.

Finally they had a witness.

CHAPTER FORTY-NINE

Dawson didn't bother to remove his jacket from the car. Both the mid-morning heat and the absence of his boss dictated it would not grace his back today.

He parked on the gravel patch between the crime-scene Transit van and Harry's low loader, which was used for transporting the ground-penetrating radar equipment. He suspected that Harry would be finished today providing he found no more nasty surprises, but the techies would be around for a few more days at least.

He tapped on the door before entering, even though they had opened the gate.

He walked into the back of Jameel, who turned and nodded in his direction. Dawson could hear The Shadows playing softly in the background.

This was one strange kid.

'Yo, man,' he said and turned back to his computer.

Dawson walked behind him and paused when he saw Catherine at the meeting table with a collection of graphs and charts spread out before her.

'You're here,' he said stupidly.

She almost smiled. 'Yes, I appear to be.'

'But how did you get in?' he asked.

He had been forced to wait a good few minutes while the officers at the cordon had cleared the press to let him through.

The arrival of forensics tended to do that. As soon as the techies turned up, the press knew there was something to find and they had been steadily growing in number since the previous evening.

The boss had filled them in on Catherine's history, and he hadn't expected to see her back at work.

This time she did smile. 'Under a picnic blanket in the back of the professor's car.'

'You told him?' Dawson asked. The boss had also been clear that they were not to say a word.

She nodded. 'A lot of what DI Stone said made sense. It's better if I work,' she said.

Dawson could understand that. Recently he'd been badly beaten while carrying out an investigation into the death of a gang member, but the following day he'd been right back at his desk.

'She's a strange one, isn't she, your boss?' Catherine asked, surprising him. It was the first time she'd spoken to him unless answering a direct question.

He felt himself bristle. 'How so?'

'There's a bit more to her than meets the eye. She's not the most likeable—'

'Yeah, you don't know her,' Dawson said, crossing his arms.

'… I was going to say on first impressions, but there's a lot going on underneath. I wasn't insulting her. She was very helpful to me yesterday,' Catherine said, gathering up her papers. 'Jameel, I'm going down to check on Elvis,' she said abruptly before brushing past Dawson and heading out the door.

The young man didn't turn or acknowledge her words in any way but mumbled something once the door closed behind her.

'Sorry?' Dawson said, taking a step back towards the office area of the Portakabin.

'Something in my throat,' Jameel said and then coughed for effect.

Dawson wasn't fooled.

'You two don't get on?' he asked. After the way Catherine had just spoken to him he wasn't surprised.

'Can't be doing with changeable women, man. The species is hard enough to understand as it is, d'ya get me?'

Dawson smiled. Oh yeah, he got that.

'Changeable?' he asked, pouring himself a glass of water.

'When she wants something she's all over you, giving you compliments and stuff, but when she's got what she wants she's cool as a penguin's belly.'

Dawson gave a small laugh. 'Mate, you'll find that's the case with all women, not just that one.' He made a show of looking around. 'Curtis Grant not with you today?'

'Nah. Good job. His aftershave was starting to get in my throat.'

Dawson smiled. Yeah, he'd noticed.

'He's been here quite a bit. Is there a lot to do to the system?'

Jameel shook his head. 'I didn't think so, but he wanted to check there were no bugs in the software upgrade.'

'Seems to know his stuff though,' Dawson observed.

'To be fair he does. His company is his life. Talks about it like it's a child.'

Dawson acknowledged his words. 'Did he do all the planning for the security provision? Siting the cameras and everything?'

'I think so. It was before I started, but Professor Wright brought him in and seems to trust him.'

Dawson finished the water and headed towards the door.

Suddenly Jameel turned. 'You got a minute? There's something I want to ask you.'

Dawson was momentarily surprised. Jameel had been totally disinterested in the activities at the site. He had asked nothing and had just kept his head down and got on with his job.

'Go on then,' he said.

Jameel put his hands on his thighs and his eyes opened wide. A quick tongue flick across the lips before he asked his question.

'I'm dying to know, Sergeant. Have you ever killed anybody?'

'What?' Dawson asked incredulously. 'You realise this is the Black Country not South Central LA?

Jameel leaned forwards. 'Yeah but have you?'

Dawson tried not to roll his eyes as the day stretched out in front of him.

CHAPTER FIFTY

Bryant pulled into the hospital car park and stealthily followed a patron to their car to nab their space.

Kim jumped out of the car and semi-sprinted to the hospital. She headed for the High Dependency Unit on autopilot.

She buzzed the intercom and pushed against the familiar click.

Doctor Singh stood at the nurses' station, completing a chart. The same ward sister from the previous day smiled in her direction before stepping away from the area with a cardboard bedpan.

Doctor Singh completed what he was writing before turning in her direction. 'That was very fast, Inspector,' he observed.

They had postponed the visit to the head teacher in favour of interviewing the live witness who had actually spent time with their killer.

'She's awake, you said,' she said, stepping past him.

He placed a gentle hand on her arm. She moved away from his touch and offered him a frown.

'Doctor, I need to speak with her immediately. She is imperative to our—'

'I understand that. It's why I called you the moment she regained consciousness.'

'So?'

'There have been, er... developments since we spoke. It's become complicated.'

Kim felt her irritation growing in spite of the doctor's gentle manner. Twenty feet away was a woman with answers she needed.

Isobel could hold the key to solving this case before anyone else got hurt.

'Look, if there's a form you need me to sign—'

'A form isn't going to help you, Inspector. Isobel may be awake, but she has no memories whatsoever of recent events. In fact, she doesn't even know who she is.'

CHAPTER FIFTY-ONE

Kim stepped back and leaned against the ledge of the nurses' station.

'That's why I wanted to speak to you before you see her. Isobel is suffering from retrograde amnesia. Sometimes the lost memories before an event are only seconds or minutes, occasionally a few years and, less often, everything.'

Kim allowed the breath she'd been holding to escape. 'Will it come back?'

He moved his shoulders in an up-and-down motion. 'I can't say yet, Inspector. In many of the cases I've worked on, the memories return like a jigsaw, randomly. She could recall something from last week and then minutes later remember something from when she was seven years old. We have many more questions to consider in the coming days. We need to assess the true extent of the damage.'

Kim was confused. 'Isn't that clear already?' The woman had no memory. What more was there to learn?

'Ah, there is a difference between memory making and memory storage,' he said and paused. 'Imagine there is a fire in a pottery and all the pots are destroyed. Your stock is gone, what has already been made is no more. But what of the potter's wheel? Does the equipment still work or is that gone too?'

Kim got it. 'She hasn't been conscious long enough for you to find out?'

Doctor Singh smiled. 'Exactly. Short-term memory can be checked after about thirty minutes. Long-term memory demands recall after a day, two days, a week or more.'

Kim shook her head, reeling.

Already she felt sorry for the battle Isobel had yet to fight.

'Thank you for your time, Doctor Singh,' she said.

'You're welcome and now you may see her.'

Kim hesitated before stepping into the ward. She was already on tiptoe to avoid her biker-boot heels thudding her arrival.

She took a deep breath and turned into the bay.

The first thing Kim noticed was the bed next to Isobel was now empty. In this ward you didn't ask why.

The second thing she noticed was Duncan gently helping Isobel to feed herself.

Kim approached the bed with a smile and touched Duncan gently on the shoulder before speaking.

'Hi, Isobel, I'm Detective Inspector Stone and would like a word, if that's okay?'

After her chat with the doctor she wasn't sure how much she was going to get.

'She prefers "Izzy",' Duncan offered with a smile.

Isobel looked from one to the other, not speaking.

Her face was pale and her eyes were dark. Her eyelids appeared heavy with fatigue. Kim could only wonder at the strength it had taken for her to fight back from wherever she had been.

Kim stepped around to the other side of Isobel. Duncan was perched on the bed, so she moved the requisite easy chair closer, taking care to lift not drag.

'Would you like me to leave?' Duncan asked.

Kim shook her head. He was helping Isobel lift her right hand to her mouth from a bowl of thin soup on the hospital table.

Isobel tried to lift her left hand to offer a handshake. Kim touched the hand and laid it back down.

She leaned forwards, resting her arms on her knees.

'Izzy, I understand that you don't remember anything, but I have to ask, okay?'

She nodded as Duncan guided her hand once more to her mouth. The effort of swallowing the murky liquid seemed to take a great deal of effort.

'If you get too tired, just let me know.'

'I don't want to close my eyes,' she said.

Her voice was weak, barely more than a whisper. Had Kim been further away she wouldn't have heard a word.

Kim could also understand her reluctance to close her eyes. Perhaps she was frightened of returning to her comatose state or even not waking up at all.

Duncan held her hand and scooped another spoonful of soup before helping her guide it to her mouth.

Again she swallowed with effort and held up her left hand to signal no more.

Duncan put the spoon back into the dish but continued to hold her hand.

'Isobel, I know this might be difficult for you to take in, but your injuries are not from any kind of accident.'

She swallowed and nodded. In the short time she'd been awake she had probably already worked that out.

'We're pretty sure you were abducted and kept against your will. Your head injury was supposed to kill you.'

A cry sounded from her throat. Kim placed a reassuring hand on Isobel's arm.

'Don't worry – you're safe. He's not going to get to you here. But we need to catch this man before he does it again.'

Kim didn't want to frighten her further by admitting that two other women hadn't been as lucky.

Isobel's look of horror turned to frustration. 'I don't...'

'Save your throat,' Kim instructed. 'I just want to see if we can shake anything loose.'

Isobel nodded, but the frown remained. Kim saw her look to Duncan for reassurance. He smiled and squeezed her hand. 'You're doing great, Izzy.'

'There are marks on the back of your legs and your stomach,' Kim explained. 'Do you have any idea where they came from?'

Isobel shook her head.

'Do you remember anything about being taken, a smell, a sound, anything?'

Isobel shook her head.

'Do you have any recollection of where you might have been taken from?'

She shook her head and then looked to Duncan who was pained that he could offer no response.

'Is there anything in your mind to do with where you were held, anything at all?' Kim asked.

Isobel's eyes filled with tears and Kim understood.

With no memory of anything she was looking into an empty space. She knew nothing about herself. Her mind was an alien place to be with nothing familiar, nothing she knew. No memories of herself or people that she cared for.

Duncan stroked her arm. 'It's okay, babe. It'll come back.'

Kim hoped he was right, not only for her own sake, and what she might learn for the investigation, but for Isobel too.

Otherwise the woman had to start again. She had to make a whole new person. Her memories would begin from about half an hour ago, providing the equipment was still working, but that was a worry for another day.

As Kim opened her mouth she caught sight of the doctor at the entrance to the bay.

He had said she couldn't take long and he was reminding her of her instruction. She couldn't tire the patient too much.

She was tempted to keep asking questions in case just one smidgeon of information had become lodged in the brain before the injury had washed it away. Just one stubborn recollection that was hanging on the end of a thought.

But it would be unfair and probably fruitless.

Kim stood and returned the easy chair to its position.

'Isobel, you're doing great, so don't push yourself to recall stuff. The harder you try the more it may stay out of reach.

'I'm going to leave my card here. If you do remember anything ask Duncan to give me a call.'

Isobel nodded and attempted a weak smile. Duncan nodded too. He looked tired and sad.

'You okay?' Kim couldn't help but ask.

'I'm fine,' he said brightening.

'You need rest too,' she advised. Hospitals were draining, and the worry was etched into his face.

'I'm okay. I'm going to fetch a few things for Izzy when I leave here.' He turned to his girlfriend. 'Pink pyjamas. You always wear pink.'

Kim enjoyed the expression of warmth that spread across Isobel's face. Facts, information, any little nugget would be gratefully received and hopefully stored.

Kim wondered how many times the finite detail of their few dates would be recounted back to her over the coming days. And each time she would learn something new about the person she was.

Kim said her farewells and headed back to the doctor.

'Sorry if I overstayed.'

'No, no, Inspector. It's not that. There's something I think you should know.'

He stepped away from the opening to the ward.

Kim followed.

'The blood tests you asked for have come back. There was a definite trace of Rohypnol in her blood, but there's something else.'

'Go on,' Kim urged.

He turned to the clipboard and consulted the notes one more time.

'Our patient has hepatitis C.'

Kim stepped back and glanced into the ward.

Duncan was helping his girlfriend take a drink of water from the plastic beaker.

She couldn't help but wonder if either of them knew.

CHAPTER FIFTY-TWO

Kim found Bryant just outside the café chatting with a broad male on crutches. She marvelled. Bryant was one of those guys who could run into someone he knew anywhere.

He saw her, shook the man's hand and joined her as she exited the building.

'Get anything?' he asked.

'She has no memory at all. Who she is, where she works, childhood, nothing. It's all blank. He did a real number on her head. She's lucky to be alive at all.'

'Will anything come back?' he asked as they neared the car.

'No one can say. We all know how tricky head injuries can be. We just have to wait and see.'

She took a breath before continuing. 'But the doc also told me she has hep C.'

He stopped walking. 'Really?'

The blood disease was infectious and affected the liver. Overall fifty to eighty per cent of people treated were cured.

But more interesting was the fact that hep C was spread primarily by blood-to-blood contact normally associated with intravenous drug use, poorly sterilised medical equipment and transfusions.

'Not sure how that helps us, guv,' Bryant said, opening the driver's door.

'Me either but let's just try and escape this bloody hospital for more than a couple of hours, shall we?'

Bryant nodded his agreement.

'Right, let's head for Stourton again, eh?' she said. Hopefully Jemima's head teacher would be able to offer them something.

'Er... not quite, guv,' Bryant said. 'I'm under strict instructions to return you to the station. Woody wants to see you straightaway and I'm not gonna lie... he doesn't sound like he wants to treat you to afternoon tea.'

Kim nodded her understanding as she slid into the front seat of the car.

'Oh and Stace wants you to give her a call back.'

Kim took out her phone and dialled.

'I think I've got her, boss,' Stacey said without a greeting. Her staff knew when brevity was the order of the day.

'Our girl?' she asked hopefully.

'Yeah, spoke to Jemima's mother. Jemima was chummy with a girl named Louise Hickman, who had a child when she was fifteen years old. I've checked with Education and I've got her last known address. It's from her school days but...'

'Read it out, Stace,' Kim said. It was a starting point.

Kim listened to the address, which was just a few miles away in Wordsley.

'Good job, Stace,' Kim said, ending the call.

Bryant already appeared to know what was coming.

'Guv, I said I'm under strict instructions to get you—'

'And I'm under strict instructions to make sure nobody else ends up like Louise and Jemima, so turn the car around, Bryant.'

She already knew why Woody wanted to see her, and she was in no rush at all for that conversation.

CHAPTER FIFTY-THREE

Dawson walked the entire width of the field one more time. The techs had uncovered nothing more than two pieces of fabric that may or may not have been connected to their victim. Given that the area had been open fields before Westerley meant it was highly unlikely. They had been logged and bagged anyway.

What he'd really been hoping for was the rock that had been used to bash their victim's head in. He was still hoping for some piece of crucial evidence that would blow the whole case wide open, and that was why he'd walked the field.

He knew that it was part of the forensic procedure to do it, but if he'd learned anything from his boss it was never take anything for granted.

As he walked back towards the grave site of their most recent victim he noted the professor's presence there.

Dawson quickened his step and sighed. He had already had to instruct the professor to leave the techies to their work on two separate occasions.

'Professor Wright, may I help you?' he said as he neared the site.

Bobby, the tech in charge, turned towards him and rolled his eyes.

Professor Wright smiled and shook his head. 'Just checking that everything is okay.'

Dawson understood that he was responsible for the site but constant interruptions just delayed their progress even more.

Dawson placed a hand on the professor's elbow and began to guide him away. 'They're fine, Professor. They're a bit of a strange bunch, not very sociable,' he said. There was no need to be offensive to the man.

He nodded knowingly. 'Oh I understand. Us scientists tend to be like that.'

'Quite,' Dawson agreed, removing his hand from the man's elbow. There was a good 150 feet of space between them and the techies now.

'Perhaps you'd like to accompany me to our most recent addition, Sergeant? A very interesting study.'

Dawson hesitated for just a minute before nodding and following the professor's lead. Anything to keep him away from the site for a while.

The professor walked in a straight line, heading for the very edge of the site.

'I'd like you to meet Quentin,' the professor said proudly.

'Bloody hell,' Dawson exclaimed, stopping dead in his tracks.

The body was burnt to a frazzle. Every inch he could see was blackened like scorched toast. He was sure that if he touched the body brittle bits of skin would fall off.

But that wasn't what had surprised him. It was the fact that the body was not lying down. It was set in a crawling motion, both hands flat on the ground and one knee in front of the other.

It appeared staged and even more macabre than the others.

'You'll see our friend here has no flowers, as this soul doesn't deserve them.'

Dawson stared at the eyes that were looking straight ahead as though he was going to continue his journey any second now.

'Why not?' he asked, unable to tear away his gaze.

'Because this man was in the process of setting a booby trap for his wife and three-year-old son. She had refused to take him back after an affair, so he was rigging up a home-made explosive device attached to the front door.'

'Jesus, what happened?' Dawson asked, suddenly just grateful it had happened to him instead. A three-year-old in this condition would have haunted him for life.

'He was in the process of balancing it when a car backfired in the street and made him jump. The bomb exploded all over him.'

'And this is how he was found?' Dawson asked incredulously.

Professor Wright nodded as he bent down. 'Yes, he did not die immediately and attempted to get away.'

Dawson finally managed to look away.

Professor Wright smiled. 'I can see that this has winded you, Sergeant. My apologies. It is strange how different things affect us.'

'What are you learning from him?' Dawson asked, eager to change the subject.

'Quentin is a joint study between Catherine and myself. The rate and pattern of decomposition in charred remains have not been studied extensively. Body regions displaying significant charring appear to decompose at a faster rate. Areas with very light levels of charring decompose at a slower rate.'

'But he is completely burnt. How can you compare?'

The professor gently turned Quentin onto his side. His pose remained the same. Dawson immediately saw that there was flesh in between his thighs that had not been burnt.

'And Catherine?'

'Again, in forensic practice burnt bodies are amongst the most neglected fields of entomological research. She is analysing the activity of flies on a burnt body in comparison to a normal body.'

Dawson collected his thoughts and forced himself to look away from the body, which looked even more macabre lying on its side.

'It takes a special kind of guy to patrol this place at night, eh?'

'None of our guests are going to harm anyone, Sergeant.'

Not the most open response.

'But you'd need nerves of steel, surely, to wander around here alone at night? There are all sorts of graves to fall into.'

'Not once you know where they are. There's something quite soothing about working amongst the dead. It's not for everyone, of course.'

'Well Darren seems to like it. He's been here how long?'

Professor Wright thought for a minute. 'I'd say a couple of years now. It was an older man before, in the twilight of his career, you might say, but suddenly Curtis brought Darren to site and told us this was our new guy. I'm not sure what happened to old Gregory. It was all rather sudden, but Darren fitted in okay.'

Dawson's antenna pricked up at this.

Anything sudden tended to happen for a reason.

CHAPTER FIFTY-FOUR

Only one car occupied the three-car drive of the spacious semi-detached property just behind the old Wordsley hospital site.

The Vauxhall Carlton was parked smack bang in the middle and appeared to expect no other company.

As they approached the roomy box porch, Kim had no idea what they were going to find.

The bell she pressed sounded a high-pitched tune beyond the front door that seemed to sing for just a couple of seconds too long.

The door was opened by a woman who appeared to have settled into her mid-fifties with ease; her frame was slender and her hair completely white.

Her lightly tanned face adopted the expression of polite refusal as she stepped into the porch and opened the door.

'Mrs Hickman?' Kim said immediately and with hope.

The woman's gaze took in both her and Bryant before a frown began to form. Kim wondered if they were looking at Louise's mother.

She nodded slowly in Kim's direction as both she and Bryant held up their identification.

'Detective Inspector Stone and Detective Sergeant Bryant, may we come in?' Kim asked quietly. The woman was about to receive some unwelcome news.

Mrs Hickman stepped aside and allowed them through.

Light streamed through from the kitchen beyond the hallway. Kim headed towards it and stepped into a kitchen that, although in disarray, was producing a mixture of smells that were delicious and inviting.

The kitchen door was open, leading into a spacious glass conservatory.

'Please excuse the mess, I have a party tomorrow to prepare for,' the woman said, wiping her hands on a tea towel.

Kim saw that her shoulders had already filled with tension.

'We're here about Louise,' Bryant said gently.

Mrs Hickman nodded. 'Of course you are.'

The woman leaned back against the counter top and slid her hands into the pockets of her three-quarter-length cotton trousers.

She appeared resigned to hearing something negative.

'Mrs Hickman, could you tell us the last time you saw your daughter?'

'December twenty-fifth in oh five,' she said immediately.

Eleven years. Considerably longer than the time since their victim had been murdered.

'You remember so clearly?' Kim asked.

'Yes, Inspector, I do. Now what can I do for you?'

'Could you please confirm that your daughter Louise gave birth to a child when she was in her mid-teens?'

Mrs Hickman nodded. 'Three days before her sixteenth birthday,' she said and folded her arms. 'Now will you please tell me why you are here?'

She appeared eager to learn what she had already ascertained was going to be bad news. Kim got the impression she had been waiting for news for years.

'Please sit down, Mrs Hickman,' Bryant advised.

'I'm perfectly fine, thank you.'

Kim took a step forwards. 'We have uncovered the body of a female, and we have reason to believe it is Louise.'

A small cry escaped from her lips. It may have been the news she was expecting, but it had impacted her all the same.

She stepped around to the dining table and pulled out a chair. Bryant held out a hand to steady her but she waved it away.

Bryant stepped back as Kim took a seat opposite the woman, whose head had fallen into her hands.

It was a long moment before she quietly shook her head and raised it. Although her eyes were red, Kim was surprised to see there were no actual tears.

'It was only a matter of time,' she whispered, staring down at the table.

'Why do you say that?' Kim asked.

'How did it happen?' Mrs Hickman asked, finally meeting her gaze. Kim saw a deep sadness in her eyes, but she couldn't help feeling that this woman had already grieved for the loss of her child.

'There is no gentle way to tell you that your daughter was murdered, Mrs Hickman,' Kim said, trying to feel her way through this situation.

'Was it drugs related?' the woman asked.

Kim shook her head. Mrs Hickman obviously thought it was a recent death and yet eleven years of absence had stood between them.

Kim wanted a better understanding of this situation before she revealed the fact that Louise had been dead for years.

'You haven't seen Louise for some years, Mrs Hickman. Would you mind sharing the reason for that?'

She nodded and stared over her head. 'I'm not going to go into too much detail, but, much as it pains me to admit it, my daughter was not a pleasant child. My late husband and I probably spoiled her as she was our only one, but by the time we realised that her behaviour was beyond precocious it was already too late.

'Every different phase we assumed she would outgrow. We tried to rein her in but she had no fear of any consequences. We tried everything, but nothing stopped the bad behaviour. It's difficult to discipline a child who simply doesn't care.

'Anyway, when she came home and told us she was pregnant and she intended to keep the child we actually hoped it would be the making of her. But she enjoyed the pregnancy more than the child.'

Kim frowned. 'What do you mean?'

'She was the centre of attention, Inspector. The only girl taking a growing bump to school. She enjoyed the attention of being unique. Until the baby was born. Of course we supported her. She lived here with Marcus and we did everything we could but once her friends stopped coming round she lost complete interest in her son.

'One day she left the house without telling me. I had no idea until I heard the baby's cries from upstairs. He was wet and hungry, and she had just left him. We argued constantly about her refusal to take care of her child, but as usual she cared nothing for the consequences of her actions.'

Kim hadn't noticed Bryant sit down at the table.

'So you took care of her child?' Kim asked.

'Of course. The time spent away got longer and longer. First a few days, then a few weeks and then months. This continued until Christmas Day eleven years ago when Marcus was five.'

She took a breath and continued. 'She stormed in on Christmas morning after being gone for almost four months. She was drunk and tried to take Marcus. He was terrified. He barely knew her. She only wanted him because she'd been told she had a good chance of getting a council flat if she had a child. Her father physically threw her out and told her not to come back until she'd cleaned up her act. We never saw her again, but we took precautions in case it happened again.'

Kim assumed they had applied for guardianship of Marcus to ensure his safety.

Mrs Hickman looked around at the baking ingredients and smiled. 'He insisted on a home-made cake like normal except this time it came with the proviso that I don't tell his friends. Her son is healthy and happy, but it doesn't mean I didn't think of Louise every day,' she said as the first tear fell from her eye. 'I always had hope that she could turn her life around but…'

Kim understood. The hope ended now.

Quietly she pushed back the chair. There were few questions to ask. This woman did not even know her daughter, had not seen her for many years before her murder.

'Thank you for being so open and honest, Mrs Hickman,' Kim said, holding out her hand.

Mrs Hickman shook it in return and made to stand.

Kim ushered her back down. 'We'll see ourselves out,' she said.

A formal identification would follow but Kim knew they had their girl.

She paused at the door that led into the porch.

A little girl with mousy brown hair and a red chequered dress frowned from an enlarged school photo.

'I've got one of mine at home looking just like that,' Bryant observed with a sad smile. 'Photographer's nightmare but a pretty little girl.'

Kim stared for a moment at the photograph and saw something that took her by surprise.

'What else do you see there, Bryant?' she asked.

'Awww… shit,' he whispered as his eyes found the same thing hers had.

A kirby grip fashioned with half a heart.

CHAPTER FIFTY-FIVE

Tracy Frost finished reading the article and placed it on the passenger seat.

It was good copy. Her editor had loved it.

She had chosen not to reveal to him that she had known she was being used. A fact that was still gnawing at her insides like a hungry ferret.

Her natural instinct was to go digging into the exact thing Inspector Stone wanted to keep hidden, and she hadn't been able to help herself completely. She had managed to find out the name of the woman who worked there as an entomologist, which had made her even more curious about what it was about Catherine Evans that Kim Stone wanted to hide.

Her fingers had been poised to start searching when she'd realised what she was doing. She had given her word and there came a time when that had to mean something. They had agreed to scratch each other's backs and Tracy knew she couldn't stop scratching just because she'd found a juicier itch. That's what had kept Bob anonymous for this long. And so she had removed her fingers from the keyboard and ripped out the page with the name so no one else could find it. A deal was a deal.

Now that she had parked, Tracy knew she eventually had to try to leave the car, but it would take another couple of deep breaths before she could even think about it.

She glanced up to the bay window. He would know she was here. His seat was to the left of the first glass pane. A spot he'd claimed as his own when he'd married her mother twenty-one years ago.

Tracy felt the rage course through her as she turned the ignition and started the car.

She still couldn't force herself to go in there.

CHAPTER FIFTY-SIX

'You wanted to see me?' Kim said, closing the door behind her.

She was not surprised to see a copy of the *Dudley Star* on Woody's desk.

'Stone, you have a leak.'

She moved closer to the desk. 'May I?'

'Carry on,' he said, pushing it towards her.

She turned the paper around. The headline screamed 'BODY FARM SHOCKER', which caused her an internal groan. Tracy had had plenty of time to come up with a decent headline.

The front page began the story, which then took up the majority of pages two and three.

She scanned it and found that Tracy hadn't done a bad job, despite the appalling headline.

'It's got everything, Stone. I distinctly remember instructing you to keep this low profile. Did you not think to pass that instruction to your team?'

'I did, sir,' she said, pushing the paper back towards him.

'Do you realise what this is going to cause? Do you have any idea of the letters, complaints and petitions that are going to flood in?'

Luckily they wouldn't be coming to her.

'I am not happy about this at all, Stone. The location of the facility has been compromised because you have a leak in your team, someone who cannot be trusted to follow a simple instruction or keep their mouth shut.'

Woody slapped the newspaper. 'It's clear that she has spoken to someone involved in the investigation and I want the name of that person…'

'It was me, sir,' she said calmly. 'I spoke to Tracy Frost.'

It was not often Kim was afforded the luxury of seeing her boss speechless, but it didn't last for long.

His disbelief turned into a knowing frown. 'No, Stone, you're covering for one of your team members, and I won't stand for it. I want to know who it was.'

'It really was me. I spoke directly with Tracy Frost and gave her most of the information. Some she dug up herself but not much. It came from me. I am the unnamed source.'

Woody sat back in his chair, shaking his head. He regarded her with an expression that demanded answers.

Even in the face of his anger, she wasn't sorry she'd done it. She'd defied a direct order, and she had no regrets.

Very few other publications would want to run the story if all they were doing was repeating the same old facts, and Tracy had included them all. Tracy was the only person who had spoken to Catherine and the entomologist wouldn't be taking any more calls from the press.

'What the hell did you think you were doing?'

She took a deep breath. 'Sir, my job is to serve and protect, and sometimes you just have to trust that I'm doing my job.'

'Is that it, Stone? Is that all I'm going to get?'

She said nothing.

'You expect me to take that explanation to Lloyd House – because that's where I'm now going first thing in the morning.'

Kim knew she had placed her boss in an untenable position. Then she remembered Catherine hiding in the lawnmower box.

'Yes, sir.'

'I've a good mind to take you with…'

His words trailed away as her phone began to ring.

His expression dared her to answer.

'So tomorrow morning you can…'

This sentence was not destined for completion as his own phone began to ring just as hers dinged the arrival of a voicemail.

He snatched up the receiver without taking his eyes from her face.

'Yes,' he snapped. He didn't offer his name. The detective chief inspector's phone didn't ring by accident.

His gaze moved from her face to a point above her head, signalling the shift in his focus.

He listened for five seconds before replacing the receiver.

'This isn't over, Stone, but right now you have an urgent message to ring Keats. This may be about your latest victim.'

Kim took out her phone. Her own voicemail was from the pathologist. The message was short and instructed her to ring him back.

'Sir, I'm going to—'

'Get out, Stone,' he said, waving her away. 'But believe me that this isn't over.'

She closed the door behind her and pressed the button to return Keats's call.

'About time, Inspector,' he said as a greeting. He sounded in a hurry.

Jesus, it had been less than thirty seconds.

'I'm on my way to Netherton Reservoir, and I suggest you might like to join me.'

Did he really think she didn't have enough work to do?

'Keats, I'm a bit pushed—'

'Well, get unpushed. I'm going to collect another customer and I'm reliably informed that this one has got no hands.'

CHAPTER FIFTY-SEVEN

Kim pulled up close to the clubhouse on the edge of Netherton Reservoir. It was more commonly known as Lodge Farm Reservoir and was used for watersports and supplying water to the canal system.

'Bloody hell, quiet day for Brierley Hill, eh?' Bryant asked as they headed around the building. She counted six squad cars and two civilian vehicles.

She could see fluorescent jackets scattered around the perimeter of the lake as the officers cleared the area. A clutch of personnel stood 150 feet to her right. She headed in that direction.

'Hey, Stone, are you lost?'

Kim recognised the bellow as the deep grumble of Detective Inspector Dunn. For this man she readily held out her hand. He took it and smiled warmly.

She had worked with Dunn when he'd been a sergeant and she a constable. His work ethic was not unlike her own.

She remembered one case where he had persuaded a woman with two children to press charges against her husband after suffering a broken arm, dislocated jaw and more bruises than the medical staff could count.

The man had been removed and charged and then bailed with a restraining order to stay away from his wife. There was no space at the shelter for the woman and her three children, and no family members would take her owing to fear of the repercussions from her husband.

Unable to get police resources authorised for protection, Dunn had finished his shift each night and parked up outside the woman's house.

On the third night, a drunk and angry Roy Bradley stumbled blindly into his front garden and had barely reached the front door before Dunn had wrestled him to the ground. The man had been back in cuffs and safely behind bars before Laura Bradley had a clue what had happened.

During her time with Dunn, Kim had learned a lot.

He was about eighteen months away from retirement and a small property in Spain. And he'd earned it.

She mirrored his smile. 'Oh you know, got a bit bored. Thought I'd come and see what you boys were up to over here.'

'Yeah, right,' he said knowingly. 'Nothing to do with you snaffling a file on one of our cold cases then?'

She shrugged. 'Thought it might be connected to something I'm working,' she said honestly. She motioned towards Bryant. 'My colleague, Detective Sergeant Bryant.'

Dunn held out his hand. 'My sympathies, Sergeant,' he said, raising one eyebrow.

Even Kim broke out a smile.

'Yeah, good job on the Ashraf Nadir case. How's the kid?'

'He's doing okay,' Kim said. She had spoken to Negib's father twice since the raid. Only the night before he had told her that Negib's older sisters were not letting him out of their sight. Normality would not return easily to the close-knit family, but the boy had a lot of love and support to help him through.

'Did your boss ever tell you she didn't make sergeant first time of asking?' Dunn said, looking at Bryant.

Kim groaned. 'Let's not rehash—'

Bryant stepped forwards. 'No, actually she didn't.'

Dunn nodded. 'Yeah, yeah, she was in line for it, a dead cert, really but…'

'What happened?' Bryant asked as Kim shoved her hands into her pockets.

'There was this raid on a flat in Hollytree. The gangs weren't prolific back then, and it was every man for himself. A car chase led to a run up three flights of stairs at Holden Court.'

'One of the maisonette blocks?' Bryant asked.

Dunn nodded. 'By the time the two chasing officers, that's your boss here and a kid named Lampitt, got to the scene, we'd had intelligence the youth was high on heroin and carrying a knife. The order was issued not to enter until backup arrived.'

'And?' Bryant asked.

'They forced entry, and the kid jumped out the window. The little shit didn't die, but he wasn't very well for a bit, and your boss here was the one that made the call to enter, said her statement. Promotion gone,' he said, opening his hands as though setting something free.

'Okay, that's enough reminiscing about the good old days,' Kim said, moving to stand between Bryant and Dunn.

Dunn looked around her. 'Poor old Officer Lampitt was first day back on shift after his missus had suffered a miscarriage and it's ever so strange that he was the one with the bruised shoulder, not your boss here.'

'I don't mark easily,' Kim said, narrowing her eyes at Dunn.

'Yeah, so you said.' He looked back to Bryant. 'Cost her a good nine months until she eventually got what she deserved.'

'Mike…' she warned.

He shrugged. 'Just thought the guy could do with knowing what kind of boss he was working with.'

Bryant nodded his head. 'Thanks for that, but I've got a pretty good idea.'

'Hey, Inspector, glad you could make it,' Keats called, looking up at her from the ground.

Kim ignored him as her eyes focussed on the thing she'd come to see. The body. This male had been dumped closer to the treeline approximately twenty feet from the water. An old condom sat three inches away from his head, leaving Kim in little doubt about some of the woodland activity.

This victim was the complete opposite of the man found at Fens Pool. She could see by the greying of the hair that they were similar in age, but this man was tall and gangly. His frame was slight and appeared undernourished.

His feet were clad in trainers that had not accumulated their filthy colour over a few days. His jeans were supermarket brand and ingrained with oil stains that would never come out. She knew all about that.

His T-shirt was plain and had once been white. She wondered if it had been washed alongside the oil-stained jeans.

As her gaze travelled up the body it met with the bloody stumps that ended at his wrists. The flies weaved and ducked around the open flesh, undaunted by the police presence. Kim was instantly reminded of Westerley.

Although the picture had walked out of a bad horror movie, no special effects had been used. Gruesome as the sight was, the stumps were unusually clean.

'After death?' Kim asked Keats as she nodded towards the wrists.

Keats nodded. 'Volume of blood indicates that the heart was no longer pumping.'

'Cause of death?' she asked as her eyes continued their journey looking for clues.

'Ahem…' said Dunn from beside her.

Damn, she had forgotten it was not her crime scene. She was here for information purposes only.

'Sorry,' Kim said and continued to walk around the body.

'Well, for whichever detective inspector cares, there is no identification on his person, and I would estimate he's been here for between fourteen to eighteen hours. I can't state cause of death yet, however there is bruising to the upper-neck area.'

Kim knew this was for her benefit and that Keats was offering any information that might help her without her having to ask and encroach on someone else's crime scene. He was also aware that she would not be able to attend the post-mortem.

'Are you finished?' Dunn asked her.

She nodded and turned away from the body. She had learned all she'd needed to know. The two murders were linked. Bob was involved in this somehow.

But good manners and ingrained ethics dictated that as it was now an active case again she should not do anything to hamper or interfere with the investigation of her colleagues.

'So this other guy from Fens Pool…?' Dunn asked.

She held up her hands. 'It's clearly your case now. I'll step away and leave it alone.'

She was surprised when he threw back his head and laughed loudly.

'Oh no you won't, not if you learned anything from me at all,' he said wryly before walking away.

She headed back to where Bryant leaned against the side of the changing rooms. Both of them viewing the body on a case that was not theirs would have been overkill.

'What's the betting his name is Larry?' Kim asked.

She couldn't help but focus on the similarity in location to where Bob had been found at Fens Pool.

'I know what you're thinking,' Bryant said, staring across 20,000 square feet of water.

'What is it that…?'

'He's luring them,' Bryant said and immediately Kim knew he was right. Both locations were easy to get to but had areas of bush, foliage and trees. The perfect place for illicit activity.

With a sinking feeling in her stomach, Kim took out her phone.

Stacey answered on the second ring.

'Guv… I was just about to call. I've described our Bob to a woman at the warfarin clinic, and I'm pretty sure his real name is Ivor.'

'Yeah, Stace, I think so too, but drop what you're doing. I need you to check and see if he's on The List.'

Stacey knew she would mean the register of sex offenders.

Dunn's recent words rang in her ear. Of course she couldn't leave it alone.

There was a pause before Stacey spoke and Kim knew why. Searching the sex offenders register was a stark reminder of just how much evil surrounded them.

'Got it, boss.'

Kim looked around and knew there was nothing more to learn.

It was time to go and see the headmaster from Jemima's school.

The answer to that case lay in the past.

CHAPTER FIFTY-EIGHT

Tracy negotiated the cobblestones that surrounded the entrance to the café. Uneven flooring was the bane of her life. Ramps, potholes, gravel and slabs with too much space in-between.

The afternoon rush had passed and the evening lull had descended. She stood at the counter feeling the additional heat from the appliances being blown towards her by a fan that was cooling no one.

She ordered a coffee that she had no intention of drinking.

It wasn't as bad as where she'd met the detective inspector the other day, but it wasn't far off. This establishment had brick walls and tablecloths. Yes they were plastic with a red and white chequered pattern that hadn't been updated in twenty years, but they were tablecloths all the same.

It wasn't the great coffee and haute cuisine that brought her here. It was about the only place from her childhood that hadn't changed a bit. Her mother had brought her to Old Hill on a Saturday morning to traipse around the markets collecting the weekly shop. Her mother had never believed in the convenience of one-stop shopping. She had liked to distribute her business. Weighed down with plastic bags of produce, they had always stopped at this café for a pork sandwich and a cup of tea.

The markets had gone but this café had remained the same, and Tracy still came here often.

She wasn't sure what had prompted the maudlin thoughts that had plagued her this week. Perhaps it was the news that one of her old classmates had been murdered. It had taken her back to a time that was not her proudest moment. A time she wished she could take back, at whatever cost to herself.

But truthfully, even at seven years of age, Tracy had been relieved when the bullies had turned their attention to someone else.

She acted as though she didn't care what people thought of her. Unfortunately for her a by-product of being bullied and tormented meant that you did care. You cared very much. Too much. There was always the paranoia that everyone having a private conversation was talking about you. Every chuckle that met your ears was because people were laughing at you. And the worst thing about paranoia was knowing you could not be proven wrong.

And just as you strived to gain the recognition and acceptance of your peers throughout school, so you continued throughout life. Self-worth couldn't be bought in the shops once you turned sixteen and escaped the education system.

Of course she knew the persona she projected, and it was intentional. It was her only form of defence. She had to show people she didn't give a shit before they laughed and pointed.

It wasn't armour she'd been born with. It had grown over her skin like a shield over the years, inch by inch, until she no longer knew how to take it off.

Of the people that she truly envied, Detective Inspector Stone was definitely up there. Tracy couldn't help the smile that tugged at her lips. Now there was a woman who really did not give a shit. Yes, people talked about her, and yes they called her names, and Kim Stone did not give these people a second thought. How did one do that? Tracy wondered.

She just wasn't sure whether the image she had shaped and honed for herself was now a perfect fit. There were days when she wanted to lower her barriers and drop the act even just a little. One day she would like to care less about what people thought, but the truth was she just didn't know how.

She needed to talk about these things, Tracy realised as she pushed herself to her feet, but she was not in the right place to get answers.

As she concentrated once more on the cobblestones, she realised there was only one person who could help her. As she headed into the underground car park, she resolved that tomorrow she would visit her mother.

CHAPTER FIFTY-NINE

The bungalow sat just off the main road that ran through Stourton and stopped short of the Stewponey lights, so named because of the pub.

The Stewponey Inn was known to have existed in 1744 when it was called the house of Benjamin Hallen. The inn gave its name to the nearby locks and bridge on the Staffordshire and Worcestershire canal, along with the octagonal toll house.

The pub had been demolished in 2001 to make way for houses.

The old headmaster's property was double fronted with a single hanging basket for decoration. Geraniums peered listlessly at the floor.

'Probably worth a few quid,' Bryant observed. Property in Stourton did not come cheap.

'Not as much as you'd think,' Kim said. From what she could see, the small back garden was overlooked by a good number of the new houses.

'How old is this guy?' Bryant asked as they walked up the driveway.

'He retired from Cornheath primary about fifteen years ago so…' she said, pressing on the bell. She heard no sound so she tapped on the glass.

The door was swung open by a woman in her mid-forties wearing a navy overall. Her hair was cut short and showed some colourful costume jewellery in her ears.

'Thank you but we don't want…'

The door was beginning to close.

'Police,' Kim explained, quickly realising the woman had taken them for salespeople or canvassers.

The door stopped.

'Identification?' she said, frowning and looking to each of them.

Both she and Bryant showed their ID. Kim had a feeling they were not getting in otherwise. The name Vera was embroidered into her overall.

Still the door did not move backwards. 'What do you want? Mr Jackson tires very easily and…'

'We need to speak to Mr Jackson regarding an investigation, and we will discuss the matter with him directly,' Kim said, pushing firmly against the door.

The woman got the message and began to back away.

'The door to the left,' she said, closing the door behind them. 'He's just had his evening meal, and he tends to get sleepy afterwards…'

'You come in and care for him?' Kim asked, pausing.

She nodded. 'His son comes every morning before going to work, and I pop in twice a day.'

Kim's heart began to sink. This man needed a great deal of assistance.

'Alzheimer's,' Vera clarified.

Kim knew enough about the disease to understand why it was called 'the long goodbye'. The cause was poorly understood, and she had read once that it was something to do with plaques and tangles in the brain.

She also knew that there was no treatment to stop or reverse the disease's progression.

'How is he with remembering things?' Kim asked.

'He's gradually spending more time in the past than the present. Sometimes he believes a memory has already happened when it hasn't. Other times he thinks an old memory is a new one. When his son comes he tends to combine two totally separate recollections and other times he confuses the people so…' She shrugged.

'Thank you,' Kim said with a smile.

She turned left into a room that was built for comfort and not style. An array of dark furniture that had obviously accrued over the years now jostled for space. Ornaments and trinkets adorned every surface.

Mr Jackson sat in a reclining armchair. His eyes were closed and his mouth slightly parted.

His face looked peaceful beneath a full head of white hair.

Bryant offered a gentle cough.

The eyes fluttered open and looked in their direction. For a second there was confusion before his eyes lit up and sparkled. It couldn't be because of her. No one was ever that pleased to see her.

Mr Jackson's gaze travelled past her to Bryant.

'My boy, come closer. How are you?'

Bryant looked her way as Vera entered, carrying a mug of something hot.

She stopped alongside Kim. 'He thinks your man there is Mr Simmons, an English teacher he mentored at Cornheath. Every man under the age of fifty is Mr Simmons, who actually died five years ago. We just don't remind him any more.'

Vera expertly placed the mug in the only space available on the cluttered table.

'Should we correct…?'

'He wouldn't believe you if you did,' Vera offered matter-of-factly.

Mr Jackson beckoned again and Bryant moved forwards cautiously.

Kim took a step. 'Mr Jackson, we're here—'

'Oh and this must be your lovely wife. How nice to meet you, my dear,' he said, nodding enthusiastically.

Bryant's expression held amusement that she would surely punish him for later.

'Yes, isn't she?' Bryant said, turning away from her. 'I was just telling my… er… wife the other day about our years at Cornheath, Mr Jackson.'

His face lit up. 'Best years of my life, son. We had some times, didn't we?'

'We did that, Mr Jackson,' Bryant said, lowering himself into the nearest seat. 'In fact, I was trying to recall the detail about that unfortunate incident with Jemima Lowe. Do you remember?'

Kim held her breath. She was normally the one for the long shot. Bryant was really throwing the net out this time.

His face saddened. 'Oh yes, I remember. Terrible business. Children can be so cruel.'

Bryant glanced her way. His look said 'back off, I've got this' and he had.

Kim retreated to the doorway. Somehow this subterfuge felt wrong. Although she had to wonder if the information would be accessible to them any other way.

Vera appeared in the doorway and Kim asked the question with her eyes. Vera nodded and leaned against the door frame.

'My memory isn't what it used to be, Mr Jackson. I can't quite remember what happened now.'

'Oh, it's your age, my boy. Happens to us all. It was those girls, if you remember. A group of them. Pinned that child down in the gym hall and lifted her dress up and held her there for everyone to come and see her privates. Awful business.'

'I don't recall how many girls there were, Mr Jackson,' Bryant said gently.

'There were four or five to start with I think. One little girl came running to the staff room to get us. Funny little thing, she was.'

Bryant continued. 'Of course, I remember now. Little Louise was there as well, wasn't she?'

Mr Jackson started to nod, but as he did so his expression began to change. His face crumpled into confusion. He looked from one to the other and then beyond them to the doorway.

'Vera…?'

The carer appeared instantly. Her smile was warm and comforting.

'It's okay, Mr Jackson. These nice people just called to see if you wanted double glazing fitted, but they're going now.'

She turned to Kim as Bryant stepped backwards. She looked towards the door. It was not an unkind gesture, but it was clearly time for them to leave.

Kim nodded her thanks and turned away, saddened.

'He'll be okay,' Vera said, appearing beside her. '*Coronation Street* will be on in a minute. It's his favourite.'

Kim swallowed the emotion in her throat and continued to the door.

'Wait a minute,' Mr Jackson called. 'I remember now. That funny little thing that fetched us. She had a limp. A terrible limp. And I think… I think her name was Tracy.'

CHAPTER SIXTY

'Guv… you don't think…?'

'Bryant, I'm willing to bet your house on it,' she said as they reached the end of the drive. She shook her head as a couple of things began to make sense. 'Those bloody stupid heels. Ring Stacey and get an address,' she said, scrolling through her list of incoming calls. She found the one she had received a few days ago around midnight. She hit the button to recall.

The phone rang and rang and finally ended with a brief message from Tracy Frost. Kim could hear Bryant talking to Stacey as she called again.

Same thing happened. It rang all the way to the message.

She tried once more. This time it went straight to voicemail without ringing.

Damn it. The phone had been switched off, and she had no way of knowing by whom.

Bryant ended his call and walked towards her. 'I've asked Stacey to check and see if Tracy Frost went to Cornheath and if she was there at the same time as Jemima.'

Kim nodded. She knew it was almost half past seven and her team had been at it all day. She also knew if she tried to send any one of them home they would refuse to go. Leads didn't always present themselves at nine in the morning.

'Have you got Tracy's address?' she asked.

Bryant nodded as he unlocked the driver's door. He hesitated. 'You do know we could be completely wrong?'

Kim had no such hesitation as she plonked herself in the passenger seat.

'Yeah. But what if we're completely right?'

CHAPTER SIXTY-ONE

'He has no idea where she is,' Kim said, ending the call. Tracy's editor had not seen her again following their morning briefing.

'You know, there are worse people he—'

'Finish that sentence, Bryant, and you and I are gonna have problems.'

No person was any better or worse, more or less deserving than the next. In their job they couldn't be. Tracy Frost was a pain in the backside, there was no doubt about that, and there had been times over the last few years Kim would have abducted the woman herself if she could have got away with it – but there was more to the reptilian reporter than she had originally believed. If Kim thought her colleague truly believed that Tracy deserved it he'd already be on his way home.

Bryant slowed as he passed QB Motorcycles. 'Is that the one?'

'Looks like it,' Kim said, checking the number of the door.

He continued to the bottom of the hill and turned into a pub car park.

Kim noted that the white Audi was nowhere to be seen.

Bryant pulled up directly in front of the house.

'Not what I expected,' he observed.

She had to agree with him. The house was a tiny terrace squeezed between two others. Together, all three might have made a decent-sized property.

Tracy's designer labels did not fit in a house like this.

She knocked on the door hard. Perhaps Tracy had the car in a garage somewhere.

She leaned down and lifted the letter box. The door led straight into a small reception room. Kim could see a television in the far corner. It was off and no other sound met her ears.

'Jesus, guv, how do we even get around the back?' Bryant asked, taking a step back and looking around.

He had a point. Tracy's property was in the middle.

A movement to the right caught her eye. The corner of the net curtain covering next door's window dropped back down.

Kim took two steps and knocked on the door. Perhaps they could get to the rear of the property via the back gardens.

The door was opened by a thin lad in his mid-teens. Gangly, milky legs protruded from multicoloured shorts covered with tropical birds. His concave upper half was uncovered.

'Yeah,' he said with the requisite attitude.

'You know the woman next door?' Kim asked, relieved she did not even have to try to raise any pleasantries.

He looked outside and glanced at the property as though he had no idea who she was talking about and had to be reminded there was a house next door.

'Yeah, I know her. Blonde, high heels, nice pair of—'

'Does she store her car anywhere else?' Bryant asked quickly.

'Yeah, in front of our house sometimes,' he said and grinned.

Kim stared back.

He shook his head. 'Nah, if she's here, the car's here.'

'Can we get to her back garden through yours?' Kim asked.

'Pfftt… not a chance. We got a six-foot fence and spikes. Fucking cats.'

Damn. They'd need to try the house on the other side, which looked as empty as the one they were trying to access.

'Me mum's got a spare key,' he said, reaching behind the door.

Her initial relief was replaced by dismay.

'You don't even know who we are,' Bryant said for her. How easily he had offered the key to two total strangers. Very secure.

He looked them both up and down then laughed out loud as he handed Bryant the key. 'Yeah, good one… Officer,' he said, closing the door.

Kim shook her head as Bryant put the key in the lock.

She stepped into a room that had appeared larger through the letter box. A two-seater sofa claimed the length of one wall facing an old gas fire. A single armchair was placed diagonally to the television set and a striped rug almost covered the worn walkway on the carpet.

Two unused pillar candles sat at opposite ends of the fire surround. In the middle was a photo. Kim took a closer look and saw it was a young Tracy, probably seven or eight, sitting beside a woman on the beach. They wore matching sombreros made of foam. Kim was drawn to the smile on the child's face. She didn't know Tracy's face could do that.

As Kim continued through the room her leg caught a pile of coupons teetering on the arm of the chair.

The only door out of the room led to a walkthrough that passed by the bottom of the stairs and then into the kitchen.

A roman blind was lowered halfway down the window above a stainless-steel sink that held a used juice glass.

An empty tin of smart-price beans peeped out of the pedal bin.

Bryant opened a cupboard door, revealing more value-branded grocery items.

A single sheet of paper was held on to the fridge door by a cupcake magnet.

'Dentist appointment,' Bryant said, taking a quick look.

There was little to learn Kim realised as she looked around, because there was very little here, full stop.

'I'm going upstairs,' she said, wondering if they would find any clues at all.

Bryant followed her. He was unusually quiet.

Kim took the door to her left and entered the front bedroom. Plain brown curtains were drawn halfway across the small window.

An e-reader and a bedside lamp occupied the only cabinet.

Kim stepped around the bed and opened the wardrobe. Hanging to the right were three designer trouser suits, one navy, one black and one cream. To the left were shelves holding tracksuit bottoms, sweatshirts and vest tops. Kim realised that she had never seen Tracy in a skirt.

Bryant bent down. 'Look, guv,' he said, picking up a high-heeled shoe. Inside was a plastic insert. As her gaze took in the identical shoes lined up in a row it was clear that every pair had its own insert.

Kim sat down on the edge of the bed and shook her head.

The sadness of the property had found a route to somewhere inside her.

'I know I moan about the missus and stuff sometimes but bloody hell, you just don't realise what you've got.'

Kim silently agreed. Her own home lacked many of the personal touches found in others but the wagging tail that greeted her more than made up for it.

It was clear that Tracy spent all her money on the bits people could see; the Tracy Frost that she presented to the world. The 'home Frost' was the polar opposite. For some inexplicable reason, it really bothered Kim.

'And I take back what I said outside,' Bryant said, as he closed the wardrobe door.

He didn't need to elaborate. Kim knew exactly what he meant.

They had to get her back.

CHAPTER SIXTY-TWO

Isobel was chasing her tail. The effort of fighting off sleep was exhausting.

The day had been tiring and, although she had escaped the dense blackness, even the light was clouded by a deep fog.

Everything in the hospital was trying to trap her into sleep, but she didn't want to close her eyes. The darkness lay waiting. She didn't want to return to it.

The lights had been dimmed and the night staff walked with a lighter step. The rhythmic beating of a machine and a soft snore reached her from the bed opposite.

Everything was trying to guide her back to the darkness.

Even awake, her stomach was in turmoil. The anxiety swirled like a tornado inside her, reaching up to touch her heart and her lungs. Occasionally she would feel the urge for a sharp intake of breath to steady the turmoil inside. Now and again the odd palpitations in her chest caused a dizziness in her head. She was learning to focus her way through the fear. See past it. Get to the other side and let it pass rather than react to it.

The worst thing was that she didn't know what she was afraid of. Except for, well, everything.

She was frightened she would never know who she was.

Only Duncan had made her feel safe. His reassuring smile and his gentle squeeze of her hand told her she wasn't alone.

He had talked her through all of their dates. She had listened intently as he'd detailed their collision outside the coffee shop, trying to recognise herself in the picture, eager for any clue.

She felt the weight of her eyelids dropping and she shook herself awake.

She had tried to understand the significance of the phrase *one for you and one for me*. What did it mean and why was it the only thing playing in her head? She visualised the words, like a sign, in her mind's eye, but the refresh button wasn't working, and nothing new was coming through.

'Hey, can't get to sleep?' asked Marion from the other side of the bed. The night sister had started her shift at seven.

Isobel shook her head and then widened her eyes.

Marion smiled knowingly. 'Can't or won't?'

Isobel felt tears prick the back of her eyes. She knew she could not hold out much longer. Her body demanded sleep and she was losing the fight.

'You won't go back,' Marion offered. 'Your brain has woken up now.'

Isobel wanted to believe the kindly nurse, but her brain had been awake before, trapped and fully functioning in a useless, defiant body.

She shook her head. 'I can't…'

Marion sighed. 'Okay, how about you just let yourself rest for…' she looked at her watch '… half an hour. I'll wake you up at half past eleven and we'll take it from there.'

Isobel considered. The thought of being able to succumb to the fatigue and allow her body to rest while someone was watching was too tempting to refuse.

Suddenly she felt like a three-year-old child in an adult body. A little girl afraid of the dark.

'Are you sure you'll…?'

'Eleven thirty on the dot. I promise.'

Isobel allowed her head to rest back fully on the bed, the dressing wedged between her skull and the softness.

Her aching neck sighed as the muscles began to relax. Isobel wasn't sure she'd felt anything sweeter.

Her eyelids slammed shut and for a split second she panicked in the darkness but it was okay, she told herself. Marion was coming to get her.

Her flesh seemed to fall away from her bones like a well-cooked chicken as she allowed the tension to ease away.

But in the darkened tunnel of her mind was a voice. No face, no form, just a whisper or an echo.

It was like trying to hear a conversation in the next room.

She tried to focus the concentration to her ears even though the voice was inside. She squeezed her eyes tightly closed, but the voice travelled further away. *Come back*, she silently called. But the sound had disappeared.

The tension had seeped back into her body, so she quickly chased it away. The voice had come when she had finally allowed herself to relax.

She shook the tension away and relaxed all her senses.

The warmth of total relaxation stole over her flesh, reaching right down into her bones. She heard the voice in the distance. It was calling a single word. She urged her body not to react, to chase it away again.

She remained as still as a statue, forcing her mind to stare beyond the voice and into the abyss. The sound was growing in volume, but she couldn't make out the word. She desperately wanted to chase after it, but she kept herself relaxed.

The voice came closer, but she kept her body and her mind still. Closer. It was two syllables.

Closer.

The word sounded like handy.

Closer.

No, the word was candy.

Closer.

For the first time she heard it clearly. And the voice was calling out 'Mandy'.

CHAPTER SIXTY-THREE

Everywhere Kim looked, she saw Tracy.

Every cupboard door she opened or drawer that she closed reminded her of the absence of life in the home of the complicated woman.

She had never liked the reporter. On occasion Tracy had shown a distinct lack of empathy for a victim or their family, choosing the urgency of the story instead.

And yet there had been other moments that had niggled at Kim's usually unshakeable opinion of the woman.

Whether by fate or accident, she had managed to save Dawson's life during a solo investigation he'd been carrying out. Faced with a group of youths from the Hollytree estate who were kicking the shit out of him and brandishing a knife, Tracy had stepped out of the shadows and intervened.

Earlier this week, when asked to leave something alone, she had done so.

These things contradicted Kim's resolute opinion of the ambitious, ruthless woman who would sell a kidney for a story and probably two for an exclusive.

And now she was missing… potentially in the hands of a killer who had murdered at least two women and had tried for a third.

Kim knew she had done all she could. At present it was no more than a suspicion and getting valuable resources committed to a grown woman reported missing by no one was an uphill struggle, even for her.

She had tried Tracy's number almost hourly since arriving home, but it continually hit voicemail.

As though she had willed it, her phone dinged the receipt of a message. Never before had she reached for her phone hoping it was Tracy Frost.

It wasn't. It was a text message from Daniel.

She gasped as she read the words on the screen: *'Got a minute? I'm outside.'*

What the hell was Daniel Bate doing outside her house? She wasn't sure herself of the guidelines in the subtle game they were playing, but she knew that turning up outside her house breached some kind of rule.

She looked to Barney as though he might have the answer. He nibbled his paw in response.

She considered ignoring the text and then wondered if it was something to do with the case but realised this wouldn't be the way he'd communicate it anyway.

The thoughts rushed through her head as she travelled towards the front door.

He stood against the driver's door facing her with his arms folded. Beneath the lamplight she could see the challenge in his eyes.

'I wondered if you'd come out,' he said.

She stood against the wall on her side of the pavement. 'Why are you here?' she asked, thrusting her hands into her front pockets.

'Took a wrong turn.'

She smiled. Yes, he had.

She waited.

'There's nothing more I can offer,' he said and paused just long enough for her to wonder what he meant. 'Keats has everything in order. The victim has been identified, so there's really no reason to stay.'

She nodded her understanding.

A moment passed where they stood, facing each other, each caught in their own thoughts.

'You do know, don't you?' he said.

She shrugged. It made no difference what she knew. It only mattered what she would or could do.

'You're such a contradiction, Kim,' he said, shaking his head.

She didn't answer.

'I'm not sure you've even admitted to yourself what could exist between us.'

Although not phrased as a question, she knew it was. A big question.

Still she didn't answer.

She finally met his gaze but neither of them moved an inch.

'You're not ready, are you?'

And that was the truth of it.

He opened his mouth to speak, but she gently shook her head. He exhaled and offered her a look of resignation.

He offered her his hand. 'Detective Inspector Stone, it's been a pleasure meeting you again.'

She swallowed and returned the handshake loosely. 'And you too, Doctor Bate.'

'I hope we meet again,' he said, letting go of her hand.

Kim had very little doubt that they would. But it would be different. The decision had been made.

There had been a moment.

And it had passed.

She turned her back and walked into the house.

Once inside, she stood against the front door and closed her eyes. She heard the sound of the truck engine start up and move steadily away. The words that had lodged in her throat, the ones she had wanted him to hear, were now lost. She had wanted him to know that if she *was* ready to take that chance, she would have chosen to take it with him.

Saying goodbye to Daniel was hard. But letting him stay would have been even worse.

It was about hope. She simply couldn't.

She had tried it once, and it had almost killed her.

She headed upstairs and sat on the bed. Barney sat at the door, looking confused. Was it bedtime? Should he jump onto the bed beside her?

Kim opened the top drawer of the bedside cabinet and took out a small white envelope.

One piece of paper was all she had. Just the sight of it was enough to bring the emotion to her throat. She held it close to her chest as though it would bring them back. Like a catalyst, the memory shot her back to three days after her thirteenth birthday.

'Make sure you give that letter to Miss Neale,' Erica said.

'For the third time,' Kim mumbled heading for the door.

Erica pulled on her jacket hood. 'Hey, little miss, haven't you forgotten something?'

Kim had allowed herself to be pulled backwards and turned into the firm embrace of her foster mum.

Most days she just rolled her eyes and accepted the inevitable. Usually she simply tolerated the display of affection that came so easily to the woman.

'Go on, off with you. Have a good day,' Erica said, walking her to the front door.

Kim adjusted her backpack and went on her way. During the short walk she resolved that tonight would be the night she would spend some time in the kitchen. Erica was always asking her to help cook and she always made her excuses and went to the garage instead. Keith's bike building always took her attention first. But it was important to Erica, so she would do it.

At fourteen minutes past eleven the head teacher walked into her History class. He whispered something to the teacher and then his eyes searched the room.

They eventually fell on her.

Kim immediately thought of the letter in her bag that she still hadn't handed in. Would Erica really inform the head?

He appeared beside her and touched her shoulder.

'Gather your things and come with me, Kimberly.'

His voice was soft and gentle and nothing like how he normally spoke to her. With a sinking feeling she knew it was more serious than the letter.

'Something has happened, Kimberly, and I'm going to take you to your… ummm… aunt's house.'

The headmaster continued to hold on to her shoulder as he guided her out of the school.

She was confused. She had no aunts. Suddenly she realised he was talking about Erica's sister, Nancy.

The sisters were not close, and Kim had met the family only twice during the three years she'd been in Keith and Erica's care.

Kim asked a dozen times what was happening during the short car journey, but he would not answer. She asked him to take her home. He ignored her. She asked him to call Keith and Erica. He swallowed and looked away.

The fear was rising around her stomach as she followed him up the path of a house she'd never seen before.

Nancy opened the door and the confusion on her face quickly turned to horror.

She looked at Mr Crooks. 'Why have you brought her here?'

'Family needs to be—'

'We're not family,' she spat. 'This child is nothing to me. What on earth were you thinking?'

Mr Crooks was clearly uncomfortable. 'I thought when you called to inform us that you wanted...'

Nancy's lower lip trembled. 'I called so you could make the necessary arrangements.'

Kim watched the exchange while the unease continued to build within her. She wanted Erica. She wanted Keith.

Finally the fear inside her exploded. 'Will someone please tell me what's going on?'

Nancy's mouth dropped open. 'You haven't told her?'

Mr Crooks shook his head. 'It's not really my place to...'

'Neither is it my...' She shook her head and sighed heavily. Finally Nancy looked at her properly.

'I'm sorry, Kimberly, but Keith and Erica were in an accident. They were on the motorway. I'm afraid they're dead.'

Kim felt her mouth drop open and although she was still looking at Nancy, Nancy was no longer looking at her.

She was looking at Mr Crooks. Her expression said 'there, I've done my bit'.

'But... th-they can't be,' Kim stuttered as her mind tried to digest what she'd heard.

She shook her head, looking from Nancy to Mr Crooks. She waited for someone, anyone to tell her it wasn't true.

Once again she felt Mr Crooks's hand on her shoulder. The tears began to bite at her eyes, and she shook off his touch.

She looked up at Nancy's face, desperate for something that said it was all a lie.

The woman took a step back into the house. 'I'm sorry but I have to… I have things to…'

Neither she nor Mr Crooks moved an inch.

Nancy hesitated for one more second. 'Kimberly, take care and I wish you the best of luck, but you're really not part of this family. Now I really must get back…'

The words trailed away as the door closed firmly in their faces.

Kim stared at the door for what seemed like hours but could only have been seconds before Mr Crooks guided her gently back to the car.

She was vaguely aware of Mr Crooks picking up the backpack that she must have dropped as she walked. Her legs faltered. Somehow she had lost the ability to put one foot in front of the other.

He held her up and bundled her back into the passenger seat. She stayed exactly as she'd been placed as Mr Crooks began to drive.

Her heart was screaming that it couldn't be true while her head knew that it was. No one would have said such cruel things had they not been true.

She wanted to throw the car door open and run along the streets back to the house she had called home and check.

The part of her heart that had finally allowed itself to break free and love screamed and cried.

They were back home. They had to be. Keith was scouring the newspapers and internet for bike parts. Erica was preparing pastry for a home-baked steak pie for supper. She tried to hold on to that thought but it wouldn't set.

It was only when Mr Crooks stopped the car that she realised she was sobbing from the bottom of her heart.

Kim never saw her home again.

By lunchtime she was back at the children's home she'd left three years earlier. Four hours later two bin liners arrived containing her clothes.

There had been no further communication from her 'family', and the funeral had taken place without her.

It was only later that Kim had learned they had been on their way back from a meeting with a lawyer who specialised in adoption.

Barney had come to sit and lean against her leg. The tears were now cascading over her cheeks, and the pain inside was as raw and powerful as it had been that day.

Kim still held the memory of those warm arms around her, the aroma of Youth Dew encasing them both.

And in the years since that day Kim had remained eternally grateful for one small detail of that morning with Erica.

On that last day, Kim had hugged her back.

Maybe Daniel didn't know the reasons that she couldn't offer so much of herself ever again or understand why she committed everything she had to her work, but she knew that it was how she stayed safe, and nothing would persuade her otherwise.

She dried the tears and placed the piece of paper back into the drawer.

She had no regrets.

There were people that needed her to be the person she was.

She took out her phone and tried Tracy Frost's number again.

CHAPTER SIXTY-FOUR

Why did you take me THAT DAY, Mummy?

How could you not have known what would happen?

After taking me to the toilet Louise stared at me all the way until lunchtime. I smiled, hoping she would smile back and she did. Kind of.

There was something about her that reminded me of Lindsay. I wanted her to like me. I wanted her to be my friend.

Louise found me a seat at lunchtime and then left me to eat on my own. She was a popular girl. Running from group to group and making them laugh. And in-between she would look over at me with a puzzled little frown on her face. I smiled and I waved, praying she would come over so that I wouldn't be on my own.

I chewed my way through sandwiches that tasted like pieces of wood. I stared down to the bottom of my lunch box. I didn't want to look around.

Finally she came and sat beside me.

'We have PE after lunch,' she said. 'You can be my partner if you want.'

I nodded gratefully. I wasn't sure what PE was, but at least I had a partner.

Suddenly I felt brave enough to ask her the question that was playing on my mind.

'Why are they all looking at me?' I asked.

'Just because you're new,' she said, snatching the rest of my crisps and walking away.

I didn't mind. Louise was going to be my partner. That meant she was going to be my friend.

The lunch bell sounded, and I followed the crowd back to the classroom and then over to the sports hall. I couldn't get close to Louise. There were too many people around her. But I told myself it was okay. She was going to be my partner. She had said so. I was already hoping that one day she would come to my house for tea.

Mrs Shaw was a thin, pretty lady dressed in a short pleated skirt. She asked me if I'd brought my gym bag. I shook my head no. I hadn't known that I'd need one.

She hesitated for a moment.

'I think we have some spare,' she said, heading out of the hall.

She got to the door and paused.

'Louise, show your new friend where to get her own gym mat,' Mrs Shaw said before she disappeared from view.

Louise turned and smiled in my direction.

But that wasn't what she did at all.

CHAPTER SIXTY-FIVE

Kim called them to order for the morning briefing as soon as the last one had sat down.

She strode out of The Bowl. 'Okay, guys, quick as you can, as I've had a message that Isobel has asked to see me. So we know Tracy Frost is either missing or has gone AWOL. She's still not answering her phone and her car is not outside her house.'

Kim had called her mobile three times already that morning and whizzed past her house on the way in to the station.

'You really think our guy has her?' Dawson asked.

Kim thought for a moment and nodded.

'Nice newspaper article,' Dawson said and then held up his hands. 'And before you ask, it wasn't me.'

Kim wasn't sure why he felt that instant suspicion would fall on him.

'I know, Kev,' she said.

'I thought I'd get the blame… because… well… I've got a big mouth, and it was clearly leaked from someone involved in…'

'Kev, it was me,' Kim said.

'What?' Bryant and Stacey said together.

She said nothing.

'You actually spoke to Tracy Frost?' Dawson said, horrified.

'Yes, I did, and now it's time to move on. So Louise Hickman was the first victim that we know of. There was then a break for a few years until Jemima returned from Dubai. He then tried to kill Isobel and now he's taken Tracy. So far we know that three of them went to the same school. There was an incident that the headmaster recalls vaguely that may have sparked this entire killing spree and two of our victims have the same hairgrip that Louise Hickman wore at school. We know that's the key.'

'Seems a bit extreme,' Stacey offered. 'We all had some shit at school.'

Kim nodded. 'I agree. We need more detail of the incident.' She paused for a few seconds before turning to Stacey. 'Find me a dinner lady, Stace. Dinner ladies always know everything and there's more to this than we have so far.'

'And the guv is almost prepared to admit she was wrong,' Bryant said with a smile.

'Am I?' Kim asked, surprised.

'Well, you heard the headmaster. He said it was a girl. Even you have to admit that we were right, and you were wrong. We're looking for a female.'

'Could be her brother, father, uncle, boyfriend, husband?' Kim offered.

'Ah, so instead of saying you were wrong you might go so far as to admit it's not the most right you've ever been?' he asked.

Kim shook her head. 'I admit nothing until we know more about what happened that day.'

'I'm still looking to see where Isobel fits into this,' Stacey said. 'I've got Louise Hickman and Jemima Lowe in the same class. I've got Tracy Frost in the class above…'

'Check middle names as well, Stace,' Kim advised. 'Some people adopt their middle names in certain situations.'

'Will do, guv.'

'I still want to know about those marks on the legs and stomach. They don't make sense and we know that both Jemima and Isobel have them. Obviously there's no way of knowing with Louise.'

The flesh around her thighs had been far too decayed to confirm.

'Talking of Isobel, she regained consciousness yesterday but has no memory of the events or her own life. Added to that, the girl has hep C. I don't know if she's aware.'

'What, that she's a druggie?'

'You're not ignorant enough to believe that's the only way to get it, Kev,' she snapped. Although, to be fair, in their experience it was the most common reason.

It was possible that Isobel was an addict who'd cleaned up. Kim had noted no obvious signs of withdrawal or track marks.

'Does the boyfriend know?' Dawson asked.

And was she going to tell him? She heard the question in the young detective's voice.

It was a question that had been nagging at the back of her own mind. Watching Duncan care for his girlfriend was heartening and meant that Isobel had someone but would he be quite as keen if he knew the truth? Eventually Kim had come to the conclusion that it was not her truth to share.

'Kev, I want you asking around at local shelters and even some of our known prostitutes to see if anyone has heard of a woman named Isobel.'

'You think she's a whore?'

Kim's head snapped up. 'I'll give you a full three seconds to rethink your terminology.'

Bryant stood before Dawson had a chance to open his mouth.

'I'm getting coffee and Stacey's gonna help me.'

Kim raised her eyebrows in agreement and folded her arms before the two of them had left the office.

'How dare you? I mean how bloody dare you refer to these women or any woman with so little respect?' she asked and then held up her hand. 'Actually don't even bother to answer, because this is going to be a conversation that requires no input from you, got it?'

His surprise was mixed with irritation.

'We seem to have this same chat every investigation, and quite frankly I've had enough of it, Kev. You have moments of pure brilliance when I'm actually proud to have you on this team and then there are occasions when, honestly, I'm not proud at all.

'You see, Kev, I get pissed off when you seem to apportion a different priority to a person based on your pre-judgement of them. The thing is, I couldn't care less about whatever Isobel was or wasn't before I met her. All I know is that I watched her moaning on the ground, fighting for breath while blood was streaming out of her head. And then I spoke to an incredibly courageous woman who has fought back from a coma, all for the pleasure of not knowing her own name.

'So when you have the audacity to refer to her as a whore it tends to piss me off a bit. Get it?'

She could see the colour rising up his neck and that only happened when he was emotional.

'It's just sensitivity, Kev,' she said, shaking her head. 'Just think before you open your mouth, yeah?'

She heard Bryant's cough from along the hallway. Subtle he was not.

'Canteen isn't open yet,' he said, taking his seat. Stacey followed.

Of course it wasn't. They all knew it opened at eight.

'Guv…?' Dawson said.

'Yes, Kev?'

'Do you think Isobel is a prostitute?'

Kim didn't hesitate in answering. She'd said her piece. 'I think she could have been. The scars on her wrist mean she's been troubled and desperate enough at some stage to consider ending her own life. The contraction of hepatitis C could indicate she's dabbled in prostitution at some stage to support herself.'

And it was a world where people came and went without having to clock in or out. She could easily have evaded the police but not other prostitutes. It was their business to know who was around.

'If she has worked the street, someone will know, Kev. Do some digging on your way back to Westerley.'

'Will do, boss. And Curtis Grant is due back there today. I want a quick chat with him. The sudden insertion of Darren James as the night-time officer seems a bit odd. And I think Curtis Grant has been at Westerley a bit more than is actually necessary this week. There's something there that doesn't feel right.'

'Well stick with it, and let me know if anything jumps out.'

Stacey ceased tapping for a minute. 'What do you want me to do about Ivor and Larry?'

Kim sighed heavily.

She knew the case was active again and belonged to Brierley Hill, yet something inside her did not want to let it go. She and her team had found out more in two days than had been discovered in three years.

They now knew that every effort had been made to remove the identities of both men. They were friends or at the very least acquaintances, and Stacey had confirmed that both were registered sex offenders.

Kim now had far less sympathy for the fact that Ivor had remained anonymous for years.

'Do some digging on their victims, Stace. They've both done prison time, but it may be that someone out there doesn't think they've done enough.'

'Yeah, me for one,' Dawson offered.

No one voiced their agreement. They didn't need to. It was a universal opinion. As was the belief you didn't get to go around killing people, no matter what they had done.

CHAPTER SIXTY-SIX

Isobel took a sip of the weak tea she'd been handed by the day nurse. She almost spat it onto the crisp white sheet before a hesitant smile began to form. Looked like she didn't take sugar after all. Fact learned.

Isobel was sorry that she'd missed Marion. The sister had been true to her word and had woken her at eleven thirty, then at two a.m. and again at five, gradually lengthening the periods of sleep. She'd been woken for the last time at seven thirty by the oncoming shift.

She'd heard the staff talking, and the snippets had told her she would be moved to a different ward later today. Apparently both her short- and long-term memory abilities were showing positive signs. She had retained the fact that she preferred toast without jam and that Duncan was her boyfriend. Her physical recovery was being hailed as miraculous.

Part of Isobel didn't want to be moved, despite all the indications that she was recovering.

There was safety in the silent, cloistered environment where foot traffic was kept to a minimum. But she was breathing without aid, her morphine had been successfully reduced and she'd managed to get some sleep.

She experienced a brief second of panic that Duncan wouldn't be able to find her. She reassured herself that the staff would point him in the right direction. She hated it when he had to leave and looked forward to his return. Just the feel of his palm against hers was a comfort.

When he returned she would ask him again about their dates. And she would keep on asking until she could remember herself. Maybe one time he would recall something different which would spark a memory of her own.

She found herself touching the scars on her wrist. There was a familiarity in the gesture. Why had she done this to herself? Before she'd been abducted, what in her life could have been so bad that she'd felt death was the answer? The irony was that she had very nearly had that wish granted by her attacker.

Her mind returned to the dreams that had taunted her during the night. Being carried, being touched but not sexually. A voice. Each time she'd been woken she had tried to make sense of the images that were no more than shadows dancing in the cave of her mind.

Isobel had now stopped grasping. She had learned that chasing the activity in her own mind was like trying to hold on to an oil-covered eel.

No, she couldn't bring the images into focus, but she knew what she'd heard.

One for you and one for me. And there was a female somewhere called Mandy.

They were two pieces of information that didn't grow, no matter how many times she looked at them. Two little nuggets that she twisted and turned in her mind, looking at them from every angle like a precious stone being inspected for its carat.

But the nuggets remained the same. Precious because they had come from somewhere inside her head, had managed to crawl out of the locked box.

The day nurse approached and checked her teacup.

'It's gone cold, love,' she said.

She opened her mouth to say something about sugar but closed it again as she saw the unmistakeable figure of the policewoman she'd met yesterday.

She had asked the ward sister to give the detective a call as soon as she'd woken, but she hadn't expected to see her quite yet.

'Hey, how are you doing?' the woman asked.

Isobel smiled at her visitor. Strangely she felt very pleased to see her.

Yesterday she'd been intimidated by the manner of the female detective. But today she was reassured. There was honesty in that face, and although the mouth didn't smile much there was a passion behind the dark eyes.

'I'm okay, I think I'm being moved later.'

The officer shook her head as she sat down. 'I've asked them to keep you here for just a little while longer. I don't think you're ready to be moved.'

'You mean you haven't caught him yet?'

The words were out before she could stop them.

The detective raised one eyebrow. 'Let's just say I'd be happier if you stayed here a little while longer.'

Isobel was not unhappy at the police's involvement. Until her memory returned she relished the safety of the cloistered environment.

'I don't like sugar,' she said, shrugging her shoulders.

'Neither do I,' the officer answered.

'I need to tell you some things, but I don't know if they mean anything,' she blurted out. Now the detective was sitting here in front of her the things she had to say seemed inconsequential. Not least because she couldn't substantiate that she'd heard either one of them while she'd been with her captor.

It could just as easily have come from her previous life.

'*Mandy*. I think he may have someone else – someone called Mandy. I keep hearing the name, but I can't recognise the voice. It might be nothing. It might be completely unrelated, and I might be sending you...'

'It's okay,' the officer said, patting her hand. 'It's up to me to decide what's relevant. Just tell me anything that comes into your mind.'

'One for you and one for me,' she blurted out.

'What?' the officer asked.

Isobel shrugged her confusion. 'I know. It's strange, but when I close my eyes the phrase plays like it's on a loop. The trouble is I don't know if that's because of me.' She felt the sigh building inside her as the tears pricked her eyes. 'I just don't know anything any more. I don't know the difference between a thought and a memory. I just don't know what's real.'

'Hey, don't get upset. You're doing brilliantly.'

The cool, firm hand was resting on her arm. The strength she felt pulsating through stemmed her tears.

'You've suffered a horrendous attack that was intended to end your life. You fought yourself out of a coma, and your body is trying to heal. So give yourself a break, eh?'

Isobel noticed the absence of any false reassurances that her memory would return. They both knew it might never happen, so the officer didn't bother to indulge in the pretence.

Her visitor stood and Isobel felt an immediate sense of loneliness. There was a security that surrounded this woman. Although her manner was brusque and unyielding, Isobel enjoyed the frankness in her face.

'Anyway, it's only the really famous that can carry off having only one name,' she said, glancing at the nameplate above her bed that stated simply 'Isobel'.

Isobel smiled at the statement as the detective squeezed her arm. 'I'll be back to check on you again, okay?'

Isobel nodded her thanks. She found the prospect reassuring.

With a final smile, the officer turned and walked away, her gait confident and assured.

Immediately the ward felt empty and dark, like a light had gone out.

Isobel had the sudden urge to shout after her to tell her she didn't want her to go. She wanted to beg her to stay.

For just a short while, she had felt safe, as though nothing could reach into this ward and get her. But as the police officer walked away she felt exposed, vulnerable.

She realised that she would feel that way until the bastard was caught.

CHAPTER SIXTY-SEVEN

'How is she?' Bryant asked as she got back into the car.

'Looking better than yesterday. Despite her improvement I've asked the ward to hang on to her for a bit.'

'You think she's still at risk?' he asked, pulling out of the car park.

Kim knew that the ratio of staff to patients dictated there was always someone close by. Unknown visitors did not get to walk around at any time of the day.

'She's not dead. So definitely not safe yet. Isobel keeps hearing the name Mandy,' Kim said doubtfully. 'I've already called Stacey to see what she can find, but it's hard to know what's real with her.'

'Any nurses or staff members by that name?' Bryant asked.

Kim shook her head. 'No, I checked and no patients either.'

Bryant sighed. 'Are you thinking we're looking for another one, as well as Tracy?'

Kim tried to make sense of what she'd heard from Isobel. 'If he had another one at the same time then where is she? We know that Westerley is his dumping ground so…'

'Could be another old one, yet to be found.'

That was exactly what she'd been thinking.

'Isobel also said something about *one for you and one for me*. She said it plays on a loop in her head.'

Kim sighed with frustration. The words meant nothing to her.

'I can hear it,' Bryant offered in a sing-song voice.

'What?' she asked.

'That change in your voice. It's very telling.'

Kim frowned at him. She wasn't aware of any change in her voice.

'It's when a case stops being a case and becomes a personal mission.'

She shook her head and looked out of the window as the car headed towards Pedmore Road. 'You really do talk some rubbish.'

'It's true. You begin each case with a desire to see justice done. Eventually, and it always comes, your motivation changes as you become more familiar with the victims and—'

'Hang on, my visit to Isobel—'

'Is not what I'm talking about, because I don't only mean the living ones. It's the same with the dead. You somehow manage to create an affinity and then the change occurs. You no longer want the killer for the sake of justice. Now it's for Jemima, Louise, Isobel and even Tracy. It's personal now. And your voice changes, that's all I'm saying.'

Kim opened her mouth to argue and then had another thought as he drove along Reddall Hill towards Cradley Heath high street.

She turned to look at him. 'How are you driving when I haven't even told you where I want to go next?'

He pulled into the supermarket car park and nodded to the other side of the street. 'Got a call from Stacey while you were in the hospital. Elsie Hinton, ex-dinner lady at Cornheath, works there.'

'You know, it would be good to tell me these things as there's a filthy rumour going around that I'm actually in charge,' Kim snapped.

She was still smarting over his inference that she was emotionally involved.

She watched as he passed space after space in the supermarket car park.

'Bryant, what the hell are you doing?'

'Looking for a parent and baby spot.'

'Just park the bloody car,' she growled.

The café sat opposite the supermarket and was wedged between a family-run carpet shop and a building society. The area inside was small, holding six tables, but was brightly decorated with black-and-white photos of Cradley Heath high street on the wall.

The smell of bacon, sausage and coffee grew stronger as they approached the counter. Kim could tell immediately that neither of the women they could see was the one they were after.

'Elsie Hinton?' Bryant asked doubtfully.

'Not here yet,' said the younger woman. 'And who are you?'

The question was direct but not rude.

'We just need a word with her. Got an address?'

She smiled as though he'd tried to catch her out. 'Nah, mate, not happening. She'll be here in about ten minutes. Park yourselves if you want.'

Bryant looked to Kim and she nodded. She took a few steps back and sat beneath a photo of the old Christ Church that had once towered over the Five Ways intersection. It had been demolished to make way for an access road to the new supermarket.

She heard the hiss and puff of the drinks machine behind her and Bryant's laugh as he shared a joke with the woman serving him.

She marvelled at his easy manner and affable nature. He was one of life's charmers, possessing the ability to relate to most people he met.

She wondered how that quality had actually been inserted into his personality. Had Bryant been the kid everyone had flocked around at school, or was it a quality that he had grown into and perfected over the years?

Whatever it was, she was grateful for the balance he offered to their team despite his ability to annoy the hell out of her.

'Double shot, latte,' he said, placing a glass mug on the table. His own beverage was a pot of tea for one.

He sat down as a girl in her late teens entered the café with a double buggy. Only one seat held a child. The other was filled with carrier bags.

Bryant stood back up and held the door while the girl folded herself around the pushchair into the café.

Kim watched as the teenage mum expertly released her son from the buggy. His arms instantly reached out to be plucked from the carriage. It was a ritual understood and executed by both.

'Storm is coming,' Bryant observed, stirring the tea bag in the metal pot.

'Good,' Kim said. The cloying heat had been building for days.

Bryant shook his head. 'You prefer rain to sunshine?'

'Yep,' she said.

'I mean, how can anyone hate the summer?' he asked, pouring the bronze liquid into a plain white teacup.

It was easy if your most traumatic memories were encased in a wall of sticky heat.

A cry sounded from the little boy as his mother placed him into a high chair. Each time she tried to sit him in it, his legs straightened so they wouldn't slide down.

Kim looked away to hide her smile. Another routine practised and perfected – this time by the child.

'We could be wrong about Tracy, you know?' Bryant said. 'She might just have needed some space to clear her head. Get away from stuff.'

Kim agreed.

A loud wail came from the little boy. He was trapped in the chair but was trying to wriggle his lower limbs free. He bucked his legs back and forth, raising them up and down.

'I just think we're making one hell of an assumption…'

'Shhh…' Kim said as she continued watching the child's attempts to escape.

He leaned forwards, trying to climb out of his trap. His stomach smashed against the food tray before him.

'Guv…?'

Kim ignored Bryant as the child again flailed his legs back and forth in an effort to get them free.

The back of his thighs bumped up and down on the wooden edge of the seat.

'Yo, guv…?'

'Bryant, shut up,' she said, unable to tear her gaze away.

The child used his chubby little fingers to grab the end of the food tray, pulling himself forwards against the edge.

'Oh, I think that might be our woman now,' Bryant said, nodding towards the door.

Finally Kim turned to her colleague, dumbfounded yet sure she was right.

'Bryant, the marks on our victims that we can't work out…'

She couldn't believe what she was about to say.

'The bastard has them chained in a high chair.'

CHAPTER SIXTY-EIGHT

Tracy put every ounce of effort she had into opening her eyes.

She felt like a weightlifter in a clean and jerk final, focussing every ounce of strength to lift two flaps of skin from her eyeballs.

She managed to raise them up, but initially she wasn't sure she had. A few seconds later, her eyes adjusted to the darkness. In the distance strange shapes were evident in the black.

'H-hello…' she whispered to the shadows that danced along the wall. The returning silence was terrifying.

She could feel liquid tracing a line from the corner of her mouth and knew that it was drool travelling along her cheek towards her lower jaw.

She tried to raise her hand, but it wouldn't move. Her fuddled brain simply caused her eyes to stare down, wondering why. She tried again before realising that her wrist was confined, but she couldn't see what was holding her.

It took a full minute before she realised that her other hand was not restrained. She shook her head, trying to clear the fog. A dozen spiders had spun webs in her brain.

Her arm lifted as though gravity was fighting it back down. She idly wondered if she was trapped in one of those dreams where your legs just won't move, however hard you try.

A flash of hope found her in the darkness. Maybe it was all a dream. Perhaps she would wake up back home.

Even while the hope tried to claim her, the logical part of her brain was coming alive too. The pain around her wrist was too raw, too jagged to be in her imagination. It cut right to her nerves. Her own thoughts, although slow, were real.

She knew she wasn't asleep and silently cursed the ray of hope that had momentarily distracted her.

She tried to scoot down in the chair. Maybe she could topple the seat forwards and somehow free her wrist, but no matter how she stretched her legs, her dangling feet met with nothing but space.

She could feel a bar in the small of her back and some kind of tray in front of her.

Tracy desperately tried to think back to the last thing she remembered.

She had left the café and had been heading back to the car. A packet of sweets had been spilled all over the floor. She was looking down, concentrating on her footing and then... nothing.

She could feel the tenderness of bruises on her skin, so she guessed she had fought.

A sudden fear clutched at her stomach. What the hell was she doing trying to make sense of the situation – all she really needed to focus on was the knowledge that she was probably going to die.

She raised her right hand and shook it. The metal hit against the wood but held fast.

She tried to squeeze the whole of her hand through the perfect circle. It wouldn't even reach her knuckles. She tried again but faster, hoping to fool the circular binding into letting her go.

A sudden bang sounded somewhere above, which stunned her into temporary paralysis; the noise travelled straight to her heart and pumped the blood around her veins.

She had waited too long. Spent valuable time trying to understand what had happened and where she was, and now it was too late. It was ironic that it was that same lethargy that had landed her here in the first place.

Tracy heard the cry that escaped from her own lips. It was desperate and strangled.

She pushed herself forwards and felt the chair rock but not enough.

She threw herself backwards. Again there was movement but not enough momentum to launch the chair.

Damn it, she had to do something – and quickly.

She reared backwards once more, using the weight of her thigh muscles. This time she felt two of the chair legs lift from the ground.

She poised to try it again as the door suddenly opened.

A shaft of artificial light surrounded a silhouette.

Her eyes stung at the sudden intrusion into the darkness. She blinked a couple of times as the shadows on the wall danced in the dim light.

The figure took two steps and switched on the light.

Tracy looked to the walls and understood the form of the shadows.

The silhouette had now moved closer. The light from behind no longer obscured her view.

Her blood froze in her veins as her eyes registered what her mind refused to comprehend.

CHAPTER SIXTY-NINE

'Nah, still can't picture it, guv,' Bryant said as the mother and child left the café.

Kim ignored him and continued to watch as the mother smoothed down the child's clothing before putting him in the buggy. She pulled down his striped T-shirt and pulled up his green shorts.

'Look, after fifteen minutes,' she said.

Bryant had to turn in his chair, but he saw what she meant. Two faint lines were visible on the back of his legs.

He shook his head. 'The marks on our girls could be from anything.'

Kim disagreed. 'I bet if you lift that child's T-shirt he has the exact same line across his stomach.'

'You're on your own with that one,' he guffawed. 'No way I'm asking her if we can inspect her child.'

Kim ignored him. A part of her thought he had a point. Why the hell would the victims be put in a high chair? And yet those marks were just too similar to ignore.

'Hey up, she's coming,' Bryant said as the woman who'd entered the café approached their table.

'You've been after me?' she said, standing between them.

Kim looked up into the worn and kindly face. Kim guessed Elsie Hinton to be mid-sixties with a lifetime of hard work behind her.

'Please sit down,' Kim said, pulling out a chair.

She nodded back towards the counter. The two women were trying to hide their curious glances.

'We won't keep you long,' Kim said, as Bryant approached the counter to explain they needed a few minutes of this employee's time.

Kim took the time to introduce them both. Elsie simply nodded with the confidence of someone who knew she had done nothing wrong.

Bryant returned to his seat as Kim continued speaking.

'We need to ask you about an incident that happened some years ago at Cornheath primary school. We've spoken to Mr Jackson, who has helped us, but we're hoping you can add to that. Dinner ladies know everything,' Kim said. It wasn't a compliment or an insult. It was just fact.

'It happened in the sports hall. One of the kids was humiliated, held down and exposed. Do you recall?'

Elsie closed her eyes as the disgust shaped her mouth. She nodded. 'Yes, I remember. There were four or five of them that pinned the little mite down. And a fair few others that watched. One of them eventually ran to the staff room and got help…'

'Tracy Frost?' Kim asked.

Elsie nodded. 'Yes, yes, I think that was her name. I didn't even know why she was trying to run along the corridor when she passed me, but I do recall the names she was being called as she went. Tears were streaming down her cheeks, but she carried on until she got to the staff room. Her disability was more obvious the faster she moved.'

Kim couldn't help the pang of regret that shot through her.

'Can you tell us the names of the other girls involved?' Bryant asked.

She looked surprised. 'Oh goodness, now you've asked me something. I'm not sure I can recall their names now. It was so long ago.'

Kim didn't want to spoon-feed the names in case the woman's memory or lack of it prompted her to agree.

'There was a girl with a name that reminded me of a doll,' she said.

'Jemima,' Bryant offered.

'Yes, that's it,' Elsie said, smiling.

'Louise?' he continued.

'Yes, there was a Louise there, I think.'

Kim stepped in. 'How about Joanna?'

She thought and then nodded. 'Yes, there was a Joanna there also.'

Kim glanced at Bryant. She was guessing she could work her way through a baby girls' name book and Elsie Hinton would agree that they'd all been there.

Bryant returned her glance with a look that said it was worth one last try.

He leaned forwards. 'And can you tell us the name of the girl being held down?'

Elsie looked from one to the other. 'Oh, Mr Jackson didn't remember it very well, did he? The child being held on the floor was a little boy.'

CHAPTER SEVENTY

It was that day that changed my life for ever.

I looked over to where the gym mats were piled high but Louise wasn't looking that way.

She was looking at me.

Her face was strange. There was a smile, but it didn't make me feel happy inside. It made me feel scared.

Louise nodded and suddenly everyone started moving towards me. Louise was in front with that excited look on her face, and the others all looked the same.

I backed away.

My stomach turned, and I didn't know why.

'Get her, Jemima,' Louise said.

I didn't know who Jemima was.

A girl with short blonde hair emerged from the pack and moved to my left. I looked from her to Louise.

My back hit the cool metal wall bars.

Jemima grabbed at my left arm and pulled me towards her. Louise grabbed at my right. They pulled me in different directions. I didn't know which way they wanted me to go.

I pushed my back against the bars.

'You two get her legs,' Louise said.

One of the girls limped forwards and reached down. I kicked out to make them stop, but the girl with the limp caught my left ankle and pulled.

I fell to the ground.

'Stop it,' I cried as a sea of faces began to gather above me, blocking out the light.

Louise's face came closer – excited, curious, determined.

'Please leave me alone,' I begged.

'Shut up,' Jemima said, removing my shoe.

'Get off me,' I cried.

Jemima shoved my sock in my mouth. My cries were muffled by the cloth.

The faces above peered closer, a ceiling of excited expressions.

I felt my pretty yellow dress being pushed up my legs. Cool air found its way to my thighs.

'Do it, do it, do it,' a few voices began to chant.

Do what? I wanted to scream.

The chatter was almost deafening. The nervous giggles were fanning my fear.

I thrashed my head trying to see into their faces. I needed to know what I'd done, and I would never do it again.

I would promise.

The chanting got louder. 'Do it, do it, do it.'

Clumsy little fingers pinched my skin as they grabbed for my knickers.

The faces got closer.

I tried to move, but there was nowhere to go. I was cocooned in a web of faces peering down at me.

The chanting was louder in my ear as the heads came closer and closer, suffocating me.

'Do it, do it, do it.'

I wanted to cover my eyes and my ears.

The stubby fingers pulled at my panties. The elastic moved down my thigh. The fabric was gathered at my knees.

The chanting suddenly stopped. For a second I was relieved. They were going to let me up now. They were going to let me go.

'Look, look, she has a willy!' Louise screamed.

The first laugh was nervous, unsure and then another joined in, and then another.

'I told you, didn't I?' Louise cried triumphantly.

The laughter grew louder. Even louder than the chants.

The faces swam before me as heat flooded my face.

I didn't know what a willy was, but somehow it sounded wrong.

The laughter was booming into my head.

Louise's face came closer to mine.

'You're a little girl with a willy,' she said, and the laughter exploded.

My tummy began to swim, and I tried to cry out against the cloth. I just wanted to make it stop.

'Little girls don't have willies,' Jemima cried.

The laughter kept growing louder, but then a small voice sounded beside me.

'Stop it,' it said.

I wondered if my thoughts had made it out of my head.

'Stop it, all of you.'

I realised that the voice hadn't come from me. It had come from the girl with the limp.

I knew it would never end. I knew that I would be pinned to the ground for the rest of my life.

My vision began to blur, and the faces all melted together. I wanted to make it stop, block it out.

I closed my eyes, but I couldn't close my ears.

The laughter and chanting went on, the faces continued to hover above me long after Mrs Shaw stood me up and led me away.

They never went away, Mummy. Every time I closed my eyes, they were there. Every time my ears held no other sound, they were there. Every time I lay down to sleep, they were there.

And it was THAT DAY I began to hate you, Mummy. For making me a fucking freak.

CHAPTER SEVENTY-ONE

Tracy tried to hide her repulsion at the figure that stood before her. She felt she might have walked onto the set of a horror film or a funhouse at the fair.

The thing wore a full-length brown pinafore dress. Two mock pockets adorned the shapeless garment.

Lurid, hairy legs protruded from the square-cut material.

But that wasn't the part that frightened her.

The hair was short but two tiny pigtails stuck out from the head, held in place by tightly wound plastic bands. It reminded Tracy of bows put in babies' hair when there was barely anything there to hold.

The make-up was heavy and striking as though applied by a child playing at dress up. All the colour without the skill.

The red slash of lipstick was untidy, giving the face a manic, terrifying expression.

The eyes were alight and bright with excitement.

'Hello, Tracy, do you remember me?'

The voice was masculine but gentle. Not unkind. It frightened her even more. There was ease, relaxation.

'Wh-what…?' she said, shaking her head.

'It's me, Graham. You knew me as Maria. You must remember my first day at school all those years ago?'

Tracy swallowed down the fear. It was what she had been afraid of since hearing of Jemima's murder.

'I'm... I-I don't... ' she spluttered. She had no idea what to say to him, to her, to it.

'I've waited a long time for this.'

The words alone were not what sent terror screaming through Tracy's veins. It was the cool detachment with which they were delivered. There was a sense of calm, which meant there was no pressure, no rush.

He turned to the side and she had a good look around.

The rows upon rows of shelves of dolls mocked her from their spectator positions on the wall. Some hung from the ceiling, dangling by a single limb, their dresses fallen over their heads.

An alcove to her left was furnished with glass shelves. The top one held a porcelain tea set. A design of tulips wound its way around cups, saucers, milk and sugar jugs.

Her eyes travelled to the next shelf down and her heart stopped.

Placed beneath the tea set were rocks. They were dark grey, almost black, and jagged as though they'd been torn like a piece of bread from a rock face. All of them were bloody. Two long blonde hairs dangled from the one on the right.

She fought down the nausea as she recalled that Jemima had been blonde.

She tore her gaze away before she threw up.

Looking down she could now see that she had been placed in a wooden contraption similar to the ones used for children. It was formed of mismatched pieces of wood and had been scaled up. Her feet dangled about ten inches from the ground. Beneath her thighs was a strip of unvarnished timber an inch wide that dug into her flesh. A serving tray was wedged against her stomach, forcing her in place. Nails that hadn't been properly hammered in protruded from most of the joints. Grey masking tape was wrapped around the front right leg. It wasn't a chair – it was a prison.

Amongst the dolls and the child-sized furniture Tracy felt like Alice in Wonderland.

The figure looked her up and down and smiled. 'Hello, Tracy doll. We're going to play a little game – but first I need to get you ready.'

CHAPTER SEVENTY-TWO

'Stace, start looking for anything to do with the name Graham Studwick,' Kim said once they were outside the café.

Kim didn't know just how reliable Elsie's memory was on the little boy's name – she had agreed with them that half the school had been involved – but it was all they had right now.

'Okay, boss, and I have something for you. When Ivor Grogan was imprisoned eight years ago he was found guilty on two counts but not guilty on a third. I've got the addresses of all the families, but that third family never got any justice so…'

'Send all the addresses to Bryant,' Kim instructed. 'And ring me the second you have anything on that name.'

She ended the call and looked to Bryant, who was shaking his head.

'Looks like we were wrong and you were right, guv, about it being a man,' he offered.

She snorted as she got into the car. 'Don't count my chickens too soon, Bryant, because at this stage who the hell knows anything?'

CHAPTER SEVENTY-THREE

The house of Stuart Hawkins lay behind the Timbertree pub at the mouth of a council estate lodged between Cradley Heath and Belle Vale, Halesowen.

The house had net curtains that were mismatched but appeared clean. The cul-de-sac was small with a thin road separating two rows of properties. With no driveways, parking space was at a premium.

Bryant had parked the car in the turning circle at the closed end of the road.

Kim was about to knock on the door when it opened. The man exiting was tall and dressed in navy overalls, with a clear plastic sandwich box tucked under his arm and a set of car keys positioned in his hand. The initial surprise at the near collision was replaced with a frown.

'Mr Hawkins?' Bryant asked quickly.

He nodded, but the puzzled expression remained.

Bryant introduced them.

He made a point of looking at his watch. 'I'm due to start my shift at—'

'It's about Ivor Grogan,' Kim said.

She had his attention. He hesitated for a second before stepping back into the house and holding open the front door.

The hallway led past a lounge and into the kitchen. What had previously been two rooms had been knocked into one and dressed as a dining room.

Stuart Hawkins placed himself on the other side of the breakfast bar and let go of his sandwich box.

'We understand your daughter had an incident with Ivor Grogan,' Kim said.

His jaw tensed and his nostrils flared. 'You mean she was sexually assaulted by the sick scumbag bastard?'

Yes, that as well, she thought, but her description of the event had been intentional. She had wanted to see his reaction.

'He was found not guilty?' Kim asked quietly.

'Only because of the involvement of the hypnotherapist.'

Kim was confused for a second, but she quickly caught up.

'How old is your daughter, Mr Hawkins?'

'Thirty-four now,' he responded. The fatigue in his voice spoke volumes.

'Recovered memory?' Kim asked.

Stuart Hawkins nodded. 'His defence made all kinds of claims of false memory syndrome or some such shit.' He paused. 'I mean, if you were gonna give yourself a false memory, would it really be one like that?'

Kim had to agree that he had a point; however she knew that there were professionals out there who had been entrusted with the safety and well-being of members of the general public and somehow used that to their own advantage. She had almost been destroyed by one such person.

'Trouble is, the memory is there now with no resolution. Ella can't get justice for what was done to her. She wishes she'd never visited the hypnotherapist, and don't even get me started on reporting it to the police.'

'What prompted Ella to go to the therapist in the first place?' Kim asked.

'She couldn't come to terms with the loss of her mother. She was fifteen when Trish died, and I could have probably handled it better. Ten years later she's still sleeping around, shoplifting, drinking heavily and even she didn't know why. After a few months with a psychologist he suggested she visit the hypnotherapist. About a year later she recalled the details of the assault.'

'May I ask…?'

'She was eleven years old, and it happened at the swimming baths,' he stated matter-of-factly. Kim realised he still dealt with it as though it had happened to someone else. If he considered the detail of what he'd just said in relation to his child, she assumed he wouldn't be quite as calm.

'How is she now?' she asked.

'Still sleeping around and drinking heavily if you want the truth. Before she recalled the memory she was doing it and didn't know why, and now she's doing it to forget what she found out. A bit fucked up, don't you think?'

'Do you think it will make any difference to her that Ivor Grogan is dead?' Bryant asked. His identity had been announced on the news the previous evening.

He shook his head. 'Not to her, but it does to me and before you ask, no it wasn't me that got him. If I had I'd admit it and do the time. Happily.'

'Mr Hawkins, that's—'

'You got kids?' he asked Bryant suddenly. 'Girls?'

'One,' Bryant answered.

Stuart nodded. 'Then don't pretend to disagree with me because you've got your work clothes on.'

He turned back to Kim.

'Inspector, if I'd done it I'd be able to look my child in the eye again. I'd shake the hand of the man who did. I'll bet he's a father too, and he showed more guts than me.'

Kim heard the bitterness. And the guilt. Had Stuart Hawkins exacted revenge for his daughter while also assuaging his guilt?

He hadn't been able to prevent the assault on his child and he had been less than perfect when he'd lost his wife.

The same person had killed both Ivor and Larry, of that she was sure… but the man in front of her had motive only for Ivor.

Kim felt the phone vibrating in her back pocket as Stuart Hawkins picked up his lunch box.

She nodded her thanks and headed back out the door.

'What've you got, Stace?' she answered.

'The name of a social worker you might like to meet,' Stacey answered.

'Dealings with Graham Studwick?' Kim clarified.

'Yeah, boss, the one that took him away when his mum died.'

'Good work, Stace. Send it to my phone, and keep digging on the name. We need all the information we can get.'

Bryant appeared beside the car as she ended the call.

'Didn't really give us a lot, eh?' Bryant said

'What it does tell us, Bryant, is that Ivor Grogan had been getting away with abusing kids for years.'

CHAPTER SEVENTY-FOUR

Tracy knew that she'd been drugged again. The thing had given her a drink. She had refused, and then his face had changed. The gentle eyes had been suffused with rage and his jaw had been set.

She had felt the danger as he had taken steps towards her, but still she had refused to drink.

He had moved behind her and yanked her head back so quickly that Tracy thought her neck would snap. Her mouth had fallen open with shock and that had been the only advantage he'd needed.

She could feel the drug travelling around her bloodstream, injecting its lethargy into her flesh. The muscles in her body felt as though they were dissolving away from her bones. Every ounce of her strength had been zapped, and she could barely lift her head.

Through the haze she heard the bang of the door above. Her heart hammered in her chest. She knew she couldn't fight him with her muscles melting away.

She wondered if she could find the strength to talk to him, beg for her life. Had Jemima begged for hers?

Tracy wanted to scream out that she had tried to help, but knew he would answer, *Not quickly enough*.

And he would be right.

The tears were hot and salty as they fell onto her cheeks, and she knew she was crying for both of them. They'd been children, stupid little children who could never have imagined the repercussions of their actions. That their one act of mindless cruelty could impact him so heavily, that the jibes and laughter could shape the person he would become.

And yet they had done the same to her.

But she had been the one, the only one that had tried to help him. She had understood him even then, had known how it felt and had wanted to end his pain.

The injustice of the situation added bitterness to Tracy's throat. She knew she was still going to die.

She gulped back the tears. She knew that she shouldn't displease him. The expression on his face and the rage that had exploded from his pores were not things she wanted to see again.

The door opened and the light went on. There were no windows in the room, which suggested they were underground, but she had no idea where. There were no sounds other than the bang from above that signalled he was on his way.

She saw that he carried a bowl of water and a small cosmetics bag over his arm. If only she had the strength to raise her legs, she could kick the contents of the bowl in his face, offering her a moment to try to get herself free. But she couldn't even wiggle her toes.

'It's time to get you clean and ready,' he said, sitting on a stool in front of her.

Ready for what? she wanted to ask, but it was clear that the affable mood had returned, and for the moment she was thankful.

He placed the bowl on the floor and opened the bag. He took out a cloth and bottle.

He dipped the cloth into the bowl and gently dabbed at her feet. He rubbed a bar of soap onto the cloth until it began to lather.

He took her left foot in his other hand and began to soap it.

His touch was gentle, and she suddenly wanted to cry. She felt every part of her foot being cleaned before he rested it gently on his leg.

A tear slipped from her eye as he dabbed gently at her toes. The smell told her he was using nail polish remover to take the red stain from her nails.

'Don't cry, Tracy,' he said, smiling up to her. 'There's nothing to be upset about.'

He took a disposable razor from the bag and ran it up and down her leg. The blunt blade pulled and tore at the short stubble protruding from her skin.

He reached into the bag again and removed a pack of baby wipes. He ripped one from the packet and another sprang up. He grabbed that one too and placed them together.

He pushed back the pink plastic chair and moved towards her, standing between her chair and the miniature table.

First he wiped gently at her forehead. Slow movements across her brow and then tender circles, small ones growing bigger.

'Close your eyes,' he said and she did.

She felt the damp wipe move across her eyelid, gently. Not enough pressure to hurt but enough to lift the stale eyeshadow and bitty mascara from her eyes. He repeated the process on her other eye.

'So much better, Tracy. You can open them now.'

She did so.

He was not looking into her eyes. His gaze was focussed on her cheek as he rubbed in bigger circles all the way down to her jaw. He moved across her chin and then up the other side and over her nose.

Finally he rubbed at both lips together.

He stepped back and assessed her face. One more rub of her lips and he was done.

He reached for the toiletry bag and took out a brush. He moved behind her and Tracy held her breath.

The prongs of the brush touched the back of her head but did not scratch it. He held her long hair firmly so that the brushing motion didn't pull at her head.

He worked his way from the back rhythmically to the left-hand side, taking care not to catch her ear as he brushed the hair down. Despite the drugs that were attacking her muscles she could feel every touch to her flesh.

He then worked from the centre of the back of her head around to the right. This time he accidentally nicked the top of her ear. Immediately he stopped brushing. She felt his hands on her shoulders as he leaned into her and planted a kiss where he had nicked.

'I'm sorry, my precious little girl,' he said tenderly.

Tracy had to work hard not to pull away. Whatever fantasy he was living, she did not want to disturb it.

He completed the brushing and once more stepped to the front of her. She could see that his left hand was clenched closed.

He reached towards her forehead and smoothed away her fringe to the side. He opened his hand to reveal two kirby grips, as her mother called them. But these were white in colour, unlike the plain brown ones that had held her mother's rollers in place.

Placed at the curve of each hair clip was a jagged heart. He slipped them both into her hair to hold back her fringe.

'That's better – now I can see your face,' he said, tipping his head. 'Now you're ready to play.'

The tenderness in his voice brought fresh tears to Tracy's eyes. She knew she was being prepared to die.

CHAPTER SEVENTY-FIVE

'I've not been here before,' Bryant said, turning the car into a car park that hugged half of the two-storey building.

The Elms formed part of the Dudley and Walsall Mental Health Partnership. This particular building focussed on Child and Adolescent Mental Health Services, otherwise known as CAMHS.

'Do social workers operate out of here?'

Kim shrugged. 'Not sure, but this is where Stacey said she's working.'

The double doors opened automatically into a functional annex with plastic chairs around the perimeter. A glass window fronted a general office area behind.

Kim approached it and tapped on the window. A second too late she saw the bell that said 'Ring me'.

A man in his early twenties with hair over his eyes approached the window.

'Can I help?' he said through the diamond of air holes drilled into the glass.

'Valerie Wood – she's expecting us,' Kim said, holding up her badge to the window.

The male looked neither impressed nor concerned. She reminded herself this was a building that dealt with troubled adolescents.

He headed to the rear of the office and made a call. He nodded a couple of times and then made a waving motion their way, indicating they should take a seat.

Kim stepped away from the window but paced around the space.

This didn't feel like any of the facilities she'd visited as a child. But she knew it was. The processes didn't change all that much. *Get it out, talk about it, you'll feel better afterwards.*

Wanna bet? Kim had always thought. She had always chosen silence.

A woman used a card hanging around her neck to key herself out of the main building and into the annex.

Kim guessed her to be late fifties with blonde curly hair that lived close to her head. Her face was devoid of make-up and a few deep wrinkles were etched around her mouth and eyes. A small gap showed between her front teeth as she smiled.

'Valerie Wood, how can I help you?'

So Stacey had asked if she had time to see them but hadn't told her what it was about.

'Do you recall a case concerning a male named Graham Studwick?' Kim asked.

Valerie's eyes widened. 'Back in my social-worker days, yes, why?'

'Could we ask you a few questions?'

She considered for a moment and then nodded. 'Come outside, I'm due a smoke break anyway.'

Kim followed as the woman headed outside and removed a small box and tiny lighter from the back pocket of her jeans.

'Terrible habit,' she said, drawing on the cigarette. 'I give up after every one.'

'So you were a social worker?' Kim asked, just to understand the relationship between this woman and their suspect better.

'In a former life – but it wasn't for me. You have to learn to switch off, and if you can't learn that, you don't last long. I didn't last long. Graham was actually one of my last cases and definitely one of the reasons I made the move to psychology.'

'Why?'

'Because that kid needed to talk. He needed more than a social worker. He needed a therapist. He needed a friend, a confidante… but with thirty-nine cases you can't be all those things. Oh, and I wasn't all that good at hiding my feelings around neglectful parents.'

Kim fought a smile back into her mouth. She suspected she would suffer the same issues in that profession.

'At what stage did you get involved?' Kim asked.

'How much do you know?' Valerie asked, demonstrating the reason Kim had never done well with psychologists as a child.

'We know that Graham suffered a horrifically embarrassing episode at school. Is that when you met him?' Kim asked.

Valerie shook her head. 'I met him when he was eleven years old. I know of the incident at school, but social services weren't called in then – God only knows why not – but he was taken out of the school system and taught at home by his mother. He never went to school again.'

'Is that legal?' Bryant asked.

She nodded. 'Oh yeah, home education is legal in all parts of the UK and always has been. It's as simple as deregistering your child, normally a simple letter, and then a proposal to the local authority of how you intend to educate your child.'

'But surely there are checks that the national curriculum is being met?' he pushed.

'It's not the responsibility of the state to educate your child, only to provide a suitable facility, should you require one. A parent is obliged to provide a suitable education for their child during compulsory school age. Schools are available to be used, but if a parent thinks they can do a better job they are within their rights to do so.'

'You're telling me that Graham's mother was able to remove him from the school system with no supervision at all?' Kim asked incredulously.

'Absolutely. The law is clear that there is no legal duty for a local authority to monitor the education provision and would only conduct a home visit in rare or extreme circumstances.'

Kim took a moment to digest this information.

Valerie continued. 'You know his mother was feeding him hormones from the age of three?'

Kim shook her head. No, she hadn't known that, but something else was confusing her. If neither the uncovering of his true sex or his absence from school had prompted the intervention of social services, then what the hell had?

'So how did the two of you meet?' she asked.

'I was the social worker that collected him from the home after the death of his mother. It was Graham that called the ambulance and the police.'

'Police?' Bryant asked.

Valerie nodded. 'Thank God he was never charged with the offence. After what his mother did to him, the kid had been through enough. He needed help, not punishment.'

Kim glanced at Bryant.

'I don't understand. Charged with what offence?'

Valerie stubbed out the cigarette on the top of the bin. 'Good grief, Inspector, you really don't know very much about him. The offence would have been murder. Graham Studwick admitted immediately that he was the one who had killed his mother.'

CHAPTER SEVENTY-SIX

Bryant showed more patience than she would have as he negotiated the rush-hour traffic building on a busy Friday afternoon.
She caught the occasional disbelieving shake of his head.

'What?' Kim asked.

'I can't believe the kid wasn't even charged.'

Kim had no trouble believing it at all. Valerie had happily
given them the detail of what had followed that day.

Eleven-year-old Graham had admitted to holding the pillow
over his mother's face until she could breathe no more. But he
had admitted it without the guidance of a responsible adult. The
young constable who had walked him from the house to the car
had asked a couple of questions that would have made the whole
confession inadmissible.

Graham had been lucky enough to secure a brief who had
known what he was doing and had got him admitted to Bromley
immediately.

The police investigation was further hampered by two inde-
pendent psychiatric reports stating that Graham's 'fitness to plead'
in Crown Court was not adequate.

Kim knew the decision of the CPS to prosecute was based on
a number of factors. Was it in the public interest? Past history,
probability of causing harm to others, need for treatment and
if that need was being provided. And the unspoken factor – the
likelihood of conviction.

Kim could understand why the CPS had chosen not to prosecute.

Bryant pulled the car straight onto the drive of the two-bed mid-terrace. The property sat back from the road in the Lyde Green area of Halesowen where it met Cradley Heath.

Only two windows were visible and both were suffocated by heavy net curtains.

Kim tried to peer through and could just make out that there were heavy draw curtains inside. Closed.

A covered entryway led to the back of the house. She headed that way and tried the gate. As it opened, Kim felt her heart sinking. Stacey had checked this was the correct address for a man named Graham Studwick, but her gut told her that the gate should have been locked if they were in the right place.

The gate opened onto a flat, long, thin garden that disappeared into a row of oak trees behind.

A decrepit shed was on her right. A quick glance inside revealed no garden tools, lawnmower or boy toys. There was no plant, bush or square foot of lawn to break up the slabbing that stretched from fence line to fence line.

'Bryant, I'm going in,' she said and tried the door. It was locked.

She tried the door to the shed. It opened. The only thing in there on the second shelf down was an upturned plant pot. She moved it and revealed a key.

'I'm just gonna check there's nothing hiding behind those trees,' Bryant said.

Kim tried the key in the door and, after a little force, it unlocked.

The back door led into a kitchen. A blackout blind held the room in total darkness.

She reached along the walls and found the light switch.

The room was empty. The counter tops were free of kettle, mugs, tea and coffee, the usual staples of a lived-in kitchen.

As she checked the cupboards each one revealed more and more empty space. The fridge and freezer were empty and switched off.

She stepped through a door to the front of the house. Again the space was dark but not dense. Two shafts of sunlight peeped around the edges of the heavy brown velour curtain, offering the minimum of light. But it was enough for Kim to see that the only thing the room contained was a carpet.

'About as homely as yours, guv,' Bryant offered.

Kim ignored him as she felt the claustrophobia of the room now it contained two of them.

She headed for the only other door, which revealed the stairs.

She took them two at a time, and after checking both bedrooms and the bathroom she found more of what she'd seen downstairs.

Nothing.

She headed back down to Bryant.

'This might be his address, but it's not where he lives.'

Kim knew that to move this case any further along she had to get a better comprehension of what she was up against.

She had to crawl inside the mind of their killer and understand how he thought. She couldn't even comprehend the mindset of a person like Graham.

Kim knew there was only one person she could ask.

CHAPTER SEVENTY-SEVEN

'Just there,' Kim said, pointing to a terraced house with a freshly painted door.

'Is this the guy you mentioned?'

Kim nodded.

'Want me to stay in the car?'

She took a moment to answer.

They were sitting outside the house of a man named Ted Knowles.

Throughout her childhood, periodically, she'd been sent to see Ted. She was supposed to talk to him so that he could help her come to terms with her pain. And she had steadfastly refused to utter a word about her life.

But he had not been like all the others.

If she'd chosen to open up to anyone it would have been Ted. More recently he had helped her get into the mind of a sociopath. And it had pretty much saved her life.

She took a deep breath. 'No, you can come in,' she answered.

Bryant gave her a long look before getting out of the car.

The twelve-year-old Citroën confirmed that the man was at home.

Two short knocks and the door was opened by a short, portly male whose head was hanging on to the last bit of hair around his ears. What he had left stuck out in a 'mad professor' kind of style. Unbelievably, in Kim's head this was exactly how he had looked twenty-eight years ago, when she was six years old.

His face broke into a smile at the sight of her and widened when his gaze rested on Bryant.

'Kim, how lovely to see you,' he said, stepping aside.

'This is Bryant, my colleague,' she said.

Ted offered his hand as Bryant passed.

'Not a social visit then?' he asked.

Despite the absence of reproach in his voice, Kim still felt a pang of guilt. She had only ever visited him when she needed something and today was no different.

'You're looking well,' she said and meant it.

'It must be those strange food hampers that come through once a month from Marks & Spencer's. Not a clue who sends them.'

She shrugged. Her lack of contact didn't mean she didn't think about him or wasn't grateful for his willingness to treat a victim damaged by the sociopath about whom she'd sought his help.

'How is Jemima's mother?' she asked.

'Making progress is all I shall say. Now you're here for something, and I'm sure you're busy so do you have time for coffee?'

Kim nodded as he reached for the mugs from the cupboard. They were all emblazoned with the insignia of the local football teams. Bryant got the Albion mug, she got the Wolves mug and Ted took the Aston Villa.

'So how can I help?' he asked.

Had Bryant not been with her, Kim knew that Ted would have delicately probed into her life. He would have asked if she'd visited her mother. He would have asked if she was talking to anyone. He would have asked if she had a boyfriend. And she would have tired of saying no.

None of those questions would he ever ask in the presence of someone else. But that wasn't why she had allowed Bryant to accompany her inside. She was a big girl and had been saying no to Ted for years.

She had allowed her colleague in because there was no reason not to. It was a matter of trust.

'We have a killer, and I need an idea of what I'm dealing with,' Kim said.

He nodded as he took his mug and headed out into the garden, which had changed very little since she was a child.

The outside border was like the Chelsea flower show. A sunken fish pond was the star of the show beneath a water-dribbling stone mermaid.

They each took a wooden chair around a circular table. Kim placed her back to the afternoon sun.

'In this case we actually know who he is – or rather was. His name is Graham Studwick and he was born male, but his mother dressed and treated him as a girl until he was eleven years old. At which point he murdered her.'

Ted showed little surprise. In his years as a psychologist there was little he had not seen.

'Okay, how about the crimes?'

'The first one occurred a few years ago. Her face was badly beaten and her mouth and throat filled with dirt. Likely to have been drugged and no evidence of sexual assault.'

'You mention the first… so there is a second?'

'The second victim was murdered this week, and she had the same injuries and dirt in the mouth. Also we have a third victim that didn't die. He was disturbed before completing what looks like a ritual.'

'You have a witness?' he asked, sipping his coffee.

'Without any memory of events,' Bryant chipped in.

'You have a history?'

Kim sipped her coffee before answering. 'All of these girls were involved in exposing his secret when he was six years old. He was held down and taunted before one of them ran away to get help.'

Ted looked off into space and nodded. 'So he's never been able to forget the looks on their faces and the things they said. What he recalls is their disgust, which mirrors his own repulsion at himself.'

'Our witness recalls the phrase *one for you and one for me*,' Kim added.

'Then it's a game,' he said emphatically.

'It's not much of a—'

'Either that or some kind of recreation. But I'll come back to that in a minute. Did either of you hear of the David Reimer case in Canada?'

Kim shook her head, as did Bryant.

'David Reimer was born in 1965. He and his twin brother underwent routine circumcision surgery at the age of six months. The surgery went wrong and David's penis was irreparably damaged.'

From the corner of her eye she saw Bryant cross his legs.

'To cut a long story short the family was referred to a Doctor Money who used them to prove his theory that nurture over nature could define a person's gender. He believed in a Gender Identity Gate, the point after which a child is locked into an identity as a male or female. He believed it to be between two and a half and three years of age.'

'What happened?' Bryant asked.

'Surgery for gender reassignment was carried out and he was raised as a girl.'

'Alongside his twin brother?' Kim asked.

Ted nodded. 'As the years passed, his natural instincts grew, as did his wish to do normal boy things. Money's answer to the fears of the parents was to treat him even more like a girl.'

'Jesus,' Bryant whispered.

'Exactly. Just imagine the confusion, the battles in his brain and his body.'

'What happened?'

'Eventually his parents told him the truth. The surgery was reversed and he began to live life as a male.'

'And he lived happily ever after?' Kim asked, raising one eyebrow.

'He committed suicide at the age of thirty-eight.'

Bryant sat back in his chair.

'By that time he couldn't live in his own head. He didn't know who or what he was any more.'

'You said about a game, a re-enactment?' Kim asked.

'It sounds like a sacrifice, an offering. He could be trying to recreate episodes from his childhood. Games he played with his mother.'

'But why all this if he hates her so much?'

'Because he loves her too and possibly misses what they had together. There would have been times in his childhood that he felt happy. There might also have been times he was humiliated. There's a great deal of conflict here, especially if he has not been helped in the right way. Bear in mind that he is unlikely to have felt disgust at himself until he saw it in someone else.'

Kim nodded her understanding. 'We think the girls have marks from being in a high chair, and they are always scrubbed clean.'

'Tea party,' Ted offered.

'Oh shit, he's treating them like dolls,' Kim said as the realisation dawned.

Ted nodded. 'A dolls' tea party is synonymous with the child-hood of a little girl. *One for me and one for you.* It could be that it was his mother's favourite game.'

'He has another. The death has not been fulfilled.'

'Then you'd better find her quickly – because just like any other game, eventually a child will get bored.'

Kim suddenly had another thought. 'How likely is he to change his ritual? I mean we have suspicions that there is another girl involved. Would he have two at the same time?'

Ted scrunched up his face and then shook his head. 'It would be highly unlikely if that's not what he's done in the past. This is not escalation, Kim. He's not growing the crimes with each one. It seems far more likely that he insists on keeping the same routine with them all.'

His answer took her thoughts right back to a girl named Mandy. Someone for whom she suspected they were too late. Forensics were still at Westerley, and it was beginning to look more likely there was something more there to find. If Ted was correct about routine then Mandy could be buried there too.

Bryant sat forwards. 'Are we definitely looking for a male?'

'In physicality, probably. In appearance, it's hard to say. There's a chance he could present as a woman or a man. He may even switch between the two. Much depends on the help he got early on. Eleven years is a long time and every year of that time is formative.'

Bryant nodded his thanks even though the answer had offered them nothing.

The situation in which they found themselves was certainly unique to Kim.

For once they knew their killer's name – yet they still had no clue who it was.

CHAPTER SEVENTY-EIGHT

'Okay, guys, let's get up to speed. I don't think we have much time.'

Kim's mind whispered that it was Tracy who was running out of time.

It was six p.m. on a Friday and the station was beginning to thin out. The shift was changing over, and the clerical staff had already said their goodbyes as they headed off for the weekend. Kim's team should have been doing the same.

'We know that Jemima was abducted on Saturday and dumped Sunday night, found by us Monday morning. Isobel was taken on Monday and dumped Tuesday night. He's keeping them one night, so…'

'Tracy was taken yesterday so will be dumped… tonight?' Dawson asked.

Kim nodded.

'So, to clarify, we know that Louise Hickman, Jemima Lowe and Tracy Frost were all present when Graham Studwick was held down and taunted at school.'

She turned to Stacey. 'Anything on the name Mandy yet?'

Stacey shook her head. 'There were seven Mandys at Cornheath at that time. I'm working my way through 'em, boss, but so far they're safe and accounted for.'

'Okay, now we believe that while he has them he's treating them like dolls and carrying out a re-enactment of a game he played with his mother… most likely some kind of tea party.

He then takes them to Westerley, smashes their faces in and kills them by stuffing their mouths full of dirt.'

'You think he'd be stupid enough to try and leave Tracy at Westerley?' Bryant asked.

'I think he has to leave her at Westerley,' Kim said. 'Just like he left Isobel a couple of days after Jemima. And there's a reason why. I just don't know what it is yet.'

'So what's the plan, boss?' Dawson asked.

'We're gonna be right there waiting for him,' Kim said.

Her whole team looked at her doubtfully, and she understood their concern. Only an idiot would risk the same location following the police presence on the property.

But following their discussion with Ted, her instinct said that's what Graham needed to do.

She just hoped for Tracy's sake she had called it right.

'Time to go upstairs and…'

Her words trailed away as her phone rang. It was a withheld number, but given the situation she decided to answer it.

'Stone.'

She stepped away from the mumbling amongst her team.

'Inspector, it's Jo… from the hospital.'

Kim's stomach reacted to the agitation in her voice.

'Is Isobel okay?' Kim asked quickly.

The chatter around her stopped and six curious eyes turned her way.

'Yes, Isobel is fine, but I thought it best to let you know about an incident we had earlier. There was a man who tried to get into the ward to see Isobel. He was refused entry, and he became quite forceful. He was banging and kicking at the doors. We had to call security to move him away from the doors. He was aggressive towards the officers and had to be physically removed from the building.'

Kim felt the hairs on the back of her neck ping.

'Jo, please tell me you managed to get a description,' Kim said, holding her breath.

'I got more than that, Inspector. He was big, burly and bald, and his name was Darren James.'

Kim thanked Jo for her help and ended the call.

She turned to her team. 'Okay, guys, get yourselves together as quick as you can. We need to get to Westerley immediately.'

They needed to find out why their security guard had tried to force entry into the ward.

CHAPTER SEVENTY-NINE

Kim didn't hesitate when she heard the call to enter the office of the detective chief inspector. He stood to the right-hand side of his desk. The brown leather briefcase handle was encased in his hand.

'Sir, I need all police and forensic activity withdrawn from Westerley,' Kim said.

He smiled. 'Stone, what on earth are you talking about?'

'I need them to stand down from the site.'

Now he frowned. 'That's impossible. The ground search is nowhere near complete and after what you said about this Amanda…'

'Mandy,' she corrected.

'Either way, we need to make absolutely sure there is nothing more to be found.'

She nodded her understanding and took two steps closer to the desk. 'I get that, but I need the area clear for tonight. The search can resume tomorrow.'

He placed the briefcase on the floor and sat back down.

'Why?'

'I think our guy will attempt to dump Tracy Frost there tonight.'

Now he laughed and she got worried.

He shook his head. 'Only a fool would be so bold. Are you thinking this killer has no access to television and newspapers?'

'Sir, there is a reason he was bold enough to leave Isobel so soon after we found Jemima. We can't track him any other way.'

'You have his name?' Woody said, as though she'd forgotten.

'Graham Studwick no longer exists. He entered the system aged eleven after murdering his mother and doesn't appear to have left again. Except we know he has, but as someone else. Knowing his name is a dead end. All we can use is his behaviour so far and up until now the site at Westerley means something to him.'

He sat back in his chair.

'Sir, I just want to make it as inviting as possible. The location is all we have.'

He nodded his understanding and picked up his pen. 'Okay, what do you need?'

She'd thought the first part would be easy. She was coming to the part where she expected a fight.

She shook her head. 'Nothing. I need to do this with as few people as possible. It will just be my team and members of Westerley staff.'

He was shaking his head before she finished the sentence. 'Not a chance, Stone. Firstly I will not have you endangering your own team to that degree and the staff there are civilians. If anything should happen to any one of those people…'

'I do understand that, but I need them for their knowledge of the site. I need to cover two or three areas, and I can only do it with their help.'

He rubbed at his chin for a few seconds.

'Sir, I do believe this is our only chance to stop him and to save the life of Tracy Frost.'

'You really believe he'll come back?'

She didn't hesitate. 'Yes, I do.'

He sighed heavily. 'Okay, but I want a team positioned no more than half a mile away and you *will* maintain radio contact at all times.'

'I need to—'

'I can add more restrictions if you say one more word.'

She quickly closed her mouth.

'If the safety of those people is compromised for even one minute you stand down. Do you understand?'

And fuck Tracy Frost, she thought.

And if anyone had told her a few days ago she'd feel so passionately about ensuring this woman's safety she would have laughed in their faces. Tracy had unveiled a great deal of herself this week without even realising it.

Like Kim's own life, the existence Tracy had made for herself didn't count for much in the opinion of others. They both had a job into which they poured everything they had. Neither of them were married or had children… but whatever Tracy's life was, it was hers and Kim was determined to bring her back to it.

In her logical mind she knew that wasn't what her boss had meant. He didn't want anything to happen to Tracy Frost, but it was always a case of safety by numbers. If one had to be sacrificed to save more then that was the equation you chose.

Only problem was, Kim had never been any good at maths.

CHAPTER EIGHTY

Oh, Mummy, it's my very favourite part of the day. I love teatime soooooo much, and I know you did too.

I would choose the dolls to come to our tea parties. I would get them all clean and ready, and you would prepare the food.

Didn't we have such lovely cakes for tea. You would sometimes try new ones for a treat, but there were some that always stayed the same.

Now and again in the summertime we had jelly and ice cream. We laughed at the wobble as you took it from the fridge. I would touch it with my fingertip to see if it bounced back. And if it did it was ready.

Do you remember when I lied, Mummy? I said it was done, and it wasn't, but I was impatient for the strawberry flavour that made my mouth water as you opened the fridge door.

You put a spoon into the dish to divide up the portion. Instead of dancing in the bowl when it landed it splodged and splashed all over the counter. I held my breath, so sure you would be angry with me. But you weren't. You laughed as the mess disappeared beneath a handful of kitchen roll. Of course you laughed. We were playing your favourite game.

I love every part of playing with my friends, Mummy, but this is the part I like the best.

It's just so sad when they have to go. But they do have to go, Mummy. Just like you had to go. I loved you, but I hated you. I loved our life together when it was just us, but you let the rest of the world in. Until then I was just your best little girl.

We tried to block them out again, didn't we? We tried to return to our own little world, just the two of us.

You pretended that one day at school never happened. And so did I.

You gave me books to read and exercises to do and everything went back to how it had been before. Almost.

The faces and laughter still haunted my dreams, but at least I had you.

Until my body began to change. There were areas I wanted to touch, explore, understand, but I didn't, because I knew you would know.

But the hormones you fed me could only prevent so much.

I called you the morning it happened.

My willy had leaked in the night, and I didn't know if it was broken.

The look on your face broke my heart. The years in between fell away as I watched your face crumple with disgust. I was back on the floor looking up at my tormentors.

I moved towards you, and you moved away, sending daggers into my soul. You didn't want to touch me, as though I was infected. I suppose to you I was. But my only affliction was being a boy.

All day you looked at me accusingly. As though adolescence was somehow my fault. And with every passing moment the child disappeared and an angry young man emerged.

Suddenly I had nowhere to belong, and I was no longer your little girl.

That expression could never be undone. Your betrayal was worse than theirs, Mummy.

Because you had made me this way.

And so, just like the rest, you had to die.

CHAPTER EIGHTY-ONE

Tracy knew she couldn't hold herself much longer. The half glasses of milk throughout the day were now backing up and filling her bladder.

She knew those innocuous little drinks contained whatever he was using to drug her. It had been a while since the last one and so the thoughts seemed clearer in her head. Easier to hold on to.

She squirmed in her seat uncomfortably, terrified the urine would come out of her.

She had no clue how much time had passed since he had last been in the room, gently bathing her. And she had no idea what was to come next.

She was sure she had been sliding in and out of consciousness. Her mother's face had drifted in and out of her mind. Always smiling, always welcoming.

Tracy felt a pang of regret course through her that translated to physical pain somewhere in her chest area. She had allowed a stranger to destroy the bond they'd once had.

She had never liked her stepfather, and he had never liked her. She wasn't sure which of those facts had been made evident first. They had tolerated each other for the sake of her mother.

After losing her real father at the age of five she and her mother had grown even closer. They had done everything together. Tracy had never even felt the effects of her friendless childhood because of the love and warmth from her mother. She had never felt as though she was lacking anything. Her mother was there for her every time the bullies chased her out of the school gates just so they could see her limp worsen when running.

Her mother had stroked her hair and dried her tears and told her everything would be okay. And Tracy had believed her.

Until Terry had moved in.

Her mother had felt that Terry was a hero, taking on a child that was not his own. But Terry had taken on nothing. There were many things that Tracy could have shared with her mother about him, not least of which was the name-calling when the woman of the house was not around.

It began just two weeks after he had moved in.

'Mek me a cup of tay then, Peggy,' he said and then laughed loudly.

She had not understood. Who was Peggy?

'Peggy, short for peg leg,' he'd clarified and then laughed again.

Humiliation had burned her cheeks and thickened her throat as she had stumbled blindly into the kitchen.

He had managed to bring the ugliness into her home, her place of safety, and it was something that could never be undone.

It became his name for her whenever her mother had left the house.

Gradually she had retreated from their company and would head straight upstairs after school, keeping the jibes and humiliations of the day to herself. She would just tell them everything had been okay.

She had moved out three days after her sixteenth birthday.

Tracy knew now that had she chosen to walk through her mother's door she would have been encased in a big warm hug as though she'd never been away. There would have been no reproach for her absence. No accusation for the weekly calls that weren't always made. Her mother would have held her, loved her and, most importantly, forgiven her.

And she'd left it too late.

Her mother loved her. She knew that.

She also knew that her mother was the only one. She had been abducted, plucked from her life and no one would even be missing her.

The door banged above and startled her. She already knew that meant he was on his way.

She almost cried out with the effort of not wetting herself. She didn't know how much longer she could wait.

The door opened and she squeezed her legs together.

He switched on the light and smiled. Tracy heard the whimper that escaped from her mouth.

Never in her life had she felt so trapped. There were moments in her childhood that could come close, but even then she'd known she was a child and that some day she would have an element of control over her own destiny. Well here she was, all grown up, and she was as trapped as she had been back then.

The knowledge lit a swirl of anger and injustice in Tracy's stomach. She had promised herself that she would never be in that position again.

'Now it's time for tea,' he said brightly.

Tracy had no idea what time it was… but if it was time for tea she knew her hours were already numbered.

Her eyes glanced across to the rocks. If only she could get her hands on one of those. She could bash it against his head and make a run for it. She didn't know how far she could run, but he always left the door to the dark corridor open. At least she could try.

He reached back into the hallway and used both hands to wheel in a trolley that was laden with a teapot, cups and plates of cakes.

Tracy's heart began to thump as he carefully placed the items one by one on the table. There was nothing she could use. Her right wrist was chained to the high chair, and she already knew she couldn't get the momentum to move the chair itself.

His smile was almost beatific as he arranged two plates side by side.

'This is my favourite time of the day,' he said as he poured tea into both of the cups. 'I love it when we have our own little tea party. Just the two of us.'

He looked around the shelves at the collection of dolls. 'No, we won't invite any of the others today. It'll be just us, okay, sweetie?'

Tracy said nothing even though her mind recoiled at his use of endearments. The thought of food brought a rolling nausea to her stomach even though she couldn't remember when she'd last eaten.

'Okay, let's start with cake. Which one would you like?'

Tracy was unable to move. The fear had deadened every muscle in her body, but her brain was coming alive.

'Which one?' he repeated.

She swallowed and nodded towards the end plate.

'Fondant fancy. Good choice.'

He took two from the larger plate and placed them on each of the smaller plates.

He put a plate before her.

'One for you and one for me.'

Maybe if she followed his instructions, did everything he wanted, he would let her go. Perhaps Jemima had angered him somehow. Perhaps she hadn't eaten the cake.

She put all her energy and focus on lifting the cake to her mouth. Her jaws were numbed by terror, but she managed to nibble the end.

The dry sponge hit the arid desert that was her mouth and would go no further.

'Are you not hungry, sweetie?' he asked.

Not knowing the right answer she shook her head.

He nodded his understanding as the last bit of the cake disappeared into his mouth. 'I think you need a cup of tea.'

Suddenly she woke to the ridiculousness of her predicament. Why the hell was she going along with everything he told her to do? Her life was at stake here. He had kidnapped her, drugged her, imprisoned her and now he was feeding her. Here she sat like one of his stupid fucking dolls with a fresh clean face and clips in her hair.

She paused as she managed to hold the thought. She had wire grips in her hair and one hand free. She had to stay present in her own mind long enough for those two thoughts to join up and become something useful.

He placed the cup before her and added the milk.

'Now be a good girl and drink your tea.'

Tracy reached for the cup, remembering how he'd reacted the last time she'd refused. The trembling of her hand caused the chipped cup to clatter around the saucer.

She remembered again how he had reacted when she'd refused to drink.

She placed the cup back down in the saucer and gently shook her head.

He sat up straight and frowned. 'Tracy, please pick up your cup.'

Again she shook her head.

He put his own cup back on the table.

'Tracy, I won't ask you again. You have to drink the tea.'

Her heart was beating rapidly, but she had to refuse. Again she shook her head.

He stood and the plastic chair fell backwards behind him.

He strode around the table and grabbed the cup from the tray. As he moved behind her she reached up and ripped the kirby grip from her hair. He grabbed a handful of her hair into a ponytail and yanked back her head.

He positioned the cup above her mouth and began to tip it towards him. She was looking into his upside-down face, and she knew she had only one chance.

The warm tea began to drip onto her lips, but this time he'd lost the element of surprise and her mouth remained closed.

The liquid ran over her chin. He paused as he realised he had a problem. He could not hold on to her hair and the teacup and prise her mouth open.

That second of confusion was all she'd been waiting for. She would have only one chance, and she had to make it count.

She threw up her arm, her hand clenched around the clip.

In her mind the motion was a snap, a whip, a thrust that took a nanosecond to execute. The actuality was like watching a slow-motion replay and all the will of her mind would not make her arm move quicker.

He loosed her hair and deflected her attempt easily and the grip, along with her one chance at freedom, tumbled to the ground.

He used his free hand to pinch her nostrils closed, meaning she had no choice but to open her mouth.

'Here, let me,' he said, lifting the cup to her lips.

He turned the cup more and most of the drink shot in a torrent down her throat.

'Good girl,' he said, smiling.

Tracy knew she'd just been fed more of the drug he'd been using on her.

Her instinct caused her to cough, but it was too late. The liquid had gone.

He sighed and tipped his head. The regret didn't reach his eyes.

There she saw a coldness she had never experienced before. Her heart began to pump quickly, and yet she couldn't tear her eyes away.

No one had ever looked at her with such concentrated hatred. It burned the colour into her cheeks.

'Graham, I was the one that helped you,' she blurted out. 'Don't you remember?'

'Of course I remember,' he said. His face didn't alter one bit. 'But it wasn't soon enough, was it?'

Tracy felt the colour in her cheeks deepen with shame. He was right, and she knew it. Initially she had been just as curious as the others and damn it, for a few minutes had enjoyed the fact they'd been laughing at someone other than her. But then a sickness had worked its way into her stomach, and she had bolted for the door.

She hadn't wanted anyone to feel the way she did. But he was right – she should have gone for help sooner.

'Graham, I'm sorry for…'

He held up his hands to silence her. 'It doesn't matter, anyway, Tracy. It's now time for you to go.'

And that was when she knew it was time to die.

CHAPTER EIGHTY-TWO

As they entered the lane that stretched the last quarter mile to Westerley, Kim began to hope that her plan had worked.

The press knew the procedure and the mass exodus of police vehicles would have signalled there was nothing else happening. There would be no further updates and no more bodies to be found.

Reporters did not hang around when there was nothing more to be gained. They had either headed home or on to the next unfortunate story.

Kim recalled the last time they had all been in her small car heading towards Westerley. It was difficult to believe it had been less than a week. The mood could not have been more different.

'You guys ready for this?' Kim asked as they approached the gate.

They all sounded a positive response.

The gate opened before Kim pressed the intercom. She groaned inwardly. Would they never learn? Just because they recognised the car approaching the CCTV camera was not a good enough reason to allow instant access.

Kim stopped the car and all four doors opened at the same time.

She couldn't help but remember the red pickup truck that had been parked there earlier in the week. It had been nice to see Lola again.

She strode towards the Portakabin and opened the door.

Professor Wright and Catherine sat at the table and Jameel stood at the computer desk, telling her that he was the one who had let them in. She really would have a word about that later.

Kim moved further into the space as her team filed in behind her. They fanned out to various points of the Portakabin.

Kim looked to the professor, who was wringing his hands.

She immediately noted the absence of the security guard. 'Darren not here yet?'

'He's called in sick,' Professor Wright answered, looking worried.

Kim glanced at Bryant, who nodded and stepped back outside. A unit had been sent to Darren's home after she'd learned of his visit to the hospital. When the constables had received no answer she had assumed he was on his way to work. They were not in a position right now to chase after him, but Bryant would instruct a squad car to keep trying.

Catherine offered her a warm smile and a nod as she stood. She wore light jeans with an embroidered design and a pastel vest top. Kim was surprised to see that she had added a little make-up too.

'May I get anyone a drink?' she asked, looking round. 'We have tea, coffee and bottles of Coke in the fridge.'

Most of the team said no. Only Dawson said yes.

A scent of flowery perfume wafted past her as Catherine reached behind her into the fridge.

'Okay, I'm assuming Professor Wright has explained to you why we're here.'

Both Catherine and Jameel nodded in her direction.

'Shortly, a backup vehicle containing a further five police officers is going to be parked up at the end of the lane should we need them.

'I want Bryant and Professor Wright at the site where Louise was found. Catherine and I will be over at the recent site where Jemima and Isobel were found, and I want Kev and Jameel in the middle.'

There was a simple logic in her plan and it all revolved around physical fitness. The professor was not as agile as his other staff members and so he was best placed at the most unlikely spot. Both Dawson and Jameel had youth and fitness on their side and could get to either of the two danger spots quickly if needed.

'Stacey, I need you here keeping watch on the cameras and monitoring the radio.'

Stacey nodded her understanding.

'We will be using the on-site radio system so Stacey can keep a check on us all. She will also be our link to the backup team down the road. Keep your torches aimed at the ground and use them only when necessary. Once you reach your designated location turn them off.'

Kim paused so that everyone could indicate they understood.

'It is imperative that we do not separate from our partners. Jameel, Catherine, Professor, you are there to assist us with guidance of the site only. Under no circumstances are you to do anything that will jeopardise your own safety or the safety of anyone else.

'If anything happens you get on the radio immediately and assistance will come. Do you understand?'

Three voices said yes.

'And finally I want a check call once you reach your designated location and every fifteen minutes thereafter. Got it?'

They all voiced their understanding.

She caught the brief look of doubt that shadowed Bryant's expression as he nodded in her direction.

She turned away, took a deep breath and offered a silent prayer. *Tracy, for your sake, I hope I called this right.*

CHAPTER EIGHTY-THREE

Tracy heard the sound above. Again she was unsure how long ago he'd left her. The thought was floating around her head like a wind-torn kite and she just couldn't grab its tail.

The tea tray had been cleared away. She didn't know when, and she didn't need to wee any more, but she wasn't wet, and she didn't smell either.

The door opened, and for a moment Tracy thought her eyes were deceiving her.

The figure that stood before her looked... normal. The make-up and the pigtails were gone. He was dressed in jeans and a T-shirt.

She had the fleeting thought that it wasn't the same person at all. That this man was here to save her. She'd been found. She was being rescued.

But then she saw the eyes. They were piercing and full of anger. The keys in his hand were being smacked against his other palm.

'Come now, Tracy, it's time for you to go.'

CHAPTER EIGHTY-FOUR

Bryant followed Professor Wright from the Portakabin into a pool of light from the one lamp to which the CCTV camera was affixed. An orange glow rained down and shone their way to the end of the gravel patch. The glow of the circle amongst the surrounding darkness reminded him of a dozen science-fiction films.

Beyond the glare their path was lit by a moon that peeked occasionally from behind the gathering storm clouds.

Bryant increased his speed to keep pace with the professor. For a portly man, he could move at speed.

As they left the safety of the glowing circle the professor activated the torch and shone it to the ground about five feet ahead. There was little point shining it directly ahead of the feet. If you were that late illuminating a hole in these fields you were going down. And in this place, you would not be alone.

Bryant shuddered at the thought of it.

He knew they were heading over to the area where Louise had been found. It was the furthest point west of the property and about three-quarters of a mile from where Jemima and Isobel had been dumped.

He understood his boss's reasons for the placement and wasn't offended by it. Although he spent time on the rugby pitch, the balance of weekends that he did or did not was tipping towards less often.

Dawson, on the other hand, visited the gym with a single-mindedness that he sometimes put into his work. Rain or shine, the guy kept his four-times-weekly commitment to keeping fit and healthy. And he was almost twenty years younger.

Although seeing the pace at which the professor moved, Bryant wasn't sure exactly where he would place his money in a sprint to the finish.

'Some weather we're having, eh?' he asked to break the silence between them.

'It is indeed, Sergeant,' the professor answered without looking at him. 'Condensation is forming in a volume of unstable air generating a deep, rapid, upward motion in the atmosphere. The heat energy is creating powerful rising air currents that swirl upwards.' He slowed and shone the torch up towards the darkness and nodded. 'There will be electrostatic discharge later, I would think.'

'There'll be what?' he asked.

'Lightning, Sergeant. It's what happens between electrically charged regions of a cloud.'

'Oh,' he said.

Ask a professor a simple question, Bryant thought.

'So how is it that you know the killer's name but are unable to trace him?' the professor said, asking a question of his own.

Unlike the professor, Bryant had no dazzling, complicated, technical response. 'He entered the system as Graham Studwick at eleven years of age. There is no record of Graham Studwick from that point on. He left the system as someone else.'

'Does that happen often?' the professor asked. 'People enter the system, as you call it, and simply disappear?'

More often than he'd like to admit, Bryant thought. And certainly more often than it should.

'There are so many different agencies involved with the care of a minor nowadays,' he explained. 'Borough councils merge or separate. Services are contracted out, medical records move amongst neighbouring health authorities. There isn't one body that oversees all aspects of a child's care.'

Bryant observed his own use of the word 'body' in a place like this.

'Ah, I see,' the professor said in a tone that indicated he wasn't really listening.

Bryant continued speaking but as they neared their designated area he sensed the distraction of the man beside him. He no longer offered any response at all to acknowledge that he was even listening.

Bryant closed his mouth and stopped speaking.

He knew the storm was coming. Could feel the threat of it in the air.

For some reason, he had the feeling that the threat of something more existed all around him.

CHAPTER EIGHTY-FIVE

'So do you think we'll see any action tonight?' Jameel asked as they headed across the gravel patch. 'I mean do you think he'll dump another one here?' he continued, giving Dawson no time to answer.

He shook his head as they entered the wall of darkness.

Only a kid who had experienced little contact with a crime scene would exhibit so much excitement at the prospect of freshly murdered bodies while normally surrounded by old, decaying corpses. It was ironic that those same words could have come from his own mouth ten years ago.

He watched as Bryant disappeared from view with Professor Wright, heading west in the direction of the area where Louise Hickman had been excavated just a couple of days earlier.

His boss was keeping pace with Catherine as they headed far east to the site where Jemima and Isobel had been left.

And here he was, travelling into no man's land between them, with a kid who could barely contain his delight at the prospect of a fresh body.

'Mate, keep the torch steady,' Dawson snapped. The lamplight on which they were now reliant was darting all over the place.

Jameel chortled. 'Oh yeah, I get ya,' he said, realising that the area of greatest importance was the ground on which they walked. At Westerley any danger to their well-being and safety originated from the graves underfoot.

'So what drew you to this place?' Dawson asked. The kid's effervescent nature and popularity on YouTube seemed at odds with the studious geek necessary for the number crunching he did in the middle of nowhere with just the professor, Catherine and a bunch of dead bodies for company.

'The data, man,' he said as though that explained everything. 'Give me a handful of numbers and I can give you data, facts, projections. Tell me your last three gas bills and I'll give you ten pages of results – history, patterns, projections. Here I get hundreds of numbers every day, and I turn them into fact. I can produce past, present and future. It's cool shit, man.'

'How'd you get here?' Dawson asked. The torchlight remained more stable when the kid was focussed on speaking.

'We were all hand-picked by Professor Wright,' he explained. 'I attended a seminar about stomach bacteria. There are one hundred trillion microorganisms in the intestines. That's more than ten times the total number of human cells in the—'

'Carry on,' Dawson advised. He didn't really want to dwell on that many living things making a home in his stomach.

'I waited until after the class and approached him about two calculations within his presentation that were incorrect by a decimal place of one hundredth of a—'

'How did you know that?' Dawson asked, following the zigzag pattern of the light source. There was no denying the kid's intelligence.

'A flaw in that particular software meant that once it reached any calculations using over one trillion it began to round the percentage up from point four of a whole instead of point five.'

Dawson was happy to take his word for it.

'I offered him a repair patch for the program, and he offered me a job.'

'Jameel, I'm not kidding about that torch,' Dawson snapped. The darkness was disorientating, but his senses told him they had to be getting close to where he'd placed the 'wet floor' signs to prevent any unsuspecting feet from falling into the shallow grave that held the delightfully rotting corpse of Cher.

'Sorry, I'm just looking for any clues.'

Dawson got the feeling he'd been landed with the booby prize. Give this guy a grocery bill and he could probably analyse your finances for the next ten years. But had the security guard turned in for work Dawson would have felt just a touch more secure in his partner's suitability for purpose.

'So what did Darren say when he called in sick?' Dawson asked. He had not yet seen Curtis Grant to question him.

'Said he'd got some kind of stomach bug. Went into a bit of detail, which was gross so I kinda stopped listening. The boss wasn't very happy and mentioned the contract renewal for the security provision being imminent.'

'What, he's going to change provider?' Dawson asked.

Jameel raised the torch so Dawson could see him shrug. 'Maybe, but the guy isn't that bad. He said he's arranged for the shift to be covered so somebody's coming, but then you guys arrived, so I just got off the phone.'

'Mate, shine the torch down,' Dawson instructed, slowing down. The light seemed to be aiming everywhere except at the ground on which they walked.

He took out his phone to call Stacey and inform her that a replacement security guard was due.

'You know, you could have bloody mentioned this earlier,' he said, scrolling to his colleague's number.

'Yeah, sorry about that,' Jameel said, as a fork of lightning lit up the dark sky, illuminating a face that didn't look sorry at all.

CHAPTER EIGHTY-SIX

The lightning lit up the Portakabin and temporarily blinded her like a brief explosion.

For a second the space fell into silence before Stacey realised the lightning strike had caused a surge in the electrics.

She counted to five before the whirring started as the backup generator kicked in. So it was more than a surge. The electrics had been temporarily disabled. The system was instructed to revert to backup only if a delay of five seconds elapsed. A surge was a split second or less.

'Jesus Christ,' Stacey whispered to herself and waited for her heart to return to its normal rhythm.

She didn't mind storms, quite liked to watch them – from the safety of a brick building with all electrical appliances switched off.

One by one the systems began to switch themselves back on. If it resembled any programming she'd ever seen it would be done in order of importance. Lighting, heating, communication equipment, security and then, finally, appliances.

Surprisingly the lighting hadn't failed, but Stacey knew that lighting was often worked from a separate circuit to everything else.

The heating wasn't switched on so there was no delay there.

The handheld phone in the charging cradle offered a single beep. The phone was back.

Next, the green light on the side of her radio base station flickered twice and then held. Great, she had radio communication from the base station. The handheld radios carried by the three teams would have continued to work amongst each other with the batteries attached but her own ability to communicate with them and vice versa would have been severed.

That only left the cameras. The screen to her right remained blank.

'Come on,' she urged.

It was not the most important of the systems but Stacey liked to know she had every tool at her disposal. Seeing the activity outside the gate and just inside the property was unlikely to assist her colleagues, as they were all at the furthest points away, but having eyes around the building and immediate area offered her comfort.

It suddenly dawned on Stacey that she was the only member of the team who had been left alone. But not for long, she realised, as the intercom beside her sounded. That would be the replacement security guard Kev had just called her about.

She smiled as the screen beside her flickered into life. It had reverted to split-screen display, showing the two camera views. Even before the voice sounded through the tinny speaker she could see the shape of the Aston Martin waiting at the gate.

Curtis Grant announced his arrival, and Stacey buzzed him through the gate.

The camera pointing over the fence to the lane beyond looked exactly as it had before the power failure. Along that lane sat a van with a team of backup officers.

A sound on the gravel outside the door met her ears.

'Hey Stacey, how's things?' Curtis Grant asked as he entered the Portakabin. 'I'm here to cover Darren's shift. Tried everyone

I could think of but no takers because it was too short notice, and this isn't the easiest gig to sell, especially at the moment.'

'But you're the boss,' she said.

'Yeah, and sometimes the boss has to come out late at night and get his hands dirty so we don't lose a valuable contract.'

He stood with his behind resting against the sink, close to the door. 'Just tried Darren again to see if he was feeling better, but his phone's off.'

'Surely you didn't need to cover the shift yourself?' Stacey asked doubtfully.

He shrugged. 'Probably not, but I would feel even more responsible if the failure to meet the contract is because of Darren… but that's what you get when you employ family, I suppose.'

Stacey was confused. Throughout her investigation she had not uncovered any familial relationships.

'You and Darren are related?'

He rolled his eyes upwards. 'Oh yeah, the irritating little shit is my cousin.'

Stacey wondered how the hell she could have missed such a connection.

Curtis Grant smiled widely and headed towards the kitchen.

'Now, how about I put the kettle on?' he asked. 'It looks like it's going to be a long night.'

CHAPTER EIGHTY-SEVEN

Kim tried to ignore the eerie feeling that was stealing over her.

The sudden lightning fork that had split the sky right in front of them had startled her and Catherine, appearing within minutes of them leaving the safety of the light circle at the top of the site.

She suspected the sensation in her stomach was not helped by the darkness and the knowledge that she was walking amongst dead bodies.

Singly, Kim could deal with either one quite happily, but perhaps it was the combination of both. Yet there was something inside her that wanted to take these bodies home. Not to her home but to Keats, where they would be treated with respect and then buried properly.

'So how are you doing?' Kim finally asked of the woman walking beside her.

Catherine held the torch, shining a path of light before them.

It was impossible not to notice the change in the woman since the last time they'd met. Bryant had done a double take and Dawson had looked more than once.

But it was more than the blonde hair hanging loose around her shoulders instead of the functional ponytail tagged to the back of her head. It was more than the subtle pink veneer that coloured her nails. Or the faint touch of lipstick and blusher that emphasised her cheekbones.

The most striking change in the woman came from within. Kim had watched as she'd offered refreshments to everyone present. Catherine had moved and spoken with a confidence that added presence to her form. The spine was straighter and the shoulders pulled back.

Kim wondered if the woman had any idea just how far into the background she had allowed herself to fade.

Kim had the feeling that if the professor introduced her as 'maggot lady' again he might expect a suitable response.

'Couldn't be better, Inspector,' Catherine answered. 'The press have gone and I don't have to hide... or leave. And that is primarily because of you.'

Kim said nothing but Catherine continued.

'I don't know how you kept my name out of the newspapers, but I am incredibly grateful that you did. My life has changed so much in the last few days. I feel like I can breathe again, even live again.' She offered a soft chuckle and the sound was attractive and light. 'Yes, I know how corny that sounds, but for the first time in years I actually feel free, as though I can now be myself. Do you understand?'

Kim thought she did. Although the difference in the woman was incredible, following their one brief conversation, Kim couldn't help but think there was more to it after the horrific ordeal Catherine had suffered as a child. The terror of her captors returning had shaped every decision she had made throughout her life. The fear had been so great she had preferred life within a closed psychiatric unit than with parents who loved her. No, these things were not erased with one short conversation, but it was not something Kim had the time to explore right now. Maybe once their killer was safely behind bars.

'How much further?' Kim asked, following the direction of the torchlight.

'Only seventy or eighty feet and we'll be back with Jack and Vera,' Catherine said.

Kim wondered how the hell she knew.

The radio on Catherine's belt cackled into life.

'Professor and Bryant to Stacey.'

While using the police radio the appropriate call signs from the phonetic alphabet would need to be adopted, but they had agreed that for use with the on-site radio system names would suffice.

'Go ahead,' Stacey answered.

'We are at location one. Nothing to report.'

'Understood.'

Three steps later and the familiar shape of the oak tree loomed ahead. The torchlight fell on the roses at its base. It felt as though weeks had passed since Kim had first noted the courtesy of the grave marker from the staff at Westerley.

'Almost there,' Catherine said.

Again the static sounded on the radio.

'Jameel and Dawson at location two. Nothing to report. Over and out.'

They both heard as Stacey acknowledged the transmission before the radio once more plunged them into silence.

Suddenly an unfamiliar sound met Kim's ears. She stopped walking and placed a hand on Catherine's arm.

Catherine came to a halt beside her.

The sound was faint but unmistakeable. To her it was the sound of tyres.

'Do you hear that?' she whispered.

She felt, rather than saw, Catherine's nod beside her.

They both stood, rooted to the spot, listening through the darkness.

'It's coming from down there,' Kim said, pointing to the dirt track at the bottom of the hill.

She strained her eyes towards the direction she felt was the road. It was the sound of tyres moving along slowly.

The dirt track was on a slight decline. It had to be their killer.

She realised that the driver must have cut the engine and was rolling slowly down the hill.

Kim moved forwards, safe in the knowledge that she was hidden by darkness.

'Look – look there,' she said to Catherine. About 300 feet back was the unmistakeable sight of dipped headlights crawling slowly towards them.

Kim felt a mixture of excitement and relief. Mostly relief. She had called it right. Tracy had a chance.

'Quick, Catherine. Call it through. Let the others know we have him.'

Catherine took the radio from her belt and spoke.

'Catherine to Stacey. We have reached location three… ' her eyes met Kim's above the torchlight '… and there is nothing here to report.'

CHAPTER EIGHTY-EIGHT

'What the hell are you doing?' Kim cried, reaching for the radio.

Realisation hit her a few seconds too late and at the exact second the first raindrop landed on her arm.

For a moment everything else was forgotten. Her colleagues, the operation, even the victims, as her brain rearranged the facts that had been fragmented around her mind.

'Jesus, you're in it together. That's why he brings them here. You help him get rid of the bodies but why…'

Kim's words trailed away as more pieces moved into place. The magnet in her mind was sucking all the pieces together, and a clear picture began to form. How could she have missed the connection between the two of them?

'You met Graham at Bromley, didn't you?' Kim asked, doing the sums in her head. They would have been there at the same time, and Kim knew full well that damaged souls managed to find each other.

Two more drops landed on her arm and the first thunderbolt sounded in the distance.

'Yes and I'll never forget it. Stupid group discussion where we were supposed to talk about our feelings and heal. Repeating our fear was supposed to help us forget it? That was supposed to make us whole?' Catherine spat.

Kim was unable to move. A lightning strike revealed the twisted, bitter face of the woman before her. Catherine Evans had perfected the art of wearing the mask that suited the occasion, but right here was the real woman. The real Catherine, who had been unable to move on from her childhood ordeal.

'There was one person there who had the courage to speak the truth. His truth... *our* truth. He spoke openly about wanting to hurt the people that had hurt him. He made no secret of the fact that he wasn't interested in forgiveness or therapy. He wanted revenge, and that was the only thing that would help.

'Yes, we had one thing in common that bound us together. Our need for revenge. We both knew that we would never live full lives until our tormentors were punished.'

'But how could you help him, Catherine?' Kim asked, stunned. 'You know the fear of being abducted, of being taken from the safety of your life. Look what it's done to you –and yet you've helped someone else do exactly the same thing.'

'Don't be stupid,' Catherine raged. 'It's different. I was a child and...'

'But even as an adult you were terrified when you thought they might come and get you again. I was there, Catherine. I saw you in that box. I helped you out. That fear was real.'

'Of course it was real. It's always been real. While those bastards were still alive, I lived with the fear,' Catherine said, as a bolt of lightning thundered past them.

'You think that's any less real to the women Graham has taken? And you've helped him. I don't understand, Catherine. Two women are dead because of the two of you. How could you do that?'

There was no hesitation in Catherine's voice and no remorse as the lightning lit up her expression.

'Because we had an agreement. That we would help each other.'

'But your captors were never...' Her sentence was left dangling between them as Kim remembered one crucial detail of their conversation at Catherine's house. The woman had forgotten herself in her fear and admitted to being terrified that 'he' was coming back. There had been two tormentors involved in her capture and abuse – but her use of the singular showed that she had known that one of them was already dead.

'It was Ivor and Larry, wasn't it? They were the two that molested you. The change in you is nothing to do with being able to carry on working at Westerley. It's because your second abuser is now dead. He was released from prison two weeks ago. You've both been waiting all this time?'

'Those two bastards took my life,' she spat. 'You can't even imagine what those fucking pigs did to me. I smell their foul, toxic breath every night; hear their perverted whispers in my ear. One after the other after the other, passed around like the bottles of whisky they shared.

'They took my childhood and my family. I could never go back to my life. By the time I was able to leave Bromley I didn't even know my parents, and they didn't know me.

'The terror they caused took over my body like a cancer. It was everywhere. There was never a choice, Inspector. For me to live, they had to die.'

Kim heard the raw emotion in her voice. Despite what Catherine believed, she would never be free of those men.

The raindrops were becoming more frequent now. The ground around them offered a cloying smell as the rain hit the dry earth.

'My life begins now, Inspector. Tonight I can live again.'

'Graham killed them, didn't he?' Kim asked, the realisation hitting her. 'That was the deal. You would help each other and that's how he helped you?'

Kim knew she couldn't call out. Any sound from her and Graham would be gone and Tracy with him. Without the link to Westerley she would never find him again. He was like a cat bringing home a mauled mouse to its owner. Without the tie to Catherine she had nothing.

Kim was struck by a sudden thought as a raindrop landed on her cheek.

'But if you're partners why didn't you warn him not to come?'

'Ooops,' she said.

'Jesus, you want him caught, don't you?' Kim said, aghast at the woman's duplicity. Graham had taken the lives of the men who had abducted and abused her, but now they were dead, Catherine wanted him gone. His purpose was complete and only two people knew the truth about her involvement with Graham.

With Graham safely caught and behind bars, that left only one person.

Kim.

The icy coldness of the woman before her chilled Kim to the bone.

Suddenly the radio hit Kim in the left temple. She tried to stay upright but she stumbled to the side.

It was the only advantage Catherine needed to push her to the ground.

Kim kicked out as Catherine threw her onto her stomach. Within seconds, her hands were tied behind her back. She kicked out again, but Catherine avoided her feet easily.

Catherine dragged her around by the hair, and she felt the plastic bouquet wrapper crunch beneath her back. The brittle stems splintered beneath and cut into her exposed skin. The thorns pricked at her skin. The grass was damp against her flesh.

Kim bucked against the tree, but with her hands tied she couldn't get very far. The wood of the tree grazed the back of her hand.

'You know you're not going to tie every loose end up neatly, don't you?' Kim asked, playing for time as an idea began to form.

She moved the plastic away from her behind and could feel the stems of the flowers beneath her.

Kim pulled her hands as far apart as she could and started to move her joined wrists up and down against the bark. The gnarly old tree might shred her skin in the process, but she couldn't wait for help to arrive.

'By my reckoning we have at least twelve minutes until the first check call, and it's not going to take long to arrange your little accident.'

Kim's blood ran cold at the absence of emotion attached to the words. If Catherine could arrange a fatal accident and then use the radio to call for help, Graham would be caught and all her loose ends would be neatly tied up.

Catherine's voice was calm and measured. 'I suspect you're going to fall in with Jack or Vera and break your neck when you fall. If not, Graham always carries a knife.'

The coolness of her speech filled Kim with dread. Her death was nothing more than a means to an end. A way for Catherine to facilitate moving on with the rest of her life – and she couldn't do that with Kim knowing the truth about her.

Kim heard a long sigh come from Catherine.

'Thank goodness. He's almost here.'

Kim knew if her hands were still bound by the time Graham reached them, she was dead.

She shook the wet fringe from her eyes and began to rub her wrists faster against the bark.

CHAPTER EIGHTY-NINE

Tracy felt herself being bounced around in the back of the van.

Minutes ago the ride had quietened, and the van had slowed down. The tyres were hitting bumps in the road, but she was no longer being launched around. The movement was rocking her to and fro.

The thought of sleep was tempting. In her haze, there was the possibility she would wake up not in this nightmare.

But she knew she couldn't sleep. Perhaps Jemima had slept. Tracy's mind was clearer than earlier, but her body still felt deadened.

She vaguely remembered stumbling down from the high chair and not having the strength to get back up. He had helped her to her feet and guided her into the van.

And she'd been grateful for his help. A rage like adrenaline shot around her body. Fucking grateful to the man who had abducted her and was now going to kill her.

The very notion evicted any thought of sleep from her mind. These could be the last few minutes of her life. Tracy was determined that if she was going to go it wouldn't be without a fight.

She had to be ready for any opportunity, ready to do what she could. If nothing else, she was not going to go quietly. Damn it, she had fought her whole bloody life. There had been moments where death had seemed favourable to life, but she had fought the feelings one moment at a time, convincing herself that eventually things would get better.

She had fought the crucifying demons of self-doubt that had never left her and focussed on her dream of journalism, determined that she would not be ruled by her past.

No, Tracy resolved, she had not fought every inch of her life to be snuffed out by some psycho loser now.

The bravado stayed with her for a whole thirty seconds. Right until the car came to a halt.

CHAPTER NINETY

Kim knew the wire was weakening against the gnarly bark.

She had slashed the skin at her wrists in the process, but she could feel the wire beginning to give. Another few seconds and she'd have her hands free.

But she didn't have a few seconds left, as Catherine yanked her to her feet.

Her left foot slipped on the mud as a clap of thunder sounded overhead. The raindrops were still slow but were much bigger. Round, heavy spots were landing all over her.

In her effort to keep Kim upright Catherine could no longer hold the torch. It tumbled from her hand.

Kim launched herself from the grip and threw herself to the ground. The torch would at least offer her some kind of weapon.

She landed on top of the torch, which dug into her breastbone. Catherine kicked her in the ribs. She coughed but stayed where she was. She would not give up the torch easily.

With her body obscuring the light she had been plunged into total darkness. The damp grass found every inch of her skin through the thin T-shirt. A brittle flower stem dug into her hip and her wrists were on fire, but she could not give up the torch.

A streak of lightning tore across the sky giving them both a clear view of each other. Catherine used the vision to land another kick, which caught her left breast.

Kim groaned out loud as the pain travelled around her torso.

'Give it up, Inspector,' Catherine hissed.

Not on your fucking life, Kim thought.

She frantically strained her shoulders pulling at the weakened wire. It was her only chance to stay alive.

The torch was now lodged in her stomach, her arms still tied behind her and her neck craned back away from the sopping mud.

Another kick – this time to her hip. The pain shot straight to her brain and then reverberated back. She was losing track of the pain sites around her body, but she couldn't think about that now. If she couldn't get her hands free she was going to die.

She pulled again at the ties. She felt Catherine's hand on her hip. Fuck, she was being rolled over onto her back.

As she turned she felt the ground disappear. There was nothing beneath her legs and nothing beneath her shoulders.

She tried to visualise it in the light of her memory. Damn it, she'd been rolled onto the bridge between the two graves. Beneath her legs was rotting Vera and beneath her shoulders was rotting Jack.

If Catherine managed to turn her around she'd be heading straight into the sunken grave to join them.

She pulled frantically on the ties as she sensed Catherine bending down towards her. She shuffled away in the darkness, careful not to turn. As long as her back remained on the bridge she was safe.

She felt her feet being lifted from the ground. A strong grip around her ankles.

'What the hell…?' Kim cried, but her voice was lost in the deafening thunder roar.

With her arms tied, she couldn't stop what was happening and she tried to kick out her feet but they were grasped firmly. Catherine had a strong hold on her ankles and was using her body like a lever to swivel her around. She felt herself being turned in a clockwise direction.

She had to pull her hands apart. It was the only way she could live.

It was coming. She knew it was coming.

She could feel the sweat mixed with the raindrops travelling down from her hairline. Catherine was using her legs like a wheelbarrow handle to turn her around.

Two more turns and she'd be lying lengthways on the bridge between the two graves and then one good kick would leave her on top of one of the corpses.

The wire would not snap.

Catherine pushed on her feet one more time and Kim realised that the woman needed the rigidity of Kim's limbs to help her make the turn. The struggling and fighting was helping Catherine to turn her to the exact place she wanted. While she was thrashing around fighting Catherine off she could use the momentum of the movement to manoeuvre her body.

The lightning struck right behind Catherine as Kim stilled her body and bent her knees. The unexpected folding of the limbs caused Catherine to stumble into her. For a brief second, Catherine's weight was resting on Kim's folded, limp legs.

She focussed her energy and shot her legs straight back out, catapulting Catherine backwards, giving her a second to try the wire one more time.

'You fucking stupid bitch,' Catherine hissed.

Kim worked frantically to weaken the wire. Catherine was disabled for only a couple of seconds. With her hands still tied behind her back, Kim remained the one at a disadvantage.

She pulled frantically at the wire behind her back. Her wrists burned from the hundreds of wire cuts that were deepening with every movement. The scars from a recent knife wound on a kidnapping case were throbbing beneath the pressure.

The first thrust appeared to have no effect on the wire at all.

Her shoulders throbbed from the effort of trying to separate her hands.

On the second burst, it came free, and her arms exploded away from her.

Kim pounced on Catherine's back and wrapped the string around her neck. Catherine's hands reached up to try to hook her fingers underneath, but Kim pulled on it hard as she slid down the back of Catherine's torso.

Catherine's additional inch or two drew Kim up onto her tiptoes. The woman tried to writhe from her grip, but Kim pulled even harder, hearing a soft choking emerging from her throat.

She dragged Catherine two steps back so that the torch on the ground would illuminate the immediate area.

The blood dripped from the score of marks on her wrist where the cuts criss-crossed and blended with each other. For a second, Kim stared at her own wrist.

It took only a moment for the pieces to fall into place and by the time Kim felt the tap on her shoulder she knew who Graham Studwick really was.

CHAPTER NINETY-ONE

Tracy writhed on the ground. She felt like a limbless worm trying to burrow along. Her arms and legs were so weak it was as though they had been removed from her body, leaving just a torso and a head.

The grass was long and slippery, and she didn't know which way would lead her to safety. She only knew that for the moment she was on her own.

Her back still smarted from him pulling her out of the van by her legs. She had managed to crane her neck and hold it rigid so the back of her head did not thump to the ground.

He had begun to drag her across the gravel path. A hundred needles had pierced her skin as her flesh was punctured by the countless bricks and stones that either scraped her bare skin or burrowed deep into it. She cursed the drugs that were paralysing her muscles but not her skin.

Beyond the thunder a sudden noise, a voice, had caught his attention and Tracy had heard it too. He had dropped her legs to the ground and started to run.

She had been left lying on her back, staring up into the night, unable to move her limbs but knowing she needed to do something.

She had ignored her arms and legs and focussed all her energy into her hip and waist area. On the third attempt she managed to rock her body to the left and then over onto her stomach, and now she had to choose which way to go.

Tracy buried her chin into the soaked ground and tried to use it to help her move along.

She could hear activity at the top of the hill.

She wanted to crawl away from the sounds. Graham had been distracted by something, and she knew it was her only opportunity to escape.

This was where Jemima had been murdered and left, and if she didn't try to crawl away, that would be her fate too.

A tear forced its way out of her eye as she remembered that fateful day at school. Just for a while she had taken the easy way out, allowed someone else's pain to relieve her of her own.

And even now, in her early thirties, she was doing the same. The article she was writing forged into her mind. Negativity, hatred, blame. Again she was pointing away from her own pain by picking at the imperfections of someone else.

The shame brought a torrent of tears she could not hold back. Some of them were for the person she was now but most were for the person lost. And some were born from the knowledge that she would never see her mother again.

The thought of her mother brought fresh, raw pain to her heart.

I wish I could have made you proud, Tracy's heart screamed into the rain.

She knew beyond a shadow of a doubt that there was danger at the top of the hill.

She sobbed uncontrollably as her gaze moved to the left and the possibility of her own personal safety.

The years of being alone had erased the instinct of putting someone else before herself.

Tracy turned her body and began the climb.

CHAPTER NINETY-TWO

Kim whipped around, still holding Catherine by the throat and looked into the face of the killer.

Although his thick black hair had been flattened against his head by the pouring rain, she was looking into the eyes of the man she knew as Duncan.

It all made sense now. Why they couldn't find anyone by the name of Isobel Jones. Because she didn't exist.

Something had struck Kim as odd when he was feeding his girlfriend. Her attempted suicide scars had been on her right wrist, meaning she was left-handed. But he'd been helping her to eat with her right hand.

He had offered false facts so they would be searching countless records, knowing they would never find her.

Kim took a step back, dragging Catherine with her. Kim could feel the fight leaving Catherine's body, but she couldn't let her go. She couldn't fight both of them.

She had missed her opportunity to call out to her team. They would never hear her now amongst the claps of thunder and pounding rain. For now, she was on her own.

'One step closer and I'll kill her,' Kim threatened as the rain poured down between them.

He shrugged as he took the step. 'Do it. You'd be doing me a favour. With you both dead no one will ever find out.'

Jesus, Catherine had held the same plan for him. Their use of each other was over and apparently so was the powerful bond that had existed between them. There was only one common denominator in both of their plans: Kim's death.

Kim took another two steps back and felt Catherine's feet begin to drag. Only another minute or two and she'd be dead, and that was not what Kim wanted.

Just one more step and she loosed the string in her fist.

Catherine fell to the ground and beyond. Her body hit against the side wall of the grave on the way down and Kim heard a loud groan and a cough as she landed on top of the corpse named Jack.

Kim knew that the radio was on the ground somewhere. She just needed to find it with her feet and that meant keeping Duncan's hands away from her.

She moved backwards, further away from the light of the torch but also further away from the graves.

The rain was beating down upon them both. Kim felt it had entered every orifice in her body.

'You went back to the hospital to finish the job, but you couldn't get in. You said you were her boyfriend, but she was being monitored too closely. You couldn't do it. And when I came you just embellished the story. And because we had you we didn't look for any other relatives or friends who would disprove your story of knowing her.'

He was listening intently, appearing to enjoy his own cleverness.

Kim continued to move one step at a time, but he had gained on her by a foot. Her vision blurred as she raised her hand to wipe the rain from her eyes.

'Catherine has been helping you bury the bodies, hasn't she? You were in this together since your days at Bromley?'

The tip of her toe met with something hard. It was the site radio, but Duncan was no more than two feet away.

Kim turned it with her foot and then leaned her weight on it, hoping she was near the transmission button.

'You made a pact that you would help each other seek revenge on the people who made your lives hell.'

She released her foot. No response. She had not activated the microphone.

'I know what they did to you when you were Graham. I understand how they hurt you, but they didn't deserve to die,' she said as she used her toe to push the radio over. She rested her weight on it again.

'Of course they had to die,' he said, smiling. His face took on a childlike innocence as though there was no other way. 'And so will the rest, once I've taken care of you…'

'How many?' Kim asked. She'd thought Tracy would be the last.

'Twenty-seven people ridiculed me that day,' he said, taking another step closer.

'Why the wait between Louise and Jemima?' she asked.

'There has to be a method, Inspector. It has to be done in order of hate and whose voice I heard loudest, whose face was most in my dreams.'

Kim realised that her second attempt to activate the radio had been unsuccessful, but she had to keep him talking.

'You killed the two men that held Catherine captive, didn't you?' Kim asked, releasing the button again.

Silence met her ears until Duncan broke it. He was no more than a foot away from her.

'We needed each other to get what we wanted,' he said.

Kim hit the radio again with her foot and gave it a good stamp. She knew she was running out of time, but her colleagues would never hear her cries through the storm.

She stepped back and the radio crackled into life.

'Boss, you all in order?' Stacey's voice sounded.

Duncan looked down to the voice that had come from her feet. Kim knew she would not be able to find the transmit button again to reply, but her failure to answer would bring assistance from the rest of her team.

'Boss, please confirm all in order,' Stacey cried.

The second call acted as a catalyst and Duncan lunged towards her.

In the darkness, she saw the glint of a knife.

She tried to duck away from his grasp, but his left hand made contact with her neck.

'You are not going to spoil this for me, bitch,' he cried. 'I've been waiting all my life to set this straight.'

Kim couldn't keep track of the location of the knife.

'Don't you fucking understand? I have to do this.'

Every word increased the pressure of his hand on the back of her neck but the words ignited a fuse within her. He *had to* do it. He hadn't done it yet. Tracy was still alive. Wherever the hell she was, he hadn't killed her yet.

She tried to prise herself away from his hand but feared for the knife.

He was struggling to hold her with one hand and keep hold of the weapon at the same time.

She gathered her strength and barged him backwards.

Graham fell onto his back, his legs flailing for balance. She turned and wrestled the knife from his grip. As soon as the knife was freed he used both hands to throw her to the ground. Her shoulder met with a puddle that sent rainwater splashing into her face and she tried to shake it away.

He sat astride her, fumbling in the grass. He leaned down onto her body, trying to find the blade around her shoulders and head.

The position reminded her of when she was riding the Ninja. His weight bore down on her.

The stems of the flowers bit into her back.

Kim knew that if his hand found that knife she was dead.

The weight of his body prevented her from moving her own. She kicked and thrashed her legs, but his thighs had her pinned at the waist. She had no weapon and only her hands free to use.

His hands were planted to the ground either side of her head. One arm was being used to keep him stable as the other hand searched for the knife.

There was only one thing she could do.

She thrashed her head against his supporting arm. The full weight of his torso landed on top of her.

Kim gasped as the wind was rushed from her lungs, but she had to make her move.

She wrapped her arms around his neck and pulled his head down, burying his face into her breastbone.

She adjusted her arms around the back of his neck, locking him in a twisted lovers' embrace.

He tried to turn his head to escape, but she held firm. His position on top of her meant there was nothing he could use to lever himself back up to a sitting position. She pulled his face right into her chest and held him close.

His hips began to rock as he tried to unlock himself from the embrace in which she held him, but she couldn't allow him to find that knife.

The wriggling of his body told her he was gasping for breath. That was exactly what she wanted. It was her only chance.

Suddenly she let go. He reared up and opened his mouth.

Her hand reached around to the side and closed around the only thing available to her.

Her palm rested around the thorns on the flower stems.

Graham's mouth was open wide as he gasped for breath. She raised her hand holding a foot-long thorny stem and used all her might to jam it into his throat.

For a split second he was still, his eyes bearing down on her, confused.

He fell to the side, clutching at his neck.

Kim knew he could pull it out, but it had bought her the minute she needed.

She reached around and finally found the handle of the torch.

Graham rose and stood, choking and staggering as he pulled the flower stem from his throat. He coughed madly and turned towards her. She shone the light directly in his face and watched as he took two steps towards her, the murderous glint back in his eyes.

Another step and his foot met with something on the ground. He shouted out as he tumbled to the floor and out of view.

Kim turned the torch to the grass. It rested on the squirming form of Tracy Frost.

Kim folded to the ground as Dawson appeared, panting, in front of her.

He shone a torch directly at her and then across to the form of the reporter.

'Jesus, boss, are you okay?' he said, kneeling down beside her.

Kim's body was beginning to let go of the adrenaline that had kept her upright. In its absence the fatigue was trying to take hold.

'I'm okay, Kev,' she said. 'Check that they're both still alive.' She didn't want them dead. She wanted to see them in the courtroom.

Dawson looked around. 'Where are they?'

She nodded towards the graves of Jack and Vera, no longer sure who was in which one.

He shone the torch and nodded. 'Yeah, boss, they're both still alive.'

The rain was starting to slow, but the storm still lingered in the air. A rumble of thunder sounded in the distance, but it was heading somewhere else.

Kim scooted along the grass towards the reporter who had escaped with her life.

'Hey, Frost, we've been looking for you,' Kim said, stroking the sodden hair from Tracy's face. She wasn't surprised by the emotion she saw in the eyes that were hooded with exhaustion. Kim knew this woman much better now than she had a week ago.

'I... w-wanted... to... had... to... help... ' she stammered.

Her hands and chin were caked in dirt.

Kim could see how Tracy was fighting the debilitating drug that was ravaging her system.

The woman could have lain low and simply waited to be found. But she hadn't. She had painfully pulled herself to the top of the hill, instead of just keeping herself safe.

Kim reached out and squeezed the woman's shoulder.

'It's all right, Tracy. You're okay. We've got you now.'

CHAPTER NINETY-THREE

The morning sun was reflected in the black marble of the gravestone. The heat of the day wrapped itself around her body like a gentle, reassuring hug. The heat was cleaner today, thinner and calmer.

The gravestone before her bore two names.

To Kim's mind it was the grave of her parents.

With her, she had two pieces of paper.

Keith and Erica West were the closest thing to a family she had ever known and although her time with them had been short, she missed them every day.

She had been hoping to visit them yesterday on the anniversary of their deaths, but she knew that they'd understand.

There had been one final thread that had needed unravelling and she had felt compelled to see it through.

After briefing Woody on the events of the night before she had headed down to the squad room on Saturday morning to find Dawson was already there.

The pile of missing-persons reports had been stacked high on his desk.

'What are you doing?' Kim asked.

'Isobel still has no name,' he answered simply.

Together they had waded through the papers, armed with more knowledge than they'd had before. Three hours later, they had found the report they were after.

Isobel was an ex-prostitute who had turned her life around two years earlier. She had been reported missing at the beginning of the week by a work colleague. And her name was Mandy Hale.

Kim had asked Dawson to pay her a visit and fill her in on her life. Warts and all, she deserved to know the truth. It was her identity, and it was her life. A less than perfect life was better than no life at all.

Catherine and Duncan were both in custody. Duncan had been charged on four counts of murder, one attempted murder and one count of abduction. Catherine was facing a whole host of accessory charges. They were both naming the other as the mastermind behind the whole thing, claiming they had been coerced as a minor. There was an amusement that even now they were offering the same justification without knowing it. Ultimately, neither of them were likely to see the free world until their early sixties and, in the case of Duncan, perhaps not at all.

He'd kept all the victims in an old corner shop that was boarded up at the end of a line of terraced houses condemned and awaiting demolition. Once he'd forced entry to the premises his activities had been seen by no one. Kim had seen the photos of the macabre room and the rocks he'd used as weapons.

There could have been a small part of Kim that was tempted to feel sympathy for these two souls who had been damaged earlier in life, but there wasn't. Both of them had suffered horrific ordeals at the hands of other people and had been powerless to defend themselves. But here was the issue for her. So had thousands of other people. She had come to learn over the years that very few childhoods were ideal. Most kids suffered some kind of emotional trauma, whether it be a simple lack of attention from a busy mother trying to do her best, to kids suffering all kinds of physical and emotional abuse. And yet they didn't all allow the cold, sharp blade of revenge to carve away their hearts.

Kim's own past was not from any storybook. She had lived with mental illness, loss, abuse and cruelty in all its forms and although the memories lived inside her, she had never succumbed to their power. Instead she used their presence as her driving force.

Kim had to wonder what would have happened if Catherine and Duncan had not been in Bromley at the exact same time. She couldn't help but speculate if Jemima and Louise would still be alive. Had the prospect of getting even ruled Duncan out of accepting help? Would he have done so without the possibility of vengeance so prevalent in his mind? They would never know.

No, Kim's sympathy did not stretch back to when the two of them were children. It was reserved for Jemima and Louise, who had lost their lives, and for Mandy, who might never recover hers.

She could not bring herself to lament the deaths of Ivor and Larry. Their crimes were horrific and not one cell of her being was sorry that they were dead. In truth she believed they deserved to die for what they had done to Catherine. But she would never believe their punishment to be the prerogative of anyone other than the justice system.

Yesterday she'd received a text message from her old mentor, Detective Inspector Dunn. She had opened it with one eye closed after having gone back on her word of leaving his case alone.

She need not have worried. The message had stated simply: *That's my girl.'*

Woody was content that the cases were solved and that there were two people to prosecute.

Westerley would continue its valuable work but with the help of another 'maggot person' and a better security provision. Curtis Grant had lost the contract at Westerley after Stacey had informed Professor Wright that Darren James should never have been working there in the first place. She had uncovered that

Darren James had been removed from working the doors after the ejection of a male from a pub had turned into a vicious assault.

The incident should have been reported to the Security Industry Authority and Darren's licence suspended. Instead, Curtis had risked his business by hiding him in the obscurity of Westerley. Both now faced investigation by the Security Industry Authority.

Kim couldn't help but think that there would be some measure of relief for Darren James that he would never return to Westerley. The sight he'd stumbled upon when he found Mandy beaten and writhing on the ground had tortured him every waking minute since. His aggression at the hospital was a result of his desperation to see her. To put a different image in his head to the one he saw every time he closed his eyes. Kim doubted he would ever have been able to go back. Dawson had admitted that he had mentioned Isobel's progress in conversation while on site at Westerley and had unwittingly given Darren all the information he needed to go and make a nuisance of himself.

Thoughts of Daniel were beginning to fade from her mind. There was still so much unsaid between them and yet, paradoxically, nothing now left to say. They both knew what the spark between them could have been, and it was that very thought that held her back. They would meet again, she felt sure, and perhaps by then she'd be whole and perhaps he'd be with someone else. But for her there was no choice, which meant there was no regret.

Kim knew she would do what she always did. Throw herself into the next case that landed on her desk.

She glanced again at the first piece of paper in her hand. It was the commendation she had received for her role in the case of two missing nine-year-old girls.

She lowered herself to the ground and placed the frame against the grave.

'This is for you,' she said as the tears thickened her voice. Had it not been for the time she had spent in their care Kim knew not what she might have become. That brief interlude in her childhood had been enough. Those three years had shown her the type of person she wanted to become. They had set her up for life.

They had shown her what it was like to be part of a family and had loved her unconditionally. And she had loved them in return.

Any award would always belong to them.

She took from her pocket the second piece of paper. The one Erica had placed in her bag on that last and fateful day.

To other people it might only have been a permission slip to attend a school trip to Dudley Zoo, but to her it was so much more.

She opened the well-worn sheet of typewritten paper that was separated in two by a dotted line across the middle.

The top half was the detail of the trip: date, day and requirements for a packed lunch. The second paragraph was a request for their 'charge' to attend.

But it was as her eyes continued down the sheet that her vision began to blur. It didn't matter because emblazoned across her mind was where they had scribbled out the word 'charge' and inserted the word 'daughter'.

For a moment she let the tears flow as she clutched the paper that was all she had left.

She took a few deep breaths and fought the tears away.

She touched the top of the headstone lightly.

'I love you, and I miss you,' she whispered softly down to the ground.

A smile fought its way through the tears. After today she would remember only the love and the good times they had shared. They deserved no less.

She sighed heavily as she walked towards her bike. There was just one last thing that remained to be done.

She took out her phone and scrolled down her contact list. She pressed to call and a voice answered on the second ring.

'Hey, Frost, it's me. How are you feeling?'

'Hello, Inspector, how—'

'That'll be Stone to you, Frost, if I remember correctly.'

Kim heard a soft chuckle on the other end of the phone.

'It's been a strange week to be honest. I feel different, you know?'

'Yeah, near-death experiences will do that to you. But you'll be back to yourself in no time.'

'Really?'

'Nah, not completely. Shit like that changes us a bit. In your case, hopefully for the better but who—'

'Hey, there's no need for that,' Tracy said with a smile in her voice.

Kim heard her mumble something away from the phone.

'Sorry?'

'Nothing, I was just thanking my mum for the seventh cup of tea of the day. Apparently it'll make me all better.'

'You sleeping?' Kim asked.

'Not so much. Not exactly nightmares but just distorted replays.'

Kim understood. 'That will pass,' she offered.

She thought about Tracy's cold, barren house, devoid of everything except for secrets. The complete absence of life and joy, family and friends.

'We were looking for you, you know. We were determined to get you back,' Kim said.

'I know,' Tracy whispered, and Kim could hear the full extent of emotion in the woman's throat in those two short words.

Kim cleared her throat. 'So when am I to expect this starring role in that article of yours?' she asked.

'Ha, Stone, what article? You really gotta stop thinking you're all that, you know.'

Kim couldn't help the chuckle that escaped from her lips. But now to the real purpose of the phone call.

'Okay listen, Frost, and listen good because this will never be repeated. *Let the past go.* The minute you decided to climb that hill defined the person you are now. Don't ever forget that – because I won't.'

The line went quiet for a second before Tracy spoke.

'Hey, Stone, does this mean we're *friends* now?'

Kim laughed out loud. 'Don't bloody push it, Frost. I'm sure we'll be banging heads again soon enough.'

Kim ended the call with Tracy Frost still chuckling in the background. She knew that the woman would be okay. She was a fighter, and she would bounce back.

Damn it, Kim acknowledged with a smile. It looked like they were alike after all.

LETTER FROM ANGELA

First of all, I want to say a huge thank you for choosing to read *Play Dead*. I hope you enjoyed the fourth instalment of Kim's journey and that you feel the same way I do. Whilst not the warmest of characters she has passion and drive and a real hunger for justice.

If you did enjoy it, I would be forever grateful if you'd write a review. I'd love to hear what you think, and it can also help other readers discover one of my books for the first time. Or maybe you can recommend it to your friends and family…

Each story is a unique journey and this one was no exception. Some begin with a clear vision and the finished product closely resembles the initial idea, and the relationship between author and story is harmonious. Other times the relationship is fraught with disagreements as the story dictates a different path to the one intended. *Play Dead* experienced many transitions before settling into the story it was always meant to be.

I hope you will join both Kim Stone and myself on our next journey, wherever that may lead.

If so I'd love to hear from you – get in touch on my Facebook or Goodreads page, Twitter or through my website. And if you'd like to keep up-to-date with all my latest releases, just sign up at the following link:

www.angelamarsons-books.com/email

Thank you so much for your support. It is hugely appreciated.

Angela Marsons

www.angelamarsons-books.com

 angelamarsonsauthor

 @WriteAngie

ACKNOWLEDGEMENTS

Every book is a separate and distinct journey. Throughout the process I invariably learn something, and this book was no exception.

In this book I wanted Kim to explore the mind of a killer whose actions while he had the victims were as important as how he chose to dispose of them.

As ever, I have to acknowledge the patience and contribution from my partner, Julie. Her belief and encouragement never wavers, and neither does her willingness to drop everything when she hears my desperate cry of 'I need a meeting'. She once told me to 'trust in the process', which has now become my mantra through the tough times. Although she doesn't realise it, these books would not happen without her.

As ever I would like to thank the team at Bookouture for their continued enthusiasm for Kim Stone and her stories. In particular, the incredible Keshini Naidoo, who will not stop until the books have reached their full potential.

A special shout-out to the unbelievably ferocious and tenacious Lorella Belli who continues to sell the foreign rights to the Kim Stone stories and has conquered fourteen territories to date.

I must acknowledge the growing family of Bookouture authors. Every single one of them is unique and talented. Their enthusiasm for each other is genuine and provides an environment of friendship, advice and support. Caroline Mitchell is one of the most dedicated and hard-working authors I know, and I am proud to call her my friend. Renita D'Silva continues to wrap me up in her beautiful, expressive prose.

My sincere thanks to my sister Lyn and her husband Clive and my awesome nephews Matthew and Christopher, who continue to offer me encouragement and support on this journey.

My eternal gratitude goes to all the wonderful bloggers and reviewers who have taken the time to get to know Kim Stone and follow her story. These wonderful people shout loudly and share generously, not because it is their job but because it is their passion. I will never tire of thanking this community for their support of both myself and my books, one or two of whom have made appearances in my books (you know who you are). They have all made social-media forums a welcoming and friendly place to hang out. Thank you all so much.

Massive thanks to all my fabulous readers, especially the ones that have taken time out of their busy day to visit me on my website, Facebook page, Goodreads or Twitter, and yes I now know the Bull and Bladder serves good food!

And finally a very warm thank you to the lovely ladies at my local libraries. In particular Rachel Hamar from Stourbridge Library and Shazziah Rock from Cradley Heath Library. Visiting and chatting with your lovely readers is a welcome reward.

Made in the USA
Lexington, KY
03 July 2016